CHRISTMAS COCOA MURDER

CHRISTMAS COCOA MURDER

Carlene O'Connor
Maddie Day
Alex Erickson

KENSINGTON BOOKS
www.kensingtonbooks.com

KENSINGTON BOOKS are published by

Kensington Publishing Corp.
119 West 40th Street
New York, NY 10018

All Kensington titles, imprints and distributed lines are available at special quantity discounts for bulk purchases for sales promotion, premiums, fund-raising, educational or institutional use.

Special book excerpts or customized printings can also be created to fit specific needs. For details, write or phone the office of the Kensington Special Sales Manager: Kensington Publishing Corp., 119 West 40th Street, New York, NY 10018. Attn.: Special Sales Department. Phone: 1-800-221-2647.

Library of Congress Card Catalogue Number: 2019940163

Kensington and the K logo Reg. U.S. Pat. & TM Off.

ISBN-13: 978-1-4967-2360-4
ISBN-10: 1-4967-2360-0
First Kensington Hardcover Edition: October 2019

eISBN-13: 978-1-4967-2362-8 (ebook)
eISBN-10: 1-4967-2362-7 (ebook)

10 9 8 7 6 5 4 3 2 1

Printed in the United States of America

Contents

CHRISTMAS COCOA MURDER

Carlene O'Connor

Chapter One

It happened during the Christmas season, in the not-so-distant past, when Siobhán O'Sullivan had just graduated from Templemore Garda College, Macdara Flannery was still living in Dublin, and rumors of snow swirled in the Irish air. The new year would bring many changes, the most exciting of all, Siobhán would become Garda O'Sullivan right here in Kilbane, County Cork. She had been advised to enjoy her last few weeks as an everyday citizen, and as usual life was filled with a thousand things to do. After all, tonight was the first showing of the Christmas panto in the town square.

Siobhán opened the door to the back garden of Naomi's Bistro, wielding a fat bone fresh from the butcher's. She waved it around, hoping to entice the family pup in from the cold. "Trigger. Come on, boy." She was late for the Christmas extravaganza in the town square, but worry had her rooted to the spot. Their Jack Russell terrier had never been away from home this long. "Trigger. Look what I've got. Straight from the butcher's shop." She sounded like a right eejit, waving a dog bone and talking to an empty garden. "Come on, luv. Come home." Had he wandered into someone's door last night, and they'd simply yet to let him out? She prayed that he was curled up in an oversized armchair, snoozing away, being well looked after, and he'd be home as soon as they realized they'd forgotten to let him out . . .

Preposterous. Everyone in town knew Trigger was their pup and they knew to return him straightaway. Perhaps he'd wandered into someone's shed or outbuilding, or even the boot of a car, and Trigger would be home as soon as whatever door he was trapped behind was opened again.

Those were the *best-case* scenarios.

"Enough," Siobhán said into the crisp night air. Her siblings were going to be in the Christmas panto. She could not afford to have her imagination running dark. Trigger would be home soon. At least her brood hadn't realized he was gone. They had been at rehearsal all day. She'd been keeping it a secret, if they knew they'd never be able to concentrate on the play.

She had already searched their back garden and shed, tried to see if there were any little paw prints to follow out back, but if there had been, the overnight rain had washed them clear away. She wondered if not being able to find the family dog was a bad omen for becoming a guard in the new year. He was such a homebody she'd often mistaken him for a rug in front of the hearth rather than a dog. Siobhán left the bone by the step, and sent a little prayer that he would be tail-wagging on the step when they arrived home, glaring at her for leaving him out in the cold. If he wasn't home by the time she returned, she and James would go on an all-out search. She locked the back door, and then exited through the front.

Sarsfield Street was beginning to look a lot like Christmas. Up and down the footpath white lights danced and pine wreaths sang from doorways. Garland and bows wrapped themselves lovingly around the iron street lamps. Fresh-cut Christmas trees were propped up outside Liam's hardware shop, their branches reaching out for their new homes. Siobhán had taken to explaining to people that Naomi's Bistro was slightly behind in their holiday decorating, and by *slightly behind* she meant she hadn't even started. Shopping. Cooking. Decorating. Baking. Entertaining. And unless Eoin and James were taking care of it, she hadn't even begun to think about Christmas supper. She had batches and batches of brown bread to bake, not to mention cookies, and maybe a sherry trifle this year. After all, she had a bit of competition.

Declan O'Rourke had made his mam's hot cocoa this year, and supposedly it was to die for, both with and without the added kick of Irish cream. He was outselling even Siobhán's brown bread, and several times she'd glanced out the window to see long lines of folks waiting to get into his pub for a hot cocoa fix. "You buy the finest squares of chocolate and melt them down with sugar, and powdered cocoa, dat's me mam's trick," Declan crowed. "Then, of course, there's the Irish cream, then top it with fresh cream. You can't beat it." She had yet to try it, but that would soon be rectified as O'Rourke's was going to have a tasting booth set up at the winter carnival. It was all starting this evening in the town square.

Up ahead she saw a wheelchair stopped in the footpath. Soon she recognized Adam Healy's mop of blond hair. A tall weed of a man stood next to him taping a flyer to the street lamp. As Siobhán neared, she saw it was a photo of Adam's new golden retriever puppy, with capital letters splashed across the top: GOLDIE MISSING.

"*Missing?*" Siobhán exclaimed. Adam turned to her as Siobhán gently touched his shoulder. Just ten years of age, Adam was the butcher's son. Ed Healy had just sold her the bone for Trigger and he hadn't mentioned Adam's pup was missing. Come to think of it, she hadn't mentioned

Trigger was missing either, for she'd been afraid saying it out loud would somehow make it real. She realized now how silly she was. She should have told her siblings, and they should be putting up flyers as well.

"Someone stole him," Adam said, his bottom lip quivering.

Siobhán turned to the man next to him. He was a man into his late sixties, with a haggard but kind face. "Are you Adam's grandfather?"

The man held out his hand. "Dave Healy. I'm the uncle."

She could see it now. He looked like an older, thinner version of Ed, the butcher. "Nice to meet you. Where you from yourself?"

"Mayo," he said. Mayo was in the west of Ireland, and it had been ages since Siobhán had been. One of these days she was going to go on a holiday around Ireland. And then everywhere else.

"Ah, lovely," Siobhán said. "It's nice to have you here."

He gave a nod and then lifted the flyers in his hand. "Didn't expect Christmas to start off with such cruelty. What kind of person would do something like this?" He glanced at Adam. The poor lad had had a rough start to life. In a wheelchair since five years of age after an illness left him paralyzed. Then last year his nana died at Christmas. His mam was called away this year to visit her sister, who was in hospital in America. Now this. That's why it took a village to raise a child; the world could be a cruel place indeed.

Siobhán knelt next to his wheelchair and placed her hand on his shoulder. "Tell me everything."

"He was an early Christmas present from Uncle Dave. Even though he's allergic."

Dave laughed. "The chemist will sort me out, lad, don't you worry about that."

"Goldie was in our garden last night. He likes it out there and Da said puppies need to get out their excess energy, so we let him be. When I went to call him in for the night, he was gone." His voice trembled and tears welled in his eyes.

"Is it possible he just wiggled out on his own?" Siobhán wanted to make it sound like everything was going to be fine, but she had a feeling that two missing dogs was no coincidence.

Dave Healy shook his head. "The garden is well fenced-in, I went around and checked before we let the pup roam about. And I did a second check after he went missing. There's no signs of him rooting around under the fence. Someone stole him." He, too, was trying to sound calm for Adam's sake, but Siobhán could hear the worry in his voice.

What does it mean? Did they have a dognapper running around Kilbane? Some kind of Grinch stealing family pets? She shuddered to think of it. Siobhán wanted to scoop Adam up and make everything better. She stared into his worried blue eyes, which seemed even larger through his thick glasses, and she tried not to melt into a puddle of goo at his feet. "Sometimes doggies have their own little adventures, do a bit of wandering around."

"But Uncle Dave said somebody *stole* him."

"We'll tell the guards, then. I'm going to be a guard myself in the new year. Finding Goldie can be my first case."

"You're going to wait until the new year?"

"No, luv. I'm going to start looking right after the panto. I promise." *Along with Trigger. Where could they be?* She squeezed his shoulder. "Try not to worry."

Adam bit his lip and gave a curt nod. "That's right. *Nothing* to worry about," Dave echoed. "We'll find him."

"Do you need help posting those flyers?"

Dave shook his head. "I'm taking him to the panto and we'll pass these out at the carnival."

"Ah, brilliant." She took a few from the pile and promised to do the same as she hurried on. She'd only managed a few steps when her eye caught another poster taped to a street lamp. This one was for a black Lab named Blackie. The next lamp featured a missing collie named Lassie. And the one after . . . a wolfhound named Wolfy. She was starting to think the Irish were a bit simple with their names, but it was no time for humor. *What on earth is going on?* There *was* a serial dognapper on the loose. Trigger hadn't run away. She knew it. And unless they found the culprit soon, it was beginning to look a lot like a blue Christmas.

As soon as Siobhán passed King John's Castle, she could see that the town square had been transformed. An enormous Christmas tree stood proudly midsquare, lights shining. Santa's throne, an elaborate golden affair, was set up in front of a red carpet. A manger was erected to the left, complete with stuffed sheep, a donkey, and Wise Men. A white tent was erected in the middle of the square, its flap closed tight with a banner above reading:

HOT COCOA DUNK TANK!
THROW SNOWBALLS!
DUNK SANTY!

"What in the world?" Siobhán said out loud. There had been some rumors about the shenanigans Paddy O'Shea, otherwise known as the town Santy, had been up to with this year's festivities. Last year, Charlesville's town Santy had brought in live reindeer from Wales. Paddy had been obsessed with besting him, and it looked as if he was attempting to pull it off.

"A dunk tank of hot cocoa," a male voice said behind her. "Wild."

She turned to find Chris Gordon behind her, holding a candy cane in one hand and a mug of hot cocoa in the other. He was their token American, a younger man with movie star good looks and enough money to bankroll the comic-book shop he'd opened down the street.

"What exactly is a *dunk tank*?" she asked, figuring if anyone knew it would be him. She was more familiar, unfortunately, with the term *drunk tank* from her brother's drinking days.

Chris smiled down at her. Siobhán was tall herself, so it was a rare experience. "Haven't you ever been to a carnival?"

"Apparently, not the kind you've been to."

He grinned in response, flashing a perfect dimple. He was way too handsome for his own good, and nothing ever seemed to knock the smirk off his face. He laughed. "I'm surprised to see one in the winter. At night. And hot cocoa—that is bizarro. Normally, it's a dunk tank of cold water on a hot sunny day. You throw balls at a target and try to knock the person in."

Was he pulling her leg? "Now, why would anyone be going and doing that?"

"For fun. To get them wet. Sometimes the proceeds go to charities."

"I see." She didn't. The rumors had been correct: Santa was flying higher than his reindeer this year. She glanced around. The Kilbane Players had erected a stage in front of the tent, and booths selling holiday wares were set up on the outskirts. She could smell the heavenly scent of hot cocoa steaming out of Chris's mug.

"Is that Declan's?"

"You bet. It's phenomenal." He thrust the mug at her.
"I couldn't."

"Don't worry, I haven't put my lips to it yet."

She wanted to remain polite and refuse, but she couldn't resist. "Thank you." She took a sip. It was the absolute best she'd ever tasted. Smooth and sweet, and he'd ordered his with the Irish cream. "Wow," she said. No wonder he had lines out the door. She wanted everyone to disappear so she could be alone with this mug of hot cocoa. If she could marry this hot cocoa right now, she would.

Chris laughed. "If only you looked at me like that."

Siobhán ignored the comment, although she could feel her cheeks light up, and his grin widened. She distracted herself in the sights and sounds. Next to Declan's tent, Annmarie was selling a colorful collection of nutcrackers. Handmade from Sligo, a coastal town in the west of Ireland, these particular nutcrackers were the talk of the town. One of them was rumored to come with some kind of prize, something about a shining star, but Siobhán was vague on the details. All she knew was that everyone seemed mad to have one. Once again, she felt the weight of everything she needed to accomplish by Christmas. Maybe she could do some of her shopping after the show. No. First things first—she would start looking for the missing dogs.

Christmas music blared from speakers hidden within the square, and folks started taking their seats for the panto.

"I hear they're going to roll the dunk tank out at intermission," Chris said. "I can't wait."

Siobhán found a seat toward the front of the row. Cormac Dooley was in an elf costume handing out programs. He was the shortest man she'd ever seen in Kilbane, and she felt bad that he was being exploited as an elf, but maybe he enjoyed it. The delusion lasted until she saw the scowl on his face.

"Dunk Santa at intermission," he barked at everyone who took a program. He seemed to be enunciating extra loud, and as Siobhán glanced around, she soon saw why. The Santa and Mrs. Claus from Charlesville were here, sitting behind Eileen O'Shea, who played Kilbane's Mrs. Claus.

Cormac Dooley caught Siobhán's staring, and he leaned in, holding the programs up to his face like a curtain. "Paddy is praying the dunk tank of hot cocoa beats last year's real reindeer." Siobhán didn't have to ask if men were putting real money on this bet, this was Kilbane. Folks around here put money on everything. The competition between the town Santas was ratcheting up.

"How did he manage to fill a tank with hot cocoa?"

"One kettle at a time," the elf said with a frown.

She wasn't sure if he was making a joke, but either way he was definitely not happy about it. A hot water tank. Poor Paddy. Why hadn't somebody noticed he needed this much help? "It's not scalding, is it?"

"He'll be fine," the elf said. "Do you know how hard it is to actually hit the target enough to dunk him?"

"I have no idea," Siobhán said. It just sounded like a waste of good cocoa.

The elf rolled his eyes. "Let's just say that by the time he goes in, it will be cooled off."

"How on earth did he come up with this?"

The elf sighed. "He's been crazed about those two." He jerked his head to the other Mr. and Mrs. Claus. "Last week he was out here pacing and muttering like a nutter trying to come up with the perfect idea. He was tipping the bottle a bit too. The guards threatened to throw him into the drunk tank."

"Drunk tank!" Siobhán said. "That's what I thought."

Cormac frowned at her before continuing. "I tried to cheer him up with a mug of Declan's hot cocoa."

"It's so good," Siobhán said, holding up her mug. "His mam's recipe. He melts squares of milk chocolate with the cocoa powder, that's the secret."

"Did you want me to finish me story, or do you want to tell one of your own?"

"Sorry. Continue."

He waited a moment to make sure she was going to keep her gob shut. She thought elves were supposed to be cheerful. "I told him how popular it was. And just like that, drunk tank became *dunk* tank of hot cocoa."

He paused and seemed to be waiting for a response. "Wow," she said.

The frown was back. He leaned in. "He had the tank 'specially made. By a man who makes giant aquariums for people who can't figure out a better way to spend their money than to build mansions for little fishies, if you can believe dat." The elf certainly had a lot of complaints. It seemed like *cheer* should have been a requirement for the job, but she kept the thought to herself, where it belonged.

One thing was clear: Paddy O'Shea was not a well man. The lights on the stage flickered; it was time to just enjoy the moment. Chris plopped next to her and soon the seats were filled. This holiday tradition always utilized a fairy tale and this year's panto was *Jack and the Beanstalk.*

Chris Gordon leaned into her, his hot cocoa sloshing, his cologne nearly overpowering her.

"What is this again?"

She sighed. Apparently, they didn't have pantos, or pantomimes, in America. "It's a *play,*" she said, explaining this to the Yank yet again.

"Pantomime?" he said. "No talking?"

"Don't be silly," she said. "They talk. And sing."

He shook his head as if it made no sense at all. It was lucky for him he had movie star good looks, for his personality left a lot to be desired. "A fairy tale," he said. "What's so Christmasy about that?"

She sighed. "They will sing Christmas songs, and wear Santy hats, and . . . you'll see." Christmas pantos were family affairs. Children and adults ate it up. How could they not? There was something for everyone. Women played many of the male roles, and there always was a man in drag. The villains would be booed and the heroes cheered on. Siobhán couldn't wait to see who would play the cow. Rumor had it that it would be Declan O'Rourke. No matter how many times she'd pressed, her siblings had kept it mum. How she hoped it was Declan! She glanced over and, sure enough, someone else was stationed at his hot cocoa tent. The audience took their seats again as her sister Gráinne strolled onto the stage, her wavy black hair hidden under a green cap. She was playing Jack. The oldest of the O'Sullivan Six, James, entered from stage left, sashaying his hips, dressed in a curly gray wig and a yellow dress. He was perfect as Jack's mother. The audience whistled and cheered. James winked and took a bow. Gráinne formed a finger gun behind his back. It was greeted with laughter, but Siobhán was pretty sure her sister had just gone off-script.

The remainder of her siblings—Ann, Ciarán, and Eoin— had accepted the role of seeds that would grow into beans. Siobhán sank a bit in her seat, because she had been offered the role of the beanstalk, but turned it down. Given that in the new year she would be a new guard, she couldn't stand the thought that for the rest of her career, behind her back, she'd be called Garda Beanstalk. As they delivered their opening lines, the sound of a young boy laughing pealed through the theatre. Siobhán turned to see Adam Healy parked at the end of his row in his wheelchair. Behind him stood his father, Ed. The faces of Ed and Dave Healy radiated joy as they smiled down at the boy. Dave had a handkerchief clutched up to his face as if already anticipating tears of laughter.

The cow lumbered out, and the audience roared. It must be Declan. He was much beloved in Kilbane, both in and out of the pub.

"Where's the milk?" James said in a falsetto voice.

"He's dry as a bone," Gráinne said, pulling on Declan's udders.

"If it's Guinness yer after, you're right, I'm dry as a bone!" Declan's voice boomed out from behind the cow head. The audience cheered. "But I've got some hot cocoa that's to die for." He finished his line with an elongated *"mooo."*

The audience howled.

"You make chocolate milk?" Gráinne said. "That's pure magic."

"You'll keep me, then?" Declan said.

Gráinne put her hands on her hips. "Are you joking me? A cow that makes chocolate milk? I have to take you to the market and sell you to the highest bidder."

More cheers rang out from the crowd.

Declan mimicked her by placing his hooves on his hips. "Whatever."

The kids in the audience wholeheartedly repeated after him. *"Whatever!"*

James pointed and flipped his curly gray hair and used his best falsetto voice. "To the market, lad!"

Gráinne led Declan-the-cow across the stage. Sheila Mahoney, dressed as a farmer, blocked their path. Ciarán, Ann, and Eoin, dressed all in green, trailed behind her.

"Wanna buy a cow?" Gráinne said. "He makes chocolate milk."

"I'll trade ya for me magic beans," Sheila boomed. Siobhán's siblings—the beans—jumped up and down. Siobhán beamed with pride. For a split second she regretted that she wasn't playing the beanstalk. She was taking photos with her mobile and trying not to cry when a loud buzzer rang, startling even those on stage.

"Do we keep going?" Gráinne yelled as the buzzer continued to blare. A mechanical whirring poured out of the white tent as a large glass tank rolled out, with Paddy O'Shea perched on a wooden board that hung over it. Above him was a target with a bull's-eye.

"Sorry, sorry," he said. "Ho! Ho! Ho! Technical difficulties." He looked around wildly as the tank kept rolling. It was on a short track that soon screeched to a stop. Loud whirring started up again, this time from the snow machine situated a few feet from the tank. "I'm afraid the timer went off too soon," Paddy said. "Can't be helped. Who wants to try and knock me into the tank?" He began yelling for the elf. Mostly Siobhán saw a sea of shocked faces, but Mr. and Mrs. Claus from Charlesville looked quite smug. Cormac Dooley scurried up and tried to work the controls to send the tank back into the tent. "We should let someone have a go, shouldn't we?" Paddy said. "Now that I'm out here?"

Siobhán stepped closer, wondering what was different about Santa this year. Was he drunk? She soon realized the most obvious difference. His Santa suit was falling off him. He was skinny. Dark circles were under his eyes. She was starting to think the cocoa in the tank was the Irish variety as well and that Santa had been drinking it, along with filling the tank.

"Somebody try and knock me in!" Santy yelled. "Don't be shy! Dunk Santa!"

"I'll do it," the elf said. He collected the snow that had dropped from the machine, rolled it into a ball, and aimed at the target. It hit the bull's-eye head-on.

Paddy O'Shea screamed as his board tilted down and he slid into the tank of hot cocoa, splashing it out both sides. The audience, thoroughly distracted from the play, cheered. Declan ripped off his cow head and stepped up. "We're taking a short intermission. If you want to drink your hot cocoa instead of being dunked in it, come visit me booth."

The elf managed to get the track working as Santa grabbed his board, effing and blinding as he tried to lift himself out of the tank. Parents slapped their hands over their children's ears and stared openmouthed as his Santa pants started to slide down, the more he pulled himself up. It was a sad day when you realized your town Santa wasn't fit to be around children. Paddy, oblivious to the reaction of parents, continued screaming at the elf. "You said it would be near impossible to dunk me!" he yelled. Cormac Dooley remained silent at the controls, but Siobhán could swear he was trying to fight a smile. Santa continued to rage as the tank rolled back into the tent. From inside came the sound of sneezing. Seconds after being dunked and poor Santa was catching a cold.

"That was awesome," Chris Gordon said. He held up his hand to high-five. Siobhán did not give him the satisfaction. All she wanted was another mug of hot cocoa of her own, and definitely with the Irish cream. She was just starting for Declan's tent, trying to fight the crowds, when the sounds of dogs barking startled her. She stopped. It sounded like an entire pack of dogs. Where was that coming from? People jostled her from behind. "Do you hear that?" she said aloud. The barking had stopped. She waited, trying to filter out the voices and the music. There it was again. High-pitched yelps. One sounded very much like Trigger. She gravitated toward the sound, and soon found herself standing in front of a small wooden shed positioned behind the manger. On the door was a crude painting of Rudolph. She yanked opened the door and a pile of tongues, flapping ears, and wagging tails clamored out, assaulting her, barking indignantly. They all had homemade reindeer antlers affixed to their poor heads.

"Goldie!" Adam screamed. Siobhán turned to find him right behind her, with his father, Ed Healy, pushing him. Ed swooped up the puppy and delivered him to his son's arms.

"A Christmas miracle!" Ed said with a nod to Siobhán as Adam covered his dog in kisses. "Who put them in here?"

"I'm not sure," Siobhán said, scooping up Trigger and holding him under her arm. He seemed exhausted from his adventures and was content just to be held. She just wanted to take him home and cuddle him. Santa had really crossed a line, and no one in their right mind would even dream of doing this.

Ed turned and glared at Santa's tent. "I'd say we know who, alright."

"Please," she said. "I don't think he's in his right mind."

"He's a thief!"

"Maybe."

"*Maybe*? They're here in his shed with reindeer antlers on their heads. Who else would have done it?"

Siobhán nodded, and smiled, hoping it would calm him. "I think Paddy is suffering from some kind of illness." *One much more serious than catching a cold.*

Ed removed the antlers from Goldie and waved them around. "You *think*?"

Her smile became strained. "I'm only asking you let the guards handle it." She glanced at Adam, who was cuddling Goldie and hanging on to every word. She stroked Trigger's head. "Believe me, I'm just as browned off as you are."

Ed's eyes were cold and hard as they flicked to the tent again. His fist balled up at his side. "That elf came into me shop and bought raw bones. Now I know why. He's in on it too."

Siobhán looked around, but could not see the elf, or Santa, or Mrs. Claus. "I bought bones too."

"He bought a dozen!" Ed stormed up to the door of the shed, turned on his mobile torch, and shone it on the ground. Sure enough, gnawed bones littered the ground. That's why the dogs had kept quiet until now.

"Leave them," Siobhán said. "The guards will get to the bottom of it." *How could Cormac do that? Was he in on the dognapping?*

"Neither of them are welcome in me shop," Ed said. Folks were catching on and rushing up to the shed to be re-united with their pups. There were eight of them. Eight stolen dogs. *Dasher, and Dancer, and Prancer, and Vixen . . .*

Music blared again, so loud that everyone threw their hands over their ears. "Silent Night" had never sounded so hostile. The dogs howled. The mechanical sound of the tank started up again, and people turned as it began to chug out of the tent yet again. Siobhán was starting to think there wasn't enough Irish cream to get through this evening.

"Mechanical difficulties," the elf screamed as he whizzed past her toward the dunk tank, the tassel on his cap flapping. Children squealed as they raced to be the first to the snowball machine. The tank chugged out and screeched to a stop. Santa was not perched on his diving board. He was already in the tank, floating facedown. Laughter rang out.

"You can't dunk yourself, Santy!" somebody yelled. Siobhán had a horrible, horrible feeling, an instinct for trouble; she felt the way some people could feel rain in their bones. Something was terribly wrong. Siobhán hurried over to the tank, pushing her way through the growing crowd. Santa was not moving. The cocoa water was tinged with a puddle of red, spreading faster across the top.

Although her mind raced to find any plausible excuse, especially when a tank of hot cocoa was bizarre enough, nothing made sense except one thing. The red tinge snaking its way through the tank of hot cocoa was blood, and Paddy O'Shea was doing the dead man's float.

Chapter Two

Siobhán raced for the dunk tank. "Somebody help me!" She spotted Mike Granger, their friend and neighbor, and motioned him to her side. The two of them leaned over the tank and pulled Paddy toward them. Mike was able to turn him over, Paddy moved easily in the water despite not moving a muscle himself.

Death was always in the eyes. Paddy's brown eyes were open, but the lights were out. Siobhán felt his neck. No pulse.

"We have to try CPR," she said. Two guards appeared at their side and took over.

"Get these people back," one called to her.

"Watch his head," she said. "I believe he was struck."

She and Mike did their best to get people to step back as the guards lifted Paddy's body out of the tank and set him on the ground. There they called 999 and started CPR.

She knew it was too late, and now they were contaminating the crime scene. But they had to at least make an attempt to revive him. Eileen O'Shea wailed from a few feet away.

"He's gone," she heard one say. "Is there a tarp in the tent?"

The other disappeared inside the tent, then came out with a large blue towel. "There's this."

"Let's get him covered."

"No!" Eileen shouted. "Paddy!"

The guards allowed her to kneel by her husband, waiting respectfully with the towel.

"Is anyone in that tent?" Siobhán called to the guard.

He shook his head. "Why?"

Was he really asking her that? "Someone struck him over the head," she said. "He was murdered."

The guard swiveled his head around. He picked up his mobile, presumably calling Garda O'Reilly who was acting as the interim detective sergeant until a permanent one could be found.

"Hey," she heard a male voice say behind her. Siobhán whirled around, to find Cormac Dooley standing in front of her, gripping his elf cap with both hands, his face white.

He swallowed. "Is he . . . alright?"

"Santa?" a child said, moving closer.

"Everyone back," Siobhán said again. "No," she whispered to Cormac. "He's not. Were you in the tent at intermission?"

Cormac shook his head. "He sent me to fetch something to eat. I came running back when I heard the tank roll out." He pointed at her. "You saw me. I ran right past you."

I did? He did streak by her, but now she couldn't remember if it was before or after she found the dogs. *Paddy could have been dead when Cormac ran out, pretending to fetch dinner.* "Was anyone else with him?"

"No, he was alone."

Her youngest brother Ciarán appeared by her side, still dressed as a bean, and she resisted the urge to kiss him and squeeze him as she handed Trigger over to him. "Go," she said as several men reached Paddy and began to turn him over. She patted his head. "You were a great bean."

"I was just a seed. I didn't get to become a bean."

"You were brilliant, now please go."

"Where?"

"Find James. Away from here, please."

Ciarán didn't budge. "What is Trigger doing here?"

"I'll tell you all about it later." *Great, I'm going to have to fess up that I knew he was missing.* That was the least of her worries.

Ciarán was trying to see past the tank. "What's wrong with Santa?"

"Later, luv. Please get back." She gently shoved her brother away.

"Is Santy coming?" she heard a child call from somewhere in the crowd.

No, luv, Siobhán thought. *Santy has come and gone.*

The first order of business was to get everyone, but the guards, out of the town square. Detective Sergeant O'Reilly fought his way through the current of exiting townsfolk, making a beeline for Siobhán. O'Reilly was a short but powerful man with ears that were hard not to stare at; they were so large and pointy. Truth be told, he would have made a good elf himself, but this was a horrible time to be having such thoughts.

"O'Sullivan," O'Reilly barked. "You don't start until the new year."

"Of course," she said. "I'll get out of your way."

"Stay," he said. "I want to know exactly what's happened here." Siobhán turned to the tank.

"It's horrible," she said.

O'Reilly made a call for the crime scene team. Unfortunately, they could not move the body in any way until the state pathologist arrived, but they could secure it as much as possible. Siobhán brought O'Reilly up to speed with everything she knew, starting with opening the shed and finding the missing dogs.

"You're saying Paddy stole those dogs?"

"I'm saying I found the dogs in his reindeer shed with antlers on them." She kept her voice steady so she wouldn't sound sarcastic. He frowned anyway.

"We need a list of every owner and dog before they take them home."

"Would you like me to do that?" Siobhán asked. She needed something to do.

"Yes. I'd appreciate if you could do that right now."

"On it."

"I'd also like the owners of the food and gift stands to stay. And if anyone in the crowd saw or heard anything, tell them to write it down and we'll be getting to their accounts as soon as we can."

"Understood."

Siobhán started for the shed, to catch the dog owners who were waiting for her to take down their information, no doubt expecting some kind of explanation. If Paddy had stolen the dogs for his show, there was no use holding a grudge. His fate had been far worse, and from what she could tell, none of the dogs were harmed. Humiliated, perhaps, by the antlers, but otherwise they were grand. She found her siblings in a clump, just beyond the barricade set up by the guards. They were waiting for her. She hurried over. James was still in full makeup and drag, even though he'd taken off the wig. She touched every one of them, Ciarán on the head, Ann and Eoin on the arms, a squeeze of Gráinne's hand, and a quick pat to James. She wanted to feel them, reassure herself they were all solid, and alive, and everyone was alright. "I have to get to work," she said. "I'm sorry about the show. You were all fantastic."

"Is Paddy O'Shea really dead?" Eoin asked.

"I'm afraid so."

"Someone said he was murdered," Gráinne said, a little too loud for Siobhán's liking. Not that everyone wasn't already whispering about it.

"Who would kill Santa?" Ann's quiet voice pierced Siobhán's heart.

Siobhán turned to James. "Will you take them straight home and lock all the doors?"

"Of course." He looked around. "Although . . ."

"*Although?*"

James gestured to all the people crowded behind him. "People don't want to go home on a night like this. You know yourself. And not everyone will want to be in the pubs. What if I open the bistro for tea and biscuits, give them somewhere to go?"

He was right. Creatures would be stirring tonight, every single one of them. "If you're alright with that, I am too." It was times like this that comfort and neighbors were needed. And Naomi's Bistro could provide it.

"What about yous?" James said, checking in with the rest of the brood. "If anyone isn't okay with it, speak now."

"Let's do it," Ann said. "I won't be able to sleep."

"Me either," Ciarán said. "And Trigger is staying with me all night."

Gráinne nodded.

"Let's go," Eoin said. "Let's be the light in the darkness." It was oddly poetic of him, but that was Eoin, always surprising her. She loved them all so fiercely.

"Keep your ears open," Siobhán whispered to James.

"Way ahead of you."

"And be careful." She didn't like the thought that the killer could come into the bistro; after all, this was someone who struck Santa Claus in the middle of a giant crowd. But life had to go on. The killer could be on the run, long gone, or biding his or her time and waiting to escape.

"We'll be fine. You be careful."

"Will do."

"Do you need anything?" he asked. James was a good big brother, even when he'd been at his worst. Now that he was sober, he was the *best* big brother.

"If you see anyone on the way home with one of the dogs, send them back to the square. I need to make a list."

"Will do."

"Try not to dwell . . ." She stopped. That would be an impossible task for any of them.

Gloved feet and hands were moving in and out of the tent. When the flap opened, Siobhán could see a pile of teakettles. Presumably the ones used to fill the tank with hot cocoa. Cormac had not been joking when he said one kettle at a time. She had collected the names and numbers of all the dog owners. "I'm on my way to speak with the booth owners," she said.

"Go home," he said. "You're not on duty until the new year."

You just asked me to do it! she wanted to say. "I don't mind," she said. "It will be good training."

"I'm not in any position to train you. I have a murder inquiry on my hands."

"I just thought . . ." *You asked me* . . .

O'Reilly held up his hand. "At this point there's nothing we can do until the pathologist arrives." It could be days.

One of the biggest challenges when it came to murder investigations in Ireland. Time was of the essence, yet they were forced to wait.

"Are you sure there isn't anything I can do?"

He took the list of dog owners from her and stared at her while she waited. Was this some kind of blinking test? She really had to blink. "Talk to Annmarie and Declan," O'Reilly said at last. "We've got the others covered." He turned his back, officially closing her out. She stared at the tank before heading off. Had it malfunctioned? Or was it purposeful? Maybe the killer wanted the distraction. A misdirection . . . *Or the killer had been putting on a show of his own* . . .

And the other Mr. and Mrs. Claus from Charlesville— where were they? The entire cast of the panto could be eliminated because they were on stage when Paddy was struck over the head. Weren't they? Her brood was on stage. She couldn't remember if all the actors were on stage. And if anyone had slipped from the audience and into the tent, she wouldn't be able to say.

Struck on the back of the head. One blow? Too quick to even cry out? Or had the noise from the music and the dogs drowned out Paddy's scream? It was awful to think about, but, in the name of justice, it had to be imagined.

"Why are you still behind me, O'Sullivan?" O'Reilly suddenly barked.

Yeesh. She made a mental note to remember that her interim detective sergeant had eyes in the back of his head, and slipped out of the tent before he had to reprimand her a second time.

Annmarie Kirby was standing behind an army of nut-crackers, wrapping and packing them in boxes. She was a voluptuous woman with sass and style. She was wearing a

sequined green dress and matching earrings. Her hair was topped with a crystal flower. "What's the story?" she said as Siobhán approached. "We were told not to leave." Annmarie owned an adorable gift shop in Kilbane; if anyone in the village kept their finger on the pulse of the town, it was she.

"I just need to get your account of the evening, luv, and then you can go home."

"Poor Eileen O'Shea," Annmarie said. "How is she?"

"I can only imagine." Siobhán took out her notebook, grateful that she carried it everywhere. "Can you take me through where you were during the intermission when the tank first rolled out, and where you've been since, including anything you've seen or heard?"

Annmarie stopped packing the nutcrackers. "Aren't you supposed to ask one question at a time?"

Everyone was a critic. "You can answer however you'd like, and if I have any follow-up questions, I'll ask them one at a time." Siobhán forced a smile. Her jaw was going to ache tomorrow from all the forced smiling.

Annmarie leaned over and placed her hand on Siobhán's elbow. Flowery perfume nearly suffocated Siobhán. "When I took over the gift shop, I had a lot to learn too. I'm still learning. I thought I'd sell a lot more of these beauties, but . . ." She slapped her hand over her mouth. "I didn't mean it."

"Of course you didn't. We're all in shock. What can you remember from this evening?"

Annmarie's eyes flicked over the town square as if she was trying to re-create her steps. "I was standing over here the entire evening. Not that I didn't want to see the panto, but these nutcrackers are too dear to leave unattended." She absentmindedly stroked the one in front of her. Siobhán eyed the colorful wooden man. "I hear they're quite popular." They had never appealed to her, and she

was astounded at how dear the price was, but her opinion in the matter was moot. It was apparent Annmarie was crazy about them.

"Handmade from Sligo," she said, holding it up. She hugged it to her chest. "And to think we might have the winner right here!"

A winner . . . "What's the story with that?"

Annmarie feigned shock that Siobhán didn't know the details. She leaned in again and lowered her voice. "The craftsman made a secret compartment at the bottom of these nutcrackers." She turned it over and showed her a tiny metal latch built into the bottom. She turned it and the bottom flap opened, revealing a hollow inside. Siobhán had to admit, she liked the nutcracker much more. "What did you say about a winner?"

"Inside *one* of them is a special shining star. Whoever receives it wins a hundred thousand euro. Wouldn't it be something if the winner is in our batch?"

Siobhán eyed the nutcracker. "What's to stop store owners from opening all the flaps to see if they have the shining star?"

"This is my sample." Annmarie flipped the nutcracker upside down revealing the secret compartment once more. "The ones in inventory have an official seal over the flap."

"What's to stop someone from opening them and re-sealing?"

"I don't know how we would get our hands on an official seal."

"I'm sure if you peel it carefully it can simply be checked then smoothed back on."

Annmarie frowned. "Garda college has warped your mind."

"You may be right."

Annmarie rubbed the secret compartment as if it was a

bottle housing a genie. "If it makes you happy all shop owners had to sign a contract that we are exempt from the winnings."

"That makes sense," Siobhán said.

Annmarie sighed and set it down on her table with a thunk. "But there's nothing saying the winner couldn't throw a little *gratitude* my way. It would be the decent thing to do."

"But these were shipped all over Ireland, correct?"

Annmarie shrugged. "I assume so. But still. The winner *could* be one of mine."

"Excellent. Can we get back to this evening?"

"I sold nearly thirty this evening, and loads more from the shop."

"Brilliant. Were you here during intermission?"

"Of course."

"Did you see anyone go into Santa's tent after the tank rolled back in?"

"I didn't see a thing. I had customers."

"Is there anything you noticed this evening that was out of the ordinary?"

Annmarie put her hands on her hips. "You mean besides Paddy O'Shea rolling out in a dunk tank of hot cocoa, and then dogs tripping out of a shed with reindeer antlers on their poor heads, and then the dunk tank rolling out *again,* only to find Paddy O'Shea floating facedown in it?"

"Yes," Siobhán said. "Besides all of that."

Annmarie shook her head and cradled her nutcracker. "Who would do that? Who would do that at Christmas to Santa?"

"That's what we need to find out," Siobhán said.

"What about the other Mr. and Mrs. Claus?"

"What about them?"

"It had to be them. No one in Kilbane would have done such a thing. Have you interrogated them?"

"I'm sure the detective sergeant will speak with them. Did you see either of them go in or out of Paddy's tent?"

"No." She chewed on her bottom lip and looked away.

"What is it?"

"I suppose it can't be the other Mrs. Claus. She was here at intermission pawing at my nutcrackers."

"Was she here the entire time?"

"No. But was the first in line. I'd say she was here about five minutes." She clasped her hands. "So it *could* still be her!"

They were getting off track. Annmarie sounded quite thrilled as if she'd just solved the mystery.

"Do you know of anyone else who had problems with Paddy?"

Instead of answering, she began packing again. "Don't be silly," she said. "Lately almost *everyone* had a problem with Paddy and the missus."

"What do you mean?"

Annmarie picked up a box, and gave an apologetic shrug. "I'm afraid I simply must get these packed up." She hurried away with one of her boxes.

It would have been much easier for Annmarie to pull her car near the boxes. She didn't. Because she couldn't wait to get away. Because she knew something. She knew someone who had a problem with Paddy O'Shea. And the missus . . .

Everyone? What ever did she mean? Siobhán sighed as she headed for Declan's tent. This was going to be a long night. Investigations would be so much simpler if they didn't involve actual human beings.

Chapter Three

Declan was pacing in front of his tent, but the minute Siobhán stepped up, he stopped to envelop her in a hug. Then he held her at arm's length. "Tell me the cocoa wasn't poisoned."

For a second she was thrown off by the question. "I don't know," she said. She nearly told him about the gash on Paddy's head, but it was vital not to give away any information. Rumors would start soon enough. Declan turned to his stash of hot cocoa stacked up in the tent. "Will I have to throw it all out? Turn it over to the guards?" She could hear the angst in his voice.

"Hold off on it for now. The guards will test the cocoa in the tank."

"Everyone was drinking it. Including m'self. Should we all go to hospital?"

She sighed. "I don't think it was poisoned."

"What happened?"

"I believe he was struck over the head." She nearly groaned out loud, already breaking her own rules. "But please don't share that."

"My word! Struck over the head with what?"

"I don't know. And please—"

Declan held up his hand. "Not a word, luv. I hear gossip, I don't spread it." He was telling the truth. Declan was the publican whom everyone spilled their secrets to, and he never told tales out of school. Kilbane was lucky to have him.

Siobhán took in the tent housing the dunk tank. Declan was quite a distance away. "You're pretty far away from the commotion. Did you see or hear anything?"

"I heard the tank rolling out, interrupting the play. I saw Cormac throw the snowball. He sure looked intent on knocking poor Paddy into the tank."

"That is the point of the tank," Siobhán said. *But didn't the elf say that it wasn't easy to do?* Seemed easy for him. But the snowball hit the target, not Paddy's head. Did any of it add up to something sinister? "What else?"

Declan raised an eyebrow. "I saw you get mauled by a pack of dogs wearing reindeer antlers."

"Hardly mauled. Poor pups."

"Is it true? Did Paddy *steal* those dogs?"

"I believe so."

He shook his head. "He wasn't well. First the threats to the other Santa, then stealing dogs."

"What a night."

Declan gave a sad smile.

"Can you take me through your day?"

"I've been here helping Paddy fill that tank, kettle by kettle."

"Where did you get the hot water?"

"I filled it from my setup here. Mind you, we didn't use the good ingredients, he just needed the tank to look like it was filled with hot cocoa. After a few kettles of it, they hooked up a hose from the tailor's shop—he has a lovely garden in the back, as you know—and we filled the rest of the tank."

"Did they test it out then?"

"They hit the target and confirmed the board tilted down. Paddy wasn't up for getting wet. Said *once* would be enough."

"Was there anyone else around? Just you and Santa and the elf?"

"It was only the three of us filling the tank, but there were others in and out of the square of course. People setting up the Nativity scene, and Santa's throne, and the like."

"Any arguments break out?"

"Paddy was being tough on Cormac. Ordering him around, hollering if he wasn't fast enough. Cormac just took it. I finally told him he was to stop it or I'd let his missus know."

Declan stood up to bullies. "Can you ever remember him like this before?"

"Never. He wasn't a well man. We should have all put a stop to Santa this year."

Someone certainly did . . . "No one could have seen this coming." Cormac had been bullied by Paddy. And Declan said Cormac had looked intent on dunking Paddy into the tank. He'd been in an obvious bad mood around her. His scowl was etched in her memory. There was no getting around that fact that Cormac was going to be high up on the suspect list.

"Did you hear or see the dogs?"

Declan shook his head. "I had no idea they were in there."

How is that possible?

The dogs must have been snuck in later. How? Where were they before that? "Do you know anyone who would want to harm Paddy?"

Declan sighed. "I know he wasn't himself this year. Ran into some trouble with the guards the other night."

"I heard."

"Almost got tossed into the drunk tank."

"Because of this rivalry with the Charlesville Santa?"

"It could be that he needed to be seen by a doctor. But he was keyed up about the other Santa, alright."

"Do you think he was drinking this evening?"

"I know he was. I refused to sell him the Irish variety of hot cocoa. But I saw him tipping a bottle." *Just as I suspected.* He'd been paranoid, drunk, and keyed up. Not a good combination. "I'm sorry I can't be of more help. Whoever it was, they were in and out of that tent during the intermission. I was only focused on my customers."

And since it had only taken seconds for the killer to strike, it was plausible the killer could have also been a customer. Everyone in attendance who wasn't on stage or in a booth was a suspect. "If you think of anything else, you know where to find me."

"Good luck, luv," he said. "The guards are lucky to have you."

She smiled and thanked him, feeling very much like she had yet to earn her wings.

"I still can't believe Santa Claus is dead," Ciarán said. He was standing in the front dining room of Naomi's Bistro, hugging a squirming Trigger.

Siobhán gripped her cappuccino. "Have you set the poor thing down once since last night?"

"Nope," Ciarán said. "Except for when I fell asleep."

"I see." Siobhán was dressed for her run, but the rest of the O'Sullivans were still in their pajamas. If Siobhán had her way, they'd stay like that forever. Eoin was cleaning up breakfast plates; James was piling wood in the fireplace. Gráinne was painting her nails by the window, and Ann was watching her, most likely vying for Gráinne to paint hers next. Ann glanced over at Ciarán.

"He's a man who played Santy," Ann said. "There's no such thing as Santa."

"I know that, *eejit*," Ciarán said, his face turning red.

"Hey, hey, hey," Siobhán said. "Let's all take deep breaths and stop insulting each other." She stared at the yet-to-be-decorated Christmas tree, which was now set up in the back dining room.

"I'm not quite in the mood," James said, turning from the fireplace and nudging one of the Christmas boxes with his toe.

"Of all the ways to go, drowning in hot cocoa never crossed me mind as a possibility," Gráinne said, holding up her painted nails to the window. "What other horrible ways to die are there that I haven't thought of?"

Eoin clunked his mug of hot cocoa down on the table. "T'anks a lot. I'm off it for life now."

"Do I have to stop drinking it?" Ciarán wailed.

"No, luv, let's all try to relax."

"Relax?" Gráinne said. "With a killer running around?"

"Yes. Because the guards will handle it. The best thing we can do is be there for poor Eileen O'Shea, and go about our business."

Ciarán stood up straight. "I'll decorate the tree."

"I'll help," Ann said.

"Thank you." Siobhán wished they could all enjoy it, but it was impossible, given the circumstances. But her advice was correct. They had to carry on. "I'm going for my run, then off to buy what we need for Christmas supper." She'd talked to James and Eoin last night. They would have turkey and ham. It was times like these that tradition was needed more than ever. She was looking forward to time with her family. Detective Sergeant O'Reilly was right. She wasn't on duty yet. They could handle this murder probe without her. "I hope all of you join in to decorate the tree. It's times like these where we need the Christmas spirit most of all."

"We will," Ciarán said. "We'll make it the best ever."

Siobhán bit her lip, afraid the tears would come. She wanted to call Macdara Flannery. Anytime anything happened, like the sun going up or coming down, he was the first person she wanted to call. But he'd moved to Dublin soon after she'd enrolled at Templemore Garda College, thus ending their brief romance. *Ending* was a relative term. In her heart she still felt him. Thoughts of him followed her like her own shadow. They had unresolved issues, but the time was piling up behind them, making the possibility of resolving their differences fade away with each passing day. Often she picked up her mobile to give him a bell, only to put it down again. There was nothing wrong with his fingers, he was quite capable of dialing her. He would hear about this murder, that was for sure. Someone was probably ringing him right now. If they didn't figure out who did this terrible deed, it would hang over every Christmas, tainting it worse than the Grinch ever could. And Gráinne wasn't wrong to be worried. The type of person who would kill the town Santa posed a danger to them all.

Eoin returned from the kitchen and knelt beside one of the Christmas boxes. "We're doing the train this year?" He lifted a shiny black engine out of the box, then looked to the ceiling. The tracks ran along the top of the wall, all around the restaurant. Their father had made the structure necessary for it to run and the lads knew how to set it up. But it took hours to do it properly. Still, the Lionel trains were always a big hit. Siobhán, for one, could sit all day by the fire, watching it chug around and around. The engine even blew smoke and whistled. She even loved the faint smell of burning smoke. "I know it's a lot of work. But we need to lift everyone's spirits up. They're bound to be shaken."

"Deadly," Eoin said. "We'll set her up."

"You're joking me," James moaned.

"It will keep your mind off Elise," Siobhán said, turning to her older brother. He had been moping around ever since she'd gone back to Waterford for the holidays. The girl was annoying, but she also grew on you. Go figure.

"You're getting quite good at delegating," James said.

"T'ank you," Siobhán called out as she headed to the door for her run. She was outside before anyone else could have the last word.

Rain the night before made the morning run a slog, yet the trip around the abbey lifted Siobhán's spirits nonetheless. The sun was just beginning to rise behind the ruined priory's five-light window, and spears of orange set the ancient stone aglow. It buoyed her. Every time she ran past, she visualized the monks as if they were still here, going about their day, brewing beer by the river, stoking the fire in the abbey. She was part of this village, these stones, this green grass, Ireland. Home was in the bones, the heartbeat, the blood. She would not let a murderer rob her village of the Christmas spirit. He or she would be caught and brought to justice. She ran faster, imagined the monks cheering her on. By the time she was back at the bistro, her running watch had five minutes left. *A record!* It was only because she was looking down at her watch that she noticed a brightly wrapped box glimmering on the bistro's doorstep. Shiny red foil and a golden bow. Siobhán nearly tripped over it. It had not been there twenty-five minutes ago. There was no tag. Who could have left it? Was it for all of them?

Siobhán glanced down the street once again, as if the person who left the surprise package might be waiting and watching. It was a medium-sized box and lifted easily. Something light. At least it wasn't Sheila Mahoney's holiday fruitcake that she guilted everyone into purchasing every year, announcing it was for "a good cause." The specifics of this good cause were never mentioned. Although Siobhán often wondered if the local dentist was in on that scheme, because if anyone did dare to bite into one of Sheila's fruit-cakes, they were in danger of mimicking a popular Christmas song and losing their two front teeth. As she picked up the prezzie, she noticed the tag. There was no *To*, only a command: *Do not open until Christmas. Love, Santa.*

She nearly dropped it. *Santa?* Whatever this was, they could not open it. It needed to be reported to the guards immediately.

She found it torture not to open presents. As a child, she'd ruined many Christmases for herself by breaking into her mam's closet, where she always stored the gifts, unwrapping them all, then wrapping them back up again before Christmas. She then had to act surprised about everyone's gift on Christmas Day. And then she had to confess her sins to Father Kearney. And then she swore she would never, ever do it again. And yet she always did it again. A wrapped box was a dare. A siren. A throbbing in her throat. She had an impulsive streak, alright, running deep through her veins. She entered the bistro with the box in hand, already imagining tearing it open. *Is this some kind of sick joke?*

She was only a few steps into the front hall when Ciarán slid toward her in yellow socks, skidding to a stop in front of the package with big eyes. "Is that for me?"

She wished she had something to cover it with. "I have to bring it to work," she said. "Just a boring present for the guards." She hated lying, but he was already traumatized that Santa was dead. She didn't want him thinking that his ghost was delivering presents to their door the day after he died.

Ciarán frowned. "What is it?"

She placed the box on the counter and turned with an exaggerated shrug. "It's a mystery." She leaned in. "It could be a fruitcake."

He scrunched up his face. "Ew."

"Exactly." She scanned the bistro floor, counting the number of Christmas boxes. "We're missing some decorations. I think they're in the crawl space on the second floor."

"I'll get them." Ciarán ran for the stairs.

"Be careful." Siobhán wanted to warn Ciarán to be careful pulling the ladder down, to be careful climbing the ladder, to be careful coming back down. If she started gushing her worries, they'd be here all morning. "Get someone to help you."

"On it." Eoin emerged from the kitchen with a salute, then glanced at the mysterious present. He was still wearing his polar bear pajamas. "What's that?"

Ciarán was out of earshot. She waved him over. "Found it on the doorstep after my run."

He read the tag and whistled. "That's spooky."

"Tell me about it."

"It's not ticking, is it?"

"Of course not." *Shoot. I should have checked.*

Eoin stared at her, a grin forming.

"What?"

"You want to put your ear to it, don't you?"

She started to contradict him, then put her ear to the box as he laughed. "I don't hear anything."

"Good on ya. You'll be a grand addition to the guards."

She swiped him with the back of her hand.

"Come on!" Ciarán yelled from the top of the stairs.

"I lied about the present," Siobhán called to Eoin. "I told him it's probably a fruitcake."

He glanced at the stairs and nodded. "I would have done the same."

Siobhán gathered her handbag and her shopping list, and then finally the present. She'd better drop it off before they accused her of hiding evidence. Who was she fooling? She'd better turn it in before she ripped it open, frothing at the mouth like a rabid, greedy raccoon.

Chapter Four

Outside, the skies were gray, brightened only by gangs of fluffy white clouds. Snow didn't often visit them during the holiday season, but everyone had been reckoning that this was the year. Siobhán and Detective Sergeant O'Reilly stood outside the garda station. An officer had just taken the mysterious gift inside. The state pathologist was on her way, and the only thing they could do was to guard the crime scene and make sure no one disturbed it. The folks of the village had decided they would set up a memorial, as well as some of the Christmas decorations at the abbey and the surrounding field. Father Kearney would preside over it and offer comfort.

"The town is gathering around Eileen," O'Reilly said, adjusting his cap. "She wants Christmas to go on in his name."

The old Paddy would have wanted the children of Kilbane to heal. Siobhán could only imagine the conversations parents were being forced to have with their children this year.

"Are you still willing to help with this investigation?"

"Of course. What can I do?" A part of her wished he would order her to open the present. *What could it be?*

"We're going to need you to go door-to-door and see if

anyone else received a package from Santa. And you'll need to collect them."

That wasn't the task she'd expected. *"Me?"*

"You said you wanted to help."

He was turning her into the Grinch. People were going to hate her. "Some people may have already opened theirs."

"You still need to collect them, find out where the package was left, what time, and if they still have the wrapping paper or ribbons. I want that too."

"Should we start by opening mine?"

O'Reilly gave her a look. "I'd like them all collected first."

"Not a bother. It's not ticking."

"Pardon?"

"I put my ear to it."

"Did you, now?"

"Yes. Just in case."

"You're acting like a pro already." He grinned.

"I don't know how I'm going to collect them all."

"I will send a guard and a car with you."

It was settled. She would be the sanctioned Grinch.

Not everyone was willing to give up their gifts. By the time they reached Sheila's hair salon, they had collected ten. They stood outside the door, for Sheila was blocking their entrance. She put her hands on her hips and tossed her hair, which was sporting green and red stripes. "A present on me doorstep?" she said, sounding as if she had to think about it. "From Santa?"

"Yes," Siobhán said. "We need it."

Sheila glanced over her shoulder. "It says not to open until Christmas."

"It's possible evidence in a murder inquiry."

"Says you. You're not even a guard yet."

The guard behind her cleared his throat. They were under strict orders to keep it moving. Siobhán turned back to Sheila. "Sergeant O'Reilly has ordered me to collect them. If it ends up not being material, I will personally return it to you."

Sheila stepped back and let them step into the salon with a shake of her head, as if she couldn't believe what they were asking of her. Siobhán saw the present right away, a box identical to the one she had received, sitting on the counter. Before she could reach it, Sheila was tearing off the paper. "Stop!"

"It's mine!"

"I'm supposed to collect them unwrapped."

"Too late." Sheila tossed the wrapping on the floor and ripped the lid off the box. She stared into it, then lifted out a hair blower. Siobhán stepped closer. "It's mine," Sheila repeated.

Siobhán reached for the hair blower. "You'll get it back, the guards need to check it out first."

"No," Sheila said. "I mean it's *mine*." She bent down and opened a drawer underneath one of the styling stations. "Just as I thought. He took my hair dryer from my drawer, *stole it,* and now he's wrapped it up and given it back."

That was odd. Siobhán stepped forward. "Are you sure?"

Sheila turned the hair dryer over. Stamped on it: PROPERTY OF SHEILA M.

That was conclusive. Why would someone steal Sheila's hair dryer, only to wrap it up and return it? She was starting to think Paddy's mental condition was even worse than they'd suspected. Siobhán eyed the blower. "I'm still going to need to take it."

"My property gets stolen, returned, and now you want to take it again?"

"Yes. I'm sorry. I'm sure it will be returned to you." Siobhán allowed the guard, who accompanied her, to take the blower, box, and ripped wrapping paper. She backed out of the shop as Sheila lit a cigarette and glared at her until they disappeared out the door.

Hours later they were back in the station standing in front of at least thirty opened gifts. Every single one of them was an item that had been taken from their homes, then wrapped and returned. From Naomi's Bistro it was salt-and-pepper shakers. Siobhán had to admit, it was a right letdown. Others included house slippers, eyeglasses, cups and saucers. A few gifts had been returned to the wrong houses.

"Just another indication that poor Paddy was suffering from a mental illness," O'Reilly said, removing his cap and scratching his head.

Siobhán was inclined to agree, but she knew it was important not to jump to any conclusions. "Are we sure it was him?"

"The tags say, 'Love, Santa.' "

"Anyone could have written that." *Or maybe it was the Charlesville Santy.*

"We can check with Eileen and see if it's Paddy's handwriting," another guard piped up.

O'Reilly turned to Siobhán with a sly grin. "Good idea. Why don't you get on that?"

Siobhán found Eileen O'Shea standing outside Saint Mary's Church, Father Kearney and dear friends huddled protectively around her. When she caught Siobhán's eye,

Eileen nodded and excused herself. "I'm sorry to inter-rupt," Siobhán said.

"Don't be," Eileen answered. "I know they mean well, but if I hear someone tell me they're sorry for my loss one more time, I'm liable to scream. Does that sound horrid of me?"

"No," Siobhán said. "Would you like to come to the bistro for a cup of tea?"

"Is this official business?"

"I'm afraid it is."

"Good." That wasn't quite the reaction Siobhán was expecting. Eileen must have read her expressions. "You're whip-smart. Top of your class at Templemore Garda College, I heard. If anyone can figure out who killed my Paddy, it's you."

"I'm certainly going to do my best." Siobhán refrained from adding that the people closest to the victims were always the top suspects. Eileen said her good-byes to Father Kearney and her friends, and the pair began their walk to the bistro.

"I suppose you want me to account for my day," Eileen said.

"Wherever you feel you need to start," Siobhán said. You could learn a lot from not only what a witness said, but what they *didn't* say. The more room a person had to frame his or her story, the more they could accidentally re-veal.

"I believe I have to start with the night before," Eileen said.

'*Twas the night before the murder* . . . Siobhán shook off the thought, loathing at times how her mind worked. Eileen was willing to talk, that was half the battle. "Please."

"The night before the winter carnival, I was upstairs in

the bedroom. I could hear the floorboards below me. Paddy was pacing for hours. He was worried the dunk tank wouldn't function properly. He wanted to test it, but he needed help, and that elf insisted he needed his sleep."

"That elf?"

"Sorry. Paddy insists we call each other by our roles during the holiday season. Cormac Dooley."

Siobhán wondered if Eileen knew how poorly Paddy had treated Cormac. She tried a subtle approach. "Did Paddy get along with Cormac?"

Eileen stopped to study Siobhán. *"Get along?"*

"Yes." An image of the elf's face rose to mind. He'd been agitated, annoyed. Was he always like that? Or had it been the strain of working with Paddy?

Eileen sighed. "I don't blame Cormac." Now she picked up her pace and Siobhán had to double-time it to catch up.

"Blame him?" *For what?*

"Paddy was very sensitive this year. Everyone but Cormac abandoned him. That's probably why Paddy kept his secrets."

"Wait. Kept *whose* secrets?"

"Cormac's, of course."

"What secrets?"

Eileen glanced around. "I couldn't. I don't know if I should."

"Anything you say will be kept in the strictest confidence." They were only a few doors down from Naomi's. "Let's get tea and biscuits first," Siobhán said gently. It was obvious Eileen was reluctant to talk, and some tea and biscuits would make it much easier to tell the widow that her husband may have been breaking into homes and stealing.

Chapter Five

Siobhán and Eileen stepped inside the bistro. The tree was dressed, baubles gleaming, white lights shining. The tables were adorned with red tablecloths and white candles set in little green wreaths. The fire was crackling, and the train was chugging along the ceiling. Siobhán had never been prouder of her siblings. Although she felt a twinge of sadness that she hadn't been able to participate in the decorating, this was just the balm her weary soul needed. Eileen gave a soft smile. "My Paddy would have approved."

Siobhán sat them by the window, with their tea and brown bread with butter. When they were finished, she gently asked Eileen about the evening before the presents had appeared on doorsteps. "Did Paddy pay any special visits to neighbors?"

Eileen set her teacup down and eyed her. "Why do you ask?"

Siobhán hesitated. It wouldn't be possible to get the answers she needed without filling Eileen in on the thefts. She tried to keep her tone as light as possible. When she was finished, the widow was already shaking her head. "I thought this was all in his head," she said. "I should have listened to him!"

"Listened to what?"

"That elf." Eileen looked around as if he might be hiding under the tables.

"Cormac Dooley?"

"Yes. This is *him.*"

"What's him?"

"He's the thief."

Siobhán did not expect that. "How do you know?"

Eileen shook her head as if Siobhán were too slow to keep up. "Paddy said he was always disappearing, never to work on time, and he was convinced he was up to something." She leaned in. "Paddy told me the elf had sticky fingers. I thought he meant he was sneaking the candy canes. Now I realize he was accusing Cormac of stealing." She sat back and folded her arms, as if that settled everything.

Siobhán was hoping for something more specific. "Are you saying you don't think Paddy stole the presents?"

"One hundred percent my Paddy did not steal presents. *He was Santa Claus!*"

He was the same Santa Claus who had been drinking, ranting, losing weight, verbally abusing elves, stealing dogs, and threatening the other Santa Claus. But Eileen was worked up, so Siobhán kept it to herself. "The tags say, 'Love, Santa.'" Siobhán pulled one of the evidence bags from her handbag and showed it to Eileen. "Is this your husband's handwriting?"

Eileen stared at it and pursed her lips, as if willing them not to speak. "I won't let you start rumors."

"Is it his handwriting?" Siobhán slid the bag across the table.

Eileen pushed it away. "I don't have my readers."

Siobhán pushed it forward again. "Are they in your handbag?"

Eileen sighed and glared at her handbag. Siobhán waited. Finally Eileen opened the bag, removed her glasses, and put them on. They perched on the end of her long nose. "It is not Paddy's handwriting," she said, taking them off, throwing them back in her bag, and snapping it shut. "It looks like Cormac Dooley's to me."

"Are you sure?"

"I am sure that it's not Paddy's. It looks like Cormac's, but I'm hardly an expert."

Siobhán was trying not to let her emotions show. The widow was defensive, she could not take it personally. "Did you receive a gift?" she asked gently.

Eileen looked startled. "No. What does that prove?"

"I'm not proving or disproving anything at this point. I am simply gathering facts."

"Then get them from Cormac Dooley. Everyone is going to accuse my Paddy of *everything*. He needed help, as you know. But this latest accusation, breaking and entering . . . Why would he steal the gifts, only to return them?" She stopped. "When did you say they were delivered?"

"The morning after the panto."

"Are you accusing my dead husband of delivering gifts *after* he's murdered?"

"Of course not. But he may have been the one to take them in the first place."

"*Never!*" Eileen pointed at Siobhán. "It's that elf!"

"We'll speak with him. Please, let's calm down." Siobhán wetted the tea and brought out more brown bread. Eileen didn't touch either. "The dogs," Siobhán said. "Do you know if it was Paddy or Cormac who took the dogs?"

Eileen's eyes welled up. "He told me the owners had all proudly volunteered their dogs."

"*He?* As in Cormac? Or as in Paddy?"

Eileen wiped her face with the back of her hand. "Paddy."

"I see." Not a single owner had even known that Paddy wanted the dogs. Plenty of folks would have volunteered them. "I don't believe he ever asked any of us for our dogs," Siobhán said. "He just took them."

Eileen shook her head. "It's that elf. I bet he lied to Paddy about that too."

Siobhán was starting to detect a pattern. Instead of a scapegoat they were now looking at a scape-elf. Only, this one wasn't being put on a shelf, he was being hung out to dry. On the other hand, Eileen O'Shea was a wife grieving her husband. His reputation was all she had left to save. Siobhán reached over and laid her hand on top of Eileen's. "I promise you. I won't make any assumptions and I will follow all leads thoroughly."

Eileen nodded, then turned her gaze out the window. Once more, the streets were filled with people and their shopping bags. "I know life goes on," she said. "But it's still a shock. For me, the world feels upside down, shifted. And then you look outside and everyone else is going about his or her day as if nothing has changed. One has to wonder if a single life matters at all."

Siobhán took her other hand and squeezed Eileen's hands. "Every single life matters. I've known your husband as Santy my entire life. Year after year he brought joy to all of us. He mattered. If he was having an issue lately with his mental state, why, it's no different than if he had been stricken with a terminal illness. He's not to blame. He was a good man, he brought joy, and he mattered. I will not let anyone tear down his name, and I will not stop until we find his killer."

Who might, Siobhán had to admit, *be sitting across from me right now, ignoring her brown bread and tea.*

* * *

Cormac Dooley lived just a few minutes outside of town in an old stone cottage. It would have been cheerful, but the front garden was choked with weeds and debris. Not a single Christmas decoration could be seen. He was pacing in the yard, speaking on his mobile, when she pulled up. He stared at her pink scooter for a moment, then clicked off his phone and studied her.

"How ya?" He squinted. "You're not in uniform?"

"I officially start in the new year, so it hasn't been issued yet. I've been called in early to help out with the inquiry into Paddy O'Shea."

He held up his phone. "I've been calling the guards. Wondering why they haven't spoken to me yet."

"Do you have relevant information?"

He nodded, then held up his finger as he ran toward her. He came to a breathless stop in front of her, then continued to hold his hand up as he dug in his pocket. He produced an inhaler and took a deep breath before shoving it back in his pocket and exhaling. "It's that *other* Santa Claus. You need to talk to him."

"Funny, because Mrs. Claus said I needed to speak with you."

He frowned. "Which one?"

"Eileen O'Shea."

He shook his head. "No. It's the *other* Santa who did this."

"The Santy from Charlesville."

"Dat's the one."

"What's his name?"

Cormac threw his hands up. "How am I supposed to know that? Tried to ask him once, he just kept saying, 'Santy, I'm Santy.' He stays in character, I'll give him that."

"What else can you tell me about him?"

"Paddy said the other Santy was *out to get him*. I thought it was just a turn of phrase. But now . . ." He looked out into the distance and sighed. "Do you want to come in for a cup of tea?"

"I just had a cup, thank you." She took a step closer. "Can you give me an account of your past week or so with Paddy?"

"He was feverish. Demanding. Determined to beat this other Santa. I knew he was working on a winter carnival theme, and I was his number two, but he was keeping me in the dark. I wasn't allowed in his workshop at home, or in the town square when he finally set up. Every day there was a new naughty list."

"He actually kept a naughty list?"

"This year he did. Practically everyone is on it!"

Siobhán wasn't on it, was she? She was dying to ask, but she was here to do a job. "Did you know about the kidnapped dogs?"

Cormac Dooley stretched out his neck, as if it was aching, then looked away. "Did I hear about them, or did I know about it beforehand?"

"I'll let you answer how you see fit."

He sighed and finally made eye contact. "I had no idea he was stealing dogs."

Is he telling the truth?

As she contemplated it, Cormac whistled. Grass rustled in the distance and then suddenly three pairs of ears were flopping as hounds bounded to his feet. Cormac knelt and began lavishing them with pets and kisses. He introduced each with a hand to the top of their head. "Bubbles, Patches, and Angel-face." He looked up at her. "I would *never* steal someone's dog. Someone's *babies*."

"Did you buy bones for them at the butcher's?"

"Of course. For Christmas."

"Are they in your freezer now?"

"They are." He squinted. "Would you be wanting one?"

He had a sense of humor after all. "I'll just be wanting to confirm they are in there."

"May I ask why?"

"Ed Healy mentioned you bought a dozen bones recently. Our kidnapped dogs were given bones in the shed to keep quiet."

"Follow me." He turned and began to walk to the cottage. The weeds were nearly as high as he was tall. She followed. When they reached the front door, he held up his hand. "Do you mind if I bring them out to you?"

"Not a bother."

"T'ank you. I've been too busy and the place is in shambles." He hurried in, barely opening the door before slipping in and slamming it shut. The dogs raced up the steps and stared up at her, tongues flopping, tails wagging.

"Sorry, pups. Official business, like." She squatted and petted them. Moments later the door opened and Cormac stepped out, holding a bag of frozen dog bones. She snapped a photo with her mobile, as they weren't really evidence of anything other than Ed Healy jumping to conclusions. "Thank you."

"I would never take someone else's dog without their permission."

She believed him. "What about someone's . . . *things*?"

He sighed as the dogs begged at his feet. "Is it Christmas Eve? I don't think so. Off with ye." He waved them away and the dogs bounded off. Trigger would have continued to beg. He was a much better trainer. "Now you're on about the stolen gifts, are ya?"

"Yes, what can you tell me about them?"

"I believe that was Paddy himself."

She pulled out the tags from the gifts. "Is this your handwriting?" Cormac looked at it, then looked away.

"We can find out. It would help if we heard it from you."

"Yes. He had me write tags. But that's the job requirement."

"Did you ask him what the tags were for?"

"It was obvious. He was giving out gifts this year. I assumed it was part of the competition."

"Why would he steal gifts, just to return them?"

Cormac's face contorted. "I didn't know he stole them! I wouldn't have gone along with that." He began to pace and patted the pocket where his inhaler had been stashed, as if worried he was going to need it again. He stopped, and must have read her mind. "I'm allergic to the dogs. I just can't live without them."

"As long as you're okay."

"Is anyone?" They held eye contact.

"We all do our best to get by."

"Exactly," he said. "I wouldn't want to live without those big eyes, floppy ears, and wagging tails." He motioned to her. "Follow me."

It was a short distance to the back garden where a small shed stood. ELF'S WORKSHOP was splayed across it in red paint. Cormac opened the door, flipped on a light, and stepped in. Siobhán followed.

It was filled to the brim with Christmas decorations. A table took up the middle of the room. Wrapping paper, ribbons, and tape covered the table. He removed a list from the table and handed it to her. It was a list of residents on one side and items on the other. Lines had been drawn from the items to the names. At times lines had been erased and redrawn, and some names and items had question marks after them. "I did the best I could."

"You returned the gifts?" The tips of his ears flamed red as he nodded. "I'm going to need you to back up and tell me how this all happened."

He sighed, then propped himself up on a stool. "Paddy pulled up to me house a few days ago, carting a big wagon behind his vehicle. In it were all the stolen items." He sighed. "He said they'd all been donated and the money would go into the winter carnival. He wanted me to sell them all to an antique dealer in Charlesville. Get top dollar."

"But you didn't?"

"I started to. And then I realized what they were."

"Stolen?"

He nodded. "Yes. Stolen."

"How did you realize that?"

Cormac took the list from her and scanned it. "There." He pointed. "This figurine. I took it into the antique shop. The proprietor took one look and almost called the guards on me. He knew the owner, and she'd already been in, warning that it was missing. I had to tell him about Paddy's declining mental state, and I promised him I would personally return all the gifts. He helped me go through the list to see who owned what. I know I made a few mistakes, but I returned every single one." His shoulders slumped. "I know it was bad timing, returning them after he'd been murdered." Cormac shivered.

"Why did you wrap them?"

A shy grin stole across his face. "I thought it would help lift people's spirits. Everyone likes surprises and presents."

Not when it's your own item stolen from your home.

He gave her a look like he knew what was she was thinking. "I just thought it was better than shaming Paddy." He pursed his lips and crossed his arms tightly. "I promised to do right by him, the *old* him, and I did." He jumped off the stool and held out both hands, palms up.

"What are you doing?"

"Cuff me. Arrest me. I did what I did."

"I'm not here to arrest you."

He dropped his arms and shrugged. "Then I have no more to say. If I were you, I'd question the Charlesville Santy."

Chapter Six

"Santa Claus?" O'Reilly said. "You want to interrogate Charlesville's Santa Claus?" His tone was one of outrage.

Siobhán stood patiently in the doorway of the detective sergeant's office and nodded. She knew why he was so worked up; he was chummy with the guards in Charlesville. "More than one person I spoke with mentioned the rivalry between Paddy and the other Santy. It doesn't have to be me who interviews him, but somebody needs to."

O'Reilly stared at the mountain of papers on his desk as if he wanted to light them on fire. "Calling the shots already, are you?"

"No, sir."

He sighed, took his cap off, rubbed his head, put his cap back on, sighed again. "I need you to be subtle. Are you capable of being subtle?"

She clenched her fists and ordered her mouth to curve upward. "Quite capable."

"Don't go accusing him of anything."

"I will stay on his nice list."

O'Reilly frowned. Siobhán grinned. Then she left as quickly as possible before her guise of subtle charm fell away and she punched him in the mouth.

*   *   *

The town of Charlesville was bustling. Shop windows were adorned with Christmas decorations, their wares calling to her. She was so behind in her shopping; she wished she were there for Christmas shopping and a spot of lunch. Would life *ever* be that simple again? The most exciting places to shop were the big cities: Cork City, Limerick, or Dublin, but the smaller towns had a cozy feel that couldn't be beat. The storefronts and streets were decorated much like Kilbane with wreaths and red bows and twinkling lights. Only here there was no hint of sadness, no folks gathered in gossiping clumps, no rumor mill churning out suspects and theories. It was just Christmas. Their Santa was named Barry Callaghan, and his wife was Aideen. Siobhán was told he could be found in town, socializing with folks as they went about their Christmas shopping. And indeed, just ahead, there he was, in his Santa outfit, which he filled out with a big belly, just as a proper Santa should. Standing next to him was his wife, dressed again as Mrs. Claus. Or maybe that's how they dressed every day of the Christmas season. Maybe they never wore anything else. It wasn't her place to judge, but Siobhán hoped they were keeping up with their washing.

She waited while he chatted with a small child, handed him a sweet, then patted his head and let out a joyful chuckle before the mother and her young lad went on their way. He caught Siobhán's eye and grinned as she approached.

"Hello, lassie. Have you been a good girl?"

"I'm a grown woman, Santa, and I'd say I've been fair to middling."

He threw his head back and laughed, he really did have the belly laugh down. "Sweet?" He held out a candy.

"I'm Garda O'Sullivan from Kilbane."

"I see," he said, exchanging a look with his wife. Siobhán gave Mrs. Claus a nod and a smile and it was returned, although it seemed to require a bit of effort. Her thick white hair was piled in a bun on top of her head, adorned with a red bow. She had the lightest of blue eyes and rosy cheeks. But there was something about her smile that reminded Siobhán of a plastic doll.

"Darling," Barry said, turning to his wife. "Why don't you find this year's nutcracker while Garda O'Sullivan and I have a chat?"

"Alright, dear." She kissed Santa on the cheek.

"This year's nutcracker?" Siobhán called after her, hoping to keep her there for a few more minutes. She got the feeling her husband wanted her gone, and that made Siobhán wish she would stay. But Aideen Callaghan was off like a shot, her backside bouncing away, as if her life depended on buying a nutcracker.

"She's an avid collector," Barry said as he watched her go. "Loves her nutcrackers."

"I see," Siobhán said. "Annmarie's gift shop in Kilbane has a wonderful collection this year. Handmade from Sligo. She was selling them at the winter carnival."

"We like to buy local," Barry said, scrunching his face as if he'd just tasted something sour. She detected a twinge of jealousy. Maybe Paddy wasn't the only one who was caught up in the rivalry.

"One of the nutcrackers has a shining star hidden inside, and whoever finds it wins a prize of a hundred thousand euro." Siobhán hadn't planned on saying any of this, but nutcrackers seemed to be on everyone's mind this year, and she wanted to establish a bond with this Santa. Suspects were more willing to open up if they felt you were on the same side.

This seemed to catch his attention. "Does it, now?"

"I'm not claiming Kilbane has been sent the winner. But it adds a bit of fun to buying one. Somebody has to be a winner."

" 'Winner, winner, chicken dinner,' " Santa said. "Although I dare say it wouldn't look good if Santa and Mrs. Claus won the money. We'd have to donate it to charity." The thought seemed to make him sad, and his posture slumped.

"I need to speak with you about Paddy O'Shea."

Santa nodded; he knew this was coming. "Cup of tea? I know a quiet spot."

"Perfect." They began to walk. He was being very accommodating. *Too accommodating? Does Santa have a guilty conscience?*

"I am terribly disturbed over Paddy," he said like an actor rehearsing his lines. "Do you have any leads?"

"It's an open inquiry," Siobhán said lightly.

"Terrible, terrible deed. During the holidays, no less. I hope you're doing everything you can to catch this killer." He stopped at a corner pub and gestured for her to enter. "We'll have a bit of peace in here."

It was dark inside and the several patrons dotting the stools barely glanced at them. The publican waved at Barry and he nodded and held up two fingers. They sat in a green leather booth tucked in the back corner; moments later the publican appeared with two steaming mugs of tea and a tin of biscuits. "That was quick," Siobhán said after the publican ambled away.

"There are a few perks to being Santa," he said with a wink.

Siobhán was already drained of the small talk, and after a few moments with their tea, she began. "Where were you right after the tank was rolled into the tent?"

Barry set his cup down. "We were walking around, looking at those nutcrackers, about to buy a mug of hot cocoa when we heard the screaming."

"I thought you hadn't heard about the nutcrackers?" It flew out of her mouth, and it was hardly important, but she'd barely been speaking to him and she'd already caught him in a lie. Maybe Cormac Dooley was right. Maybe there was more than one Bad Santa in Ireland this year.

"I didn't know about this shining star, or anything else, other than me wife spotted nutcrackers at the carnival." He squinted at her. "Are you accusing me of something?"

Siobhán smiled. "Sometimes words come out of my mouth the wrong way. Not at all." He continued to stare at her. She decided to plow on. "Didn't you hear the dogs before the screaming?"

"I suppose I did." He scratched his chin. "I didn't think much of it, to be honest. I hadn't realized at that point the dogs had been taken without their owners' permission." He crossed his arms. "Never thought I'd see the day when a man wearing this uniform would resort to stealing pups out of people's gardens."

"I don't think he was in his right mind."

"It's a disgrace to the profession."

"I heard that you and Paddy had become more than competitors as of late."

"Whatever do you mean?"

"Rivals," Siobhán said. "I heard you were rivals."

"That sounds very sinister." He held up his hands. "I won't say a bad word about him." He crossed himself.

"I'm trying to find his killer. If there's a bad word to be said, then so be it."

"He was an angry man this past year. Do I go all out to help this town celebrate Christmas? You bet I do. Was I

trying, as he accused, to humiliate him? That's ludicrous."
He leaned forward. "He created a dunk tank of hot cocoa.
That's mental."

"He may have had a mental illness, a treatable one, but
he didn't knock himself over the head, a killer did that."

"*Knocked over the head* you say?"

Shoot. She'd done it again. "It's an expression."

He leaned forward. "Is it, now?"

"We're still waiting for the state pathologist to issue her
report."

Barry frowned. "It was so quick. The time between the
tank rolling back into the tent the first time, and rolling
out the second time."

"It was very quick." *Either someone got lucky with an
impulse kill, or the evening had been premeditated. Right
down to the technical errors . . .*

"What's your current theory?" Once more, he looked
very eager for gossip.

"I can't comment on an ongoing inquiry."

"'Course you can't. I apologize." He finished his tea. "I
don't know how else I can help."

"Can you think of anyone who wanted him dead?"

"Blunt, aren't you?"

"When I have to be." She leaned forward. "Who do you
think would have wanted him dead?"

"I have no clue. I know of no one. Including myself. I
enjoyed the competition."

Another lie. The other Santa was dead and he was still
competing. "Why were you there that evening?"

"*Why?*" He leaned forward. "Paddy invited us. I thought
he was extending a holly branch. We had no quarrel with
him." He sighed and leaned back. "We didn't have to go. It's
a busy time of year. I was hoping it would be the beginning
of a truce."

"Did you or any of your friends place any bets in relation to this healthy competition?"

"Is that what you're getting at? A motive for murder? Money?"

"I asked a simple question."

"If you breathe one word of this to anyone . . . these preposterous theories. I play Santa Claus. I can't be painted as a murder suspect. Are you trying to ruin our Christmas too?"

"No. I'm trying to catch a killer."

"How many times are you going to say that?"

"As many as necessary."

He sighed. "Good luck to you. I wish I could help."

"Where were you at intermission?"

"We didn't move from our seats. I wanted to be close to the action when Paddy got dunked."

"I thought you said you were looking at nutcrackers?"

He cried out and banged the table with his fist. The bartender stopped polishing a glass and glanced over. Barry held up his hand as if indicating he was alright.

What do they all think? That I'm going to accost Santa Claus midafternoon during tea?

He leaned in and lowered his voice. "I've had quite enough."

"Enough of what?"

"You're confusing me. Trying to trap me."

"If you need more time to answer, then take it. I'm trying to ascertain the facts."

He sighed. "I know I was in my seat during most of the intermission. The wife went out to look at the nutcrackers. Truthfully, I was waiting because I wanted to be the first to dunk him."

That was the first thing out of his gob that had rung true. It meant he had been sitting close to the tent, facing the entrance. "Did you see anyone go in and out of the tent?"

"The elf," he answered right away.

"Did you see him go in or out?"

"I saw him roll in on top of the tank, and a few minutes later he dashed out."

"Did you pay attention to where he went?"

"No."

"Did you see him come back?"

"No. By then, we were watching you and those dogs with antlers. Did he do that because I brought in live reindeer from Wales last year?"

"I don't know." *He so did.*

"It wasn't easy getting them here, I tell ya that. If only they could really fly." He winked. He certainly sounded proud of himself.

"You didn't see anyone else enter or leave the tent?"

He stroked his beard. It was long, and white, and it was the real deal. "I can ask the missus, but I only saw the elf. I tell ya, that was more like a circus than a Christmas celebration. My reindeer were the talk of the town. I was on the news. What was he thinking?"

The rivalry definitely wasn't as one-sided as Barry Callaghan wanted her to believe. Some adults never stopped being children at heart. She suddenly didn't know what else to ask. Two years at Templemore Garda College and there hadn't been any tips on interrogating a narcissistic Santa. She jotted her digits down on a piece of paper and slid it over to him. In the new year she'd have proper calling cards. "If you think of anything else, let me know."

"If there's anything else I can do . . . Would you like me to visit Kilbane as Santa this year?"

"I don't think that would go over very well."

He sighed. "I suppose not. Please give my sympathies to Eileen, will you?"

"Of course."

"I'll walk you back to that pink scooter." They headed out. When they arrived at her scooter, he seemed to be checking it out. "Did Santa bring you that?"

"No," she said. "My paycheck did."

He grinned. "I'd say second to flying reindeer, that's a very nice ride."

As she motored away, she noticed Mrs. Claus run up to her husband and cling to him. The two of them stayed, heads bent toward each other, whispering and glancing her way. Siobhán hated to say it, but there was no way she could cross Santa and Mrs. Claus off her naughty list.

Chapter Seven

"You're to watch only," Sergeant O'Reilly said to Siobhán as they stood outside the crime scene, donning paper booties and gloves. The square was still closed to the town, cordoned off with yellow tape. They were about to enter Santa's tent. Every object in the tent had already been photographed and bagged as evidence, including every teakettle. There hadn't been any snow that evening, and the square was made of cobblestone, so footprints would be impossible to find. O'Reilly had guards in the process of pulling all the CCTV cameras from nearby to see if any of them caught anyone going in and out of the tent. Paddy's body was covered in a sheet. Unfortunately, it had to remain where it lay until Jeanie Brady, the state pathologist, arrived from Dublin to declare it a crime scene. The only thing they could do was drain the dunk tank to see if there were any clues to be found within. Samples of the water had already come back clean. No poison. The blood was confirmed to be Paddy's.

Once they removed the tent and mapped where they would allow the water to drain, special glass cutters had been delivered to cut holes into the tank. As Siobhán watched, she felt a squeeze of pity for Paddy. Despite his mental instability, he'd gone to a lot of trouble to come up with this dunk tank. The scent of cocoa filled the air, making the task deceptively sweet. Cocoa snaked through the cobblestones like a meandering creek. When it was drained, there was nothing to see but the Santa cap, and a vibrant blue paint chip. It had survived in a tucked away crevice, and the color had not faded away. The hue was unique. Everyone stared at it.

"Something blue," Sergeant O'Reilly said.

"Would you call that sky blue?" a guard asked.

"Aqua," someone else offered.

"Teal," Siobhán said.

Sergeant O'Reilly shook his head. "Are we done spinning the color wheel?"

"Does it mean something?" a guard finally asked.

"It could be from the murder weapon," Siobhán said. "And in that case it means we can narrow down our search until we match the color." She hesitated, knowing she shouldn't, but unable to resist. "Which I believe is teal."

O'Reilly pushed past her. "Let's bag it, see if we can figure out where it came from." They searched the rest of the tent and the surrounding area, but found nothing that matched the blue chip of paint. O'Reilly bagged it, and Siobhán asked permission to take a photo. He sighed. "If you must." She snapped a picture with her phone. "Let's process the shed. All we can do after that is wait for the state pathologist."

Inside the shed they found the pile of raw bones. O'Reilly pointed at them. "Bag the bones and take them to the shop," he said. "See if Ed remembers who bought them and when."

"*Me?*" She hadn't meant to sound so surprised.

"You said you wanted to help."

"Yes, of course."

"Then take the bones to the shop."

"Do you want them back?"

"They're in evidence bags, aren't they?"

"Yes, sir."

"Stop calling me *sir.*"

"Yes, Sergeant."

He tipped his hat and walked away. She headed for the butcher's.

Once again, the butcher shop was jammers as folks vied for their holiday meals. Dave Healy was at the register checking out customers as Ed handled the product. Siobhán had to wait off to the side until the shop emptied out, a brief lull before the next wave.

"I have a feeling you're not here for more rashers this soon," Ed said.

Siobhán smiled. "I'm afraid not. I'm helping out Detective Sergeant O'Reilly and he wanted to know if you sold Paddy O'Shea a half a dozen raw bones." She produced the evidence bag by her side and held it up. "These bones."

Ed Healy squinted. "No." He wrapped a package of rashers as he spoke. Siobhán wished she were at home having brekkie with her brood. "Must be Dooley's purchase."

"I just spoke with Cormac Dooley and he showed me the bones he purchased. Someone else bought these."

"I'm sorry, but I can't identify customers from the bones of the meat I sell."

When he put it that way, it did sound ridiculous. But this was a small shop. He'd been in business for over thirty years. He was an old-fashioned man who had never embraced the Internet or smartphones. But he had a wicked memory. He knew who came in, and what they ordered, especially a dozen dog bones purchased only a few days ago. He was being dodgy. "These aren't from your shop?"

"I sell those, yes. But I didn't sell them to Paddy."

"How can you be sure?"

"Because he hasn't been in here since we had a falling-out."

Siobhán stepped forward. *"A falling-out?"* This was the first she'd heard of it. "What happened?"

Ed threw a weary glance to his brother, Dave. "Can you handle the shop for a minute?"

"Of course."

He took off his gloves, threw them away, then wiped his hands on his apron and motioned for Siobhán to follow him out the back door to their garden. She smiled at Dave as she passed, but he wasn't looking at her. She got the feeling he wasn't happy she was here to question his brother. Perhaps once she was a guard, no one would ever be happy to see her again.

The back garden was overgrown with weeds. An old shopping cart was abandoned in the middle of the yard, and had been overtaken by plants and vines. Cigarette butts were dropped on the ground. She was grateful Ed always wore rubber gloves when handling the meat.

Ed sighed. "What I am about to tell you stays between us."

"If by *us* you mean the guards, and whatever we need to do about the information, then yes."

"Paddy owed me money. A lot of money."

"I had no idea."

"They are proud people, the O'Sheas. Too proud. Eileen didn't want to admit Paddy was deteriorating. But I could see it. Anyone could. Skin and bones, and usually raving about something."

"He would come into the shop like that?"

"He wouldn't come into the shop at all. Eileen would. And for the past several years I was keeping her tab."

"My." *Several years?* She could only imagine how much they owed. It was very nice of Ed. He had a big heart. "And then Paddy found out?"

He stared at a cigarette butt on the ground like he longed for it. "Not exactly."

"Go on."

"I had no choice. Adam needs things. Physical therapy. A new wheelchair. There's a rehabilitation program in Limerick I want to sign him up for. It's expensive. I've been watching every pound, trying to save for it. Hoping insurance would kick in. But it's too dear. I make too much to qualify for assistance, but not enough to pay. How do you like them apples?"

"I'm sorry." If it were one of her own, she'd want them to have the best care too. "Maybe we could start a fund-raiser."

"Not a chance."

"Why not?" But she knew why not. Ed Healy was a proud man. He'd never take it.

"Are you going to raise over a hundred thousand euro?"

"That is dear."

"I'm sorry. I didn't mean to sound harsh."

"Please continue." She would leave the subject of Adam's rehabilitation for another day, and perhaps speak with others about a fund-raiser. It was worth a try.

"I had to call in the O'Sheas' bill. That's when Paddy found out."

"Did they pay it?"

"Paddy stormed in, spitting and cursing at first for daring to let his wife run a tab."

"He didn't know?"

"The husband is always the last to know."

"I see."

"By the time he left, he said he'd have the money to me before Christmas."

Before Christmas . . .

Is that when he started stealing objects from homes? Cormac Dooley said Paddy wanted him to sell the items to an antique store in Charlesville. Could it have been to pay his tab? Who else did they owe? Was anyone angry enough to kill over it?

"Was that the last time you saw him?"

" 'Twas. Except for at the panto." He shook his head. "You know yourself."

"These bones have to be from your shop."

Ed glanced at the bones. "I keep those in the back freezer. I don't remember anyone but Dooley purchasing them recently, but he only bought half a dozen."

"Should we ask your brother?"

Ed lifted an eyebrow. "We were just inside. If my brother had sold Paddy those bones, he would have said so."

"I'm sure you're right. But I'm just doing my job. I have to ask and document the answer."

Ed nodded, and turned to go back in. "I don't want to embarrass Eileen about the tab. I hope that information stays with the guards."

"I'll see to it."

When Ed and Siobhán returned to the front of the shop, they found it empty and the register abandoned. For a second Siobhán felt she was in a dream. Wasn't this place just packed with people? Ed sported a similar bewildered look. Dave Healy had locked the front door and turned the sign to CLOSED.

Ed glanced at the clock on the wall and frowned. Then looked at his watch. "He's had some banking issues back home. Perhaps he had to return a call."

"I'm sure whatever it was, it was important."

Ed flipped the sign to OPEN and unlocked the door. "This is why I don't go online. Anyone can steal from you. Someone on the other side of the world. It's madness."

"'Tis." Siobhán mainly stayed off social media except for hosting a page for Naomi's Bistro. Social media could also be a helpful tool for law enforcement. But she saw the drawbacks. Her parents would have hated all this screen-time business.

"One more thing." Siobhán pulled out her mobile and opened the picture of the blue paint chip. "Do you have any object this color?"

Ed took the phone and brought it close to him. "What am I looking at?"

"It's a distinct color. I'm wondering if you've seen it anywhere."

"*Anywhere?*" He shoved the phone back at her. "Not that I can recall."

"T'ank you."

He shrugged as if he wasn't sure what she was thanking him for, showed Siobhán out, and returned to his post.

Hours later, as the bistro swelled with customers, Siobhán didn't have time to ponder Ed's revelation that the O'Sheas had been in desperate straits the past few years. She wished they would have known. The church would have taken up a collection. The village would have rallied around their Santa and Mrs. Claus. Then again, wasn't Adam Healy a better cause?

No matter the recipient, Irish pride was strong, if not stronger than Irish kindness. There were times when being from a small village drove her mad, but other times, like these, it was a welcome blessing to be surrounded by familiar faces. It made her miss Macdara. She missed their conversations; she missed his blue eyes, his messy hair, his wink, his laughter. Did he ever think about her? How was he celebrating Christmas? Did he like Dublin? She was grateful the case was keeping her occupied, for the moments when she started obsessing on him were the worst.

She was just clearing a table when she noticed Mike Granger seated at the two-top by the window. It was the shopping bag by his feet that caught her eye. Sticking out from the top was the head of a nutcracker, wearing a vibrant blue hat. *That shade of blue is unmistakable . . . isn't it? One might even say it is teal . . .*

"You alright there, chicken?" Mike asked when he caught her staring. "Are you thinking I've got the winner?" He grinned.

"I'll be right back." Siobhán hurried to bring the plates to the kitchen, then returned and stood by Mike. "May I see it?"

He appeared puzzled, but bent over and removed the wooden man. "Annmarie is selling them in her shop."

Once she drew closer, she could see it was an exact match from the blue paint chip found in the tank. "May I?" She gestured.

"If you want to fondle me nutcracker, I won't be stopping ya," he said with a wicked grin.

She ignored the improper joke and picked up the nutcracker. The wood was thick. Substantial. Hard enough to kill. She examined it carefully, including flipping it over and noticing the thick seal across the bottom flap. When she was satisfied there were no chips, she returned the nutcracker to the bag. "I hope it's a winner." His nutcracker wasn't the murder weapon, but one of them very well could be. It made sense. Annmarie had been selling them at the panto. And her shop. Either the killer had brought it with him or her, or they had purchased the murder weapon minutes before striking Paddy over the back of the head. "May I take a photo of it?"

"Be my guest. But maybe Santy should bring you one of your own, seeing as how you're so transfixed."

Chapter Eight

Sergeant O'Reilly was already waiting for Siobhán in front of Annmarie's. The wind was picking up, delivering a stinging bite to their cheeks. A bell jingled above the door as they entered. Annmarie was just handing a customer a shiny bag. "Happy Christmas," she called as the customer exited. There was a moment of silence as they regarded each other. "What can I do for you?" Annmarie said, a hint of worry in her tone despite her smile. Siobhán showed her the photo of Mike's nutcracker. "Yes," Annmarie said. "We had quite a few with that color blue."

"*Had?*"

"Those went first. It's a unique color."

"Would you say it's teal?" Siobhán said. O'Reilly nudged Siobhán with his foot. She let it go. "Did you keep a list of everyone who bought one?"

"If they paid by credit card, I would have the transaction, but it wouldn't list the color."

Detective Sergeant O'Reilly took off his hat and scratched the top of his head. Siobhán sighed. It would have been so much easier if Annmarie could hand them a nice little list. "Besides Mike, can you remember who purchased ones with this particular teal on its head?"

Annmarie squinted. "Isn't it more of a sea blue?"

"Sea blue," O'Reilly said, suddenly cheered. "I like dat one."

"Can you remember or not?" Siobhán hoped it hadn't come out too harsh. *It is definitely teal. What is wrong with people?*

Annmarie mulled it over even as she shook her head. "Adam Healy was quite taken with them. He and Ed were in. But they didn't buy one. Ed said he'd come back without the young one."

"Did he?"

"Not while I was here. Sarah Murray has been helping me out. I can ask her."

"Please do." Sarah Murray was in college at Limerick University, but she helped out at the shop whenever she was home on break. Whenever Siobhán saw her, her face was shoved into the screen of her mobile, so the chances of her remembering anything was very low. Maybe Ed Healy had a point about the drawbacks of technology.

"Can you give her a bell right now?" O'Reilly asked.

"Of course." Annmarie took her phone and stepped to the side as she made her call. She returned moments later. "She does not recall Ed Healy coming back to buy a nutcracker."

"Who else can you remember?" Siobhán asked.

"Sheila Mahoney bought one, I remember because she wanted to haggle with me on the cost. I told her these were handmade from Sligo, and because of the shining star in one of them, I expected them to sell out. Then, of course, you already know Mike bought one for his aunt. I think it's the spinster one who lives in Killarney. I haven't been to Killarney in ages. I wish I was there right now." She gave Siobhán and O'Reilly a look that suggested *they* were the reason she wished she were there right now.

"Who else?" Siobhán said, inquiring before Annmarie got too far off track.

"Cormac Dooley, and Eileen O'Shea bought one." She sighed. "I guess we'll no longer be referring to them as the elf and Mrs. Claus. If I knew what that poor woman was going to go through, I would have given it to her for free."

"She paid for it?" Siobhán blurted out.

O'Reilly shot her a look. Luckily, Annmarie didn't seem to pick up on it. "She paid cash. Is that important?"

"Only to the extent you don't have a card receipt," O'Reilly said.

At the mention of the elf and Mrs. Claus, something was flitting in and out of Siobhán's mind. The *other* Santa Claus said his wife was crazy about nutcrackers. "Did the Charlesville Santa come in to buy one for his wife?"

Annmarie brightened. "How did you know?" She clasped her hands together. "Those reindeer from Wales last year were so wonderful, weren't they?"

Sergeant O'Reilly took off his hat and rubbed his head. "Seems we were better off asking who *didn't* buy a nutcracker."

"I told you. They are very popular." Annmarie gestured to the shelves. "Only a few left, if you fancy one yourself."

The image of poor Santy's head rose to mind. "No, thank you," Siobhán said.

"I didn't mean you. You don't need one."

"Pardon?"

"Never mind. It's nothing." Annmarie busied herself in a drawer and started humming. Siobhán took a step forward.

"It didn't sound like nothing."

"Am I required to tell you everyone I remember who bought a nutcracker?"

"Yes," O'Reilly said.

Annmarie chewed on her lip. "Eoin bought one." She glanced at Siobhán and shrugged. "Surprise!"

"Eoin bought one? My brother Eoin?"

"Yes. Your brother Eoin."

"I had no idea."

Annmarie grinned. "I hope you'll have the winner. You deserve it."

The prize! Eoin, of course, would buy one. Her brood loved daydreaming about winning money.

"I'll question Eoin," O'Reilly said. "You have an obvious conflict of interest."

"Not a bother." Siobhán wanted to assure him that Eoin had nothing to do with knocking Santa Claus over the head, but she kept her gob shut. She was a guard now and had to do everything by the book.

Annmarie leaned on the counter, her large chest holding her up like cushions. "Does this have anything to do with the murder?"

Siobhán patted her on the shoulder. "You know we can't say. But it's very important that you go through your records, and your memory, and make us a list of everyone who bought a nutcracker."

"I will do." She sighed. "I sold a lot. This is going to take a while." She glanced around the shop, which was once again starting to fill with people.

"Where is Sarah?"

"She's busy with the family."

"Do you want me to see if Gráinne could offer you some holiday help while you sort it out?"

Annmarie brightened slightly. She always liked Gráinne's roguish ways. "That would be lovely," she said. Her face turned serious for a moment. "But she can't argue with the customers. Not during the holidays."

"I'll let her know."

"And none of those short skirts."

"Understood."

"Or tight or low-cut tops."

"I see."

"If she could go easy on the makeup . . ."

Siobhán sighed. "Shall I send Ann instead?" The youngest of the O'Sullivan Six had none of the challenges Annmarie had listed.

Annmarie exhaled with relief. "Please do."

As soon as they exited the gift shop, O'Reilly took a call. He hung up. "Jeanie Brady has arrived."

"Thank goodness."

"Come along, you can watch, but keep your gob shut and stay out of the way."

"Of course."

"Will you go back into the shop first and buy a nutcracker? I'd like Jeanie to know we think it's possibly the murder weapon."

"Of course."

He dug some euro out of his pocket and handed them to her. "Get a receipt and meet us back at the crime scene."

"Right away." Siobhán started back for the shop, and then stopped. "Wait."

O'Reilly waited, although one could hardly call his stance patient. "Yes?"

"What if it's a winner?"

He frowned. "What if?"

"Who wins it?"

"It will belong to the garda station."

"Makes sense, I suppose."

"We'd put it to use." He tipped his hat and left. Siobhán hurried back inside and bought the nutcracker, checking first to make sure it was sealed. It still bothered her, the thought of someone abusing the seals. Did the maker simply not care? Or was the craftsman counting on folks to be so wrapped up in the Christmas spirit that they wouldn't dare try to cheat? It was a careless set-up if you asked Siobhán. She wasn't the type of person who would break the seals looking for a winner, but make no mistake, those types were out there. Those were the types who would soon be keeping her employed. Maybe Annmarie was right. Her mind had been warped. As it should be. Guards had to be able to see the worst in people to be good at their jobs. The thought made her sad. This was why she should be enjoying Christmas, using the little time she had left to see the best in people instead. At the register she hesitated. They were selling fancy boxes of pistachios in red and green, the ribbon-adorned bags propped up in tiny wooden sleighs. Jeanie Brady had a mad pistachio addiction, and it was Christmas after all. Siobhán purchased it separately, thrilled to be buying her first Christmas gift of the season.

"For me?" Jeanie Brady's eyes lit up at the pistachios. She was a short and round woman, with bright eyes and a vibrant personality. "It's perfect." They stood just outside the tent, standing sideways to brace themselves from the biting wind.

"Not a bother."

"Do you mind keeping it for me so I won't be tempted?"

"Of course."

Jeanie nodded, and kept her eyes on the gift bag as she donned gloves. She pointed at the sleigh. "I'll be seeing you soon." She turned to the tent. "Now." She entered and began her initial task, which was simply declaring it an official crime scene and doing a preliminary examination of the body. "We'll have to check his lungs to see if the blow killed him, or if he drowned."

"We sent the cocoa water in to check for poison," O'Reilly said. "It came back clear."

Jeanie nodded. "No need for poison when a blow to the head and drowning would certainly do the trick." She held up the evidence bag with the paint chip in one hand and the nutcracker in the other. Theirs wasn't a winner; Siobhán had broken the seal and peeked the minute she purchased it. To be fair, it hadn't taken awhile to remove the seal, so maybe it wasn't as careless as she first thought. "First glance, I'd say you found your murder weapon, alright. I'll measure the wound to the head with the nutcracker and render my findings."

"Technically, it's not the murder weapon," Siobhán said. "The real one will be missing a chip off the old block."

Jeanie nodded. "Indeed. Thank you for clarifying." She added a sarcastic smile. Siobhán clamped her lips shut, hoping the pistachios would earn her some good graces.

It didn't take long before the van came to take the body. It would be transported to the only funeral home in town, Butler's Undertaker, Lounge, and Pub. There Jeanie would conduct the autopsy. She took the sleigh of pistachios from Siobhán as soon as the van left with the body. "Thank the stars the cocoa wasn't poisoned," she said with an affectionate pat to Siobhán's shoulder. "I've heard it's magic in a mug."

" 'Tis. You'll have to stop into O'Rourke's for a mug before you leave."

"Will do."

Siobhán remained at the crime scene and scoured it again, just in case she'd missed a stray nutcracker. There were none to be found. The killer had taken it with him or her. Cases often took one step forward and two steps back. Forward step: they now had a bead on the murder weapon, and Siobhán suspected it wouldn't take long for Jeanie Brady to confirm it. Back steps: many in town, including her brother, had purchased a nutcracker, and they had no idea where the exact murder weapon was now.

She paced the square as she tried to piece together what they knew so far. Either someone had just gone shopping, then happened to enter Santa's secret carnival and . . . what? An argument broke out and the murderer pulled the nutcracker from his shopping bags and struck? The injury was toward the back of the head, which suggested a kill from behind, so that didn't quite fit. Unless they argued, then Santa turned his back for a second and the killer struck.

They were only looking at a fifteen-minute window of time.

What kind of argument could it have been to ignite that kind of rage in such a short time? The evening had been cheerful. Festive.

The second possibility was that Paddy's murder was premeditated. The killer was already in a rage, and determined to confront Paddy. He or she figured the best place to do it was surrounded by everyone in town. Everyone would have the same alibi, too much commotion to notice someone slipping into Santa's tent during intermission. Quite cunning. If the O'Sheas owed Ed Healy money, who's to say they didn't owe others? Eileen was going to have to be thoroughly questioned. It was heart-wrenching to put a widow up as a suspect and start digging into her darkest secrets, but finding the killer took precedent. This business was not for the faint of heart.

But what if it wasn't the blow that killed Santa? What if it had only succeeded in knocking Paddy unconscious and he'd died by drowning in the hot cocoa? If that was the case, had it been intentional? Did the killer think the tank would help hide evidence? Paddy had kept his dunk tank very secret. Either this murder was impulsive and the killer used the tank to his or her advantage at the last minute, or . . .

The killer was someone who knew about Paddy's dunk tank.

Mrs. Claus? The elf? The *other* Santa and Mrs. Claus? The man who made the tank who normally made mansions for little fishies? Maybe *he* hadn't been paid, and she could only imagine what kind of money was involved in building a dunk tank from scratch. Why hadn't she thought of this before? She needed to get the name of the maker straightaway.

Chapter Nine

Once the crime scene tape was removed and the town square was once again open to the public, candles and flowers and mass cards were placed on Santa's throne. Soon folks began leaving copies of pictures of children taken with Paddy over the years. Siobhán had added a few of her own. Paddy O'Shea had been a vibrant and chubby Santa much longer than he'd been a thin, raging one. Siobhán was thrilled to see everyone recognizing that fact. Eileen stood with Father Kearney and her dear friends, going through all the photos, and reminiscing. Residents took to putting antlers on their dogs and bringing them along to show they had no hard feelings.

Back in town, Declan advertised hot cocoa of the Irish variety, which folks were happy to purchase. He had both a Baileys, an Irish cream, and a whiskey version. Siobhán found some quiet morning time to make batches of brown bread with cranberries. Every season she tried to add a different touch. It came out divine, if she did say so herself. Meanwhile, the town was scrambling to find a replacement Santa for the children. Siobhán would leave it to them, as she had more important work to do, not to mention she hadn't even started her Christmas shopping. Eoin and James had volunteered to handle Christmas supper so that was one less burden to bear. Annmarie had done her best to make a list of everyone she remembered who bought a nutcracker, and then they split the list among the guards. O'Reilly was looking into the maker of the dunk tank and the finances of the O'Sheas. The guards were like reindeer, preparing to pull the sleigh of justice. She kept this observation to herself, one of the many thoughts that was best kept to herself.

Jeanie Brady had confirmed that a nutcracker was a match to the blow to Paddy's head and that his final death had been caused by drowning. It was horrible to hear, but every fact would help lead to the killer. The morning after Jeanie's report was issued, Siobhán finished her run, changed her clothes, and headed out to speak with the folks known to have purchased a nutcracker. Ed Healy remained on the list, simply because he'd mentioned he'd planned on buying a nutcracker. It was possible he'd sent someone else to do it. Ed wasn't one of the people on Siobhán's list. However, she had decided that when this murder probe was over, she intended on speaking with the sisters at Saint Mary's Church to see about raising money for Adam's rehabilitation. She had no idea whether or not Ed had been exaggerating the cost, so she placed a call to the rehab center in Limerick and left a message about her inquiries. No one was available, but she was assured they would return her call as soon as possible. For now, she was on her way back to Charlesville to speak to the other Mr. and Mrs. Claus.

Siobhán secretly had more than one reason to return to Charlesville. One was to follow up on Aideen Callaghan's nutcracker collection, and the other reason was to visit the antique store where Paddy had told Cormac Dooley to sell the stolen items. She was surprised to find that Aideen and Barry Callaghan lived in town above the antique shop. She didn't know why, perhaps stereotypes of Santa were influencing her, for she had imagined them in a North Pole–like farmer's home, complete with elves, and reindeer, and sleighs, and, of course, Santa's workshop. Instead she found herself climbing the steep stairs above the shop, and by the time she reached their red door at the top, she was out of breath. She was going to have to step up her runs.

The door was opened by Aideen Callaghan, still dressed as Mrs. Claus, and for a second Siobhán had a hard time focusing on her, for the small flat behind her was jammed with Christmas. Multiple Christmas trees, nutcrackers, knickknacks, a train going around the floor, and every bit of space on the wall was filled with stockings. Mrs. Claus was smiling and waiting patiently; she apparently had this reaction often enough that she knew to wait for it.

"I don't know what to call you," Siobhán admitted. "Do you prefer Aideen or Mrs. Claus?"

The woman smiled. "It's the holiday season. Whatever you like, but I'm used to Mrs. Claus, pet."

"Mrs. Claus it is."

"Come in, come in, have a cup of tea."

It took Siobhán a second to realize the invitation hadn't come from Mrs. Claus, but rather a large colorful parrot perched on a rocking chair in the middle of the Christmas explosion.

Mrs. Claus laughed. "Bobby is right. Please do come in."

"Cup of tea," Bobby said as he spread his wings and ruffled his feathers.

Ciarán would go mad over a bird like this, Siobhán thought. Especially as a Christmas gift. That was all they needed, another mouthy-mouth to feed. "It's very . . . festive in here."

Mrs. Claus sighed. "We go overboard. Some call us Christmas hoarders, but we can't help it. We love Christmas!"

Siobhán had to watch her feet as she followed Mrs. Claus through the living room and into the kitchen. Even the teacups had tiny sleighs on them.

" 'Jingle Bells'! 'Jingle Bells'!" the parrot chirped.

"My husband said you'd be paying me a visit," Mrs. Claus said when they were situated with their tea and biscuits. "I don't know what I can tell you. But we feel just awful. And I hope it doesn't sound like I'm only thinking of ourselves, but do you think we're in danger? Is the killer after *all* Santas, or was it specifically Paddy he was after?"

"I'm actually here to see your nutcrackers," Siobhán said. "Mr. Claus told me you had quite the collection."

Mrs. Claus looked startled, her eyes darting about the room as if she were counting her collection. Siobhán brought out her phone. "Do you have any with *this* color?" She showed Mrs. Claus the chip of blue paint. "Most say it's teal."

"I'd say that's sea-glass green-blue."

"There's no such color with that name." Siobhán was getting irritated and they were getting off track. "Regardless, do you have any this color?" *Teal. It's teal!*

"Funny, you mention it." She rose and navigated toward a back shelf in her living room, where she began shuffling nutcrackers around. "I know it's here somewhere. That sea-glass color is very distinct." After a few moments of looking, she turned back. "It's gone!"

"When did you see it last?"

"It's the latest in my collection." She began to scan the room, anxiety stamped on her full cheeks.

"Has Paddy ever been inside your flat?"

Mrs. Claus frowned. "As a matter of fact, he and his wife were here. Just after I put out the decorations." This was news.

"Why were they here?"

"He said he wanted to mend fences. He was horrible to me husband last year. Jealous as a toad, he was. But it was only right to accept his apology. He was so skinny, I kept trying to feed him more biscuits. Where is that nutcracker?"

"By any chance, was Cormac Dooley with them?"

"Who?"

"He played Paddy's elf."

"Yes, he was. A delightful fella. Bobby really took to him."

Siobhán had a feeling she knew what had happened to the nutcracker. She still wasn't sure if Cormac or Paddy was the thief. Both had blamed each other, and only one was left who knew the truth. If Cormac was the thief, he'd hardly admit it. It would be the height of irony if Paddy had stolen the nutcracker that killed him. "I'm sorry to worry you. I hope you find it."

Siobhán didn't mention the nutcracker was the murder weapon. She had to be careful about giving away information pertinent to an ongoing inquiry. And she had no proof that Paddy, or his elf, had stolen the nutcracker. Who was to say which Santa or which Mrs. Claus stole it? What if this Christmas-addicted Mrs. Claus was a killer?

" 'Jingle Bells'! 'Jingle Bells'!"

Mrs. Claus sighed. "I'd better play the song or he'll harp on it all day."

"Go right ahead."

Mrs. Claus was heading to the radio when her mobile

rang. She excused herself and left the room to take the call. Siobhán walked up to the parrot.

"Happy Christmas," Siobhán said, feeling a bit foolish.

"You fraud!" the bird screamed.

Siobhán was gobsmacked. She took a step closer to the bird. "Happy Christmas," she repeated.

"You're no Santa."

"Happy Christmas," she said yet again.

"Fraud!" Bobby stretched his wings and ruffled his feathers. "Fraud!" He began to scoot back and forth on his perch, bobbing his head. "What did you do! What did you do!"

"What did you overhear?" Siobhán said, mostly to herself. "Who are you imitating?"

Siobhán heard a thud and turned to find Mrs. Claus staring at her. "I'm afraid I have to go," Aideen said.

Siobhán pointed at the bird. "*Who* was he mimicking? Who called who a *fraud*?"

Mrs. Claus folded her hands and straightened up. "No one. He picks up random bits from telly and the radio."

"I don't remember any show on telly where someone screams that Santa is a fraud." "*What did you do . . .*" *What is that all about?* "Did Paddy O'Shea threaten your husband?"

"Let the man rest in peace."

"He won't be in peace until we find his killer."

"I'm afraid I cannot help you with that."

"It sounds like an argument took place here in front of Bobby." Siobhán glanced at the parrot. He had his head cocked and he was watching Siobhán intently. He could hardly be used in a court of law, but so far, he was the most honest witness she'd ever come across. But before she could question him or Mrs. Claus any further, she felt a hand on her arm, and she was escorted to the door.

"I'm going to kill you," the parrot called after her. "I'm going to kill you, I'm going to kill you!"

Siobhán stopped. "My word." She pointed at the bird. "How do you explain that?"

"Law and Order," Mrs. Claus said, then slammed the door.

Chapter Ten

Siobhán was still fixated on the parrot when she entered the antique shop. If only she had recorded it. There was no way that had come from a show on telly. Had Barry Callaghan found out that Paddy was stealing and confronted him? How would he have learned? Perhaps from his downstairs neighbor, the owner of this antique store. She forced her attention back to her surroundings. The lights in the antique shop were so dim, Siobhán had to wait for her eyes to adjust. *Law & Order. As if!* If it was so innocent, why had Mrs. Claus ushered her out the minute Bobby started talking?

The shop was jammed with stuff, much like the Clauses' flat. In the middle of the store, an old man was hunched over a newspaper spread out on the counter, and he didn't even look up as he spoke to her. "Do not touch anything."

What customer service! If she were a regular customer, she would have turned around and walked out, but not before touching as many things as possible. A character flaw of hers—this temper—but, nonetheless, her fingers were itching to start mauling at old wooden dressers, porcelain dolls, and dusty candlestick holders. She used to whittle to control her anger. She was going to have to get back to it. She approached the clerk, stood in front of him, and waited for him to look up. When he did so, it was with a heavy sigh.

"I'm Garda O'Sullivan from Kilbane."

His eyes flicked over her. "You're not in uniform."

"Not until the first of the year," she said.

He frowned. "What can I do for you?"

"I understand that one of our residents came in a short while back and tried to sell you a number of household items. You recognized one as being reported stolen."

"Finally," he said. "I've been waiting for someone to follow up."

"Here I am." In truth, she had come here on a whim. But this was the first bit of enthusiasm he'd shown and she wanted to keep that going. "Was one of the items a nutcracker?"

He frowned. "No."

"Are you sure?"

"Of course I'm sure. If it had been, I would have thought of Aideen Callaghan. She's a collector, you know."

"Yes, I know."

"That's how I'm sure."

"Tell me what you remember about the day Cormac Dooley came in."

"Cormac Dooley?"

She sighed. "The elf." She wanted their real names used, but it was difficult when they dressed as their characters all season. If she spent all her time trying to be correct, she'd get nowhere.

The clerk leaned over the counter. "I told that elf I knew his items were hot and I was going to call the guards."

"How did you know?"

The clerk continued speaking, as if he hadn't heard the question. "He talked me out of it over my better judgment, said he was going to return the items."

"And he did."

"Not all of them, he didn't."

Siobhán stepped closer. "What do you mean? And how did you know the items were stolen in the first place?" She was starting to feel like Bobby, the parrot, repeating the same things over and over.

The old man stood up, maneuvered around the counter, and headed to the back of the store. Siobhán followed just in time to see him pick up a small figurine. It was a lad in overalls. "It looked just like this. It's German. Worth nearly eight thousand euro."

Siobhán gasped. "That?"

He glared at her. "You've no eye for antiques. Yes. *That*. At the right auction maybe even more."

"How do you know it wasn't returned?"

"Because the owner was in here when it first went missing, and asked if anyone had brought it in to me. At that time, no one had. But the minute that elf came in with stolen items, I knew it had to be him."

"You're saying he admitted he was bringing you stolen items?"

"He blamed it on Paddy O'Shea. Claimed they were all donated."

"But you didn't believe him?"

"I told him it smelled fishy. That he should double-check with the owners to make sure they were donated free and clear."

"Then what?"

"He promised he was going to check with every owner, and get documentation if the item had been donated."

Cormac Dooley didn't mention this when I spoke with him. Why not?

"I gave him a chance to honor that promise. But the woman was in again last night, crying her eyes out. Said she didn't get her figurine back. I told her to report it to the guards."

"I promise I will follow up on it." She would too. If Cormac Dooley was holding on to this figurine, he was the one guilty of stealing. It didn't necessarily make him a murderer, but he would need to be held accountable for the thefts.

The clerk made a clicking noise with his tongue and teeth. "I've heard that before."

"Cormac claimed he tried to return all the items, but he mixed a few up. Maybe the figurine simply arrived at the wrong doorstep." But even as she said it, she wondered. The guards had collected as many of the wrapped gifts as they could. Opened and catalogued every one of them. She didn't remember seeing this figurine. Did the elf know how valuable it was? Had he kept it? Or was it still sitting innocently in his shed and he'd simply overlooked it?

Or what if it *had* been returned, and the owner was lying so she could double-dip. "Would an owner insure something like this?"

"If they're smart."

"Do you know if this particular owner insured it?"

"I don't see why she'd be crying to me if she had."

Siobhán sighed. "I'm going to need her information."

"Do you have a warrant?"

"*A warrant?*"

"I can't just give out information about my clientele."

"I thought you said she wanted the guards involved."

The clerk headed back to his counter. "She was going to make an official report. If you're so official, either ask them for it, or come back here with identification, or a warrant . . ." He stopped and looked her up and down. "Or at least a proper guard's uniform."

* * *

"Let me get this straight. You think Mr. and Mrs. Charlesville Santa are hiding something because a little birdie told you."

Siobhán gave a terse smile and counted to five in her head. She was standing in O'Reilly's office, filling him in on her recent excursion. "Not so little."

"Pardon me?"

"He's a normal-sized parrot. With a big mouth."

"Sounds familiar," O'Reilly said with a smirk. "Anything else?"

"The clerk at the antique shop."

"We have no report on file about a missing figurine. Is that it?"

She couldn't believe he wanted to ignore everything she'd just learned. *Is every day going to be like this? Is it because I'm new?* "Parrots mimic what they hear."

"He heard it on telly, then, like she said."

"What about Cormac Dooley?"

"I told you I don't have a report about the item in question. If we have proof that he stole it, if you learn who this mysterious woman is, or if a figurine turns up, we'll make sure it's returned to this mysterious owner and he's charged with theft."

"It's possible he's the murderer."

"He's the size of a child. Paddy was hit on the back of the head. The only way it was him is if he carried a ladder in, along with the nutcracker, and somehow set it up and climbed up on it right behind Paddy without him turning around." He had a very good point, and Siobhán felt like a right eejit. "Anything else?"

"What else do you need from me?" she asked.

"Nothing."

"I see."

He sighed. "You start in the new year. You have a rare chance to enjoy the holidays without the stress of this job. Go. Enjoy it."

"Yes, Sergeant." She left the office, not at all enthused about being ordered to enjoy the holidays. Perhaps she shouldn't have told him about the parrot.

On her way home Siobhán tried to follow orders. She commanded herself to enjoy the decorations in the windows, the garland-wrapped street lamps, the feel of Christmas in the air, but she couldn't help but ruminate over the case. If only they could figure out where the killer stashed the murder weapon. Had the nutcracker been tossed? Buried? Cleaned up and stuck back on a shelf? Was this all because of a possible hundred-thousand-euro prize?

Was there any way Cormac Dooley could have struck Paddy on the back of the head without Santa first turning around? He hadn't been found with headphones or a radio. Loud music playing while he worked could have drowned out the approach of the killer. Could the elf have perched on the diving-board portion of the dunk tank? It seemed far-fetched, and he would have had to have knelt on the diving board and reached forward to strike Paddy. Required coordination, but it was plausible.

O'Reilly wanted her to stay out of it.

She could either stay out of it or find a way to speak with Cormac Dooley. She definitely shouldn't have mentioned the parrot.

A man was standing in front of Naomi's Bistro, staring at the CLOSED sign. As she drew closer, she saw that it was Dave Healy. He was holding a bag from the butcher shop. He turned and nodded on her approach. "How ya?"

"Grand, how are you?"

"Ah, I'm alright. Ed wanted me to drop off those chops he promised you."

"It wasn't necessary."

"We're very grateful you found Adam's pup."

"So am I." She opened the door and gestured for Dave to enter. Eoin was stoking the fire. She handed him the bag. "Do you mind putting these in the fridge?"

"Chops," Eoin said. "Deadly." He grinned at Dave.

"What have you done with your siblings?" Siobhán asked her brother.

"James is at a meeting. Gráinne took the young ones door-to-door."

"Door-to-door?"

"They're recruiting Santas."

"Pardon?"

"Gráinne's idea. She wants to audition Santa Clauses."

"You're kidding?" She prayed he was kidding. It was hard to tell with Eoin—he had a fabulous poker face.

"I think she plans on holding the auditions here after brekkie tomorrow."

"Here?"

"She said it would also be good for business."

"She did, did she?"

"They even made flyers." He nodded to the counter. Siobhán went over and picked one up: BRUNCH WITH PROSPECTIVE SANTAS.

Siobhán groaned. *"Tomorrow?"* It was going to be hard to relax and get ready for Christmas with prospective Santas being grilled by Gráinne.

"The job does need filling right away."

Siobhán sighed. "I wish someone would keep me in the loop."

"I just did." Eoin took the box and ambled into the kitchen.

She turned to Dave. "Sounds interesting," he said. "I'll bring Adam." He turned and glanced at the entrance.

"We should have a ramp," Siobhán said. "But in the past we've managed by carrying Adam in, and then folding the wheelchair and carrying it up separately."

"That will do."

As soon as they had funds, she would hire a contractor and look into what it would take to make the bistro accessible to wheelchairs. These older buildings had narrow entries, but maybe one could be set up in the back. "Would you like a cup of tea?"

Dave removed his hat and stroked his head. "If it's no bother."

"No bother at all. Do sit."

Dave chose a table near the fireplace and sat rigidly. He wasn't used to social calls. "I've been hearing quite a bit about your brown bread," he said.

Siobhán laughed. "I'll get you a slice with your tea."

He smiled. "Much obliged."

They sat with their tea and brown bread, and filled the space with the polite conversation of strangers. He lavished praise on her brown bread, which wasn't necessary, for his plate with nary a crumb told the story. "Is the winter carnival still being held in the town square?"

"Heavens, no. We're moving to the abbey."

"Oh," he said, sounding somewhat puzzled. "I suppose he was just gathering his things, then."

"Pardon?"

"Never mind, I shouldn't have said anything."

"Too late now," Siobhán said, doing her best to sound cheerful. "Out with it."

If she wasn't mistaken, Dave Healy was actually squirming. "I saw the elf running around in there."

"Running around?"

"He seemed very busy. That's why I wondered if the carnival was still happening."

"When was this?"

"Just before I arrived."

Siobhán stood. So did Dave.

"Dear me," he said. "Should I have said something sooner?"

"It's a crime scene. We can't have anyone scurrying around." Should she call O'Reilly, or just pop over there herself? It had been made quite clear they were using every guard on duty. If she sent them, and the elf was nowhere to be seen, she'd catch the blame. "I hope you understand I must go and have a look."

"Of course, of course. I thought you didn't begin your work as a guard until the new year."

"Good memory. For a case this serious they've brought me in early."

They headed for the door. "The poor fellow was obviously not in his right mind," Dave said. "May he rest in peace."

"Yes," Siobhán said. She wouldn't rest. Not until she found his killer. "Give my love to Adam and be sure to thank Ed for the chops."

"Will do. And I'll be back in for more of that brown bread."

"Anytime." She turned, and began jogging for the square.

Chapter Eleven

The carnival was no longer cordoned off with crime scene tape, which meant the guards had finished processing the scene. Even so, there was no sign of an elf . . . *"Not a creature was stirring, not even a mouse . . ."*

The dunk tank had been drained and taken to a warehouse, just outside of town, and the tent had been taken down. Now only a mound of teakettles was left in the spot where the tent stood. Hot chocolate tins had been found among the kettles. They were pretty tins, a cocoa color, of course, outlined in gold. It was a pity the tins were evidence as well, for they made nice keepsakes. As a girl she used to love engaging in craft projects. She should be sitting down with Ann and Ciarán, making ornaments for the tree or cookies. She would make a point of carving out time. There seemed to be so little of it. Much less for some than for others. Death had a way of forcing you to embrace life. "What happened to you, Paddy?" she said softly. "Who did this?"

If the elf had been here, there was no crime in it; the guards were finished with the scene. But that didn't help her from wondering what he was doing here. Dave Healy said he'd been scurrying around. That sounded like someone in a panic. She headed back to the bistro. She needed her scooter. It was time to pay another visit to Cormac Dooley.

Christmas lights were down from his windows and along the roof. The snowman in the yard was now a puddle of plastic on the ground. Even as she parked the scooter, and ran back to the workshop, she knew that he was gone. As expected, the workshop was empty. Not a stitch was left in it. She ran up to the cottage and pounded on the door for good measure. Silence greeted her. *Where are his dogs?*

She looked in the one window where the curtain was parted. It was empty. Not just quiet, but bare to the bones. Not a single rug, sofa, or chair. Cormac Dooley was on the run. He'd need to pawn those items. She picked up her mobile, as this did require a call to the guards. But what was her excuse for being here in the first place? A social call with one of their top suspects? O'Reilly said to let him follow up on the figurine, so that excuse was out the window. She'd have to come clean about Dave Healy's visit and mentioning seeing Dooley in the square. She'd have to admit that led her to Dooley's cottage to check it out. No harm in that. Hardly investigating at all. She picked up her mobile and called the detective sergeant.

"I don't have time to be cross with you," O'Reilly said. "But I did warn all of our suspects not to leave town, so I'll send guards over to his place."

"He's gone."

"I heard you the first time."

Siobhán ignored the comment. "If he's running away and he's our thief, he's going to need to sell his items. I think I know where he'll be doing that."

"The antique dealer in Charlesville?"

"Yes."

"Why would he go back there if the clerk turned him away in the first place?"

"I don't think our clerk is as honest as he'd like us to think. He wouldn't give me the name of the woman missing the figurine."

"You think he wants it for himself?"

"It's as good a reason as any."

"What are you suggesting?"

"Either he was telling the truth, and he'll talk to me if I look official, or he's going to pay Cormac Dooley for the figurine."

O'Reilly sighed. "You couldn't stay out of it, could you?"

"His eyes practically glowed when he talked about that figurine. I think he plans on buying it from the elf, unless we stop him."

"I'll talk to the Charlesville guards. We should let the sale go through and then arrest them both. Normally good citizens turning bad over greed angers me almost as much as the hardened criminals."

O'Reilly was showing a rare moment of emotion, and this time his anger wasn't directed at her. He edged up a notch in Siobhán's eyes. "In the meantime, I'm going to get you a uniform—it might not be the right fit yet—but let's send you back to stake out the antique shop, and this time you'll have your credentials. I will see if I can get a temporary ID for you as well."

"Thank you."

"You won't be thanking me if you fail."

"Yes, Sergeant." She hung up the phone and felt a slight sense of relief. He'd finally believed her about something. But he'd meant it, if she failed, he wouldn't be so quick to support her again. Not the best way to start out her career as a guard. One way or another, she was going to get something useful from the antique clerk, maybe even catch a runaway elf.

Siobhán felt like a total eejit as she traversed the passageway between the antique shop and the flat next to it in her ill-fitting uniform. The jacket was too short. The pants were too big and too long. She had to roll them up, and they kept coming down. The white blouse was her own, so she was good there, and the garda cap, with the *An Garda Síochána* gold emblem, was class. The passageway was only a few feet wide, but from here she could see the footpath in front of the antique shop. Hopefully, she would catch Cormac Dooley if he entered. The Charlesville Guards were not keen on staking out one of their locals, but if Cormac entered the shop, Siobhán was to alert them, and they would presumably show up. It sounded like a bad plan to her, but the truth was that Cormac might be long gone by now. Still, she had her mobile out and was ready to send the text. As she waited, she was reminded how exciting stakeouts sounded compared to how mind-numbingly boring they actually were. She had to stare at the footpath, watching bundled-up locals passing by, wishing she'd brought chocolates and a bag of crisps. She still hadn't done her Christmas shopping. She hated that she wanted to buy something for Macdara. Was he thinking about her too? Or was his life in Dublin so fabulous there was no room for the past? She doubted that. Then again, he'd done a pretty good job of staying away from her these past two years. *Two years.* She really had to move on. She was doing it. Granted, she was doing it in an outfit that looked more suited for a costume party than a day at work, but by the new year she'd make sure she had a uniform that fit.

An hour later she was shivering from the cold, and bored

out of her mind. No wonder O'Reilly gave her this assignment. It wasn't because he believed in her—it was because no one wanted to stand in a passageway freezing for hours on end. She was tired of singing "Jingle Bells" in her head, and yet she couldn't stop. "*Dashing through the snow . . .*"

Snow . . .

Snow!

It was snowing! Was she hallucinating? Is that what happened when you started to lose all feeling in your fingertips? She really should have remembered gloves. It was true. Little white flakes were falling from the sky. She wanted to whoop with joy. And just as she thought it, a child on the footpath did it for her. Everyone stopped and craned their necks upward and the word started passing from person to person. "Snow!"

"It's snowing!"

"A white Christmas."

It was that second, the second that Siobhán allowed herself to look up, that she made her first big mistake. Just as she stopped staring at the flakes, she caught a streak of green headed for the door of the antique shop. It was either a child dressed in green or it was Cormac Dooley still in his elf costume. Perhaps he thought he looked innocent in it. No one would suspect him of anything devious. By the time she noticed him flying by, the door to the shop had already slammed shut with a bang. She gripped her mobile. If it wasn't him, she'd look like an idiot. She needed to verify first. Should she sneak in through the front of the antique shop, or try to catch Dooley making a run for it out the back?

If she entered through the front, she'd be spotted in seconds in her garda uniform. How long would Cormac stay in the shop if it was him? She needed a disguise. Her eyes landed on a shop across the street. There it was, in the window. A mannequin. Dressed like Santa. She'd never had the urge to play the legendary character. But she had to get into that store without being recognized. She hurried across the street, wishing she could take a few moments to frolic in the first snowfall they'd had in years.

The bell dinged as Siobhán entered the antique shop, dressed in her Santy outfit. Just ahead, at the counter, Cormac Dooley was accepting an envelope from the clerk. Then he turned and began to walk to the back exit of the shop. Maybe she'd chosen the wrong option.

"Stop!" Siobhán called. She almost yelled out that she was a guard. But when Cormac turned and saw Santa, the elf in him must have reacted out of instinct, for he did stop. He cocked his head and waited. *What am I supposed to do now?* The Santa costume was so bulky, it would take quite a bit of fumbling to reach her mobile; by then, the elf would have caught on.

"You're needed down the street," she said, trying to disguise her voice as a man's. She wasn't too bad, if she did say so herself, maybe she should have been in the Christmas panto.

"Do I know you?"

"Everyone knows me."

Cormac frowned.

"Ho, ho, ho," she added.

"I'm retired," he said, then turned to go.

"You'll be letting down children," Siobhán said. "It's less than an hour of your time. I'll pay you."

He hesitated again. Siobhán was now moving closer. "It's snowing, and what better time for Santa and his elf to make an appearance?"

He looked up at Siobhán, as if trying to get a good look at her face. The clerk watched them pensively. She could see the figurine on the shelf behind him. He knew it was stolen and he didn't care. This was not the Christmas spirit. The clerk wasn't an innocent bystander, that's why he wouldn't tell her the name of the woman who owned the figurine. *What is wrong with these people?*

"I was a good friend of Paddy's," Siobhán said. " 'Tis a shame what happened to him."

The elf started, and then bolted for the back door. Siobhán kicked into high gear. Dooley knocked a coatrack into the aisle. Siobhán hopped over it. He shoved over a wooden shelf, sending it crashing down in front of her. Books, vases, and knickknacks careened across the floor. The clerk screamed. Cormac threw open the back door and disappeared as a gust of wind blew snow into the shop. Siobhán fumbled for her mobile as she stepped over the debris and kept running. It was a contest between wanting to catch up with Dooley and needing to call for backup. She made the call, yelled into the phone, and then hung up before they could respond. They would either show, or they wouldn't, and the elf was getting away.

Chapter Twelve

In the passageway behind the shop she could either go left or right. Footprints in the snow led left and she was about to follow them, when she noticed the same footprints off to the right. The sneaky little elf had tried to trick her. She looked to her right and caught a glimpse of a green-tasseled cap ducking behind a parked car on the next street. She took off at a run. Snow was beautiful, but slippery. As she reached the end of the passageway, she slid, her arms became windmills flailing to keep her balance. She landed on her arse with a thud in the middle of the street.

"Santa!" she heard someone yell, and for a moment she wondered where Santa was. Then she remembered *she* was Santa. She hated the job already. Dooley peeked out from behind the parked car. Siobhán scrambled to her feet, slipping a few more times as she made her way to him. He took off again, running down the footpath. But this time Siobhán wasn't far behind and her legs were much longer. Her running habit paid off. She overtook him, grabbing him and bringing him down.

"Who are you?" he said as he squirmed underneath her.

"Father Christmas," she said in her own voice.

"Bah, humbug," he said.

"You're going to be arrested," she said. "What I need to know is, will theft be your only charge, or did you kill Paddy O'Shea?"

"*Me?*" he sputtered. "*Kill Santa?* You take that back!" Although she was sitting on top of him, he began to pummel his fists. "He was good to me. He didn't turn me in. Unlike some people."

"He was going to turn you in to the guards for stealing?"

"I'm not the thief! I was trying to do a good deed."

"Nice story, blaming Santa when he's not here to defend himself."

The elf stopped fighting her. "It's not Santa," he said quietly.

"What?"

"If I tell you, do you swear to go easy?"

"No."

"Then I won't tell."

Siobhán's mind reeled. Either he was lying or . . . he was protecting someone else. Someone like . . . *Mrs. Claus* . . . "Eileen," Siobhán said. "Eileen O'Shea is the thief."

She let up on Cormac, then stuck out her hand to help him up. He hesitated, then took it. She took off the Santa cap and brushed back her hair.

"You," Cormac said. After brushing himself off, he sighed and met Siobhán's gaze. "Yes. She has a problem. Paddy found out what she did and ordered me to return the gifts."

"He didn't tell you they were donated and asked you to sell them?"

"That was Mrs. Claus."

"Why did you lie?"

"Because she's not a killer. I thought if I told you the truth, you would think she was."

"Leave the investigating to the guards." Siobhán recalled what Ed Healy said about the O'Sheas' dire financial situation. Is that why she was stealing?

"Who stole the dogs?"

"That was all Paddy. He'd been given some free chops by Ed Healy, and when he was finished, he got the idea of luring dogs to the square with bones. Using them as reindeer."

"Why didn't he just ask the owners? I'm sure they would have volunteered their pups."

"He thought success hinged on the element of surprise. He was crazed trying to make the winter carnival perfect."

And it got him killed . . . Why? "Do you know of anyone who had reason to kill him?"

The elf looked away.

"Eileen?" Siobhán said. "But you just insisted she didn't do it."

"That was before."

Siobhán took a step forward. *"Before?"*

Dooley crossed his arms. "I don't want to think it."

"Go on."

"They had financial difficulties. Paddy recently bought a hefty insurance policy."

Siobhán didn't have time to process what that could mean. Sirens wailed closer. The guards were almost here. She had more questions for Dooley. "A little birdie told me an argument broke out at the Callaghans'. What was that about?"

Cormac sighed. "Barry Callaghan heard about the stolen figurine from the antique dealer downstairs. Like everyone else, they accused Paddy of being a thief."

"The parrot said, 'What have you done?' "

"That was Barry. He was horrified that another Santa would be stealing from homes."

"Who said, 'I'll kill you'?"

"Paddy. He didn't mean it. He couldn't have Barry going around accusing him of being a thief."

"One more question."

"Do I have a choice?"

"Why were you rooting through the town square earlier?"

His eyebrow shot up. "I wasn't."

"Someone saw you."

"They didn't see me. Or he or she was lying."

"Why would a person lie about that?"

"You're the detective. You figure it out."

Siobhán opened her mouth to say she wasn't a detective, but she was interrupted by the approach of the Charlesville Guards.

"We'll take it from here."

Siobhán stepped back. "Just tell them the truth," she said as they started to lead Cormac away.

"By the way, Garda O'Sullivan," he called over his shoulder. "Paddy brought one more item into the tent that evening. One his dear wife had stolen. *Twice*."

"What?"

The guards were opening the doors to their car and ushering him in. The doors shut. The guards got in. The window came down slightly and she could just see the elf's eyes. He lifted his mouth to call out the window. "A nutcracker with a teal head."

Teal. She knew it was teal.

O'Rourke's was a welcoming place at any time, but Siobhán was never more grateful for it and her brood than this moment. She had done her duty, and had caught the elf. The figurine would be returned to its rightful owner. Eileen O'Shea would be brought in for questioning, and

O'Reilly swore he'd look into the insurance policy, and the nutcracker she'd stolen. Something was gnawing at her about the nutcracker, and Siobhán was itching to stay involved, but O'Reilly wasn't having it. She was left with no choice but to try and enjoy herself, and having drinks and a bite at O'Rourke's was just what Father Christmas ordered. Declan delivered her an Irish version of the hot cocoa, which was so delicious it should be a sin. For a few moments the table was filled with normal chatter of the snow—and because James didn't drink, and Gráinne was the only one besides Siobhán old enough to partake in Declan's Irish hot cocoa, the sisters were enjoying a special bond. That didn't mean the others were left out. Declan had made versions of hot cocoa for them with a hearty dose of whipped cream without the alcohol. They raised their mugs and toasted.

"Sláinte!"

"I want to go sledding and build a snowman," Ciarán said. Declan had a turf fire going just behind them, and Ciarán's eyes glowed from the reflection.

"I don't think we're to get more than a dusting," Siobhán said. "But at the abbey they may be setting up the snow machine."

"Yes!"

The rest of the O'Sullivans laughed at his enthusiasm and he didn't even grumble when several hands went to ruffle his mop of red hair.

"Liam's has some nice paint sets," Ann said. "And lovely paper."

"Do they, now?" James said with a grin. He glanced at Siobhán. "Do you think Santy is listening?"

"I think he's listening, alright," Siobhán said, taking out her biro and notepad. "Who else has noticed lovely things around lately?"

Her brood happily started reciting their wish lists. Siobhán was relieved when nobody asked for a nutcracker.

She stole it twice. That's what the elf had said. Or something close to it. What did he mean by that? She stole it once from Aideen Callaghan . . . Wait, didn't Aideen say that Eileen and Paddy O'Shea had given her the nutcracker? What if Paddy had given it to her, and Eileen had stolen it? That meant they were regifting something that had already been stolen. But from whom? Who is the original owner of that nutcracker?

"What about you?" James said, interrupting Siobhán's meanderings. "What do you want for Christmas?"

Macdara Flannery. His name popped into her head before she could stop it. She wanted to call him and ask him about the case. Or e-mail him. It wasn't possible that he hadn't heard about the murder. And he'd stayed out of it. She, for one, wasn't going to drag him back in. She never thought it possible that they would stop speaking to one another. "Maybe a new pair of runners," she said. *So many bad guys to chase after.*

"That's it?" Gráinne said, eyeing her up and down. "I'd say an entirely new wardrobe and accessories for starters."

Her brood laughed, and Siobhán opened her mouth to protest, then realized Gráinne had a point. "Surprise me," she said. Gráinne rubbed her hands together and her brood laughed again.

As her siblings started to chat, Siobhán took in the pub. The snow had driven in the crowds, and the atmosphere was surprisingly jovial. All but one corner was lit up in chatter and laughter. In that one corner a woman sat, hunched over her table. It took Siobhán a minute to recognize Eileen O'Shea. Were the guards finished with her already, or did they not believe the elf? *So much for O'Reilly believing me.* If she had been in charge, she would already have Eileen in for questioning. They were pinning it on the elf, taking the easy way. It was true that Cormac Dooley could have been lying. He'd done it before. Had they learned there was no insurance policy and dropped the rest of the inquiry on her? Or were they too afraid to grill Mrs. Claus at Christmas?

Siobhán glanced at her again. Eileen was in a back booth, with a bottle of half-empty whiskey. She seemed to be muttering to herself.

"Excuse me," Siobhán said. She headed up to Declan first. "How long has she been like that?"

Declan sighed as he ran a rag over the counter. "She's been here for ages. I watered half the bottle down when she wasn't looking. But she refuses my offer for a ride home. I tried getting some folks in here to cheer her up, but she turned them away. Then I tried to see if she wanted to speak with Father Kearney. I tell ya, I never thought I'd hear such words come out of Mrs. Claus at Christmastime. I've decided to let her be. If you're thinking of going over there, I'd say have another Irish cocoa and think on it some more."

Siobhán sighed, her mind coming back to the insurance policy. Couples bought insurance; it didn't mean they were murderers. But somebody had to ask her about it, and at this moment that somebody was Siobhán. At the very least the grieving widow looked like she needed some comfort. She headed over to Eileen's table. "Hello," she said softly. "May I sit down?"

Eileen's head snapped up. Her eyes were tinged with red. "I told you Paddy said that elf had sticky fingers! And yet you blamed my Paddy! And now he's blaming me!" So the guards had at least spoken with her.

Siobhán sat down. "I have to keep my options open," she said quietly. "It's me job."

"We all know that's a bunch of malarkey. You're just like everyone else in this town. Kick a man when he's down, even if it's Santa Claus." Her white hair, usually in a neat bun, fell over her face; her housedress looked as if she'd been wearing it for days; her winter coat was sewn and mended at the elbows.

"He did take the dogs," Siobhán said softly.

"He was going to give them back."

"I know," Siobhán said. There was too much shame around mental illness. Had Santa Claus come down with a physical ailment, everyone would have rallied around him, and then some. "If you want to come to the bistro for tea or coffee—"

Eileen lifted her bottle of whiskey. "I'm sorted."

"You're not going to find any peace at the bottom of a bottle," Siobhán said. "We're just next door, if you change your mind."

"I'm getting out of this town." She poured herself another drink, sloshing most onto the table. "As soon as I get a few things sorted."

Like the insurance policy? If the guards were still researching it, they would have Siobhán's head for alerting her. "You won't be able to leave until we've finished our investigation, but when you go, I wish you well."

"Are you saying *I'm* under investigation?"

"Everyone is under investigation in a murder probe. I know it's frustrating, but if you want us to catch the killer, you'll cooperate so that we can eliminate you."

"It's not enough my husband is dead, you want to nail me for it, is that it?"

Siobhán stood, then hesitated. Declan came over to the table with a plate of chicken fingers and chips. "It's on me, luv," he said. Eileen barely glanced at it. Everyone in town had been kind to her. Ed Healy had kept her tab. Declan had probably been feeding her. And if Cormac Dooley was telling the truth, then both the elf and Santa had tried to protect her reputation when they learned she was stealing.

"Cormac said your husband had brought a nutcracker into the tent. One with a teal head. He said it had been stolen twice." She managed not to say who had been accused of stealing it twice. "What do you know about it?"

"Nothing," she said. "I know nothing. And you shouldn't believe a word that elf says."

"If you change your mind, I'm ready to listen. I know what it's like to have your world fall apart. I know what it's like to not know how you can afford to keep living a life you've grown accustomed to."

Eileen looked up, her eyes swimming with pain.

"I heard about the argument when you went to visit the Callaghans."

Eileen's face scrunched into rage. "Barry laughed at Paddy's winter carnival. Said he couldn't wait to see him fail. Said he had big money riding on it. Paddy lost his mind. Threatened to kill Barry. He was only ranting and raving, it didn't mean anything. But what if Barry believed it and killed me Paddy first?"

"And the nutcracker?"

Eileen let out a sigh and her shoulders slumped. "After the argument I stole it back from Mrs. Callaghan. Paddy gave it to them as a housewarming gift." She sniffed. "That woman didn't deserve it. I took it back is all."

"Who did you steal it from in the first place?"

Her eyes flicked away, then back at Siobhán. "I don't know," she whispered.

"What do you mean?"

"It was sitting next to the register at the butcher's. The

place was jammers and nobody was paying attention. It could have belonged to anyone in the crowd. Nobody noticed when I took it."

"Paddy noticed."

She sighed. "Yes, Paddy noticed. I told him I couldn't return it, because I didn't know whose it was."

"Did you open the bottom latch?"

Eileen bit her lip.

Siobhán stepped forward. "Eileen?"

"It doesn't matter now! It's gone!"

Siobhán sank into the booth and grabbed Eileen's hand. "This is very important. Did Paddy bring that nutcracker to the panto, knowing there was a shining star inside worth a hundred thousand euro?"

Tears filled Eileen's eyes. "We needed the money. He should have listened to me."

"But he didn't."

"He insisted we were going to find out who it belonged to. I told him there was no way of doing that. Once they found out it was the winner, everyone would say it was theirs."

Siobhán stood. She leaned in. "Drink some water. Sober up. I don't think you killed your husband. Go to the guards and tell them everything you told me."

"Where are you going?"

"Don't you worry about that." Siobhán was headed to Annmarie's shop to see if there was a way of validating that Kilbane had received the winning nutcracker. Worth a hundred thousand euro. Eileen O'Shea may have stolen the winner. And, in retaliation, this winner had extracted much more than a chicken dinner.

Chapter Thirteen

"Not even the craftsman knows where the winning nutcracker was sent," Annmarie said. "No one has claimed the prize yet, but that's to be expected." Siobhán was in Annmarie's shop purchasing accessories for Gráinne and Ann. Annmarie's nutcrackers were sold out. She couldn't help but think of the shining star that resided in one of them, and how this year it may have guided a killer to his victim.

"Because presumably the winner will open it on Christmas Day," Siobhán said.

"Presumably?" Annmarie arched an eyebrow.

"There's nothing to stop someone from purchasing the nutcracker as a gift, opening the seal to see if they have the winnings, *before* they stick the seal back on and give the nutcracker as a gift."

Annmarie sighed. "You make me sad." She said nothing else, proving to Siobhán that sad or not, she couldn't refute that someone would do that. Nor was there anything illegal about it. Grinches and Scrooges could be found in every corner of the world. "Do you really think the winning nutcracker is right here in Kilbane and it was a motive for murder?"

"What do you know about the people who set up this

contest?" Siobhán already knew a few things about them. They were total eejits for not developing a better system to protect the nutcrackers. Or they had a naive-like devotion to the good in human beings during the holiday season. Someone had to say it. *Bah, humbug.*

"Only that they're handmade in Sligo."

"What are the steps if one finds a shining star in their nutcracker?"

"First, the star is unique. Only the craftsman can verify the true winning star. She's agreed to travel to the winner to verify, and write them a check for a hundred thousand euro."

"She?"

"The craftsman is a woman."

"You know her?" Annmarie looked away. Siobhán stepped forward. "This is important."

"I've been buying from her for years."

"How did you first hear about her?"

Annmarie chewed on her lip. "It was a long time ago."

"Go on."

"I really don't think it's important."

"Let me do the thinking." Annmarie frowned. Siobhán grabbed her hand. "I swear. If it's not important to the investigation, I won't breathe a word."

"You swear?"

"I swear."

"Ed Healy recommended her work years ago."

"Ed Healy?"

Annmarie nodded. "On one of his visits to Dave, they went to her shop. He said she was very talented and thought her work would sell well in Kilbane. He was right. I've been ordering from her ever since."

"Thank you."

"Ed isn't behind this. He wouldn't take charity from anyone. You know yourself."

Siobhán did know. Ed Healy was the last person to rig a contest in his favor.

Annmarie watched Siobhán pace. "I just want the killer caught by Christmas. Is that going to happen?"

The question stopped Siobhán in her tracks. "Given what day it is, I highly doubt it."

Annmarie nodded and thrust Siobhán's purchases at her. "Happy Christmas Eve."

Siobhán was heading out for her run when the rehab center in Limerick returned her call. The woman on the line quickly got to her point. "It's lovely you wanted to start fund-raising for Adam Healy. But I'm thrilled to report his treatment has been paid in full. He'll start in the new year."

"Wow," Siobhán said. "May I ask who paid for it?"

"I'm afraid we can't give away that kind of information."

"You may need to give it away to the guards," Siobhán said. "What is the cost of the treatment?"

The woman wouldn't answer, but she didn't need to. Siobhán had a pretty good idea. It was a hundred thousand euro. The same amount as the prizewinning nutcracker.

She went for a run, needing to work out all the thoughts in her head. This case was all about a theft . . . and a nutcracker. And money. And a preordained winner. Who wouldn't have been privy to the plan because he would have rejected it. She ran faster.

Someone needed to give someone else money. Only *this*

someone would have been too proud to take it. Even if it was for a very good cause: a handicapped child's rehabilitation. It had bothered Siobhán that the woman who crafted the nutcrackers and this contest had been careless when it came to protecting them. A simple seal over the flap that could easily be removed. But now it made sense. She wasn't worried about folks cheating, because she knew exactly whose hands the winning nutcracker would wind up in.

The elf said he heard Santa sneeze as he was leaving the tent. Siobhán had heard it too, and assumed it was Santy getting sick. Instead, it was the killer. Cormac had allergies to dogs, but his manifested in a wheezing chest, for which he used an inhaler.

The sneezer, the killer. Another person who was allergic to dogs. Dave Healy.

He had snuck into the shed and removed the bones that he'd originally placed there to keep them quiet. Once he removed the bones, he counted on the dogs to start barking. He then slipped into the tent to find his stolen nutcracker—the one with the shining star. Stolen from the counter at the butcher's. Right out from under his nose as he worked the register. When Siobhán had spoken with Ed in his back garden, they'd returned to find Dave gone and the shop closed. Ed mentioned he was having problems with bank fraud. Most likely, he was contacting the craftswoman to let her know the prize had been stolen. Bet they were sorry the nutcrackers hadn't been better protected then. Dave hailed from Mayo, only forty-five miles from Sligo. And Ed had been friends with the craftswoman for years. Why wouldn't the craftswoman and a devoted uncle concoct a sweet little contest to benefit a disabled boy at Christmas? What could go wrong?

When did Dave Healy glom on to Paddy O'Shea as a

thief? He must have heard rumors while working in the shop. And then, at the panto, he'd seen Paddy O'Shea bring a nutcracker into his tent. *One with a distinct teal head.* It was a spur-of-the-moment rage that must have ignited him; he'd mistakenly assumed Paddy had stolen the nutcracker on purpose. He would have known about their running tab at the butcher's. It must have infuriated him.

Dave Healy had planned the perfect Christmas. A new puppy and top-notch rehab for his nephew. Dave was the one Cormac heard sneezing. He must have been hiding in Paddy's tent, waiting for intermission to take back his nutcracker. Was the shining star already gone? Was that what caused him to strike the minute Paddy turned his back?

Paddy must have known the shining star was in the nutcracker, for it was one of the few items he *didn't* task the elf with returning. The other was the valuable figurine. Given their financial difficulties, he'd been too tempted; and as far as the nutcracker was concerned, he may not have even known to whom it belonged. He wouldn't have been afraid to see Dave Healy in his tent.

Siobhán was surprised to see she was almost home. She'd been so absorbed in her thoughts, she'd run on autopilot. She intended to go into the bistro, then shower and change. Afterward, she'd confront Dave Healy, see if she could get him to turn himself in. He wasn't an evil man. He wouldn't kill her. Would he? Just in case, she'd pick a public place. She'd invite him to O'Rourke's. But just as she was opening the door to Naomi's Bistro, she saw a sea of red behind the windows. The café was filled with men auditioning to be Santa Claus. She'd forgotten all about Gráinne's scheme.

Is Dave Healy among them?

Had he heard that Eileen was now being questioned and he was worried she would squeal about finding the shining star in the stolen nutcracker? Or did he have the shining star now, ready to be opened by Adam on Christmas? *Tomorrow.* He had to keep his plan going until tomorrow. Was he in one of those Santa outfits milling around the bistro?

"You need to work on your *ho, ho, ho,*" Gráinne said to the Santa standing in front of her. "I didn't believe you."

"Excuse me," Siobhán said with a smile to the poor man, who definitely was *not* Dave Healy. She took her sister by the arm and pulled her away.

"Hey, I'm busy."

"Is Dave Healy here?"

Gráinne frowned as her eyes flicked over the Santas. "He's the skinny uncle of Adam, right?"

"Yes."

"Adam's here." She pointed. Adam was in the back room in his wheelchair, looking up at the train going around the room. Kneeling next to him was a skinny Santa. "That him?"

"Yes," Siobhán said. As they spoke, Dave Healy looked up and locked eyes with Siobhán. He couldn't possibly have heard her say his name from across the room. And yet there was a warning in his eyes. Maybe she should go straight to the guards.

"You better not be vying for him, because this time we're getting a fat Santa." With that, Gráinne pulled away and went back to her interview.

Siobhán needed to think. It wasn't smart to confront him here. She wished she had the backup of the guards, but all she had was a theory and the fact that Adam's rehab had been paid for. And an allergic, loving uncle. It wasn't *proof.* She certainly wasn't going to confront him in front of Adam. She needed evidence. Her mobile rang as she was mulling over her options. She could barely hear the caller over the din of the Santas. She excused herself and took the call in the back garden.

"O'Sullivan?" The voice was muffled, hard to hear.

"Yes?"

"O'Reilly here. I've had a report about a break-in at the warehouse."

"A break-in?"

"Someone messing with the dunk tank. It's probably lads acting the maggot. I'm sending every guard I can, to check it out. Are you free?"

"I'll be right there." *Finally. He's finally seeing me as part of the team.* Christmas would come early this year. She wondered if she should run upstairs and change into her uniform. Time was of the essence. She would grab her torch and head over straightaway.

The warehouse was located a few miles outside of the main part of town. She took her scooter, and arrived just as the sun was going down. The area around the warehouse was deserted, except for sheep and cows grazing on the soft hills around it. She thought she was the first to arrive until she saw the warehouse door was ajar. "Hello? Garda O'Sullivan here." When no one answered, she stepped in. It was pitch black, but when she turned on her torch, nothing happened. She shook it and tried again. Nothing. She unscrewed the bottom. No batteries. Classic mistake. Someone had probably switched them out recently. They were all doing that. She kept the torch in her hand, anyway, and tried to visualize the location of the light switch. On the left, about ten steps in. She stepped in, hoping the door would stay open at least until she reached the light, but it slammed shut the minute she was inside.

She whirled around. The door had been ajar. Why had it suddenly shut? "The guards have been notified," she said. "They're on their way."

There was no response.

The guards are on their way.

Unless, that hadn't been O'Reilly on the phone.

She wasn't necessarily afraid of the dark, but she also didn't want to trip over anything and land in hospital with a broken ankle. She walked three steps toward the light switch, and a loud click sounded from the door. The sound of a lock being turned—from the inside. She whirled around, still blind.

"Who's there?" She waited, her heart beating in her ears. "It's Garda O'Sullivan. Who's there?" She turned again and sprinted for the light switch. Dave Healy had called her from inside the bistro, pretending to be O'Reilly. He'd taken one look at her and knew that she was onto him. This one mistake could be the last she'd ever make. Her eyes were starting to adjust, and the hulking form of the dunk tank could be seen just ahead. A gurgling sound, like water, echoed through the warehouse. *What was* that? She pawed along the wall. *Come on, switch, come on.* She felt someone behind her, but before she could turn around, a sack covered her head. She screamed.

"I don't want to hurt you." It was *him*. Was he telling the truth? She stopped struggling for a moment. The hood stayed on, but didn't tighten. "Hands behind your back."

She hated herself in this moment. She hated that guards couldn't carry guns. She hated that she didn't know whether or not to try to kick behind her. He grabbed her hands and yanked them behind her back. She felt heavy rope and he began tying her hands together. She was full-on sweating behind the sack he'd thrown over her head. It smelled like oats. At least he hadn't used something that had stored raw meats or bones.

"Let's talk," she said. Her voice was muffled.

"If you listen, you won't get hurt. I promise you."

"You're just adding to your sentence."

"I'll be gone soon. They won't find me."

"It's not too late to do the right thing."

"Walk."

He shoved her forward. She walked. "What are you doing?"

"No more talking. I do the talking. A few more steps." After a few more steps he told her to stop. To her surprise, he whipped off the hood. Dave Healy stood in front of her, his gaunt face nearly skeletal in the dark.

"What are you doing?" she said. Her voice was still firm, she would not plead.

"I just need a head start." He pulled out a flask. "Drink this."

She shook her head. She turned to see where he had marched her. They were in front of the dunk tank. The ladder was propped against it. It was filled with water. "How can that be?" she said. "There are holes cut in it now." And yet it was filled with water.

"It's not the greatest patch job, but it will hold long enough."

She didn't know what he had in mind, but she didn't like it. "Go," she said. "Get your head start."

"You need to drink this."

"I will not."

"It's not going to kill you."

"I don't believe you."

"It's Declan's hot cocoa. With a little twist."

"Just go. The guards are on their way." They weren't, but maybe she could make Dave believe that they were.

"O'Sullivan?" Dave said, mimicking the voice on the phone. "O'Reilly here." *Or maybe he would see right through her lie.*

"Please," Siobhán said. "You were only trying to help your nephew. You don't want to hurt anyone else."

"Two hours of sleep and then you'll be awake." He shoved the flask near her mouth. "Drink it."

"I won't."

"You have no choice." He reached behind him and pulled out the nutcracker. "I used it once, I'll use it again."

"You did this for Adam."

"I had it all worked out, and that fool almost ruined everything."

"You funded the contest with the craftswoman so your brother would accept the money for Adam's rehabilitation."

"And he will."

"He's going to find out what you've done."

"Are you going to stand there and keep telling me things I already know, or are you going to drink this?"

"Just leave. It will take me a while to get myself untied. Or take my scooter. I'm not drinking that."

"I don't want to knock you out. I might accidentally kill you."

She didn't want that either. "I have a family," she said. "I have young ones to mind."

"I know. You're a good person. I used to be. The world did this to me. It's a few sleeping pills from the chemist. If I were you, I'd take it over a box to the head. You've got seconds to decide."

He pushed the flask to her mouth and backed her up against the tank. "Easy," he said. "Drink."

He was forcing it into her and she didn't want to choke.

She drank. He made her drink it all. "Why didn't you just turn Paddy in to the guards?"

"He had the nerve to bring the nutcracker to the panto. I spotted him go into the tent with it. If he had just let me take it back, he'd still be alive. I'd snuck in just before intermission. When the elf rolled the tank back in, I hid in the corner. They didn't see me. I thought I'd get out clear. The elf left to fetch something for Paddy to eat. That's when he saw me. He tried to grab it out of me hands. I told him it was mine. He let go, and said *he* was getting the guards. Said he'd have *me* arrested for theft. Isn't that rich? A man stealing things out of people's homes and dogs out of their back gardens. A young lad's dog. The minute he turned around, I didn't think. I struck. Maybe harder than I intended. He began to fall. The blood . . . I wasn't expecting it. I panicked. It was pure adrenaline and the fact that he was as skinny as me that made it easy for me to lift him high enough that I could put him in the tank." He looked her over, then glanced at the ladder. "It's almost time," he said. He turned her toward the ladder. "Climb."

"What?"

"Climb the ladder and lay down on the diving board."

"I need my hands."

"You can't have them."

"I can't do it. Not without my hands for balance."

"You graduated from Templemore. I know the drills they make guards-in-training do. You can do it."

She gritted her teeth and began to climb, leaning forward slightly to keep her balance. When she reached the top, she nearly panicked. "How?"

"The board is right in front of you. You'll have to shimmy onto it, laying on your belly."

She wanted to argue, but she could feel her limbs falling to sleep. She didn't want to fall in the water. He might just leave her there. She leaned forward onto the board.

"That's it. Inch forward. I'll tell you when to stop."

"I can't."

"Lie flat and stick your legs out. I'll give you a push."

She was too sleepy to argue. She flattened herself on the board and soon felt him pushing her legs until she slid forward.

"Good night," he said. "I'm sorry."

She heard him climb back down, and take the ladder away. She wanted to yell. She wanted to cry. She wanted a do-over. She prayed she would wake up, and prayed she wouldn't roll into the water, and sank into sleep instead.

Her head throbbed and her face was smashed up against something hard. Her hands were tied behind her back. She lifted her head with a cry, nearly tilting herself into the water. She wasn't dead, but she nearly wished she were. How long had she been out? Her throat was dry. *Now what?* She gave herself a few minutes just to breathe, and then slowly began to move parts of her body. She wiggled her fingers. She moved her feet. Her head. There was a tank full of water below her and no ladder behind her. The floor of the warehouse was cement. Dave Healy had intended for her to lie up here until someone found her. He was probably already on a bus, or a train, or a plane.

"Hello?" she called, because she just wanted to hear a voice, even if it was her own.

One wrong move to either side and she would go into ten feet of dark water with her hands tied behind her back. She was grateful he'd removed the hood, but he was still off her Christmas list. The only choice was to inch backward and take the drop off the side of the tank. It was, she guessed, at least a fifteen-foot drop. She stilled her mind, took a deep breath, and made her first attempt at inching back. The board wobbled. Had she moved at all? It was hard to tell. She tried it again. The board tilted to the left, and she moved to the right, fighting her pounding heart and her fight-or-flight responses, which were urging quick and decisive movements. It took forever, but soon she was near the end of the board. Her clothing was bunched at the top, nearly off her, but otherwise she had done it. She paused to think through the jump. Normally, her hands would fly out to protect her from this fall. Being tall was an advantage, but the cement floor had an advantage too. It was cement.

The key to falling was to stay loose, but the body always tensed. Once again, she would have to fight her natural instincts. She relaxed her mind and imagined herself in the bistro surrounded by her brood, fire roaring, feet up, mug of tea and brown bread in hand. Her best bet was her bottom. The worst option, her head. A broken tailbone could certainly ruin not only Christmas, but the new year too. Softly on her bottom. For once, and perhaps the only time in her life, she wished she had a bigger bottom.

Her backside took the brunt of the drop. It hurt. It really, really hurt, but she was still alive, her head stayed up, and she was pretty sure nothing was broken. It took another several tries to pull her legs in, roll over, and attempt to stand without using her hands. He had so much rope wrapped around her hands; there would be no cutting it off herself, or rubbing the rope against something sharp in the warehouse. She just wanted out, so she could reach the first person she saw and alert them that their killer was on the run. She headed for the warehouse door, limping from the hit her left-lower half had taken during the fall.

Opening the door to the warehouse took several attempts. She had to turn backward, get her hands on the doorknob, then use her body to help turn it. She would never take her arms and hands for granted again. When she finally got the door to open, she tumbled out, and landed on the ground. She heard voices in the distance.

"Siobhán? Siobhán?" It was James. She wanted to cry. "How did you know I was here?"

"I heard you talking on your mobile," Gráinne said. "I heard something about a warehouse." Her sister actually did listen sometimes.

"This is the only warehouse I could think of," James said.

Another Christmas miracle. "Here," Siobhán said. "I've fallen and I can't get up." She began to laugh into the ground, and the more she tried to stop, the harder she laughed. Soon her entire brood was surrounding her, including Trigger, who licked her face as James and Eoin began to undo the knots.

"Are you drunk?" Gráinne said.

"No," Siobhán said. "I've just been waiting my whole life to say that."

Chapter Fourteen

The abbey positively glowed in the night. Hundreds of little white lights adorned the surrounding trees, and candles glowed from tables set in the field. The snow machine was running, sending magical flakes raining down on upturned, little faces. At least fifty Santas roamed the grounds, ready to hear children's wishes. Gráinne, despite her hard exterior, had a soft heart, and she hadn't been able to reject a single Santa, so she'd hired them all. If there was any year they needed a village of Santas, it was this one.

Dave Healy had taken a bus out of town, and was quite surprised to see a blockade set up and a line of guards ready to arrest him when it pulled up to its first stop. Siobhán and her brood had personally brought Adam to the festivities, and everyone in town had agreed not to mention that his uncle was the killer. He was told the bad guy was from out of town, he was caught, and he would never hurt anyone again. When he was older, he would learn the truth, but enough of his childhood had been stolen, and no one wanted him to feel any burden for his uncle's actions. This was the main reason Ed Healy was going to continue with Dave's last gift: the rehabilitation facility. Adam's face was beaming as he passed around the shining star he'd found in his nutcracker. Made of tiny crystals, it positively glowed as he passed it from person-to-person while chattering about the new skills he would be learning at the rehab center. Siobhán knew this was a kid who was going to go far. He deserved it.

Siobhán brought glasses of bubbly over to a quiet corner where one Santa was planted, as if keeping an eye on the festivities from a distance. "Champagne?" she offered to the Santa.

"T'ank you." His voice was deep but muffled behind his fake beard.

"You're welcome." She sat. "I'd ask who you are, but I'm sure tonight you're just Santy."

"Dat's right." His outfit was good. Besides the long beard, and overpadded suit, his curly white wig practically covered his face. He wore thick glasses that were cloudy and white gloves.

"So, Ms. O'Sullivan," he said. "What would you like for Christmas?"

Siobhán laughed softly and pointed to the crowd. "How could I ask for more?"

"Gratitude is a gift," he said. "But it's just you and Santa here. There must be something."

Siobhán hesitated. "There might be *someone*."

"And who is this someone?"

"You can't give me a *person*, Santa." She smiled, patted his gloved hand.

"Tell the stars, then," he said, pointing at a twinkly one above.

She tilted her head up. "Merry Christmas Eve, Dara," she whispered to the stars. "Wherever you are."

She stood, kissed the Santa on the cheek, and patted his back. "Come to Naomi's Bistro for hot cocoa and brown bread," she said. "We're staying open late."

"Not too late, I hope," he said. "Santa is on his way."

Her laugh filled the night with warmth. "Not too late, Santa," she said. "I promise."

Macdara Flannery watched Siobhán O'Sullivan walk away, his heart swelling. He'd pretended to grant her a wish, but he'd just been given one. All he wanted in the whole world was to come home. And home, he'd come to realize, was wherever Siobhán O'Sullivan was. He was determined this was the last Christmas he'd ever be apart from her. He continued to watch from a distance as carolers began to fill the night air with song, and children cried out in glee.

"Snow!"

At first, Macdara thought they'd turned the snow machine on, but then he tilted his head and saw the flakes dancing down as the moon shone above. In the distance Siobhán O'Sullivan stood with her brood, swaying as they sang.

"Happy Christmas," he said as he tipped his Santa cap to the moon.

Hot Cocoa—An Irish Variety

1½ tablespoons of unsweetened cocoa
1½ tablespoons of sugar
¾ cup milk
2 ounces *Baileys Irish Cream
Whipped cream, freshly made

Stir, heat, enjoy! Garnish with chocolate sprinkles, a candy cane, and a good book!

*Can also use Kahlúa, vodka, flavored rum, butterscotch liqueur, any of your favorite spirits.

Happy Christmas to all, and to all, a good night!

CHRISTMAS COCOA
AND A CORPSE

Maddie Day

Chapter One

This close to Christmas, I'd assumed we'd have a smooth, joyous next few days leading up to the holiday. But as Mom used to say, to assume only makes an *ass* out of yo*u* and *me*. She was absolutely right this time.

In my best poetry-reading voice, I began, "'Twas the Sunday before Christmas and all through the country store, tiny lights were atwinkle and in through the door came . . . customers!" I unlocked the front door of Pans 'N Pancakes and pulled it open at exactly eight o'clock. Sure enough, at least ten eager diners waited on the wide covered front porch. I stepped out.

"Good morning." My breath made little clouds in the air as I viewed the crowd and spied three new faces. "I'm Robbie Jordan. Welcome to my country store." The last two in line I knew well, Howard and Sean O'Neill. I welcomed a hug from Howard, my boyfriend Abe's father, and exchanged a fist bump with Abe's fourteen-year-old son.

"Come on in and sit anywhere." I followed them into all the delectable aromas of a breakfast restaurant: sizzling meat, sweet syrup, sautéing onions and peppers, pancakes on the griddle. I gazed around my festively decorated store

and restaurant, where my assistant, Danna Beedle, tended
sausages and bacon at the grill. Greenery swags, beribboned
wreaths, and strings of white lights brought the place alive,
and the tree in the corner shone with ornaments and col-
ored lights.

I bustled around with the coffeepot and my order pad. I
funneled orders for omelets, banana-walnut pancakes, and
today's special, Holiday Eggnog Oatmeal, over to Danna
as fast as I could. When I finally neared the O'Neills' four-
top, a gentleman I hadn't seen before was walking with a
shaky gait to the table. He shook hands with Howard and
took a seat.

"Coffee?" I asked when I got there.

"Yes, please." Howard gestured to his cup. "Robbie,
this is Jed Greenberg, a former associate of mine. Jed,
Robbie Jordan. This is her store and restaurant."

"Nice to meet you, Jed." I poured coffee for him, too.

"Likewise." Jed looked a bit younger than Howard's
sixty-four, and had a permanent frown wrinkle between
bushy eyebrows. He didn't return my smile, instead tapping the table in a nervous rhythm.

"Sean, we're offering a yummy Mexican hot chocolate
this week. Interested?" I smiled at the teen. Since I was a
native of California, I was well acquainted with the rich
spicy hot cocoa made south of the border. It was going
over well as a special drink, and I'd made up packets of
the mix to sell in the store, too.

"Sure." At a glance from his grandfather, he added,
"Yes, ma'am." Sean's big brown eyes and dimple echoed
Abe's, but his skinny frame still had some filling out to do.

I held pen to pad. "What can I get you all to eat this
morning? The specials are on the board on that wall, Jed."

He twisted to look. "Eggnog oatmeal sounds terrible.
Give me a cheese omelet with white toast and bacon."

No "please," and insulting my specials all in one breath. *Wonderful.*

"I think the oatmeal sounds great, Robbie," Sean piped up. "Can I have that, please, plus biscuits and sausage gravy and a cheese omelet with a side of bacon?"

Ah, the legendary appetite of the growing boy. I checked with Howard.

"Whatever he wants is fine. For me, the pancakes with the yogurt topping, and sausages, please." Howard smiled up at me, his appearance how I imagined Abe would look in another few decades: curly walnut-colored hair shot through with silver, the same dimple as Abe's, and deep smile lines around his dark eyes making the elder O'Neill look kindly even when he wasn't smiling.

"Coming right up." I hurried the order over to my tall young co-chef. She'd been my right-hand person since I'd opened more than a year ago.

Danna was a two-armed wonder, pouring and flipping and pushing things around on the grill. "That order needs hot chocolate and two OJs, and that one's ready to go, too." She gestured with her chin at the top of the counter in front of the grill, where we set finished plates. "I see Mr. Greenberg is here," she murmured, her lips curled as if she'd tasted moldy bread.

"You know him?" I asked in a low voice as I ladled out hot chocolate and loaded up a tray.

"Kind of. Wish I didn't."

"Tell me later, okay?"

When she nodded, off I went. After I delivered an order of sunny-side up with bacon and a Kitchen Sink omelet to two older women in slightly garish holiday sweaters—one embroidered with dancing elves and reindeer, and one appliquéd with interlocking wreaths—the white-haired one pointed to my lit-up Christmas tree in the corner.

"What're all them cute cardboard skillets you got hanging on the tree?" she asked.

I smiled. "They're part of the gift tree project for the Mothers Cupboard Community Kitchen. Each ornament has a child's first name, their age, and one thing they need or really want. You can take the ornament and donate that item to the charity. They like them wrapped and labeled with the child's name, but you can also deliver just the gift and they'll put it in a gift bag." It had been a no-brainer when the organization asked me if I would be a sponsor for the project. Even people who didn't donate in any other way during the rest of the year felt the urge to help others during the holidays.

"Is it clothes or toys and such?" the other woman asked.

"Some of everything," I said. "One of them simply has *Books* written on it. I have a big box behind the tree if you want to bring stuff back here, or you can take it to their center in Nashville."

"I'm going to get me one now." The first woman stood. "Sis, you want I should grab one for you, too?"

"You bet your sweet bippy I do. Helping some poor little children at the holidays. Heck, I'll take me two."

"Thank you both," I said. "It's a great cause. Enjoy your breakfasts, now."

When the O'Neills' plates were ready, I carried them and Jed's to their table. A tall woman with spiky white-blond hair arrived at the table at the same time. It was Karinde Nilsson, a woman I'd been introduced to when she ate here earlier in the year. I hadn't seen her since.

"Hi, Karinde," I said. "Are you joining these gentlemen for breakfast?"

"Hi, Robbie. No, I just need a word with Mr. O'Neill." She glared at Jed as she spoke, the color high in her cheeks.

Howard stood abruptly. "Let's talk over there." He hurried her away from the table.

Sean looked as confused as I felt, but when I set his food down, his eyes lit up.

"Thanks, Robbie. This looks, like, perfect."

Jed, on the other hand, didn't thank me. He picked up his fork, but his gaze had followed Karinde and Howard to where they spoke in my waiting area.

Chapter Two

A few minutes later, we had a momentary lull in the action. All our customers were served and seemed content, and nobody new had arrived. Howard had returned to his table after Karinde departed. Clicks of flatware on porcelain, pops of sausages, and the murmur of conversation combined to make my favorite soundtrack.

I looked up at Danna, who was more than half a foot taller than me. Today she was working in a red cotton sweater, an Indian-print wraparound skirt, orange tights, and black Doc Martens, with a green scarf wrapped around her reddish-gold dreadlocks. Plus a store apron, of course, whose royal blue didn't match any of the rest of her outfit. Me, I settled for a long-sleeved store tee and jeans under my apron. I paired it with blue tennies and threaded my thick curly ponytail through a store ball cap. The store part of the country store did a surprisingly brisk business in the blue shirts and caps. The logo featured a cast-iron griddle held by a grinning stack of pancakes.

"So, how do you know Jed Greenberg?" I asked Danna.

She raised one pierced eyebrow. "My mom doesn't like him at all."

Danna's mom being Corrine Beedle, mayor of South Lick, our town nestled in scenic Brown County, Indiana.

"He owned some piece of real estate, and Mom said he was trying to, like, avoid paying taxes on it or something. She introduced me one time we were out and I hated the way he looked at me. I was only fifteen and it was like I was a piece of meat or something." She shuddered. "Ick."

"*Ick* is right."

"Plus, I heard a rumor he had some connection with a place where they breed dogs and cats in really terrible conditions."

"That sounds awful." I grabbed a rag and wiped down the counter above the grill and then the one next to it. "*Connection* meaning he owned it, or he worked at it?"

"I'm not sure. I think Mom said nobody found any, like, real evidence to connect him to it, but I'd have to ask her."

I spied Howard approaching us. "Everything all right with the meal?" I asked.

"Absolutely, Robbie. Delicious, as always. Good morning, Danna."

"Hey, Mr. O'Neill." Danna smiled. "How's the AP bio class this year?"

I knew Abe's father taught science at South Lick High School, but I hadn't realized that included advanced placement biology.

"Not as good as when you were in it," Howard said. "Any college applications in the works?"

"Nah. I'm doing what I love."

Danna had told me when I'd hired her over a year ago as a recent high school graduate that all she wanted to do was cook. Her mom and her teachers had urged her to continue her academic education, but Danna was firm in her choice to work for me, at least for a while. I couldn't be happier to have her, even though I knew I'd lose her to either culinary school or a higher-end restaurant one day. I was a decade older and fully regarded her as my equal.

"Good." Howard turned to me. "Robbie, my wife and I would like to invite you and Abraham to dinner tonight. Can you make it? Fredericka has the house all decorated and wants to share it."

"That sounds lovely. Have you checked with Abe?" I took a swig from my rapidly cooling mug of coffee.

"Not yet, but I will. I wanted to be sure you were free."

"I know I am, and I'm pretty sure he is, too. What can we bring?"

"Let's see. I'm making beef Bourguignon, and there will be six of us. How about a bottle of red?"

"You got it." I'd been the beneficiary of Howard's excellent cooking before.

He glanced over at Sean. "And you can meet his Christmas present."

"Oh?" I asked.

"That blond woman who came in? She rescues dogs, and she has a puppy for us that we're giving Sean. She's going to bring it over tonight."

Aha. I hadn't known that about Karinde. "And it's a surprise?" No wonder Howard wanted to talk with her away from the table where Sean sat.

"Trying to keep it one. Freddy's idea, of course." He shook his head, a fond look on his face. "It's a chocolate Lab."

A customer held his coffee mug in the air, and a family of six dressed in their church clothes, with ruddy cheeks from the cold, pushed in.

"Thanks for the invitation. I'd better get back to work."

"Great. See you at six tonight, then. Oh, and I wanted to buy some of your Mexican hot chocolate packs for stocking stuffers." He gestured toward the display near the door. "Can you add six to my ticket? I'll pay for Jed's breakfast, too."

"Of course. Enjoy the rest of your day and we'll see you tonight."

Chapter Three

"So Sean's with his mom tonight?" I asked Abe as he drove us to his parents' home that evening.

"Yes, until tomorrow, then he's with Mom and Dad until I'm off for Christmas. Jan and I alternate years having Sean for the holidays."

Jed Greenberg and his wife, Willa Mae, had apparently been invited for the meal that evening, too. Abe and I arrived at the same time as the couple, and he introduced me to them on the driveway. We enjoyed drinks in the O'Neills' living room while Howard put the finishing touches on the meal. Willa Mae's red wool skirt, which she'd paired with black boots, was festive. Freddy wore a simple green dress with Nordic wool clogs, and I'd selected a red sweater and black pants for the dinner, my hair loose on my shoulders for once.

I admired the Christmas tree decorated with tiny white lights and a diverse array of ornaments. "I love all these," I said, pointing to a small red cable car hanging from a branch. "Is this from San Francisco?"

"Yes. We collect one from every place we travel." Freddy pointed. "See, here's a kiwi from our trip to New Zealand, and this is a little polar bear from Alaska."

"When did you go to Alaska?" I asked.

"A couple of years ago." She went on to regale us with funny stories of life on a cruise ship.

"Soup's on," Howard announced to the group about twenty minutes later.

I was behind Jed as we made our way into the dining room, which had been added onto the back of the house. A light outside showed snowy woods stretching into the darkness. It hadn't snowed recently, but so far it had been cold enough for the previous snow not to melt, as happened some winters. Jed seemed unsteady on his feet as he walked, the same as he had in the store earlier.

Lovely hand-painted Nativity figures populated a crèche scenario on the sideboard. I peered to look before I took my seat and stifled a giggle when I saw a little Snoopy figure peeking out from behind a ceramic cow and a tiny Bert from *Sesame Street* keeping a Magi's camel company. A plastic chicken perched in the eaves of the stable, too. Irreverence was just fine in my book. Abe saw me looking. He winked at me as he pulled out my chair and waited for me to sit.

Howard had set steaming plates at every place and fat wineglasses were all half full with a red vintage.

I lifted mine. "Here's to the cook."

"To the cook!" Abe echoed the sentiment.

After we all clinked around, I tucked into the meal, savoring the first bite of Howard's wine-flavored beef stew.

"Too bad my wife can't cook something this good," Jed said.

My wife? Willa Mae, sitting across from me, winced. Surely Jed knew her name.

Freddy let out her tinkling laugh. "I say leave the cooking to the menfolk, don't I, How?" Her big blue eyes sparkled at her husband.

Jed curled a corner of his upper lip, but didn't argue with his hostess.

"I love to cook and Dad taught me well, but I sure don't try to compete with the best chef in the county." Abe pointed at me, then gently nudged my elbow with his.

I opened my mouth to dispute the last claim, but closed it and smiled at Abe, instead. "The Bourguignon is truly a masterpiece, Howard," I finally said. And it was. The rich dark sauce was thick with tender pearl onions and mushrooms. Chunks of beef fell apart on the fork. The buttery parsley-flaked potatoes he'd served with the dish made a perfect accompaniment, as did the crusty bread that soaked up sauce as if that was its purpose in life.

Willa Mae had barely said a word in the hour since we'd arrived. Not while we enjoyed our drinks. Not here at the table, either.

"What do you do for work, Willa Mae?" I asked.

She sat up straighter. "I'm a plant toxicologist. I work at a lab in Bloomington." She looked about fifty, with neat light hair framing a round face, her pale green sweater exactly matching her eyes.

"That sounds really interesting," Abe said. "Like botanical poisons, that kind of thing?"

"Pretty much." She smiled at him.

"I always worry she's going to put something in my scrambled eggs." Jed's laugh was harsh and he rolled his eyes at Howard in an *only men understand* kind of look.

Willa Mae gave him a tight smile and sipped her wine. She addressed me again. "I really love puzzles, and my work is sometimes like solving a hard puzzle."

"I love puzzles, too, particularly crosswords." I smiled at her. "We should talk more about that sometime."

Howard stood and walked around the table refilling

glasses. When he sat, he lifted his own. "Here's to a peaceful holiday season, both right here and around the world."

"A merry Christmas and a happy Hanukkah to all," Freddy added.

Jed's nostrils flared. "Hanukkah ended a week ago."

"Thank you, Freddy. It's the sentiment, Jedediah," Willa Mae admonished.

When he turned his glare on her, she shrank into herself.

Howard cleared his throat. "Freddy's playing in the *Messiah* tomorrow night, did you know?" He beamed at his wife.

"At Indiana University?" I asked. Petite Freddy was a concert cellist. She'd played with the Indianapolis Symphony and was a regular at classical performances in neighboring Bloomington, at the flagship Indiana University campus. I'd seen her walk with her cello in a rolling case and it always looked nearly as tall as she was.

"No, this is the Brown County Symphony Orchestra." She laughed again. "It's an elite group, if you want to call a bunch of amateurs elite. Well, amateurs except for me. We just formed this fall. The county has a number of talented musicians who wanted to up their game. Since I have experience, I agreed to shepherd them along. I wouldn't expect the Met, but we have fun and put on a pretty good show. We're playing at the new Maple Leaf Performing Arts Center."

"The *Messiah* is an ambitious project to start with, isn't it, Mom?" Abe asked.

"Yes, of course. But why not aim high?" She swooped her fork up to point at the ceiling, showering her hand with parsley.

"I play the oboe," Jed said. "Maybe I should join your little group."

Freddy blinked, her always-congenial expression slipping for a moment. "Let me consult the others. I'm, ah, not certain we need an oboe at present. And we do have an audition requirement." Her smile returned.

Or maybe she simply didn't want Jed in the group?

"I'm not sure I have time, anyway." Jed lifted his chin.

"Howard, this morning you said you and Jed were former associates," I said. "Do you teach music at the high school, Jed?"

Once again, Jed's expression turned to disdain. He was about to speak, but Howard beat him to it.

"No, we were partners in an investment property."

I caught the hint of an eye roll from Freddy.

"I wouldn't dream of being a teacher." Jed lifted his chin. "All those recalcitrant teenagers? Please. No, I have my finger in several other more lucrative pies."

"Except ours. It ended up not being a great investment." Howard lifted a shoulder. "You win some, you lose some."

I sneaked a glance at Abe as he rubbed his knee against mine under the table. Something was up about that investment, and I planned to ask Abe about it on the way home.

Chapter Four

We sat around the table enjoying hot chocolate and a platter of crisp sweet Christmas cookies. Some were cut into stars, trees, and bells, with red and green sugars glistening and crunchy. A dozen were chocolate rounds, with white granulated sugar, while others were nutty shortbread squares dusted with powdered sugar. Abe and I had cleared the table and scraped the plates. We'd rejoined the others while Howard prepared some of my hot chocolate for everyone. He'd whipped cream and added a dollop to the top of each small cup.

"I have a choice of Armagnac, Frangelico, or Kahlúa." Howard set out the three bottles, one shaped vaguely like a monk with a piece of actual rope tied around the bottle's waist. He brought a tray of tiny glasses, too. "You can have it in your hot chocolate or next to it."

"Frangelico is hazelnut, right?" I asked.

"Yes."

"I love Kahlúa," Willa Mae said. "I'll take some of that, but no thank you to the hot chocolate."

She'd barely touched her wine during dinner, but maybe she preferred alcohol on the sweet side. Come to think of it, she'd had sherry as her before-dinner drink.

I looked at Abe. "You're driving home?"

When he nodded, I said to his father, "Frangelico, please. I love hazelnuts." Plus, it was Italian, and I was all for indulging in food and drink from my father's birthplace.

"I'd take whiskey if you have some, O'Neill," Jed said.

Howard got up to fetch a bottle of Scotch. He poured from the friar's head for me, and I thanked him. He handed a glass of Armagnac to Freddy without asking her, poured the Greenbergs' drinks, and looked at Abe.

"As the lady said, I'm driving. I'll stick with virgin hot chocolate."

"These are so light, Freddy," I said, nibbling my second cookie, this one shaped like a bell.

"Thanks," Abe's mom said. "I use my mother's sugar cookie recipe. I've been making them my whole life." She looked at Willa Mae. "The chocolate cookies are tasty, Willa Mae. Did you try one?"

Willa Mae shuddered. "Sorry. I know it's unusual, but I don't like chocolate at all."

"Mom doesn't cook dinner often, but, boy, can she bake," Abe said. "My other grandma always made these Mexican Bridecakes." He picked up one of the squares. "Robbie, you could offer them for a lunch dessert in the restaurant. They're easy, because you make them by the panful. They bake in under fifteen minutes, too."

"Good idea," I said. And it was. Maybe Danna and I could whip up a few batches during the lull tomorrow morning. "Can I get the recipe, Freddy?"

"Of course. Just remind me before you leave."

Howard stood. "And speaking of passing things along, I have a little something for Jed and Willa Mae." He left the room and came back with a bundle wrapped in red ribbon. "To warm up your winter." He handed the bundle to Jed.

Jed held it up. "Well, that's good of you, O'Neill. Thanks."

"What is it?" Willa Mae craned her neck to see.

"It's the hot chocolate mix Robbie has been serving in her store." Howard pointed at me. "Quite tasty, too, as we've just experienced. It was brilliant to think of selling it, too. I'm sorry I didn't know about your aversion to the stuff, Willa Mae, or I would have found something else." He looked sheepish.

"No worries. It's a lovely gesture, Howard," Willa Mae said. "We thank you, and Jed will enjoy it, I'm sure."

"I decided to sell it because everybody's always looking for small gift items at this time of year," I said.

"Is it a special mix, Robbie?" Willa Mae asked.

"Yes," I said. "It's a Mexican mix, or my approximation of it. The real stuff involves grating a thick bar of chocolate, adding cinnamon and a touch of cayenne, and beating the mix with a special kind of wooden whisk. It's fabulous, but not very practical."

"I didn't even know you brought those packets home, How," Freddy said.

"I figured the packets were good stocking stuffers and such." Howard turned to Jed. "Have you been watching any holiday movies?" He glanced at me. "Jed's a big classic-movie buff."

Jed's face lit up. "Despite my religion of origin, I'm a huge fan of Christmas movies. I think this year's viewing of *Miracle on 34th Street* puts me over fifty times. And *White Christmas*? I can't get enough of it. Boy, did they know how to make films back then."

For the first time, Willa Mae had a fond look for her husband. "He studied film in college, you know. There isn't a movie made he isn't informed about."

"I'm partial to the *Muppet Family Christmas*, myself,"

Howard offered. "And *Mr. Magoo's Christmas Carol* is a real classic in my book."

"I'm not as big into the cartoon movies, but I'll grant those are becoming classics." Jed gave a grudging nod. "Including *A Charlie Brown Christmas,* of course."

"What about *How the Grinch Stole Christmas*?" I asked. As I said the last few words, the doorbell rang.

Howard stood. "I'll get it." He headed toward the front door.

Yipping and the sound of toenails on the hardwood floor greeted us a moment later. "Look who's here." Howard held a leash connected to an energetic little bundle of dark brown fur wagging its tail and weaving in three directions almost simultaneously.

Karinde followed them in, carrying a cloth bag that looked heavy.

"Aw, come here, cutie." Freddy held out her arms and boosted the puppy into her lap. Its floppy ears hung flat and the downward slope of its big eyes made the puppy look sad, or at least confused.

"Karinde, this is our son Abe, and our friends Jed and Willa Mae Greenberg," Howard said. "I think you know Robbie already. Everybody, Karinde Nilsson, dog rescuer *extraordinaire.*"

Abe stood and shook her hand. "Thanks for doing such good work."

Karinde nodded, but didn't smile. Her gaze lingered briefly on Jed and landed on Willa Mae with what I could swear was a look of pity. If Karinde knew and disliked Jed, no wonder she would feel bad for his wife.

"Can you join us for some dessert, Karinde?" Freddy asked.

"Thanks, but no. I have to get going. The bag has the

food the puppy is used to. He's pretty well trained, but you'll want to take him out frequently at the beginning. You've already signed the paperwork, and, Howard, you said you'd gotten a crate, right?"

"Yes." Howard nodded.

"Good. He's been crate-trained, and they don't like soiling where they sleep, so he might even make it through the night, but I wouldn't count on it for the first few days. There's also a blankie in the bag, for lack of a better term. He's used to sleeping with it and it'll be something familiar for him."

"The blankie will be important," Willa Mae said. "I fostered puppies before I was married."

"Then you know." Karinde knelt and petted the dog's head. "I've been calling him Cocoa, but you can change his name if you want. Just be consistent. He needs a lot of loving right now." She kissed his head and stood. "We found him at a filthy puppy mill." Her words came out through a nearly clenched jaw and her gaze bore down on Jed with a fury. He didn't look back, instead regarding the wintry scene outside the window.

"That's terrible." Willa Mae shook her head.

Maybe what Danna had said about Jed was true. Karinde must be aware of it, but it seemed that Willa Mae wasn't. Howard showed her out.

When he returned, Freddy said, "I think Cocoa is a perfect name for him, Abe. Don't you, with that coloring?"

"Sure." My guy smiled, his dimple creasing his cheek. "Sean is going to go nuts over him."

Freddy unclipped the leash and set the wriggling puppy on the floor. "Go explore, cutie."

Cocoa prowled under the table, sniffing our feet, checking for crumbs. I laughed when he nibbled gently at my ankle. He trotted up to a three-foot-tall vase that sat on the floor and headed behind it. The vase wobbled, with Howard catching it just in time.

"We're going to have to do some dog-proofing around here," Howard said. "It's been a decade since we had toddler Sean in the house."

The puppy scampered into the next room. "You'd better follow him, How," Freddy said.

"I'll watch the little dude," Abe said, standing.

The next moment brought the tinkling of a bell, the sound of glass breaking, and a mini-bark. Abe and I both rushed in to see a broken ornament under the tree and Cocoa sniffing the trunk, about to raise his leg.

"Oh, no, you don't, buddy." Abe scooped him up.

Willa Mae and Freddy hurried in, too, followed by their husbands.

"Puppies will be puppies," Jed said, raising an eyebrow.

"You guys remember you have Sean tomorrow," Abe said to his parents. "The dog isn't going to be much of a surprise on Christmas morning."

"I know." Freddy, who had knelt to pick up the pieces of the broken ornament, wrinkled her nose and sat back on her heels. "We wanted Karinde to deliver him on Christmas, but she said this was the only day she could bring him, and she just let us know today."

"We haven't had a minute to find a place to board him," Howard added.

"Let me take him," Willa Mae said with a sidelong glance at her husband. "I'm good with puppies, and, of course, we don't have a tree set up."

"What do you think, Freddy?" Howard gazed at her.

"Sounds perfect." Freddy gave him a thumbs-up.

But was it perfect? What if Danna had been right, that Jed had been involved in abusing animals? That—combined with Karinde's look at him—didn't bode well. Was Cocoa safe at the Greenbergs' home? I supposed if Willa Mae kept a close eye on him, he would be. It was only for a couple of days. And it wasn't my decision, anyway.

"I'll bring him over on Christmas morning anytime you want," Willa Mae offered. "We have nothing going on that day except the annual Jewish Christmas feast, Chinese takeout." She finally smiled.

"Okay with you, Greenberg?" Howard asked Jed, who stood with arms folded on his chest.

"If that's what the wife wants, it's fine."

Chapter Five

Danna and I were full steam ahead in the restaurant at eight-thirty the next morning, with Christmas carols playing softly in the background and frozen wind whistling through the windows. Thank goodness I'd upgraded the heating system when I'd renovated the dilapidated country store that was now my pride, joy, and income stream.

Our number three in the Pans 'N Pancakes kitchen, Turner Rao, was off with his parents and sister on a trip to visit his father's family in India, with my blessing. The store would be open only a few more days before we closed for the week between Christmas and New Year's. I knew Danna and I could manage. I'd been able to get the Mexican Bridecakes dough mixed up before we'd opened this morning. It was chilling in the walk-in, and the cookies would be easy to press out and bake before the lunch rush. For now? It was the usual menu, our specials, and the rest. Rinse and repeat.

I'd deposited a load of dirty dishes in the sink an hour later when Lieutenant Buck Bird ambled in. After I smiled and waved, he acknowledged my greeting, but didn't smile back. *Odd.* He'd become a friend over the past year. Plus, he kept my budget in the black with his hollow leg. The man was a foot taller than me and could eat like a Tour de

France rider. He didn't show an ounce of it, also like a pro bicyclist. Or like a teenage boy, except the officer was in his late forties. He hung his South Lick PD winter jacket on the coat tree near the door and pointed to his favorite two-top at the back wall. I nodded, heading his way with the pot of full-strength coffee. Something was up. It couldn't be a disaster involving my aunt, away for the holidays, or Danna's mom. If it was, Buck would have come straight to us. But I tasted negative news in the air.

I greeted Buck and filled his mug. "Something bad has happened. I can feel it."

He nodded, his face somber. "A South Lick resident was found dead a little while ago."

My mouth formed an O. "Somebody I know?"

"Not sure. He was apparently a friend of Abe's folks, though."

No. My eyes widened. "Was it Jed Greenberg?"

Buck squinted at me. "How did you know?"

"I didn't. But we had dinner with Jed and his wife at Howard and Freddy O'Neill's last night. I think the Greenbergs are the only friends of Abe's parents I've met." Abe and I had been an item for less than a year, and while I'd spent time with Howard and Freddy, plus Sean, of course, I hadn't yet been invited to a gathering of the older generation and their friends until last evening. "Did he have a heart attack or something? He wasn't that old." Poor Jed, and poor Willa Mae.

"The death appears to have been accidental." Buck tapped the table and frowned, as if he had doubts about what he'd just said.

Whew. "I hope so. Because, another murder in South Lick? No, thanks. Still, it's really sad. What kind of accident was he in?" I thought about what he'd said. "Wait. Did you say it *appears* to be accidental?"

"Can I get me some breakfast real quick before I tell you, Robbie? I'm so hungry I could eat a cow between two bread vans. And I got to get back to the office lickety-split."

"Sure. The usual?"

Buck glanced at the Specials board. "Huh. I'll take me some of that there oatmeal. It's colder than a polar bear's toenails out there, and oatmeal will warm me up fast. Plus biscuits and gravy, and two over-easy with sausages and rye toast, please?" He looked up at me, sounding hopeful.

"You got it." Definitely an appetite as legendary as a teenager's. "Don't go anywhere."

"I'm too plumb weak with hunger to move, Robbie."

I snorted as he hauled out his department-issue cell phone and started jabbing at it with his index finger.

I brought his order to Danna. I lowered my voice. "Buck just said Jed Greenberg was found dead this morning."

"Really?" She brought her hand to her mouth.

"Buck said it was an accident. Or that it looked like one, whatever that means. I feel bad for Jed's wife, Willa Mae. Did you ever meet her?"

Danna shook her head. "I don't think so."

"I met the couple only yesterday. Buck's going to tell me more after he gets his food."

"Because he's so hungry his stomach thinks his throat's been slit?" She rolled her eyes, but it was an indulgent look. "I'm on it, Madame Chef."

I cruised about, clearing tables, making change, freshening up coffee. A party of four women, white-haired as well as dye-jobbed, found a table and gave me their orders. Three of them beelined it straight for the shelves of vintage cookware I collected to sell, their excitement palpable.

"We're down from Indy to shop, but, you know, most

of the stores in Nashville don't open 'til ten," the last one told me. "One of the girls had been to South Lick before and she raved about your store and the restaurant. We just had to start our day here!"

"I'm glad you did. I'll come get you when your food is ready."

"Thanks, hon."

After almost five years in southern Indiana, I was finally used to nearly everybody older than me addressing me as "hon" or "dear," which hadn't been a custom in California—and still wasn't, as far as I knew.

Danna dinged the Ready bell for Buck's order. I swapped the slip for the shoppers' and carried a tray holding enough breakfast for three of me to Buck. He tucked his blue cloth napkin into his collar and his fork into a gravy-laden biscuit. A customer across the room caught my attention, so off I went to attend to him. Fifteen minutes elapsed before I got back to Buck. He'd made short work of the food. The bowl of oatmeal was empty and only a few smears of gravy remained on the biscuit plate. He was using the toast to make sure he didn't leave behind even a trace of egg.

"Now can you tell me what happened, Buck? Please?" I kept my voice low, even though nobody else sat directly adjacent.

He swallowed and swabbed his mouth with the napkin. "Welp, seems Mr. Greenberg was out walking a puppy before dawn this morning. Man fell on a patch of ice and hit his head hard on an iron fence. Between that and the frigid temperatures, he was a goner by the time somebody found him."

"Where was the fence? Who found him?"

"Behind the library. That lady who works there, a, uh . . ."

He checked the display on his phone. "A Ms. LaRue was out emptying the overnight box. She saw him and called it in."

"I know Georgia." I pictured the walkway behind the library. In fact, it faced north and the pavement might not get any direct sun at this time of year. "That must have been hard on her, to find a dead person. Was Cocoa okay?"

He gaped, half-chewed toast still in his mouth. "Now, how in Sam Hill do you know the doggy's name?"

"Shut your mouth when you have food in it, Buck." I cleared my throat. "I was at the O'Neills' when Cocoa was delivered last night."

Buck wrinkled his nose as if that was too much information to take in. "Anywho, pup was fine, although his leash was all tangled up in the corpse's legs. Might coulda been what killed Greenberg. Trip over an energetic puppy and you're a goner."

"Ouch. I did notice yesterday and last night, too, that Jed seemed a little wobbly, like he had poor balance, even before we started having drinks. He didn't sound drunk, but I suppose he could have been. I have no idea what caused his wavering when he walked."

"We'll check into it. Good thing the dog was wearing a tag, so the patrol officer had somebody to call. Ms. O'Neill told us the Greenbergs was keeping the pup until Christmas."

"Right. He's supposed to be a surprise Christmas gift for Abe's son," I said. "Jed's wife, Willa Mae, offered to keep Cocoa until Christmas morning."

"So she told me. A lot to sort out." He scratched his head and stood. "I'd best get back to the station. I got men securing the scene until Oscar shows up and commences his investigation."

"Oscar Thompson?" I stared up at Buck. "But he's a state homicide detective. Why is he taking over?"

Buck looked down—way down—at me over the bridge of his nose. "You should oughta know by now, Robbie. Unattended death? A man essentially in his prime? We're obliged to call in the big guns, as far as that goes. No three ways about it."

Chapter Six

News spread fast in a small town like ours. The restaurant buzzed with rumors and gossip about Jed's death for the rest of the morning. We barely had our usual ten-thirty lull, the time when we did necessary things like use the facilities, grab a bite to eat, and do lunch prep. Diners kept stopping me as I passed.

"What do you think, Robbie?" one regular asked, a gentleman retired from a career in aerospace. "Was Greenberg's death really a accident?"

I gritted my teeth at the use of *a* rather than *an*. Even after nearly five years in the area, some of the local expressions drove me a little nuts. I mustered an innocent look. "That's what the police said. Why should I doubt them?"

" 'Cause you're some kind of PI, aren't you?"

"No, sir." I laughed. "Not at all. I'm a chef and business owner, not a private investigator." Despite having discovered that I did, in fact, have a knack for figuring out murders over the last year, I'd much prefer never to need to.

"Do you think he was murdered?" The man's white eyebrows went nearly into his hairline. "I heard he was messing around in more than one piece of dirty business."

Interesting gossip, but I wasn't going there. Relieved to hear Danna hit the Ready bell, I said, "If you'll excuse me, I have some hot food to deliver." I hurried over to the grill. "We have to swap out. Everybody thinks I'm a detective and is asking me if Jed was murdered. Sheesh."

"Sure, boss." She slid out of her apron and donned a fresh one. She pointed at the grill. "That's the Adam and Eve on a raft, and the cowboy with whiskey down is for the same table. I haven't gotten to the next two orders yet."

"Got it." I washed my hands, smiling at her diner jargon, which she'd learned at her previous job. *Adam and Eve on a raft* was two poached eggs on toast. A *cowboy* was a western omelet, and *whiskey down* meant rye toast. I'd picked up most of the expressions, but she still stumped me on occasion, like when she'd delivered a slip at lunchtime and said, "*Noah's boy and run it through a Wisconsin garden.*" She'd laughed out loud at my bewildered expression and patiently explained, "Ham—you know, like, Noah's son—and cheese—Wisconsin—sandwich with lettuce, tomato, and onion. That's the garden part."

By eleven-thirty I'd managed to bake three big pans of the cookies. I dusted them with powdered sugar and cut them into inch-and-a-half squares while they were still warm. We could serve three on a small plate and call it dessert. Danna wrote the cookies on the Specials board, and added the pea soup I'd whipped up yesterday afternoon, too. It was a pretty green with a mix of split peas and fresh frozen ones. Tiny chunks of ham added flavor, and we'd fine-chopped red pepper to sprinkle on it before serving, so it looked festive.

Abe set the front-door cowbell to jangling at a few minutes before noon. His expression wasn't a happy one. We'd had a flood of customers come in over the last ten minutes and there was exactly one small table left open. Danna was still handling the front, taking orders and filling drinks as fast as she could. Abe gave me a quick squeeze around the waist, then stepped back from the grill.

I laid on two beef patties and a turkey burger. "What's going on? Do you want lunch?" I stole a glance at his face, ruddy from the cold, but with worry lines between his dark eyebrows, and spied his electric company work shirt under his jacket.

"I'm on my lunch break from work, and, yes, I'm hungry. But some serious stuff is going on." He grabbed the black watch cap off his head and ruffled his hair with his other hand.

"So tell me." The patties sizzled.

"You heard about Jed."

I nodded.

"My dad got other bad news this morning. He'd had an audit done on the books for the property he and Jed owned. The one they sold not too long ago. Turns out Jed was cooking them. Stealing money and disguising it."

I faced him. "No. Really?"

"Truth. Dad thought something was fishy, but he could never find it. He finally got the report a couple of hours ago."

"Wow. Did Jed know your dad was getting an audit done?"

Abe shook his head. "I don't think so. Dad called him this morning, but, of course, Jed was already dead, so he didn't reach him."

"Last night, Howard said it hadn't been a good investment. That must have been why." I turned back to the waiting orders. I assembled a grilled cheddar and tomato on whole wheat bread—otherwise known as a *mousetrap on brown with a slice*—and laid it on the hot surface. "Your dad must be really upset. Was it a lot of money?"

"I think it was."

I scrunched up my nose. "Has he let the police know? If Jed was ripping off your father, he might have been cheating other people, too."

"Dad's over at the station now."

I flipped the burgers and the grilled cheese and ladled out two bowls of soup, sprinkling the pepper bits on top. "They wanted him to come in? I would have thought he could just put them in touch with the auditor."

Abe didn't speak for a minute. He cleared his throat. "Detective Thompson insisted."

"I don't like the sound of that."

"What's he doing on the case, anyway? I heard Jed slipped on the ice."

I threw a handful of sliced onions and green peppers onto the grill. "Buck reminded me that it's because Jed's death was unattended, and it's not like he's an old guy who died in his sleep. The police are required to investigate it."

"But what if the police make a fuss about the fraud and people think my father killed Jed?" Abe asked softly. "What if they think Dad had a motive?" He jingled the change in his pocket faster than he picked his banjo.

"Abe, one step at a time. We both know your father wouldn't hurt an atom on a flea. They can't charge Howard if he didn't do it. Plus, you don't even know that Jed's death wasn't an accident." I slid the burgers onto their buns and checked the order slips. I dragged two of them *through the garden*, so to speak, loaded up four plates with pickle spears, burgers, and *a mousetrap*, and dinged the bell for Danna. "Sweetie, I really have to focus on cooking. We're packed and we don't have Turner."

"I know. I'm sorry." He blew out a breath. "I'm just kind of worried right now."

"I hear you. But everything's going to be okay. Trust me." I gazed into his eyes until he nodded. "Now, what do you want to eat?"

Chapter Seven

A text came in at one-thirty from Abe. Things were getting worse.

Heard from Mom. Thompson suspicious of Dad giving Jed your chocolate mix. Kept him at station for more grilling.

My Mexican chocolate mix? Yikes. They must think Jed had been poisoned. But what about hitting his head? And did they really imagine cheery, mild-mannered Howard would have murdered someone? What did they think he did, open the packet he'd bought from me, insert a powdered toxin, and then seal it? That was so stupid, and would have run the risk of poisoning Willa Mae, too, or instead. No, wait. Last night, she'd said she hated chocolate. But Abe's dad hadn't known that before he'd wrapped the gift.

I gave a quick glance around the busy restaurant. Rumors of poison in a food product was as bad as evidence of rats for a restaurant's reputation. This place would be empty in a New York minute if a toxin was found in my special chocolate packets. All I could do was hope it wouldn't be.

Danna dinged the bell. We continued to be swamped with customers. Normally, business waned by this time of day. But it was vacation week, and people still had three shopping days until Christmas. Also, it was too cold out to do much of anything. I was going to have to put in a re-supply order and soon, or we'd run out of food by Christmas Eve. I shoved the phone into my back pocket and hurried to the kitchen area.

"Can you believe it?" Danna asked. "I don't think I've ever seen us so busy. And if I don't get to the girls' room, I'm going to—"

I held up a hand. "Don't tell me. Just go."

She tore off her apron and nearly sprinted to the restroom. I loaded up a tray with three lunch orders and delivered it, then hurried back and washed my hands. I slid easily into the cook's role. We served breakfast all day, and next up were a *double wreck on a raft, three stacks—one with logs* and *two with pigs*—and a *moo.* Translation, two scrambled eggs on toast, three orders of pancakes—one with sausages and two with bacon—and a milk. Good thing I didn't offer creamed chipped beef on toast or we'd be uttering a bad word over and over. We'd have to abbreviate it as *SOS,* or maybe say *stuff on a shingle,* instead.

When Danna emerged, she took over waiting, busing, and taking orders while I worked spatulas in both hands. I glanced up when the cowbell jangled, hoping it wasn't a party of ten. If it was, they'd just have to wait. What I saw was possibly worse. State police detective Oscar Thompson clomped toward me in his usual black suit and matching cowboy boots. This time, he wore a red Colts scarf around his neck and a Colts watch cap, instead of his summer ball cap. He was an odd bird personally, but a competent detective. After my being somewhat involved with more than one murder investigation in the past, we'd finally gotten on a first-name basis, too.

"Good afternoon, Oscar." I flashed him a smile. "We're pretty busy, but a table should open up fairly soon."

He did not return my greeting. "I'm not here for lunch. I need to confiscate all your hot chocolate packets." He grabbed the hat off his head, leaving thin hair plastered to his head.

My heart sank. "You do? Why?" I sniffed. Time to focus on my cooking. The pancakes needed turning a minute ago.

He cleared his throat. "One or more might have been tampered with." He pulled out a folded piece of paper. "It's all official. Got the search warrant right here."

"You must think Jed Greenberg was poisoned," I murmured. "Why? I thought he slipped on the sidewalk."

"The man had chocolate spilled on his shirt. It had an odd smell. He was apparently nearly universally disliked, and we have to cover all our bases."

I nodded once. "What about a security camera? Does the library have one out back?"

"We've requested the footage, of course." He opened his mouth to say more, then shut it again. He didn't quite glare at me, but almost. "I'm not free to discuss any more about the case, Robbie. As you well know. Where do you stock the packets?"

"Am I going to get them back?" I asked. I pushed around the scrambleds, then scooped them onto a plate with two pieces of buttered wheat. "They've been really popular."

"Maybe, if they aren't contaminated. I'll give you a receipt from the state."

I stared at him. The Board of Health probably wouldn't let me sell them after they'd been examined, anyway. *Wonderful.*

Oscar tapped his hand on his thigh. "Ms. Jordan, I don't have all day."

"Just hang on. I'm a little busy, as you can see." When Danna approached, I said, "Can you please show Oscar the chocolate packets real quick? And then these orders will be ready."

She raised the eyebrow threaded through with a tiny silver ring, but nodded. She beckoned to Oscar. "Follow me, Detective."

Several customers watched with interest—way too much interest—as Oscar slid the packets into a bag and headed out. Two women shot me glances as they murmured to each other. Just what I didn't need, gossip about one of my food products being carried away by a law enforcement officer.

I wanted to stomp my foot in frustration, but restrained myself. The packets had been a great draw into the retail part of the store, especially for customers who'd had the hot version with their breakfast. Phil had even drawn a custom logo for me that I'd had printed on the wrapping. Instead of my usual store logo, this one had the grinning stack of pancakes wearing a Mexican sombrero. Instead of a skillet, the pancake person held a steaming mug topped with whipped cream. I could just picture Oscar's team ripping my carefully assembled mix open and subjecting it to whatever kinds of tests they would do. My whole enterprise could go down the drain if they found something. If they could pin it on Howard, his life would, too.

Chapter Eight

My hand was reaching to turn the OPEN sign on the door to CLOSED at two-thirty when the door pushed in toward me. I stepped back.

"I'm sorry, we're—" I halted midsentence when I saw Freddy was the latecomer. With everything going on, she was welcome.

"Robbie, I know you're closing," she said. "I'm not here to eat, but I have to talk with you." Strands of hair crept out of her topknot onto her black wool peacoat, and she blinked watery eyes.

I flipped the sign and held out my arms for a hug. "I heard about Howard," I murmured.

"That's why I'm here." She hugged me, then stepped back and gazed around the restaurant.

The only remaining customers were two men playing chess at the table I'd painted with a chessboard, plus one four-top with two young moms and two babies. Both little ones slept in their strollers and the women were catching up on girl talk while they could, from the looks of it. Danna scrubbed the grill.

"Come, sit down." I headed for my little office corner and plopped into the wheeled chair at the desk, rotating to face out. "I'll have to finish up with those folks when they're ready to leave, but it looks like we have a little while." I caught Danna's eye and pointed to Freddy and myself. My assistant nodded her understanding.

Freddy took the armchair opposite me, shrugging out of her coat. She wore a blue Indianapolis Symphony fleece sweatshirt with faded jeans.

"Are they still questioning him?" I asked.

"Yes." She swore softly. "Robbie, Howard thought he was doing the right thing. We've been waiting for the auditor for months. Naturally, it had to be this morning that he finally sent the report. There were all kinds of discrepancies, and he was able to trace some of the missing money to Jed. Of course Howard thought he should tell the police. And now they're making like he killed Jed!"

"So it wasn't just an accident on the ice?"

She threw up her hands. "I don't think they know. If it was an accident, why are they keeping my husband there all day?"

"But questioning Howard doesn't make sense." I rubbed my forehead. "If you only got the report this morning, well, Jed was already dead. Right?"

"Tell me about it. But listen, will you help me figure out what really happened to Jed? I know you've looked into murders in the past." Freddy sat forward, elbows on knees, hands clasped. "I have to get my husband home. It's Christmastime, Robbie. Time for family to be together, not to be stuck in a police interrogation room."

"I guess I can try to help, but I'm not sure how. I will tell you that Oscar Thompson, the state police detective, came in earlier and confiscated all my Mexican hot chocolate packets."

She nodded slowly. "They showed up at the house and took the rest of the ones How had bought from you, too."

"Ugh. We all drank some last night after dinner, too. All except Willa Mae. I bet they were interested in that."

"Yep. They wanted the cup in which Howard had served Jed's hot chocolate, but it had already gone through the dishwasher." She shook her head. "It's nuts. I mean, I admit nobody was in the kitchen while my husband prepared the hot drinks, but it would be supremely stupid for him to add poison to Jed's hot chocolate right there in our kitchen. And Howard is not a stupid man."

I drummed my fingers on my knee, thinking. "Freddy, did you notice how Jed seemed rude to Willa Mae? It seemed like he put her down more than once."

"You think maybe he'd been abusive and she poisoned him?"

"It's a stretch, I know. But if they find a toxin in the autopsy, somebody put it there, right? And she said she works with botanical toxins or something like that." I tapped my fingers some more. "Except Jed couldn't have been very sick. He took the dog out for an early-morning walk while it was still dark, after all."

"I know." She blew out a breath.

"What was in that bag you gave Willa Mae as we were all leaving? I just thought of it."

"Just some dried wisteria pods. She'd seen a few still hanging from the vine outside and she wanted to spray them gold and silver as seasonal decorations. I had collected and dried a bunch in the fall, but I never got around to doing anything with them. I like decorating for Christmas, but my patience doesn't extend to making the actual decorations. I'm no Martha Stewart."

"Something about what Buck told me has been bugging me," I said slowly. "He said Jed slipped on a patch of ice. But it hasn't rained or snowed in a while, a couple of weeks at least. Why was there ice on the sidewalk?"

Her eyebrows zoomed up. "You're right." She scrunched up her nose. "Unless it was a patch of snow nearby that melted and ran onto the sidewalk?"

"I'll go by and check it out when I get a chance."

The moms stood and looked like they were getting ready to leave.

One of the chess players announced, "And mate." The two men shook hands and scooped the pieces into the wooden box.

"I have to get back to work." I stood. "Listen, let's talk later. You learn anything, call or text me. I'll do the same. All right?"

She stood, too. "Yes."

"And don't worry. Howard will be home for dinner, I'm sure."

"Good thing we have lots of leftovers. I have my concert tonight on top of all this." She pulled a wan smile. "Thank you for listening."

"Any time." I headed back to the work of being a restaurateur and business owner, but my thoughts were on an unpleasant man's death. If it hadn't been an accident, who might have killed him?

Chapter Nine

At a little after three-thirty, I stashed the day's consider-
able cash in the safe I kept in the bedroom of my
apartment behind the store. I started a load of store laundry—aprons, cloth napkins, and dish towels, all by design
the same shade of blue. After I poured myself an IPA and
flopped into a chair, my little tuxedo cat, Birdy, promptly
jumped into my lap. I stroked his long smooth coat with
one hand and lifted my glass with the other. It had been a
long day and it wasn't over yet. The cool beer went down
just right, and the warm air coming up through the register warmed my feet. I set down the beer, running my hand
over the beautiful table my late mother had made. All I
had left of her were pieces of her handmade fine furniture,
a few photographs, and a quarter century of memories of
the best mom, ever.

I let out a sigh. "Birdy, I thought we were going to have
a nice restful holiday." A holiday week that now included
the confiscation of my hot chocolate packets. I'd paid
good money for the custom order, and nobody had blinked
at the markup. Money now down the drain. Several customers had asked about them after Oscar had left. I'd
merely replied that I had sold out and directed them to

other gifts in the store, like the colorful hats my aunt knitted from her own sheep's wool, as well as the array of cookware ornaments I'd stocked. "It's gone all wacko out there," I told my cat.

He replied with a happy purr, closing his eyes in a Sphinx pose, but staying alert in case a snack might be in the offing.

As soon as those last few customers had paid and left earlier, I'd remembered to put in an order for all kinds of things we'd nearly gone *eighty-six on*—more diner jargon for running out of a dish or ingredient. Danna and I had come up with a green-and-red breakfast special for tomorrow—an asparagus, cherry tomato, and sharp cheddar omelet—and a Ho-Ho-Ho-Hoagie for lunch, with provolone, Genoa salami, and thin slices of tomato and green pepper on toasted sub rolls. Hot chocolate, Mexican or otherwise, was not going to be on the menu, though. Luckily, the supply company had given me a delivery time of later this afternoon. Otherwise, the breakfast special would have had to wait until Wednesday—Christmas Eve.

Checking my phone yielded nothing new from Freddy or Abe. I poked around for news about Jed's death, but found only one item in the local online paper, which said a South Lick man was found dead this morning behind the library.

The library. Buck had said Georgia was the one who'd encountered Jed's dead body. I'd agreed to help Freddy if I could. I could go talk with the library aide now, see if she would tell me any details about her grisly discovery. I yawned out loud as I looked up the library's number and tapped it into my phone. A minute later, I disconnected. They'd told me Georgia had only worked until two o'clock and had gone home, but that she'd be in again the next morning. With any luck, I could pop over there tomorrow. What else could I learn without leaving the comfort of my own home?

I set Birdy down and shifted myself and the beer glass over to my laptop at the desk in the living room. For more in-depth searches, I preferred a real keyboard and a bigger screen than what the phone provided. As the system started up, I gazed out the window at the pale skim-milk light filtering through the trees beyond my driveway. I'd been too busy today to even be aware of what was going on outside except for the cold air that blew in every time the door opened. At least it wasn't snowing.

I started to search for readily available poisons that acted quickly and were undetectable in a cup of cocoa. If the NSA ever monitored my Googling, I'd be in big trouble. *Gah.* There were so many botanical toxins. The poison in castor beans and rosary peas. All parts of the lily of the valley plant. Datura in trumpet vines. Who knew?

One entry caught my eye and chilled my blood. Saponin had a bitter taste and could cause plenty of damage to a person's health, including death. And it was found in wisteria seedpods. Was it too bitter to be disguised by Mexican chocolate? My mix included dark cocoa, sugar, cinnamon, and a dash of hot pepper, so maybe it wasn't. Had anybody told Oscar that Freddy had a supply of wisteria pods and had given some to Willa Mae, plant toxicologist? Probably not, or both of them would be at the station being questioned, too.

I pulled up Oscar's number to text him, but hesitated. I hated to implicate Abe's mom in this.

"Birdy, what should I do?"

He gave me the slitty eye, but not a word of advice. I blew out a breath and tapped out a text.

Willa Mae has dried wisteria pods. Check out their toxin saponin.

There. Mostly the truth. It was his job to find out where she'd gotten the pods. I flashed on the dirty look Karinde had given Jed in the restaurant. Had she said something about him later? No, but she'd mentioned that Cocoa had been rescued from a filthy puppy mill and had glared at Jed in the same breath. She surely wouldn't have left Cocoa if she'd known Jed and Willa Mae were going to keep him for a few days. And Freddy wouldn't have asked them to take the dog if there was something to the story, so maybe there wasn't. Howard had been in business with Jed, after all. Danna had mentioned something about a puppy mill, too. I could ask her in the morning if she knew the name of the place.

Maybe it was time to create a crossword puzzle. Doing so had helped me in the past to lay out everything I knew about a case: clues and suspects and motives. My brain liked putting together the pieces, and seeing the elements of the investigation on a piece of graph paper often clarified the issues.

My phone dinged with an incoming text at the same time as the washer dinged that the cycle was finished. *Oh.* The delivery was already here, which set a record for them even though they'd promised it today. They must have added extra drivers for the holiday cooking season. Fine with me. I probably should have hired on a temp cook to replace Turner. Too late now.

I abandoned my Googling in favor of letting in the delivery person. By the time I'd stashed all the veggies and perishables in the walk-in cooler, it was five o'clock. I stood in the refrigerated compartment with my gaze on the two gallons of split pea soup I'd put away after lunch. Willa Mae had just lost her husband. I could bring her a pint of soup and condolences. And maybe learn something while I was there.

Chapter Ten

Aﬀter texting Freddy for Willa Mae's address, I headed out. On the seat next to me, I stowed a cloth bag containing a plastic container of soup and a half dozen fresh biscuits I just whipped up. My ancient Ford Econoline minivan had finally taken its last rattling, dysfunctional ride in October. The store was doing so well, I'd treated myself to a frankly adorable brand-new Prius C in a bright blue. It drove like a dream, included Bluetooth technology and heated leather seats, and the moon roof was a fun touch. The miles per gallon were awesome, too, averaging over 50 MPG even on Brown County's hilly byways. I would add a bike rack on the back when the weather warmed up.

The Greenbergs' home was a few blocks beyond the center of town. I could have walked, but the curtain of night was already falling, and the icy wind had chilled me simply walking out to the barn to get my car. During the short drive, I realized I had no idea if the Greenbergs had adult children. If they did, with any luck, at least one would have been summoned to grieve alongside Willa Mae and provide support, or perhaps other relatives were with her. Either way, it was always nice to bring condolence food. It was what folks did around here, and being a food-centric person, I approved of the custom.

I cruised by the library on my way. Turning into the parking lot behind it, I pulled to a stop. The after-hours box abutted the walkway, and a black iron fence stood three feet tall outlining the parking lot. Maybe movie lover Jed had walked by here because he often dropped a loaner DVD in the box.

Yellow police tape was strung in a wide circle around where Jed must have died. It included the box and blocked the walkway in two places about ten feet apart. I didn't see any obvious piles of snow nearby. But the twilight didn't give me a good glimpse of the ice, so I drove on. How the walkway got icy was still a puzzle.

At the Greenberg ranch house, it looked like every light inside was turned on, including the one over the front porch. I rang the bell and waited. When Willa Mae pulled open the door and saw me, she blinked.

I proffered the bag. "Hi, Willa Mae. I was so sorry to hear about Jed. I brought you some soup and biscuits."

She peered at me. "Oh, it's you, Robbie. Do you want to come in?"

"Sure. Just for a minute, if I'm not interrupting anything." She hadn't taken the bag, so I kept hold of it.

She stepped back and I followed her into the living room. The temperature felt like it was set at eighty degrees. She shut the door and pointed to the couch. "Please sit down."

I set the bag on a coffee table full of newspapers and *New Yorker* magazines and sat. In the light, I looked more closely at Willa Mae. Last night, her hair had been fluffy and neatly arranged. Now it lay limp and mussed, like she hadn't bothered to brush it all day. She wore a black turtleneck under an old IU sweatshirt with black yoga pants.

Her face was bare of makeup, but her eyes weren't red or watery and her gaze was sharp. Her feet were bare, too.

"Thank you for bringing food." She perched on the edge of an armchair at right angles to the couch. "I haven't been very hungry, but I know I should eat something."

"You're welcome, of course. Do you have children with you, or other family?"

She shook her head once to each side. "We never had kids. Just as well, really. And my family is in Illinois and Iowa. I called my sister and she's on her way, but she's driving from the western side of Iowa. It's going to take her a day, at least."

"It must have been such a shock to hear the news. Did Buck Bird come and tell you?"

"The tall goofy one?"

"He's definitely tall." *Goofy?* I guess some of his colorful phrases could prompt a person to think he was goofy, but he really wasn't.

"I'd barely woken up when Lieutenant Bird arrived. When he told me the news, I couldn't believe it. I almost didn't answer the door." She gave a shudder and rubbed her thumb against her first two fingers in a fast motion that looked like a nervous tic. "I don't like policemen."

"I can vouch for Buck, Willa Mae. He's a good man. He talks kind of like a yokel, but he's smart and an excellent officer."

She shrugged. "Anyway, Jed must have gone out for his walk at six in the morning like he always does. The man is—or, was, I guess—a total creature of habit. This morning, he must have taken Cocoa, too. Last night, he'd said he would. I guess that was the last thing he ever said to me."

"You didn't see him this morning?"

"No. We have very different schedules and biorhythms.

He goes to bed early and gets up early, and I'm the complete opposite. Plus, I apparently snore like a foghorn." She gave a little laugh. "We've slept separately for years."

I ran my finger around the neck of my sweater. I was getting overheated in here. "Buck told me Jed fell and hit his head. How sad."

"That's what the officer told me, too, and that Cocoa's leash was tangled in Jed's legs. My husband had been having an issue with balance recently. His doctor hadn't figured out what caused it yet. He probably shouldn't have been walking a puppy at all."

I glanced around. The kitchen and dining room at the back of the house were open to the room where we sat. In the dining area, the table was covered with newspapers and an array of irregularly shaped seedpods, some shining with silver paint. The wisteria, no doubt, but no sign of Cocoa. "Where's the puppy?"

"The police called Freddy to pick him up. She phoned me and I said I'd be happy to keep him, since we'd offered to, but she said I would have too much to do, that she'd figure something out. I mean, I need to plan Jed's burial, but the police said they have to keep his body for a while." She shuddered. "I hate to even think of his body all cold and in the morgue or wherever."

"I can imagine. I'm so sorry."

"That's why I have the heat so high. I know it doesn't make sense, but I can't help it. I kept shivering when it was set to sixty-eight, like I usually have it." Willa Mae scratched at silver paint on the back of one hand. "It's crazy. I've been doing a craft today. It helps keep my mind off what's going on."

"That's not crazy. What's the craft?" I asked, even though I knew.

"Freddy O'Neill gave me some interesting seedpods when

we were leaving their house the other night, remember? I'm spray-painting them." She waved a hand toward the dining table.

As long as this plant toxicologist wasn't grinding up the wisteria pods and putting them in her husband's hot chocolate.

Willa Mae continued. "It was either that or work on a really hard puzzle."

"Puzzles are a great distraction. How long were you and Jed married, if you don't mind my asking?"

"Nineteen years." Her fingers resumed the rapid rubbing.

I nodded. "You seem to be doing pretty well with this sudden news."

Her fingers quieted as she gazed at me. "I don't mind telling you, he and I hadn't gotten along very well for quite a while. I'm not quite sure why I stayed married to him. We didn't have children to tie us together. But I didn't wish him dead. No way." She pushed first one and then the other sleeve up to her elbows.

I stood, nearly staring at a healing bruise on her forearm, but made my eyes keep moving up to her face. "I'm afraid I need to get back to my store and do prep for tomorrow. Please call me if there's anything I can do for you, okay?" I dug one of my Pans 'N Pancakes cards out of my bag and scribbled my cell number on it.

She took the card. "Thanks, Robbie. This was real nice of you to drop by. I don't belong to a church, you know, the kind of folks who usually step up when somebody passes. My only friend in town moved away last year. And Jed had alienated our neighbors something bad, so they haven't been by, either. Or maybe they don't know he's gone yet."

Chapter Eleven

In my thoughts, as I ate dinner back at home, was that healing bruise on Willa Mae's arm. I pictured it while I fed and played with Birdy and during a quick phone check-in with Abe while he drove to his banjo group practice. Jed had seemed overbearing and controlling with his wife. Had he been physically abusing her, too? I didn't know Willa Mae well enough to ask her. And a lot of abused spouses didn't want to admit it, anyway, although it might be different if the abuser was dead. Still, she'd pushed her sleeves up as if she wanted me to see the bruise. Maybe Freddy knew more.

By seven o'clock, I was in the restaurant prepping for the next day while the laundry finished drying. On my list were the usuals, like biscuit dough and the dry ingredients for pancakes. Tonight I also had to cut up asparagus and cherry tomatoes for tomorrow's omelets. Pre-slice sub rolls. And accomplish all the other prep tasks of a breakfast-and-lunch chef.

I wrinkled my nose. Did we have a lunch dessert? My friend Phil usually baked cookies and brownies for the store, but he, like Turner, was away on a family vacation.

I mentally drummed my fingers on the counter as I chopped asparagus into half-inch pieces, perfect to quick cook in an omelet. The vegetable wasn't in season, of course, but I didn't adhere to a strict farm-to-table policy, where all ingredients had to be local and in season. For starters, I wouldn't be able to serve coffee—which you couldn't grow outdoors anywhere in Indiana—and without a cup of joe, a breakfast joint couldn't survive.

The question of dessert remained. Oh, heck. I could whip up more of Freddy's Bridecakes. Why not? I stowed the asparagus in a covered container in the walk-in and emerged with three pounds of butter in my arms.

I froze at the sound of knocking on the front door. It was dark out. Very dark. Jed might have died accidentally, or someone might have killed him. Didn't matter. No way was I opening the door of my store to an unknown visitor.

A text dinged into my phone in my back pocket. I dropped the butter on the counter and checked the name. Howard O'Neill? I laughed out loud. The message said he was on the front porch. I hurried over to the door and unlocked it to find a harried-looking Howard and an excited Cocoa standing together, Cocoa straining at his leash.

"Howard, please come in." I stood back.

He blew in with a gust of wind. I shut the door against the weather. Cocoa sniffed everything he could reach.

"Robbie, I'm in a major bind."

"What's going on? I heard you were questioned by the police half the day."

"I sure was. Right now, Freddy is at her concert and I'm supposed to pick up Sean and get over there, too. But she got the dog back this morning, and Sean's supposed to come home with us, because his mom is leaving town and Abe's working. I don't know what to do with the puppy. Any chance you can keep him for a day or two?"

"Me?" In my little apartment with Birdy? And me in the restaurant? *Yikes.*

"Please? I didn't know who else to ask. I tried finding a place to board him, but they're all either full or don't take puppies. I'll come over tomorrow and walk him, if the police don't invite me back, that is." He stole a glance at his watch and swore under his breath.

"I guess so. I've never taken care of a dog before, though." I wanted to ask him why he and Freddy hadn't asked a neighbor to help out, but I didn't want to seem uncooperative. Howard and Freddy had a pretty big chance of becoming my in-laws one day. Which, I supposed, might be the reason they felt comfortable asking me for this favor.

Howard handed me the leash and gave me a quick hug. "You're an angel. I'll get his stuff out of the car."

He was back in a flash carrying a metal cage and a cloth bag. "Where do you want the crate?"

"He can't be in the restaurant." I grimaced. "It'll have to be in my apartment. Come on back."

We set up the crate in the living room. Birdy arched his back and hissed at Cocoa when he saw him. Cocoa whined and pulled at his leash, so I kept a firm hold on the puppy. Poor Birdy ever so slowly backed up until he could safely dash into the kitchen.

"Cocoa already ate tonight, and he took a leak outside when we got here," Howard said. "You'll have to take him out one more time before you go to bed. Give him half a cup of puppy kibble and water in the morning. And thank you."

"Can he go into the crate now? I have work to do in the restaurant." And laundry to fold after that.

"Sure." Howard coaxed Cocoa into the crate with his blankie, unclipped the leash, and latched the door.

The puppy started barking and I groaned inwardly, but by the time we went back into the restaurant, he had quieted. *Whew.*

At the front door, I said, "I hope you'll let me know the train of Oscar's questioning when you get a chance."

"You're on a first-name basis with the detective?" Howard paused, his hand on the doorknob.

"Kind of. Does he think Jed was murdered? And suspects you for it?"

"Frankly, it was a bewildering day, Robbie. All I did was bring them the report from our auditor. Jed had been ripping me off for a year and hiding it. But I didn't find out until after he was dead. The whole thing was ridiculous. I finally got my lawyer in there and she put a stop to their grilling." He looked at his watch again. "I gotta go. Thanks again. See you in the morning."

And he was gone.

Chapter Twelve

I was *so* not a dog person. I got up at my weekday usual of five-thirty the next morning, yawning from my restless sleep. As I jacked up the thermostat, Cocoa awoke and barked a few times almost immediately. I groaned aloud. Instead of lounging with coffee in my pj's, playing with Birdy, I pulled on socks, a knit hat, my long down coat, and my winter boots. I clipped on the puppy's leash and donned fleece mittens before stepping out the back door with him.

It was a dark morning, with not a hint of dawn, which wouldn't happen for another two hours. True, the stars were silver glitter overhead, but my breath came out in clouds of condensation that looked like they wanted to freeze midair. I followed Cocoa around the small yard until he relieved himself.

"Let's go, doggy." I was already shivering. Once inside, I reversed the warm wraps, but kept socks and hat on until I warmed up. I didn't care how silly it looked, I was still chilled. I set up Cocoa's food and water dishes on newspapers near his crate, instead of in the kitchen. I didn't want Birdy to get freaked out any more than he already was—although, for now, he was still snoozing on the foot of my bed. I closed the bedroom door and let the puppy off leash to eat and explore a bit while I made coffee and ate a toasted English muffin with peanut butter. Cocoa ended up snoozing on my foot for a few minutes, exactly where Birdy liked to sit, too.

By six o'clock, I was showered and dressed. Cocoa was back in the crate, Birdy was fed, and it was time to get breakfast for the masses under way for the seven o'clock opening. Sunday was the only day we delayed opening until eight. By the time Danna arrived at six-thirty, I had biscuits baking. I'd beaten dozens of eggs, which were now in a pitcher waiting to be transformed into omelets and wrecks. And a pot each of caf and decaf perked into their carafes.

"Hey, Danna."

She gave a little wave, but her eyes were only half open.

"Late night?" I asked.

She nodded wordlessly as she slipped on an apron and washed her hands before heading into the cooler to bring out the caddies of jams, sugars, and condiments that went on each table. We set the tables before leaving the day before, but kept the caddies in the cooler so we didn't tempt any critters to sneak in and dine overnight.

I smiled at her. Danna was as reliable an employee as they come. She and her boyfriend often went out on weeknights, but she never skipped out on work the next day because of it. By the time she needed to be alert and on the job, she always was.

"I cut up all the asparagus and tomatoes last night," I told her. "And I ordered in grated cheddar for the omelets."

"Mmm."

"And I made up more Bridecake dough, too, for lunch desserts."

She nodded.

"So I temporarily acquired a puppy last night."

That got her eyes open. "You did? Can I see it?"

"Sure, but not now. He's a Christmas present for Abe's son, but they're trying to keep it a secret until Christmas morning. We'll have to walk Cocoa a few times this morning, and I'm happy to let you do the honors."

"Cocoa's his name? That's adorbs." She got out the big ketchup bottle with the pump and topped up some of the red squeeze bottles.

"He's definitely adorable and is a chocolate Lab, so the name fits." I emptied the pancake mix into the big mixer bowl and started cracking eggs into it.

Danna finished with the caddies. After setting one on each table, she asked, "Me start grill?"

"Yes, Jane. I already got out the meats."

"Any news on the death? Like if it was an accident or not?"

"Nothing official. Yesterday you mentioned something about a business Jed might have been associated with. Someplace that raised animals in bad conditions?"

"Yeah." She lit the grill burners. She laid out bacon in neat strips, and a line of sausages next to it.

"Do you know the name of the place?"

"No. Lemme text Mom. She remembers everything." She thumbed a quick text and stuck her phone back into the pocket of the calf-length denim skirt she wore today. It had been cut apart and reassembled with flowered gores of what looked like flour sack fabric interspersed with the denim so the skirt flared out toward the hem. Red tights and a green waffle-weave shirt completed the outfit, with a green-and-red flowered scarf tying back her hair. The girl owned flair.

Buck waited on the front porch when I opened the door at seven. I greeted him.

"Mornin', Robbie. Man alive, am I ever famished." He ambled in.

"Are you ever not hungry?" I asked.

"Don't suppose I'm not."

Nobody else had followed him in. *Huh.* Yesterday we had a crowd. Had word gotten out about the confiscated cocoa? I hoped this wasn't a sign that my business was about to take a nosedive.

Inside I asked, "Any news?"

He turned his back on Danna. "We was checking into a lady by name of Karinde Nilsson. You know her?"

I nodded. "A little. She's big into animal rescue."

"That's right. Seems she had some contentious history with Greenberg. She don't got no alibi for his time of death, neither. Lives alone out in the woods and such."

Interesting. "But isn't that only relevant if Jed was murdered, Buck?"

"Yuperoo. They're going to do a rush autopsy this morning, Thompson said. We should oughta know more in a couple few hours."

"Good."

"And by the by, we seen that cam footage. All's it shows for the time in question is Greenberg slipping and hitting his head."

An older couple pushed through the door, followed by several construction workers who ate breakfast here nearly every day. *Whew.* We had customers, after all.

"Let me know the autopsy results after you hear?" I murmured even as I smiled and nodded at the newcomers.

"You bet. I know by now I can trust you, Robbie."

Trust me to do what? I didn't ask.

Chapter Thirteen

We still weren't as swamped today as yesterday. Maybe people were starting to travel elsewhere for the holidays. Or maybe they were avoiding a place that might have been selling very bad chocolate.

Three local businessmen lingered talking over their meals. I refilled their coffees for the third time and had turned my back when my ears perked up.

"Howard O'Neill?" one said. "He was thick as thieves with the dead guy. I heard O'Neill's trying to pick up a new investment property."

"I wouldn't do business with him. Greenberg was a crook and so isn't O'Neill," one of his breakfast companions said.

I casually turned back and slowly headed for the table beyond them.

The third man made a tsking noise. "It's a crying shame. A teacher, of all people." He wagged his head.

The crying shame was that kind of malicious gossip, that kind of guilt by association. Poor Howard. We had to clear his name, and fast. Fuming in silence, I headed back to make another pot of coffee.

Buck consumed his gargantuan breakfast and departed. Our omelet special was popular with those who did come in. There was more buzz about Jed's death, but since it hadn't publicly been deemed murder, it was a quiet buzz. I didn't pick up any more slurs on Howard's character, thank goodness.

Danna headed into my apartment to let Cocoa out at around eight. She said she was going to spend a few minutes playing with him after he did his business.

"That's fine," I said. "And thanks."

While she was on puppy duty, Abe came in, holding a folded newspaper. He made a beeline for the grill and gave me a quick hug. I was working, so I had to tamp down the rush I always got from touching him, but I did hang on slightly longer than I should have.

He smiled down at me and tucked a stray curl behind my ear. "Thanks for taking Cocoa. Dad texted me from the concert last night."

"It's working out okay. Birdy's a little freaked, but it's only for another day. Danna's with Cocoa right now."

"You can spare her?" He glanced around the restaurant.

"We're not overly busy, as you can see." The gossiping men had finally left, too. I decided not to mention to Abe what they'd said. He had enough on his plate.

"I'd offer to help, but I have to be at work by nine. At least it's my last day until next week. I managed to stay off the emergency call list for once."

"Good." I smiled at him. Nobody should have to work on Christmas, but obviously a lot of people did, and electrical line workers were among them. "We're fine, at least so far."

"So you know Dad's lawyer got him sprung."

"Yes, he told me last night. And Buck told me they're doing the autopsy on Jed this morning." I flipped three pancakes and turned a couple of sausages.

"Paper declares it an accidental death." Abe unfolded the paper to show me the headline on the *Brown County Democrat.*

I peered at it. "So they do. I'm sure Oscar wouldn't want to spook the murderer if that was what happened. The authorities can always change their tune after the autopsy if they need to."

"I guess."

"Hungry?" I asked.

"That's one reason I'm here, yes."

"What's your pleasure? We have a cheerful omelet that's tasty, plus all the usuals."

"I'll take cheerful, please, with wheat toast and sausages. Thanks, darlin'." He picked up the coffeepot and headed to an empty table, pouring his own mug full before returning it.

By ten, the place was nearly empty. Danna wiped down tables and reset them while I loaded the dishwasher.

"Danna, I'm going to take Cocoa for a quick walk. Okay?"

"Of course. I'll bake the cookies while we're quiet."

Five minutes later, I was suited up in warm clothes and heading toward the library with an eager puppy. I figured he could use the exercise, and I could use a quick chat with Georgia. I'd be back well before the lunch crowd showed up, if we got a crowd. Storefronts blared Christmas music, and the bells and wreaths the town had hung from lampposts gave the town a festive air. The crisp air in front of a bakery smelled of fresh-baked cookies. Last-minute shoppers toted handled bags and smiles. I paused to admire a working train set making its way through a miniature holiday village in the front window of the toy store. The bookstore next door had set up a Christmas tree of books with red and green covers in their window. Everybody seemed to be in the spirit this year.

Along the way, Cocoa stopped and did some serious business in front of the octagonal gazebo. I scooped up the poop with a plastic bag, which I plucked off a little roll attached to the leash, a handy invention. The gazebo, the site of the former Jupiter hot spring South Lick was named for, had had a giant menorah set up in the middle of it for the week of Hanukkah, with a ceremonial lighting every evening at sunset. The town was an equal-opportunity holiday celebrator, at least for Christians and Jews.

As we continued toward the library, a tall, slender woman came toward us and smiled.

"What a cute puppy." She stooped to pet Cocoa. She looked somewhere around seventy. Her nails were painted a brilliant scarlet red that matched a stylish short leather jacket over black stretch pants. "How old is he?"

"I'm not sure. A few months, I think."

The woman raised an impeccably shaped eyebrow as she straightened. "You're not sure?"

Something about her seemed familiar to me, but I couldn't place it, and I didn't think I'd seen her in the store before. I smiled. "He's not mine. I'm just keeping him for friends for a couple of days."

"Well, he seems like a sweet one. Your friends are lucky. You have a lovely holiday, now." She gave Cocoa one more pet and moved on.

I dropped the bagged poop in a municipal trash can in front of the library, and we trotted up the steps. I hoped it was okay to bring him in for a few minutes. If not, maybe Georgia could step outside while we talked.

She stood behind the front desk, scanning the bar codes

of a stack of books. When the man checking them out left, I picked up Cocoa and stepped forward.

"Is it okay to bring him in for a minute?"

"Sure, Robbie, it's cold out. What a sweet dog. I didn't know you had one." Georgia was a well-padded woman on the far side of forty, with bottle-blond hair and a huge warm smile.

I laughed. "I don't. I'm dog sitting for a couple of days."

"Hey there, sweetie." She reached across and petted Cocoa's head. "How have you been, hon? I haven't made it into the restaurant in a while."

"I'm fine." I glanced around, but no patrons were within earshot. "I heard you found Jed Greenberg yesterday. That must have been really hard."

She brought her thin eyebrows together. "It was, for sure." She looked more closely at Cocoa. "Oh. That's the same doggy, isn't it? His name is Cocoa."

"Yes, that's right, you already met him. I forgot about that." Which was pretty dumb of me, come to think of it. He wriggled in my arms, so I set him down, but kept the leash tight so he didn't roam.

"I was so glad he had a tag with his name and his owner's. But, Robbie, the strangest thing was the ice."

"Because we haven't had snow or rain lately?"

"Exactly." She lowered her voice to a whisper. "I empty that bin every morning we're open. That pavement has been as dry as my hometown in northern Kentucky. Where on earth did the ice take and come from? I think somebody must have poured water on that there spot overnight. I told the detective, but he didn't seem to pay me much mind." She shook her head. "Now the why of it has me stumped. What do you think?"

"I'm not sure, unless somebody dumped their soda or emptied their water bottle. You don't have any enemies, do you?"

Georgia laughed. "Little old me? I get alone with purt' near everybody. Why? You think somebody knew my routine with the returns box and wanted me to slip and get myself bonked upside the head?"

I flipped open my hands. "It was just a thought."

"Nah, I don't have no enemies." She sobered. "But that Mr. Greenberg sure might could have had himself some. He was as unpleasant as they come."

"Did Jed come into the library a lot?"

"From time to time. Mostly for movies, not for books, though."

"I heard him talk about how he loved classic movies. Was that what he checked out?" I asked.

"Yes. Well, all kinds of movies, really. Sometimes it would be our newest releases. You know we don't have a theater here in town, and the Brown County Playhouse in Nashville only has showings four or five times a month. Sometimes people don't want to go all the way to Bloomington to watch a flick on a big screen. Mr. Greenberg said he actually had a screening room in his basement at home, with a big screen and surround sound and all whatnot."

"That makes sense for a movie buff. You said Jed was unpleasant. What did you mean?"

She looked down at the counter, straightening a pile of already-tidy papers. She met my gaze. "I shouldn't speak ill of the dead, but I found him demanding and rude, and that's a fact. Why, he came in with his wife once and lost his temper even with her. She backed away from him like she was frightened. Of her own husband!"

"Jed didn't win any charm awards, that's for sure."

The antique tall-case clock rang once. *Ouch.* It was already ten-thirty. My phone dinged with a text from Danna.

Where are you? We're slammed.

I had to get back. I thanked Georgia and hurried out with the puppy and my new piece of information. Where had the ice come from, and how could I find out?

Chapter Fourteen

Business had really picked up in my absence. I was pretty sure the full-sized tour bus sporting a red maple leaf that was parked across the road had something to do with it. I rushed to give Cocoa a drink of water in my apartment and stow him safely in his crate. Back in the store, I donned an apron and scrubbed my hands. It was only ten-fifty and every table was full. We'd never had a full house at this time of day.

Danna, wild-eyed and cooking at high speed, gave me a pair of raised eyebrows worthy of a scolding mom. "Your people want you." She gestured at the room with a spatula.

"Sorry. I owe you."

"Yes, ma'am, you do. Now go."

I went. I smiled, greeted people, took orders for food and drink. I calmed impatient diners and directed cookware fans to the for-sale shelves when they asked. Even customers short on patience were polite, though, and the accents I heard were clearly not local to this part of the country.

One white-haired lady stopped me. "Miss Jordan, we've heard of your restaurant all the way up in London. Canada, that is."

"Please call me Robbie. That's amazing. You're all Canadian, then?"

"Yes, indeed. Can't you tell?"

I could. Her vowels were clipped in a way that made me think of a Scottish accent. "How far is London from here?"

"Nearly eight hundred kilometers."

I scrunched up my nose, trying to do the math.

She laughed. "It's about five hundred miles, but we stayed in Indianapolis last night. Now, that's a city with hidden treasures." She paused. "I read on Facebook a man was murdered near here yesterday. You must be terribly frightened. I assumed he was shot dead?" She widened her eyes, awaiting my response.

She's getting her local news from Facebook? *Yikes.* "Uh, no, that's incorrect, ma'am. A man tragically did die behind the library Monday morning, but the police say it was an accident. And no firearms were involved."

"I'm glad to hear that. You know, we hear so many stories about the epidemic of gun violence down here in the States."

I sighed, but silently. Unhappily, so did we. "I'm sure you do." Three of her bus mates were waving menus in the air and Danna had dinged the Ready bell twice. "You'll have to excuse me. Did you already give Danna your order?"

"I did, thank you."

"Let me go see if it's ready, then." I sped away and spent the next hour doing nothing but fetching and serving. Delivering orders to Danna and the finished products to diners. Making change and answering questions. My meager breakfast seemed like ancient history, but I felt guilty about taking the time to even snag and wolf down one sausage. I did it, anyway, and encouraged Danna to eat a bite, too.

And then, presto. At eleven-thirty, the tour guide stood in front of the door and blew her whistle. "Five minutes to board. Five minutes, people. We have a tour in French Lick next and we need to arrive promptly."

They were making a tour of the Licks, apparently. Luckily, everyone was finished eating by then and most had already paid. I scurried around to those who hadn't, and collected money hand over fist from shoppers, too. I sure wished I still had the hot chocolate packets, but that was water under the Beanblossom Covered Bridge. The hot chocolate ship had sailed yesterday, through no fault of my own, and there wasn't a lick—South or otherwise—I could do about it.

"Wow." Danna sank into a chair after the door closed behind the last tour participant and she'd paid a visit to the all-important facilities. "What do you think about posting a sign saying, 'No Tour Buses'?"

I sat opposite her. "Sounds appealing, but it would be ever so bad for business. Come on, you know if Turner had been here, we'd have managed just fine." Or mostly fine. Even with three of us, we'd have been run ragged. I breathed deeply and resolved then and there to pay out a Christmas bonus. And hire emergency help next time.

"You took a long time walking Cocoa," Danna said. "I bet everybody wanted to stop you and pet him."

"A few did. But what I did was pop by the library and have a little chat with Georgia, the library aide who found Jed Greenberg's body."

Danna pulled a face. "Poor lady. Is she okay?"

"She is. Jed had been a library patron, she said." I frowned. "But what's worrisome is the patch of ice he slipped on. Georgia says she walks on that pavement every day and it hasn't been icy for weeks. Neither of us can figure out how it got that way."

"Yeah. That's funny, huh? It's been cold, but super dry. Somebody must have dumped out their water. I know if I leave water too long in my bottle, it gets stale."

"That could be."

"Or maybe a dog peed on the grass and it ran onto the pavement?" Danna snapped her fingers. "My grandmother, my mom's mother, lives in the building next to the library. You know that old school that's been made into condos? Her place looks out directly onto that walkway where the returns box is. Plus, she's a total insomniac. She posts on Facebook at, like, two in the morning about convening the Insomniacs Club, and then all her sleepless old lady friends chime in. It'd be kind of funny if she didn't hate being awake in the middle of the night so much."

"So you'll ask her if she saw anything?" I tapped the table between us. "Or maybe she even saw Jed fall." I wondered if the police had done a door-to-door search. People would have been up by then. Maybe somebody else saw the accident.

"She might have. I'll ask her as soon as I leave here. Josie's a fun lady, Robbie. Josephine Dunn, but she insists on being called Josie, even by me. She reminds me of your aunt Adele. I go over and play Farkle with her sometimes. She's a genius with dice and she beats me nine times out of ten." Danna didn't look like she minded losing in the least. "I bet she saw something."

"Thanks. Text me or call if she saw anything, will you?"

She made a clicking noise and gave me a thumbs-up even as the cowbell rang and five hungry locals pushed through the door. The lunch hour had arrived.

Chapter Fifteen

By one-thirty, I was frankly irked. Last evening, Howard had said he would return to walk Cocoa this morning. Except I hadn't cast eyes on Howard, nor had he called or texted—and neither had Freddy. Twenty minutes ago, I'd sent Freddy a quick text, telling her we needed puppy relief, and fast. Danna and I hadn't had time to take the dog out since I'd come back from the library. I really hoped he hadn't peed in the crate. It couldn't be good for a puppy to be cooped up like that.

Contributing to my dark mood was Buck's apparently false promise to share Jed's autopsy results. The tall lieutenant was also in absentia, and he'd missed his daily midday meal. Something big must be up for that to happen. Plus, the lunch service had slammed us as intensely as the tour bus had. The fresh-baked cookies were gone and we'd resorted to offering fruit salad with a spray of canned whip cream for dessert. We'd eighty-sixed turkey burgers and split pea soup, making me almost rue my delivery to Willa Mae yesterday. Nearly every table in the restaurant was full. The one small blessing was that nobody was waiting to be seated, and most of the seated parties had been served.

Freddy rushed in, cheeks matching her pink hand-knitted cat hat, and hurried up to me where I was flipping burgers at the grill. "I'm so sorry, Robbie. Howard only now told me he'd promised to help with the puppy, but then he wasn't able to. Is Cocoa okay?"

"I don't know. I took him for a walk earlier, but it's been a couple of hours. Go on into my apartment there in the back." I pointed to the adjoining door, marked PRI-VATE, DO NOT ENTER. "It's unlocked. We've had so much business we couldn't spare a minute to check on Cocoa. He's in the crate." Or I hoped he was. I'd stuck him in there so hastily earlier, I might not have latched the door securely. If so, my apartment could be in shambles.

"Got it." She zoomed toward the door.

I turned four hot dogs and gently folded over a Christmas omelet. I buttered two hot pieces of toast, scooped out slaw for the hot dog orders, and dished out three servings of fruit salad. Another order wanted a *heart attack on a rack, with two pigs in a poke,* so I laid out two more wieners and topped a split buttered biscuit with sausage gravy.

Ten minutes later, Freddy reemerged from the back. "I took him out, and he'll be good for a while. Sorry about that. Listen, I have an errand to run and you're clearly busy. But if I come back at about four, will you have time for us to catch up on . . ." She glanced around. "You know, on what's happening?"

"Yes, I think so," I said. "Howard's not back at, uh, headquarters, I hope?"

"No, but it's not all smooth sailing. I can't talk about it right now." She set her lips in a grim line and hurried out.

At least Cocoa should be set for another couple of hours. I focused on orders again. I poured, I turned, I scooped, I dinged the bell, and started over. Danna performed all the

corresponding actions: delivering food, clearing and reset-
ting tables, jotting down orders and running them over to
me, taking people's money. My bank account was going to
bask in fullness after this week.

The charity donation box was filling up, too. A thirty-
something woman came in with three children, each of
their arms full of wrapped packages.

"We heard we could drop these off here," the mom
said.

"We got pwesents for the kids who don't have vewy
much," the youngest lisped, a little girl whose curly black
hair matched my own.

"That's very nice of all of you. The box is behind the
tree." I pointed. "Can they have candy canes?" I murmured to the mother.

"Of course."

I handed each a small candy cane from the box I'd stuck
near the cash register. "Merry Christmas."

Polite to a one, the children thanked me and returned
the greeting before Mom shepherded them out. I smiled
after them, my mood lightened by their generosity.

It was a few minutes before two o'clock when Buck finally made his entrance. Had he brought conclusive news
about the way Jed died? I sure hoped so. I waved, flipped
two beef patties just in time, and grabbed a sub roll from
the toaster for a Ho-Ho-Ho-Hoagie. They'd been a popular order today. So far, we hadn't run out of any of the ingredients.

Buck ambled over, hat in hand. "Boy, howdy, Robbie.
That samwich sure looks good. Can I get one of them with
double the stuffing? And maybe a hot dog on the side, too."

"Of course." The anticipation was killing me. "So do
you—"

He held up a hand. "No, I do not, I'm sorry to say."

"What? But you said they were going to do a rush job early this morning." I sniffed and swore under my breath, scooping up the burgers just in time for them to be still edible.

"Guy got called out on an emergency," Buck went on. "Don't worry, Greenberg's still on today's schedule. Autopsy just ain't happened yet."

Chapter Sixteen

"Okay to leave?" Danna asked at three-thirty.

I surveyed the restaurant. Even though I'd turned the sign to CLOSED an hour ago, we'd had customers linger until three o'clock. But now the place was clean, swept, and quiet. The dishwasher hummed and the tables were all reset.

"Sure." I smiled. "One more day, then we get a week." I deposited my apron in the dirty-laundry box.

"What about dessert for tomorrow?"

"I'll have time to bake tonight. Brownies with green and red sugars? Or wouldn't that go? I want something I can bake pans of and not have to make individual cookies or whatever."

"The brownies sound fine, but how about with crushed candy canes on top? You can harvest all the ones on the tree." She gestured with her chin.

"I like that idea. I'll add peppermint flavoring in the batter, too."

"Have a good night, Robbie. I'm off to go ice-skating with Isaac. He said the ice at the outdoor rink is perfect."

"Sounds fun. See you in the a.m."

Danna pulled open the door, only to reveal Freddy. They greeted each other before Danna slipped out.

"I'm glad you're back." I strolled to the door. "Come on in and have a seat." I locked the door behind her.

She sat on the edge of a chair. "Did you get news from Lieutenant Bird?" Her eyes were bright.

"No, darn it. He said the guy got called away to something more urgent, but Jed's autopsy was still on today's schedule."

Her posture slumped.

"I know, it's frustrating," I said. "Hey, I was going to have a beer. Can I get you one?"

"Sure. That sounds perfect right now."

"Why don't you come back to my apartment and we can let Cocoa out of his cage."

"It's called a crate, Robbie."

I laughed. "I know, but it sure looks like a cage, doesn't it? Actually, let me grab my cash and walk the laundry back, too." I emptied the day's take into a bank bag. I left only tomorrow's starting cash in the ornate old-fashioned cash register. I laid the bag on top of the laundry. "Can you get the door?"

Cocoa started yipping as soon as we walked in. Freddy opened the crate and was beset by a wriggling licking puppy.

"I'll take him out back for a minute before I take off my coat." Freddy clipped the leash to Cocoa's harness and led him out.

I bustled around my house. I gave Birdy a couple of good pets and a treat in the kitchen, having closed the door to the living room. I started the laundry and locked the cash in the safe. I'd take the week's till to the bank after we closed tomorrow. Finally I grabbed two beers and two glasses and made it back into the living room, where Freddy and Cocoa had just returned.

"Cheers." I handed Freddy a glass and lifted mine.

She clinked it, but said, "Not much cheery about this week. Except for this little guy, of course." Cocoa was busy sniffing every corner of the room.

"I guess. So, what's up with Howard?"

"It's not the police, thank goodness. But How has to see if he can salvage any of the accounts where Jed deposited the money he stole from their partnership. He's been meeting with a financial lawyer."

"How well did Howard know Jed before they went in on the investment together?"

She pulled a wry look. "Not well enough, clearly. They'd met back in college. When Jed moved to this area a few years ago, he contacted Howard. Sometimes they played tennis together and went for a beer afterward. Frankly, I don't think Howard did his due diligence checking out finances when Jed proposed the deal."

"Has Detective Thompson cleared Howard yet?"

"I don't think so. Everybody must be waiting for the autopsy and lab results. They still think he might have poisoned the packets he gave Jed. The detective claimed Howard could have known about the embezzlement before we got the auditor's report. I ask you, would we have invited Jed to dinner if we'd known he'd stolen money? Jeez, Louise." She tapped her glass. "And now people are looking at How like he has three heads or something. He was looking into a different investment opportunity, but the other guy pulled out just today. He made some lame excuse, but I know it's because of Jed's death."

"That's no good. I actually heard a bit of gossip like that in the restaurant this morning."

Freddy blew out a breath and sipped her beer. She didn't ask for details.

"I saw my friend at the library earlier," I said. "She said that spot of pavement had no reason to be icy." I took a sip and savored the cold hoppy bubbles. "Freddy, how well do you know Karinde Nilsson?"

"Karinde?" Freddy peered at me. "Why are you asking about her?"

"She alluded to Jed having abused animals in the past, and she's really passionate about rescues. If the autopsy shows Jed was murdered, I've been wondering if she killed him."

"Isn't that kind of a stretch, Robbie?"

"I guess."

"Anyway, I don't know her well at all. We met first when we visited the shelter at her house. Then we saw her when she came to the house to approve us for the puppy adoption, and the only other time was when she delivered Cocoa." Freddy patted her leg and Cocoa trotted over to her. "But she never got close enough to Jed to poison what he ate or drank."

"Good point. But she could have iced the walkway. Buck did say she didn't have an alibi for that night or early morning because she lives alone."

Freddy took a long drink of beer, then set down the glass. "How would she know he was going to walk there?"

"True. And why would she kill him now the puppy mill is shut down? Unless Jed got involved in another one."

"How will we know if we don't ask her? I know where she lives, out beyond Nashville."

"I like how you think, Freddy. And I have to drop off the box of donations at the charity in Nashville, anyway. I almost forgot." I tilted my head, thinking. "Karinde living out there means she'd have had to come all the way into South Lick in the middle of the night to ice the sidewalk." My phone pinged with a text.

Abe had written, **Dinner tonight? I can bring takeout. I miss you.**

He'd finished with a kissing happy face.

I tapped back, **Perfect. Romantic evening of folding laundry and baking! 6:30?**

I hit Send.

"Why do I get the feeling that was from my son?" Freddy asked with a smile in her voice.

I looked up at her, my cheeks warm. "You have remarkable powers of intuition. Now, about that field trip. I happen to be free as soon as I finish this beer."

"You and me both. We can say we know someone who likes Cocoa so much they're wondering what other puppies might be up for adoption. We'll bring this little guy to say hi, too."

"We'll have to be careful in what we ask her," I cautioned. "And how we phrase it."

"Because if she is a murderer, we don't want her to know we think so?"

"Exactly."

Chapter Seventeen

By four-fifteen, we were in Freddy's Subaru wagon heading out Route 45, east of Nashville, having just dropped off the box of donated gifts. Freddy had a car harness for Cocoa that attached to the seat belt.

"That's a cool thing," I said.

"We had it for our previous dog."

"I've never thought about keeping dogs safe in cars. Of course they'd be damaged worse than humans would by flying through the air in an accident."

After ten minutes, we skirted Nashville and kept going past Gnaw Bone BBQ & Original Gnaw Bone Tenderloin, a place that made the best breaded tenderloin in the known universe.

"So Karinde operates a shelter at her house?" I asked. "How did you learn about her?"

"A friend in the symphony got a dog from her last year. Karinde comes highly recommended."

"I only met her once in the restaurant last winter when she came in with a girlfriend."

"And, yes, she has a kind of shelter at her home," Freddy said. "When she hears of animals that need to be rescued, she and a team of volunteers go get them. Karinde

houses them until they can be fostered out. She gets donations of food and has volunteer vets who treat them. She
set up a whole system of bathing and cleaning the dogs'
coats, which they all need." She shuddered. "They come in
with fleas, lice, ticks, you name it."

"Does she rescue cats, too?"

"Not at her place, but somebody else takes them in."
Freddy slowed, peering at the side of the road. When a
green sign for CROOKED HILL RD loomed, she turned right
onto the road, which wound up a hill. She pulled up at the
very last house before the road ended in a patch of woods.
The nearest neighbor had been back a few hundred yards
and wasn't visible around the bend.

"She is out here all by herself," I observed.

"Maybe it's so neighbors don't complain about dogs
barking around the clock."

I glanced into the back seat. Cocoa sat up alert and gaz-
ing out the window as if he recognized his prior home.
"We didn't exactly finish planning our story."

"We can wing it. Leave it to me, Robbie. I've always
been good at making stuff up."

I sure hadn't. I didn't have an imaginative mind. Freddy
could take the lead.

She unhooked Cocoa from the car harness and made
sure she had a good grasp of his leash before letting him
out. Stretching out to the left of the nondescript cottage
was a long plain structure with several doors set into the
wall facing us. In front of the length of the building ran a
covered walkway enclosed with a six-foot chain-link
fence, like an open-air hall.

We made our way up a flagstone walk and rang the
doorbell. Cocoa barked when he heard it chime within.

Karinde pulled open the door. Her eyes widened. "Cocoa?

You okay, buddy?" She knelt and rubbed his head with both hands, which were remarkably big. I hadn't noticed them at the O'Neills'. She glanced up at Freddy. "What's going on?"

"Cocoa's fine. We were in the area and decided on the spur of the moment to bring him by so he could say hello." Freddy beamed.

Karinde stood, her head cocked like she didn't believe her. "Ohhh-kay. Come on in." She stepped back.

The living room held half a dozen dogs. Two puppies in a big crate looked a lot like Cocoa. A small white dog slept on a sheet-covered couch, and a skinny greyhound lay on a braided rug. An old brindle mutt, with rheumy eyes, stalked up to sniff us. A ten-inch tall Buddha statue sat in the center of the mantel, but the rest of the dog-centric room was filled with chew toys and dog beds everywhere, plus a rack of leashes was mounted on the wall near the door. The air smelled of canines, too, but the scent wasn't overpowering.

A big black dog rushed in from another room and barked at us, loud and accusing. Karinde grabbed it firmly by the collar. If a dog could glare, this one was glaring. I took a step back. She'd better have control over it, or I'd be sprinting for the car.

"Let me put this one in the back." She didn't ask us to sit and disappeared with the black dog through a door that clicked shut after her. She was back in a moment, sans dog. "Let Cocoa loose. These girls are his sisters." She pointed to the crate.

After Freddy released his leash, Cocoa ran up to the crate and rubbed noses through a gap with one of his littermates. The other one pushed in front and got her kiss, too.

"So?" Karinde folded her arms.

"My cousin heard about Cocoa," Freddy began in a bright tone. "And she wants one, too. I told her I'd come by and see what other puppies are available."

"You know they're all on the Web site." Karinde narrowed her eyes. "Where does she live?"

"She's out in the country and the Internet reception is just awful." Freddy lifted a shoulder in a *what can you do* gesture.

"Yes, but yours isn't," Karinde said. "I don't get this visit, ladies."

I swallowed. "When you dropped off Cocoa, you said you'd found him at a filthy puppy mill. Where was it, and how did you learn about it?"

Her nostrils flared. "It was up in Morgantown. I got a tip from somebody who drives by the place. She was suspicious, and I was, too. I took some volunteers, a truck full of crates and carriers, and the animal control officer for that county. We shut the place down. And guess who had a financial stake in that disgusting business?"

"I don't know," I said.

"That despicable dinner guest of yours, Freddy. Jed Greenberg had no heart, no conscience. I can't believe you invited him to your home."

"I had no idea he was involved in such an enterprise," Freddy said, "or we never would have invited him and his wife."

Or sent Cocoa home with them, either.

"I heard he died the next day. I say good effing riddance." Karinde dusted off her hands.

I had the feeling if we were outdoors she would have spat on the ground.

"It turns out he was also stealing from my husband over the course of several years," Freddy said. "I personally wouldn't have wished him dead, but he was an unscrupulous man, no doubt about it."

"Unscrupulous doesn't even begin to describe his evil," Karinde said. Cocoa came over and sniffed her leg, then rubbed up against it. She scooped him into her arms and kissed his head. She lifted her chin. "I wish I'd killed him myself."

Chapter Eighteen

After Abe and I finished our pad Thai and fish curry with rice, we put Cocoa in his crate and headed into the restaurant. Abe carried the basket of clean laundry. "I'll fold while you work."

He folded the napkins, aprons, and dish towels at a table as I prepped cut butter into flour for biscuit dough.

"Your mom and I paid a visit to the dog rescuer this afternoon. Cocoa got to see his sisters."

Abe squinted one eye shut. "Lemme guess, you were trying to worm information out of Karinde Nilsson."

"Pretty much. But the only thing she told us was that she wished she'd killed Jed herself."

He whistled. "That's pretty out there."

"I know. I think you're about the same age as Karinde. Did she grow up in South Lick or in the county, do you know?" I wrapped the biscuit dough and turned my attention to peppermint brownies.

"I guess she is in her early thirties, come to think of it. But I believe she didn't grow up around here, unless she went to a private school. She wasn't at South Lick High with me, anyway."

I added peppermint extract instead of vanilla to the brownie batter and slid two big pans into the oven.

"I'm done with the laundry, darlin'," Abe said. "Can I help with prep?"

"Sure, thanks. How about washing and trimming that asparagus and then cutting it into half-inch pieces?"

"I'm on it." He washed his hands and got busy with a knife across the counter from me.

We worked in companionable silence for a few minutes.

"I have to say, this investigation has really hit Dad hard." Abe shook his head.

"I can imagine. I heard some unpleasant gossip about him this morning. I didn't tell you when you came in."

"You can tell me now."

"It was guilt by association, tying him to Jed and his un-scrupulosity. I just made up that word, but it's true." I spread candy canes between two layers of waxed paper and took a mallet to them. *Bam.* "Take that, nasty men." *Bam-bam-bam.*

Abe laughed. "Easy, now."

"Well, it's not right. Your father is a good man. I hate it that people are saying otherwise." When the timer dinged, I drew out the brownies.

"You and me both. I heard a bit of gossip, too. A couple whose line I fixed asked me if I knew anything about poison in your restaurant."

"Of course they did." I groaned as I sprinkled the warm brownies with crushed candy canes. "When a state police detective arrives in the middle of the rush and confiscates my special hot chocolate packets, why wouldn't folks be talking?"

He set down his knife and came around to my side of the counter, wrapping his arms around me from the back and laying his chin on my shoulder. "It's all going to be fine, Robbie. You wait and see."

I leaned back into his comfort. "I guess I'm going to have to."

He sniffed. "Those brownies smell like heaven. Need a taste tester?"

I laughed. "Of course." I cut us each a square.

"Ten thumbs-up." Abe reached for the brownie knife after he'd swallowed.

I gently swatted his hand away. "Hey, those are for tomorrow." I offered him a kiss, instead.

Abe took Cocoa out before we went to bed, and I made sure the doors were securely locked, just in case. We blessedly retired early enough to have some sweet time together before we slept.

Chapter Nineteen

The next morning found Danna and me doing our cook-and-serve dance as we always did, except we both wore Santa hats, instead of her usual scarf and my usual ball cap. Supplies were dwindling, but that was fine, since we were going to be closed for the next eight days. We ran out of sausages at a few minutes before nine. Danna wrote it on the Specials board and then drew a big red X through the word. I did make up a fresh double batch of biscuits when those ran low. Flour, eggs, and butter didn't go bad, and I always had a ton on hand.

Now at nine-thirty, I watched Buck come in at his usual slow pace. Was this finally going to be the verdict on whether Jed was poisoned or not? Did he have lab and autopsy results in hand, at last? He gave a little wave and headed back to his favorite two-top, available because we were only moderately subscribed at the moment.

The next time Danna approached the kitchen, I said, "Swap out? I need to talk with Buck."

"Sure."

"By the way, did you learn anything from your grandmother?" I asked her. I'd forgotten to earlier.

"No, she was busy. But Josie said she would come in for

lunch and you can ask her whatever you want." Danna grinned. "She's a hoot. You'll like her."

"I love the name." When I had a daughter, Josie was definitely high on the list of names I would consider. I smiled to myself, picturing being married to Abe and starting a family.

I changed out of my grease-splattered cooking apron into a fresh one and grabbed an order pad. It took me a while to get to Buck, though. A gentleman over here hailed me for more coffee. That lady asked for her scrambled eggs to be drier. A mom needed another milk for the one her toddler had spilled, despite my serving it in a cup with a tight lid and a paper straw. I also brought a wet rag and several dry ones to clean up the mess. I finally arrived at Buck's table, where he sat frowning and poking at his phone with an index finger nearly long and skinny enough to double as a chopstick.

"Good morning, Buck. Dare I ask?"

"We got some results, but it's kind of a crazy mixed-up bag, Robbie." He set the phone down with a frown.

"What do you mean? Was Jed poisoned or not?"

"Welp, didn't find no evidence of toxins in Greenberg's body. So, no, he apparently wasn't poisoned."

Huh. "At least that's information, right?"

He bobbed his head once "But the lab ain't done with the chocolate mixes yet. Turns out, some of them tests take a while to react or some such thing. I don't know laboratory science from Adam's off ox, 'course, so I just gotta believe the experts."

"But if Jed didn't ingest any poison, why does it matter?"

Buck regarded me. "Because we could still nab somebody for attempted murder. Like O'Neill. The wife, of course. Or, in theory, you."

"*Me?*" I screeched in a whisper, cranking my eyes open to maximum.

"Look. I know you wouldn't have done such a thing, but you did assemble them mixes, am I correct?"

I nodded as I set my fists on my hips. "I would never do something like that, Buck, and Howard wouldn't, either. He's a good man."

"I know, I know. We got higher-ups to satisfy, though, and the court system, too, as you're well aware."

"And what about the ice on the sidewalk?" I asked. "Is Oscar looking into why it was icy despite zero precipitation for the last couple weeks?" I kept my voice low, but even I could hear the ire and impatience in it. "And is he checking who knew—besides Willa Mae—that Jed walked that way every single morning? His wife told me he was a creature of habit, that he always followed the same route."

Buck pressed down the air with one hand. "Calm yourself down, now, Robbie Jordan. All in due time. And speaking of time, I got a hole in my stomach bigger than the Grand Canyon, and if I don't eat a triple breakfast right quick, I won't make it back to the major powwow at the station at eleven. Any chance you could scare me up some food?" He smiled with a hopeful look.

"If you'll tell me what the big meeting is."

"You know." He pulled his mouth to the side. "Oscar. My boss. The staties' commander. Madame Mayor. Heck, maybe other mucky-mucks. They want this thing solved yesterday. Can't blame 'em, really. It's near Christmas."

"I'll bring you breakfast." I blew out a breath. "You want to pick or you just want a bunch of food?"

"A bunch of food. Thanks, hon. You're the best."

I turned away. Right now, I was feeling a lot more like the worst. Jed hadn't been poisoned. That was good. But the fact that nothing was really solved made me queasy. As

I headed to the kitchen area, I realized Buck hadn't mentioned what I'd texted Oscar about Karinde saying she wished she'd killed Jed. I almost turned back to Buck's table, but kept on going. I didn't want him going all hangry on me. I'd mention it when his food was ready.

"Any three breakfast plates for Buck, Danna, please," I said when I reached the grill. "Whatever we have the most of. He didn't seem to care except he needs to eat a lot and then leave."

She lowered her voice. "Did he tell you something upsetting? Things looked a little dicey between you and him."

I nodded. "You could say that." Four women stood. One waved their check like the group was eager to pay and leave. "Tell you when I get a chance."

Chapter Twenty

"Where's your grandma?" I asked Danna at a little before one o'clock. "I thought she was coming in for lunch?" I was antsy to find out what Josie Dunn knew.

"Yeah, she said she was. I'll text her." Danna worked her phone. "She's a pretty busy lady. Still running her own IT business and stuff."

Business was waning on this Christmas Eve afternoon, which was fine with me, even though I still had six lunch orders to fill. If we got a chance to close early, I wouldn't complain. I'd written a bonus check for Danna before she'd arrived this morning and tucked it into her gift bag back in my apartment. I'd assembled a selection of small games and local gifts for both her and Turner: a South Lick Celebs game like Authors, except it featured cards with photographs of people like Corrine, my aunt Adele, and Buck. One of Adele's multicolored knit hats. A little jigsaw puzzle of Brown County. Plus a fat candy cane, a jar of local honey from my Mennonite beekeeper friend, and a box of mocha fudge from Nashville Fudge Kitchen. The gift bag was one of the new blue Pans 'N Pancakes totes I'd ordered, but Danna and Turner were the first to have them. The bonus check would be the real present for my hardworking and inspired young employees, though.

Danna's phone dinged. She glanced at it, then pointed at the front door with a raised eyebrow. "There she is."

The woman who had petted Cocoa on my way to talk to Georgia walked in. *Aha.* That was what had seemed familiar to me, her resemblance to her granddaughter and to her daughter, Corrine, too. Danna hurried over to greet her. I flipped a beef patty and positioned a slice of cheddar on it, cracked two eggs for a sunny-side up order, and laid four strips of bacon on the hot surface.

"Josie, this is Robbie, my boss and the best cook around," Danna said, her arm linked through the older woman's. "Robbie, Josephine Dunn, grandma *extraordinaire.*"

I extended my hand. "I'm delighted to meet you, Ms. Dunn."

She shook with a firm grip. "I'm Josie, Robbie, and that's that. Now, I think you were walking a puppy yesterday, if I'm not mistaken." Her green eyes, only slightly faded with age, bore into mine.

"That's right." I had a moment of panic, thinking I'd forgotten to let Cocoa out, until I remembered that Abe had taken the puppy with him when he left early this morning. He'd said Sean would be with his grandparents all day, and Abe had the day off to finish shopping and wrapping, so he could mind Cocoa. *Whew.* "It's so nice to meet you, Josie. Your daughter and granddaughter are both super. I couldn't run this place without Danna, and we all know how much Corrine does for South Lick."

That eyebrow of Josie's went up again. "As my daughter is so fond of telling anyone who'll listen."

"Josie," Danna chided. "You know Mom works hard."

Josie's gaze at Danna was fond and indulgent. "Of course, my dear."

"Can we get you some lunch?" I asked.

"Dan, here, has been lauding the place since she started. I'm afraid I've been traveling so much with my consulting company I simply haven't made the time to come in and eat." Josie glanced at the list of specials. "The hoagie sounds nice, but only a half, please. And a glass of chocolate milk."

"You got it," Danna said, then turned away to attend to customers.

"Oops." I worked my stove for a minute rescuing a few nearly burnt items. "I'll get that sandwich out to you in a sec. Please sit wherever you'd like."

"I understand you have some questions for this insomniac," Josie murmured to me.

"I do, and I'll appreciate whatever you can tell me."

It took me five minutes to finish up the last of the open orders and to assemble the half hoagie. I carried it and the milk to where Josie sat with the *Wall Street Journal* open on the table. She closed it and stashed it in a roomy leather bag on the floor.

"Please sit with me if you can." Josie gestured to the opposite chair.

I surveyed the store and decided I could. "Thanks."

She chowed into her sandwich with the enthusiasm of a hungry Buck. I smiled to myself.

When Josie finished chewing the first mega-bite, she began. "Danna told you I'm awake a lot at night, I believe."

I nodded.

"I don't actually seem to need much sleep in my advanced years. Sometimes I work or read a memoir, my favorite kind of book."

"My aunt is the same," I offered. "She'll sit up knitting or reading a mystery when she can't sleep."

"I know Adele. We went to high school together, did you know that?"

"You did?"

"Yes. She's only a couple of years older than me. I liked her then and I like her now. She's always been one of my inspirations in life." Josie took another bite.

"She's sure one of mine."

She swallowed. "Anyway, I also like to sit at the window in the dark and look at the night sky. I'm on the third floor—the top one—and no trees obstruct my view of the firmament. But there's one annoying streetlight down behind the library, near that returns box they have."

Where Jed met his end.

"Sunday night, or perhaps it was early Monday morning, I was looking for the Ursids meteor shower, and I saw a woman do the oddest thing."

My heart rate increased and I sat as still as one of those spray-painted living statues. I sensed customers leaving, Danna moving around clearing and cleaning, the big school clock ticking, but my attention was locked on Josie Dunn—with the key tossed down the drain.

She took a sip of chocolate milk. "The person parked in the lot and approached the returns box. But instead of a stack of books, she carried something heavy in one hand, something sort of big and round. You can believe my attention perked right up."

I didn't dare interrupt.

"She proceeded to tip the thing over the walkway. It must have been water. On the walkway, I tell you! Well, I felt like I was back in the *Mary Poppins* book I read as a child, with the woman who had fingers made of barley sugar and the uncle who floated to the ceiling when he laughed. You know? Why was she watering pavement? I almost expected red poppies to sprout from the concrete." She gazed at me.

Except this wasn't magical realism. This was murder. I cleared my throat. "What did this woman look like? Hair, height, shape?"

"Aha, now there's the rub." She tapped one of those red fingernails on the table. "I'd taken out my contact lenses, of course, because I don't sleep in them. I'm not as near-sighted as I used to be, but I'm afraid I'll need cataract surgery before long. Plus, no one's eyes work as well in the dark at seventy as they did at twenty. My plain answer is that the woman's form—height, weight, appearance—was on the fuzzy side. When she was under the light, she was bending over, and it was only for a minute or two."

"So, how do you know it was a woman and not a man?"

Josie laughed, a raucous sound that reminded me of Corrine's enthusiastic cackle. "That much I could see. Last time I checked, men don't tend to wear red skirts."

Chapter Twenty-one

Stunned at Josie's revelation, I knew exactly who had caused the icy pavement. I stared at her. "When you heard about Jed's death, did you tell the police what you'd seen?"

"I didn't hear about his demise until this morning. I left town on business Monday morning and didn't get back from California until yesterday. Right before I saw you walking the puppy, in fact." She raised a single elegant eyebrow. "A death in a town like South Lick doesn't exactly make the national news."

"No kidding. Thanks for sharing that information." I wanted to take action, but the restaurant didn't empty out like magic, so I kept working.

Josie ate and departed, giving Danna a hug and me a handshake. I refused Josie's offer to pay, of course. The rest of the customers settled up and left. The clock read one-thirty. I looked at Danna. She looked back. I gave her a thumbs-up and hurried to the door. Once it was locked and the sign turned to CLOSED, I exchanged a high five with my employee.

"We did it," I said. "Now for some well-deserved time off."

"I can't wait. Let's do this cleanup in double time."

I cranked up a playlist of reggae Christmas carols. We cleared and stashed and scrubbed. By two-thirty, we had all the chairs upside down on the empty tables, ready for the cleaning folks I'd hired to come in next week to deep clean, and to wax and buff the floor, too. Any food likely to spoil in the eight days was either tossed or packaged up and ready for Danna and me to take to our respective homes and consume—not that my home was very far away.

"How about a beer to celebrate?" I asked her. "I know you drink a little." She was still nearly a year shy of twenty-one, but hey. It was Christmas.

"Like obviously, Robbie, I'd love to. And I'm walking home, so no worries."

"Come on back." I took my share of biscuits, bacon, and cut-up veggies to my apartment fridge. Birdy crouched, wary, near his empty food bowl. "Hey, kitty cat. Doggy's gone, okay?" I poured pint glasses of beer for Danna and me at the kitchen table, then served Birdy his wet food of the day. I sank into a chair and raised my libation. "Here's to a great team, and a totally relaxing holiday."

She clinked, sipped, and set down her glass. "We should think about bringing in a substitute whenever one of the three of us is gone. That got nutso for a while there this week."

I poured tortilla chips into a bowl and popped open a new can of cashews before I answered. "You're absolutely right. Who we could hire is always the question. But we can work on that."

She munched a few cashews. "What'd you think of my grandma? Isn't she dynamite?"

"She's a pistol, all right." I pictured her sitting awake in the dark, looking with her bad eyesight down onto the walkway.

"Did she help? Did she see anything?"

"Only sort of. A woman poured water on the pavement between the box and the iron fence. But Josie said her vision wasn't up to more details than that."

Danna uttered an obscenity and then ducked her head into her shoulders. "Oh, sorry."

I snorted. "Like I haven't heard or said it before."

"I know, but I'm trying to get out of the habit of swearing. It totally doesn't go over well with customers."

"True."

"Anyway, too bad Josie couldn't see more, right?" Danna asked.

"Very much too bad," I agreed. "Still, I think what she did see might be of use." It might very well be of use.

"At least she said it was a woman. How did she know that?"

"She said she saw a red skirt. Hang on while I text that to Oscar. I should have done it earlier." I tapped out the message.

Josephine Dunn, Mayor Beedle's mother, lives by library. Said she saw woman in red skirt pour water on pavement night before Jed Greenberg's death.

"There." I set my phone on the table and munched a chip.

"And are there women who are suspects?"

I nodded. "Jed's wife, Willa Mae, and Karinde, the woman who rescues dogs. I've only met Karinde a few times. I don't think she's the skirt-wearing type, but I could be wrong. Enough talk of suspects. It's Christmastime. Hang on a sec." I rose and went into my bedroom, emerging with Danna's gift. I handed it to her before I sat.

"What's this? I love the cute bag."

"Thanks. I'm going to offer them for sale, but you got

the first one." I watched as she unpacked it, crowing over every discovery.

"Robbie, this is so sweet." Her cheeks glowed. "You're wicked awesome, you know that?" She pulled a little green box tied with a red ribbon out of her skirt pocket. "I got you something, too." She pushed it across the table.

"You didn't have to do that. But I'm not waiting until tomorrow to open it." I untied the ribbon and removed the lid. On a square of puffy cotton sat a pair of round earrings an inch in diameter. They were blue, with our store logo enameled on them in white, with silver wires. "My gosh. Where did you get these? I love them!" I slid out the small gold hoops I wore every day to work and threaded the new earrings through my lobes.

"Etsy. You can get anything on Etsy."

"Thank you, Danna. What a treat." I pointed at the bag. "There's one more thing in your bag."

She peered into the bag until she drew out the envelope.

"You earned that, and more," I said. "Don't open it now. Turner's getting one, too. And Merry Christmas."

"Thank you, Robbie," she said, her voice thick. "This is the best job I've ever had." She stuck Adele's hat on her head and grabbed her phone. "Christmas selfie?"

"Your arms are longer than mine. You take it." I scooted around to stand next to her. She was so tall I only had to bend my knees a little to align my face with hers, and she was sitting.

"Cheers!"

Chapter Twenty-two

"Thanks for coming along, Freddy," I murmured an hour later as we stood on Willa Mae's front porch. I'd asked Freddy to accompany me, with a quick stop at the bank, and I hoped the new widow was home. All the lights inside were lit up again, even though night hadn't yet fallen. "I didn't want to do this alone."

"Sure. I haven't offered my condolences yet, so the timing was perfect."

I'd already rung the bell twice. I raised my hand to knock, but then the door opened.

"Robbie, Freddy." Willa Mae looked from me to Abe's mom and back. "Is everything okay?" She looked like she was wearing the same black turtleneck and yoga pants she'd had on two days ago.

Freddy stepped forward. "I haven't gotten a chance to tell you how sorry I am about your husband's death." She touched Willa Mae's arm.

I reached into my bag and switched on the tiny recorder I'd brought.

Willa Mae blinked bleary eyes. "Thanks, I guess." A sharp gust of breeze blew by and she shivered. "Won't you come in?"

We followed her in and waited while she shut the door. On the coffee table sat a bottle of Scotch and a half-empty highball glass.

"Sit anywhere." Willa Mae plopped onto the couch.

I set my bag on the coffee table and slipped out of my coat, too, since the heat was once again set way too high for comfort. My comfort, anyway. The air smelled stale, too. I knew the feeling of not wanting to clean, to shower, to do anything except cry. After Mom had died so suddenly, I'd been a basket case for weeks.

"How are you getting along?" Freddy asked, shrugging out of her coat.

"Like crap, what do you think? That detective keeps dropping by to talk to me. When I go out, everybody stares. The police won't tell me when I can bury my husband. Jews are supposed to inter the dead promptly." She picked up her glass with a shaky hand and took a swig of the whiskey.

"If there's anything I can do to help, please let me know," Freddy offered.

"Thanks. I doubt there is." She gestured to the bottle. "You girls want a drink?"

"No, thanks," Freddy replied.

"Not me, either." I swallowed. This wasn't going to be easy. "Willa Mae, I spoke with someone today who said she saw you pour water on the pavement behind the library the night before Jed died." I half hoped Oscar would already have arrested her, so I didn't have to do this. Since Willa Mae was here, I was going ahead with my plan.

Willa Mae's jaw dropped. Freddy stared at me. I hadn't told her my plan, simply that I was going to see Willa Mae and wanted company.

"You're kidding me," Willa Mae said, slumping into her shoulders.

"No." I kept my voice gentle. "And those bruises on your arms? You didn't get those from running into door frames, did you?"

Willa Mae drew her knees to her chest and hugged them, resting her face on them for a moment. She looked up at Freddy and me. "He'd been beating me again. He used to, when we were first married, and then he stopped. But he started up again earlier in the year after the partnership with Howard broke up. My husband broke my rib, ladies. He busted my nose and I had to pretend to my work colleagues that I'd tripped and fallen." She rubbed her nose, then held out both forearms. "He grabbed me by the arms and threw me against the wall."

"Did you ever take pictures of your bruises, or go to the hospital?" I asked.

"I had to go after he broke my nose. I lied to the doctor, but I'm not sure she believed me."

Willa Mae had said Oscar had been repeatedly visiting her. I wondered if he suspected Jed had been abusing her. Maybe he'd asked the hospital for any record of Willa Mae being treated.

"Why didn't you leave Jed?" Freddy asked softly.

"I don't know if you can understand this. I loved him *and* I hated him." Her eyes filled. "My life was a nightmare. But he'd stopped abusing me once. I thought he would again. He said he loved me and was going to start counseling. But that night after we went home from dinner?"

"Where you'd been wearing a red skirt," I added.

"He nearly strangled me to death." She pulled down the neck of the shirt.

I winced at the sight of the three-day-old bluish-purple marks. Freddy gasped and brought her hand to her mouth, her own eyes filling.

"I just snapped," Willa Mae continued. "He went to

bed. A couple of hours later, I grabbed a few gallons of water and headed out. Behind the library actually wasn't the only spot I watered, but I didn't think anyone would see me back there." She choked out a harsh laugh. "Jed never, ever varied his walking route. He'd been having balance problems, some neurological thing, and all I wanted was for him to have a really bad accident. I wanted him to be hurt so bad, he couldn't hurt me any more. I didn't mean to kill him."

Chapter Twenty-three

The poor woman. I'd heard of the classic abused-wife syndrome, where the abuser kept saying he would change, and the woman kept saying she loved him, sometimes until he killed her. I didn't blame Willa Mae for wanting it all to stop.

"Did you tell Detective Thompson any of this?" I asked.

"Him?" Willa Mae scoffed. "Like he would be sympathetic. He'd have had me in handcuffs and out of here before I could put shoes on."

I glanced at Freddy. *Do we call Oscar right now?* We had to. I had my recording, but I had no idea if what Willa Mae had said would be audible through the fabric of the bag. Plus, it probably wasn't admissible in court, anyway. I'd texted Oscar about what Josie had told me, so the decision was already out of our hands.

"I thought I would feel so good, so free, after I heard he was dead." Willa Mae put her feet back on the floor and sat slumped, her glass in both hands. "But I don't. I don't feel good at all."

The doorbell rang. I rose. "I'll get it."

Willa Mae snorted. "Probably some snoopy neighbor pretending the reason she's bringing a casserole is out of sympathy, but really she's just a nosy parker."

I paused. "Do you want me to answer it?"

"Go ahead." She waved me away.

I pulled open the door to the tall sight of Buck, with Oscar hovering behind him.

"Hello, Robbie." Buck frowned. "You should not be here. No way."

"Call it a condolence call?" I winced. He was right, of course. "I came with Freddy O'Neill."

Oscar pushed forward. "We're here to see Willa Mae Greenberg. Bird is right, Robbie. You could be in danger here, you and Ms. O'Neill, both."

I simply stepped back and got out of the way. Buck stepped in, removing his hat. Oscar followed and did not remove his knit cap, until Buck elbowed him, then he pulled it off his narrow head.

"Hey there, officers." Willa Mae's glass was now empty and her speech was sloppy from the whiskey. "Join the party."

"Ms. Greenberg," Oscar began, his hands limp at his sides. "Based on an eyewitness report, we have obtained additional security footage from the South Lick Library. It indicates that in the early morning of your husband's death, you deliberately poured water on the pavement to cause icing. You are under arrest for the murder of Jedediah Greenberg." He told her she had the right to remain silent and the rest.

Good. He'd followed up on the tip from Josie. And it must have taken this long because he'd needed to confirm her story with the footage.

"I just told these nice ladies the whole story," Willa Mae said in a low voice. "If you knew how many times that man tried to kill me, you wouldn't blame me for wanting to put him out of commission. But I wasn't attempting murder. Just harm."

"I recorded everything she said," I told Buck. "You can check with the hospital for a record of some of her beatings."

Oscar beat his hand against his leg, the picture of impatience.

Buck nodded. "Thanks, Robbie. The recording won't be admissible, but get it to us before long. We'll see if we can use it somehow." He gave Willa Mae a sympathetic smile as he pulled out handcuffs. "Ma'am, if you'll stand, please?"

She stood. "Robbie, will you get my shoes? They're by the door."

Buck waited until I brought Willa Mae her winter boots, as well as a coat hanging on a hook above the shoe rack. After she was ready, he cuffed her hands behind her back.

"Thank you, kind sir." Willa Mae blew out a breath. "I'm ready to roll."

Oscar headed for the door. Buck took Willa Mae's elbow with a gentle touch and guided her out.

Before the door closed, she called back, "Turn down the heat and switch off the lights, will you, girls?"

"We will," Freddy called back.

The door clicked shut. Freddy and I exchanged a look.

"Willa Mae is something," Freddy said. "She's not exactly acting like a widow, but not like a murderer, either."

"I know. Her emotions must be so confused." I got up and turned the thermostat down to fifty-five. Willa Mae wasn't going to be back any time soon. "Not quite the condolence call you bargained for, I guess," I said.

"No. Not quite."

Chapter Twenty-four

I sat back in my chair at Howard and Freddy's dinner table at eight that night. "I can't manage another bite." My plate still held a piece of the best turkey I'd ever eaten, a few bites of stuffing, a smear of cranberry sauce, and a stray garlicky green bean. "What a perfect Christmas Eve dinner."

"Dad, you outdid yourself with that turkey," Abe said. "Marinated and smoked is a winning combination."

"Thanks, kids." Howard beamed and drained his glass of Chardonnay. "I learned it from a Puerto Rican friend."

Sean, who'd been as excited as a three-year-old when Abe and I had arrived with Cocoa a couple of hours ago, slipped the puppy at his feet a sliver of turkey. Cocoa scarfed it down.

"I saw that," Freddy scolded. "Not too much of people food for the little guy, Seanie. You surely don't want him upchucking on your bed tonight."

"Yes, Grandma." Sean popped in a huge bite of stuffing and washed it down with milk. "I'm going to take him out for a walk." He stood. "Come on, Cocoa Puff."

"We'll have cookies when you get back," his grandmother called after the two.

After the door shut, Abe set his elbow on the table and

chin on his hand. "All right, Robbie, now that Sean's out of the room, dish. On the way over, you said you'd had a newsworthy afternoon and part of it happened with Mom. Tell us what went down."

I exchanged a glance with Freddy, who pointed back at me. "All right," I began. "Howard, you must have heard that Jed wasn't poisoned. Buck came in and told me this morning."

"Yes," Howard said. "But they were still waiting to see if any of the chocolate had been tainted."

"Right. Danna's grandmother, whose condo overlooks the back of the library, came into the store a little later and told me she kind of saw a woman in a red skirt pouring water on the pavement."

"Kind of saw?" Abe asked.

"One, her contacts weren't in. Two, she has cataracts. Three, she's seventy. So, yeah, saw but not clearly."

"Then Robbie asked me to go with her to visit Willa Mae this afternoon, but I had no idea what I was getting into," Freddy said.

"Willa Mae wore a red skirt to dinner here Sunday night," I said. "Karinde Nilsson hated Jed, but she never wears skirts. I didn't want to visit a murderer alone."

Abe squeezed my hand. "Smart move."

"I took a little digital recorder in my bag and turned it on."

"The poor woman." Freddy wagged her head. "Jed had been beating Willa Mae badly. She told us she did pour the water. She knew he would walk by there, because he never varied his routine. And he'd been suffering from imbalance. She said she just wanted to hurt him." She glanced at me.

I nodded. "Enough so he would stop hurting her. She said she didn't mean to kill him."

"Makes your heart break, doesn't it?" Abe asked. "I can't understand men who hurt their women, or anybody." He blew out a breath.

"But why didn't she simply leave him?" Howard asked.

"We asked her that," Freddy said. "It's a terrible syndrome, hon. And love is a strong emotion."

"Willa Mae had been to the hospital at least once with her injuries, so the abuse is documented," I said. "I'm sure by now medical practitioners know the difference between a bruise from actually walking into a door and one caused by another person."

"Good." Howard nodded.

"To top it all off, Buck and Oscar showed up with a warrant for her arrest. They'd gotten security cam footage from the library that showed Willa Mae doing the deed more clearly than Josie Dunn's eyesight had."

"Did she go calmly?" Abe asked.

"Yes, with the help of a whiskey or five she'd had beforehand. I hope they'll let her off lightly."

Boy and dog blew in through the door with a gust of cold air. "Cookies?" Sean asked.

Cocoa barked. Freddy laughed. Abe and I stood to clear the table.

We ended the evening with hot dark cocoa—spiked for the grown-ups, including Abe and me, since we were staying overnight—and cookies. Sean stood in front of the lit fireplace and recited "The Night Before Christmas," which Abe said was the family's annual ritual ever since Sean had been in preschool. The teen didn't seem the least bit embarrassed by the attention, even when his changing voice cracked from low to squeaky.

When he was finished, the family began singing carols, one of my favorite things to do at Christmas. Freddy played the piano beautifully, and I discovered something new about my man—he had a strong and clear baritone singing voice. I must have never heard Abe sing before. Just one more thing to love about him.

I had a pang, picturing Willa Mae alone in jail tonight. I would do what I could to help her get a fair trial. In a misguided way, she'd been trying to save her own life, but she would probably end up in prison for years. I hoped she could find happiness, somehow, somewhere.

Recipes

Mexican Hot Chocolate

Californian Robbie makes up packets of this mix to sell in the store at Christmas. Too bad half of them were confiscated by the police.

Ingredients

1½ cups granulated sugar
1 cup all-natural unsweetened dark cocoa
1 teaspoon kosher salt
1 teaspoon ground cinnamon
¾ teaspoon cayenne pepper (use ½ teaspoon if you want more heat)

Directions

Whisk together all ingredients in a medium bowl. Store in an airtight container for up to 2 months. To make 1 serving of Mexican Hot Cocoa, heat 1 cup whole milk in a small saucepan over medium just until hot and milk begins to steam, about 5 minutes (or in a microwave for about a minute and a half). Remove from heat. Whisk in 2 tablespoons cocoa mix. Serve immediately with whipped cream and a dusting of cinnamon.

Mexican Bridecakes

Freddy O'Neill uses her mother's recipe for these easy buttery cookies. The original recipe comes from my grandmother Dorothy Henderson.

Ingredients

1 cup butter, softened
2 cups unbleached flour
¾ cup powdered sugar
1 cup pecans or walnuts, finely chopped (optional)
1 teaspoon vanilla
¼ teaspoon salt
¼ cup milk

Directions

Preheat oven to 375° F.
Mix all dry ingredients.
Cut butter into them until fine.
Add vanilla and milk and stir with a fork until mixed.

Form into a flat disk with your hands and chill for twenty minutes to a day.

Press or roll onto a cookie sheet to an even ¼-inch thickness.

Bake for about fifteen minutes, watching closely for browning.

While warm, sift powdered sugar over the top and cut into one-inch squares.

Eggnog Oatmeal

Robbie offers this seasonal oatmeal as a holiday breakfast special. Note: steel cut oats are chewier and more flavorful than rolled oats.

Makes two servings.

Ingredients

1 cup milk
1 cup eggnog (commercial or homemade using the recipe of your choice)
¼ teaspoon salt
⅔ cup quick steel cut oats
Nutmeg

Directions

Bring dairy just to a boil. Stir in oats and salt, reduce the heat, and simmer uncovered for 6 minutes or until desired texture. Sprinkle nutmeg on top. Serve hot.

Dear Readers,

I hope you enjoyed *Christmas Cocoa and a Corpse.* I had fun setting a story featuring Robbie Jordan and her country store during Christmas in southern Indiana. I loved thinking up tasty specials for her and Danna to offer every day and to imagine Pans 'N Pancakes all decorated for the holidays. The Nativity scene at the elder O'Neills' home comes directly from my own, right down to the irreverent additions of plastic figures like Snoopy and Bert. The life-sized menorah is modeled on the one in the gazebo in my own Massachusetts town.

If you haven't read any of the Country Store Mysteries yet, this is the seventh installment. The series begins with *Flipped for Murder,* which takes place on the first day Robbie's country store is open for business. But after a difficult South Lick town employee is found dead—with one of Robbie's cheesy biscuits in her mouth—opening week gets a lot more complicated. You can make the biscuits from the recipe in the back, or sample Robbie's signature Banana Walnut Pancakes. The next book is *Grilled for Murder,* which occurs a little more than a year before *Christmas Cocoa and a Corpse.* It's the week after Thanksgiving and Robbie is horrified to find a body in her store the morning after she hosts a welcome home party for a local woman. The apple-spice muffins are baked, not grilled, and are an easy addition to your breakfast.

In *When the Grits Hit the Fan,* Robbie and a friend are out snowshoeing when they encounter a corpse frozen in a lake. The creamy cheesy grits recipe will warm your insides even as you read about Robbie and her new guy trapped in the woods in an ice storm facing a killer with a gun. Book four, *Biscuits and Slashed Browns,* takes place during the Maple Festival. But when a man is found dead at a maple syrup farm, things get sticky for Robbie and her new helper, Turner Rao. The recipe for Chocolate Biscotti doesn't have maple in it, but is perfect for an Italian brunch or just a midmorning snack.

Death Over Easy, the next book, shows Robbie's Italian father coming to town during a big bluegrass festival, when not one but two murders take place. If you make the Sugar Cream Pie, it goes down easier than finding the killer—or killers. *Strangled Eggs and Ham*, book six in the Country Store Mysteries, takes place during a steamy August, with controversy over a proposed real estate development in the county and Robbie's septuagenarian aunt Adele leading a protest group. A cool cucumber-dill soup is a perfect accompaniment for both the weather and the heated controversy that leads to the murder of one of the protesters.

So a Christmas novella slides perfectly into book time. The seventh in the series, *Nacho Average Murder,* releases next year. Robbie heads back to her native California for her ten-year high school reunion in February. She samples new recipes featuring avocados and tortillas for her restaurant back home—and maybe digs up the real story behind her mother's premature death.

It makes me so happy to write about Robbie, her cast of friends and family, and the delightful fictional town of South Lick in Brown County, Indiana. I lived in the neighboring county for five happy years a few decades ago, and I love being back in that slower-paced corner of the country. I get a kick out of including quirky regional sayings from Lieutenant Buck Bird and Robbie's aunt Adele. And, within the confines of the story, I like exploring deeper questions of small-town life, family ties, and what would drive a regular person over the line to actually commit murder.

I'm always delighted to hear from readers. Please find me on Facebook on my Maddie Day page, on Twitter and Instagram at @MaddieDayAuthor, and on my Web site, edithmaxwell.com (my birth name and alternate author name). I blog and Facebook group with the Wicked Authors—we'd love to have you join us. If you're reading this book close to the winter holidays, may you and yours have a warm and cozy season. And if you picked it up a different time of year, enjoy!

Cheers,
Maddie Day

DEATH BY HOT COCOA

Alex Erickson

Chapter One

Snow crunched underfoot as Rita Jablonski and I made our slow way toward the large building ahead. It looked like a warehouse, but it sat out in the middle of a farm on the outskirts of Pine Hills, which made it seem out of place against the backdrop of fields. Icicles hung from the gutters running along the top of the building, along with a string of colorful Christmas lights of alternating red and green.

"Are you sure this is the right place?" I asked Rita as I eyed the place. She was giddy with excitement, practically dancing in place as we walked.

"Of course I am, dear. Lewis holds these things a couple of times every year. Everyone knows it."

Everyone but me, apparently.

I pulled my coat tighter around my shoulders as the wind picked up briefly. "I really should be getting the house ready for Dad and Laura." I spoke with only a mild chatter to my teeth. Why couldn't the parking lot be closer to our destination? It was way too cold to be outside. My poor nose felt like it was going to fall right off my face if I didn't warm it up soon.

"Oh, pah." Rita waved a heavily mittened hand at me. "This should only take an hour. You'll be back in time to make sure everything is set to rights for James and *that* woman."

I glanced at her out of the corner of my eye, but refused to comment. Rita was infatuated with my dad, who just so happened to be her favorite mystery writer. She hadn't taken it too well when I'd first told her he had a girlfriend. It might have been months ago, yet it appeared she was still bitter about it.

We reached the building a few moments later. It had no markings on it to identify it as anything but a big ware-house, which made me imagine a gigantic room filled with dusty old boxes. With some trepidation, I stomped my way up the three stairs to the door, which, thankfully, resided beneath a roof. I shook the snow out of my hair as Rita reached for the doorknob.

Hot air blew out at us as the door swung open. I closed my eyes and made a low groan of pleasure as we stepped inside.

There were already four other people in the room. Christ-mas lights were strung along the walls, and a tree stood in the corner, complete with wrapped gifts sitting snugly be-neath it. I was assuming they were mere props, not part of the festivities, but what did I know?

"Rita, I'm really not sure about this," I said. "I've never done one of these before."

"You'll be fine," she said, pulling off her mittens and shaking them out. Water dripped to the floor, as the snow had already melted, thanks to the heat. "I bet you'll have the whole thing solved in mere minutes." She elbowed me and grinned. "It's what you do."

"I serve coffee." I'd taken the day off from Death by Coffee, the bookstore café I co-owned with my best friend, Vicki, to be here with Rita today.

"Escape rooms are a big deal these days," Rita said, as

if that should make everything better. "It'll be just like solving a murder, just without the body!" She rubbed her hands together in anticipation.

I had my doubts about that, but I let it drop. Nothing was quite like a murder investigation. The fear, the constant worry that a killer might spring out of a dark corner and put an abrupt end to your investigation. No, I seriously doubted an escape room could compete with that.

"Besides, you can't back out now, even if you wanted to," Rita said. "I already pre-registered us for it. Lewis has put a lot of work into this and I, for one, don't want to make it more difficult for him."

The door opened and two more people entered. The couple appeared to be in their mid-twenties, and in the cute and cuddly stage of their relationship. The woman leaned on the man's arm, giggling and staring at everything with wide-eyed wonder. The man was smiling, though I could tell he wasn't comfortable with her hanging on to him like that. Some men just didn't know how to show their feelings, especially in a room full of strangers.

The two newcomers walked right past Rita and me, and past a man who stood against the wall, tapping his foot. He wore an ugly red, green, and gold sweater, which would have been right at home in an ugly sweater contest. His eyes found mine, narrowed briefly, before he turned away.

Nearby, two men stood by one of those electric heaters that was made to look like a real fireplace. They were both wearing suits, which I found odd at a place like this. The thinner of the two men wore sneakers, while the bigger guy wore polished dress shoes, which clashed with the décor of the place. He looked as if he'd come straight from a business meeting.

The door next to them opened and a man strode through.

He was tall, and was dressed in a way that I could only describe as a Christmasy butler. His hair was combed back from a face full of harsh lines, and was tucked beneath a green Santa hat. His suit was likewise green with red lining, and his shoes were a matching scarlet.

He scanned the group, and then his eyes suddenly hardened. The scowl that found his face was enough to dispel any notion that he was enjoying the holidays. He took an angry stride forward, jaw so clenched, I was afraid his teeth might shatter.

"Lewis, my friend!" The foot-tapping man pushed away from the wall and came to a stop in front of the scowling man—Lewis, apparently.

"I think we're nearly all here," Rita said. "Lewis only appears once everyone's arrived. He doesn't like people all that much, if you can believe it."

With how hard he was glaring at the man jabbering at him, I most definitely could.

Rita glanced around the room. "I think we're waiting for one more. The limit's eight for this room, I believe. And he wouldn't accept anything less. It would ruin the whole event if someone weren't to show." She tsked.

"What will he do if we're short?" I asked.

Rita's eyes widened like she couldn't believe anyone would dare risk it. "Well, I don't know. I expect he might postpone until we find someone to fill in."

I groaned just a little inside, but was relieved of my worry when a door at the opposite end of the room opened and a plump older woman in a white sweater slipped out. She saw the rest of us looking her way and she winced.

"You!" Lewis shouted, jabbing a finger her way. He took two quick, angry strides away from the foot-tapping man. "What are you doing?"

"I was just looking," the woman said, gaze bouncing

around the room as if she was too embarrassed to meet anyone's eye. "No one else was here and I thought—"

"That is a violation to the rules!" Lewis's face turned a bright shade of red as he cut her off. "I should disqualify you and cancel the whole thing!"

"What? For taking a peek?" The woman pressed a hand to her chest. "There was no harm in it. I didn't look at anything, just at the room to see how it was laid out."

"It's against the rules. You accepted them when you signed up. Or did you not bother to read the form?"

"There was a form?" I whispered to Rita, who gave me a sharp glare.

Lewis stared hard at the woman before he huffed. "Fine. I'll let it slide this time, but one more infraction and I'm calling it off."

The woman nodded, her face a deep scarlet as she edged away from the now-closed—and, apparently, off-limits— door.

"Welcome, everyone, to this year's Christmas escape room," Lewis said, his voice adopting a more cheerful tone as he raised it to address us all. "I am your host, your guide, Lewis Coates. I'd like to go over the rules briefly before allowing you to get to know one another."

Everyone moved to stand in a loose semicircle around Lewis. The couple who'd come in last stood immediately to my right, with Rita and the woman who'd just gotten yelled at to my left.

"First, I will ask that everyone leave their cell phones, purses, and any other valuables in the lockers behind here." He motioned toward a desk. Lockers that looked a lot like the kind you'd find in a school hallway lined the wall behind it. "Take the key with you. Once the escape room is complete, you will be able to retrieve your things."

"Why?" This from the bigger man in a suit.

Lewis's mouth drew into a fine line. "Because I don't want anyone cheating or becoming distracted by staring at your phones. Your belongings will be safe, as you will have the only key to your chosen locker."

The big man crossed his arms and frowned, but didn't otherwise complain.

"You are to all work together in this, which is why I will allow for a few moments for you to get to know one another before I take you to the start of your adventure. Do not fight. Do not destroy the property. Anyone doing so will be removed from the room and banned from ever returning."

Someone grumbled under their breath. I didn't see who.

Lewis checked his watch, which I noted had Mickey Mouse on its face. "I will return in five minutes. We can then begin." Without another word, he strode through the doorway the woman had exited from a moment before.

"Guy's a jerk," the foot-tapping man said the moment Lewis was gone. "Always has to be in control, and if he isn't, he freaks out."

"I can't believe he yelled at me," the woman next to Rita said. "I was just looking. There's no harm in that, is there?"

"He's a control freak," the man went on. "He works security and thinks that gives him the right to look down on everyone else."

Not wanting to continue with the negativity, I held out a hand to the couple next to me. "Hi, I'm Krissy Hancock, and this is my friend, Rita Jablonski. This is my first time here."

The woman was the one to reach for my hand. "June Blevins," she said. "And my boyfriend, Troy Carpenter."

"Pleasure."

"This is our first time here too," June said. "I've always

wanted to do one of these things. When I found out Troy was coming, I insisted on tagging along, didn't I?"

"That you did." He didn't appear amused, though he did put his arm around her and smiled.

"What do you two do for a living?" I asked, genuinely curious.

"Nothing exciting," June said. "I work in my parents' store." She looked at Troy, pure adoration in her eyes. "Troy's a banker."

"I do investments," he said. "Pretty boring stuff."

I was surprised, but guess I shouldn't be. He might be young, but that didn't mean he couldn't have a real career.

I looked past them to the foot-tapping man. "And you are?" I asked him.

"Yuri Vance," he said. He didn't offer to shake hands.

"Have you done one of these before?" I asked.

Yuri shrugged. "I've done some. Not here, though."

"It's my first time too," the big man in a suit said. "Bob Mackey, accountant." He grinned. "I'm not sure what to expect, but figure it might be a fun little distraction."

All eyes turned toward the man next to him, who blushed at the attention.

"You can call me Jerry," he said, eyes dropping to his sneakers. "Jerry James."

"Don't mind J.," Bob said with a chuckle. "He's got to work on being more assertive. It's holding you back, J., it really is."

Jerry's blush deepened as he nodded.

"I'm Carol," the woman in the sweater said. "Most everyone still calls me Mrs. Kline, though. Habits are hard to break, I guess." She tittered.

"You're a teacher?" I guessed.

"Was. Retired a few years back. With what they're doing to education these days, most of us are getting out while we still can. The politicians are making it so that most of us can't actually teach the kids anything anymore." She shook her head sadly. "It's a real shame."

"We'd better get our stuff locked up," June said. "We only have a minute or two left before he'll be back."

And with how Lewis had reacted when he'd caught Carol sneaking out of the escape room, I doubted he'd be thrilled if we weren't ready for his return.

Troy and June led the way to the lockers. The rest of us lined up behind them, waiting our turn. I took off my coat and gloves and hung them on the hanger inside my locker, once I was able. I considered slipping my cell phone into my pocket so I'd have it with me, but decided it wasn't worth it; I didn't want to face Lewis's wrath if I were to be caught. I slid it into my coat pocket before I closed the door and took the key, which I tucked away into the front pocket of my jeans.

The escape room door opened again a moment later. Lewis stepped through, closed the door to prying eyes, and then turned to face us.

"It's Christmas Eve," he said in a dramatic voice that would have been perfectly in place on the stage. "Snow is falling, coating everything in a soft blanket of white." His hand drifted slowly across our view, setting the scene.

"You, Santa's elves, have worked hard to provide toys and gifts for all the children, yet one remains—a gift so magical, it must be locked away, lest those filled with greed attempt to steal it. This gift will be presented to Santa himself, if you can unlock it." Lewis met my eye. His gaze was intense. "Follow me, and I will show you to your rooms."

He opened the door behind him. The hallway beyond was lit by bright Christmas lights. The hall itself curved, and was obviously built for just this occasion. I could smell freshly cut wood and dried paint. Doors were placed periodically along the hall on the left side. I assumed there'd be eight in all, but with the curve, I couldn't see them all to be certain.

"You have woken in your rooms," Lewis said, motioning toward one of the doors. A small removable plaque on it read, CARP. "Because of the valuable nature of your gift, you have locked yourselves in your rooms, and must work together as one to enter the main room, where Santa's gift has been kept safe from prying eyes."

"We've got to go in alone?" Jerry asked. His eyes were a little too wide.

Lewis nodded. "Find your rooms. They will unlock as one and then you may enter." He bowed his head slightly, and then vanished back the way we'd entered.

"This is so exciting!" Rita said, clapping her hands together. "Where's my room?" Before anyone could so much as look, she was off, hurrying down the hall. "Krissy, here's yours!" she called back to me. "Oh! And mine's right beside it!"

"Who's Carp?" Bob asked.

"That's me," Troy said with a shrug. "Used my old high school nickname when I registered." He stepped up to his door, which got everyone else moving.

I found Rita four doors down, practically dancing from foot to foot. My room was right before hers, Bob's before that. Jerry glanced back at Bob at least three times before he vanished around the corner in search of his room.

"Nerves," Bob chuckled. "J. needs to get over it." While Jerry had taken off his suit jacket, Bob had left his on. He patted his chest pocket once before turning to face the door.

All the lights in the hall flashed twice. And then, all at once, locks clicked, and doors sprang opened. Taking a deep breath to calm my nerves, I took hold of the door-knob, pulled the door open the rest of the way, and then stepped inside my first-ever escape room.

Chapter Two

The room was surprisingly big. It wasn't quite as big as, let's say, a normal living room, but it was close. There were small end tables, shelves, and a chair, all with Christmas-themed knickknacks and drawings scattered atop them. A door stood on the opposite side of the room. Glancing behind me, I noted the door I'd entered through had no doorknob on this side. There was only one way out of the room, and I was pretty sure it wouldn't be as easy as turning the knob.

"Okay." I spoke aloud to calm my nerves. I could hear shuffling sounds and thumps coming from the rooms on either side of me. "Now what?"

There was so much to look at, it would take all day to sort through it all and make sense of it. I needed a guide, something to tell me what I was supposed to be doing.

"Oh, Lordy Lou, would you look at that?" Rita's voice was muffled, but audible from the room beside me.

Noting a timer in the corner, counting down the minutes, I decided I'd best get moving. I had just under fifteen minutes remaining, which seemed like a lot of time, but with no idea what to do, it might as well have been quad zeroes.

I went to the door first. I tugged on the doorknob, but as expected, it was locked. There was no keyhole, so I wasn't looking for a key. It was then I noticed the small rectangular box on the wall next to the door. There was a small keypad beneath it and just enough spaces for a three-digit code. Above the box were symbols, each lined up with the spaces for each number. The first symbol was a Christmas tree, the second was a Santa hat, and the third, a reindeer.

"Well, usually, there's only one tree," I muttered, entering 1 into the keypad. "And Santa has only one hat." Another 1 followed. "And, counting Rudolph, there were nine reindeer." I typed in 9. I then checked the door, thinking it was painfully easy if it worked.

Still locked.

"Okay, then." I turned to take in the room. My eyes immediately landed on the Santa hat sitting in a rocking chair in the corner. I hurried over and picked it up. There were no numbers written on the inside or the outside of the thing. I felt around the fluffy white edge, but nothing was tucked inside there either.

Since the hat had been on the chair, I went ahead and checked it too. It was an old wooden rocking chair, the kind you could imagine someone's grandmother sitting in with knitting in her lap. I was careful as I tipped it back to check underneath, afraid that it might be as frail as it looked.

Nothing.

Setting the chair back in place, I took a step back to give the room another good look. It took only a moment to note one of the drawings hanging on the wall was of a cheerful-looking Santa standing beside a square house with smoke curling from the chimney. Santa's hat was a bit overlarge, but I figured it still counted for my purposes.

"That's two," I said. Now that I understood what I was to do, I began searching for hats in earnest.

I took a good couple of minutes checking every item in the room. Nearly everything was Christmas themed, and that included the small bowl of candy sitting next to the rocking chair. There were no Santa hats inside it, however, though I did steal a chocolate bell and popped it into my mouth.

I glanced at the clock, and noted I had twelve minutes remaining. I chewed my chocolate and considered the rest of the room. I had yet to find a single Christmas tree or reindeer. Did that mean the other two numbers were zero?

It seemed odd, but I went with it. I hurried to the lock, typed in 0, 6 (the number of hats I'd found), and one more 0. I checked the door once again, but it remained stubbornly locked.

It was then I noticed the two microphones.

They were attached to the wall, just under a small black speaker. There was one on either side of the room, and I had a feeling they fed directly into the rooms on either side of me.

I hurried across the room to my right and spoke into the mic. "Rita? Are you there?"

There was a long moment of silence where I could *feel* the seconds draining away. I almost abandoned the mic to check the other one when she finally responded.

"Krissy? Lordy Lou, this is a challenge!"

"I think I've solved it," I said. We already were under ten minutes remaining, and if I was wrong, we'd be wasting a lot of time.

"Really? You've unlocked your door?"

"No, not yet. But I think we need to work together to get them open." I glanced back at my lock to double-check the symbols before turning back to the mic. "Do you happen to have any reindeer around your room?"

"Let me check."

Seconds ticked by. I fought down the urge to pace as yet another minute passed, and then one more.

"Rita?" I asked. She was taking her grand old time searching. "Hurry."

I was dancing from foot to foot by the time she said, "Got it! I see three reindeer."

"Okay, great." I mentally catalogued the number. "Look at your passcode box. There are three symbols above it. The first symbol is what I'll need to look for. Then use the mic on the other side of your room to talk to your other neighbor. Tell them the third symbol, while asking for their first. Whatever symbol is in the middle is your item. You should find them in your room."

"Snowballs," Rita said. "It looks like snowballs."

"Got it. Tell your neighbor. I'm going to let mine know and get counting for you."

I hurried across the room, eyes scanning for snowballs. I saw one immediately, a soft, plush one in the corner. I pressed the mic as my heart started to pound. Time was quickly running out. Those fifteen minutes drained away awfully quickly and I wondered if the clock was running fast.

"Hey," I said, mind blanking for an instant before I remembered the name of the man next door. "Bob, are you there?"

Seconds ticked by.

Then a few more.

I scowled and pressed my ear to the wall, listening for any sounds from the other side, but his room was completely quiet. There wasn't even the faint shuffle of him going through the stuff in his room.

Did he somehow get out?

"Bob?" What if the mic wasn't working? Would we get more time? If we couldn't communicate with one another, then there was no way we'd be able to escape. "Hey, are you there?" I raised my voice, just in case he could hear me through the wall like I'd heard Rita earlier.

Another handful of seconds ticked by, and then, finally, there was a click.

"Sorry. I'm here," Bob said. He sounded out of breath. "I didn't even know these were here."

"It's all right," I said. "I think I know how to unlock our doors."

I gave him a quick rundown of what to do and told him to look for Christmas trees for me.

"Candy canes," he said, once I finished explaining. "Looks like you need to find me some candy canes." He grunted into the mic. "This whole thing is kind of clever, isn't it?"

"It is," I said, even as I hurried away from the mic and started searching for both candy canes and snowballs. I had six minutes remaining. I had no idea what happened when time ran out, since Lewis hadn't told us beforehand. I was guessing we failed and Santa wouldn't get his gift.

I was determined not to let that happen.

I went through the room twice, double-checking my count. The items weren't all that hard to find, and none of them appeared to be hidden inside other objects, which was a relief. Once I was certain I had them all, I headed for Bob's mic. Just before I could tell him my count, he said, "Four. There's four trees."

"Eight candy canes," I responded.

"Got it."

I took a moment to set the first number of the code at 4, leaving the 6 hats in place, and then I adjusted the reindeer

number to 3. Then I moved to the other side where Rita
would be waiting.

"Two snowballs," I told her. "Got that?"

A handful of seconds passed before, "I do."

"Great. I'm going to try my door."

A strange sense of excitement washed over me as I double-
checked the code and reached for the doorknob. I was un-
sure about doing an escape room at first, but now that I
was actually doing it, I found it was kind of fun. It was
like a puzzle, but on a grander scale. I loved puzzles of all
kinds, and this one was already exceeding my expecta-
tions.

My fingers brushed the knob, and with a big grin, I
turned it.

The door refused to budge.

"What?" I almost screamed it. I was positive I was on
the right track, so how could that have not worked?

I checked the code once more, even went as far as to adjust the numbers and reset them, before I tried it again.

It still didn't work.

"What went wrong?" I asked aloud. I turned and counted
my hats again, and came up with the same number.

But what about the one on the wall?

Could the code symbols count? I added one to my total
and tried again.

Still locked.

Glancing at the clock, I added 1 to both Rita and Bob's
count. Less than five minutes to go. I tried the door, and
was once again rebuffed.

 I hurried over to one of the mics. "Rita, are you out?"

"Almost," she said. "I was double-checking my number.
I had to find sleighs, if you can believe it. There's actually
a life-sized one in here!"

"You said three reindeer, right?"

"I did."

"Are you sure that's right?"

"Well, it's what I found."

Four minutes.

"Can you check again? My code's not working and I can't think of any other way to get out."

Rita made an exasperated sound, but said, "Give me one sec."

While she recounted, I darted across the room and asked Bob the same thing in regard to the Christmas trees.

"I've already double-checked," he said. "There are four. Let me try my code and I'll let you know if it works."

"All right."

My fingers drummed on the shelf next to the mic. Three minutes and counting. If I'd gotten it wrong and caused us to fail, I'd be sick. This was supposed to be something I was good at.

There was a shout from the center room. It sounded like Carol, but the door was thick, as was the wall on that side, so I couldn't be sure.

A moment later, Bob returned. "It unlocked. I'm good to go."

"Can you count your trees once more?" I asked. "I have Rita checking for more reindeer. My code isn't working."

"Will do. But once we're down to a minute, I'm getting out of here. I'm not sure if those who fail to escape are eliminated or not, and don't plan on being left behind."

"Understood," I said, before leaving the mic and hurrying to Rita's side. Two minutes to go.

The commotion outside got louder as I called for Rita to hurry. After a few seconds, she returned.

"You won't believe this, dear, but I totally missed one of

your reindeer! It was sitting right in front of my face and I looked right over it."

"So, there's four?" I asked. I could feel every tick of the clock. Lewis wouldn't eliminate me for Rita's error, would he? If she got to continue and I didn't, I wasn't going to be happy.

"Four," she said. "I'd swear to it."

Bob's voice came from the other side, echoing Rita. "Four trees. I'm getting out of here."

I rushed to my code. I had less than a minute remaining, and I was terrified I'd be the only one not to get out. I adjusted the numbers on either side to 4, made sure the hats sat at 6, and then reached for the door, just as a loud "Oh, my Lordy Lou!" came from the room on the other side.

"Here goes," I said, turning the knob.

The door opened. I just about threw myself through as the timer hit 0.

The first thing I noticed was the giant package sitting atop a table in the center of the room. It was wrapped, with a big green bow on it and a tag that read, SANTA. All around it were smaller gifts, eight in all, that were obviously meant for the eight competitors. Each had a tag with our names on them.

My eyes moved from the gift table to the people in the room.

Carol was standing near one of the open doors, hands over her mouth, eyes nearly popping from her head. Next to her, June had her face buried in Troy's chest. His own face was pale, with a trickle of sweat running from his brow. Across the room, both Bob and Jerry stood next to one another, talking in quick, hushed tones, while Yuri sat in the corner, head hanging, knees up by his ears.

All eyes were locked on something on the other side of

the table from me, right next to where Rita stood with a shocked expression on her face.

Trepidation growing, I circled the room until the object that had captured everyone's attention came into view.

Lying upon the floor, amid a still-steaming spill of what smelled like hot cocoa, was an unmoving, unblinking Lewis Coates.

Chapter Three

"Do you think it's part of the game?" Jerry asked from across the room.

No one made a move toward Lewis. He hadn't so much as twitched since he'd been found, which told me we were most definitely not dealing with part of the escape room here. Even if he was faking his death, he would still have to breathe.

"Is anyone a doctor?" I glanced quickly around the room, not wanting to take my eyes off of Lewis for long, just in case he made a subtle movement of some kind. The only response I got were shaking heads.

"It could be part of the game," Jerry continued. He sounded frantic, half out of his mind. I didn't blame him. I'd feel much the same if I hadn't already dealt with a few dead bodies in my time. "It could be like that horror movie, the one where the guy pretended to be dead, but really wasn't, and was, in fact, the killer all along."

"This isn't a horror movie, J.," Bob said.

"Yeah, but he could've gotten the idea from it, right?" He met my eye. "Right?"

"I don't know." But you didn't make dead bodies, real or not, a part of a Christmas-themed event.

"I think I'm going to be sick." This from Carol.

"Has anyone checked him for a pulse?" I asked. I needed to remain calm. Out of everyone here, I was probably the person with the most experience around dead bodies. It didn't say much about my life choices, but it wasn't like I went out of my way looking for them.

"No," Carol said. Her voice was quiet, subdued. "I found him when I escaped my room. He hasn't moved so much as a finger. No one has gone near him either."

"Okay." I took a deep breath. "I'm going to check him, just in case." Then, hoping that Jerry was right, and it was all part of the show, I raised my voice. "Hey, Lewis. If you're alive, could you, I don't know, move a hand or something?"

I held my breath, as did seemingly everyone else in the room.

Lewis's hand remained stubbornly still, as did the rest of him. I willed his back to move, an eyelid to blink, but nothing happened.

I swallowed and then started slowly forward. I could feel everyone's eyes on me, which made me worried I'd somehow mess this up. I wasn't trained for this kind of thing, and I was most definitely not a cop. No matter how many crimes I'd solved in my time in Pine Hills, I was still just an amateur. One misstep and I could destroy an important piece of evidence.

Slow down, Krissy. I wasn't even sure the guy was dead yet, let alone murdered. I couldn't let my past experiences influence my thoughts about what was happening now.

Careful not to step in the cooling hot cocoa, I knelt next to Lewis. There was no blood, as far as I could see, which was a good sign that this might be an accident. "Are you okay?" I asked. When he didn't respond, I reached out and gently pressed my fingers against his neck.

He was still warm, but there was no pulse I could detect. I moved my hand and held it under his nose in case my untrained fingers had missed their mark. I felt no air movement of any kind.

"Okay," I said, sitting back on my heel. "He's not breathing."

"Oh, no." Carol backed up until she bumped into a Rudolph standing near the wall. She gave a little yelp as she hopped away from it.

"Does anyone know CPR?" I asked, though I was pretty sure it was already too late.

"I know a little," Bob said. He made no move toward the body. He eyed Lewis's corpse as if he was afraid it might leap up and attack him if he got too close.

I stood and gave him room. The way his eyes tightened, I knew he didn't want to touch Lewis, but with everyone watching him hopefully, he couldn't refuse either.

Bob strode forward and gently rolled Lewis onto his back. With the rest of us looking on, he got to work.

"Does anyone have their phone with them?" I asked, patting my pockets in the vain hope that I'd somehow forgotten it there, though I knew it was tucked away in my coat.

"I left mine in my locker," June said. She glanced at Troy, who said, "Me too."

"We all did, dear," Rita said. "It was one of the rules."

"I know," I said with a sigh. "But I hoped that someone decided to break the rules this time." My gaze flickered to Carol, but she shook her head.

"It's no use," Bob said, standing and taking two quick steps away from Lewis. "The guy's dead." He rubbed his palms against his slacks.

"Does he have his phone on him?" Jerry asked. "He didn't have to follow the same rules the rest of us did, so maybe he has it."

When no one immediately moved to check Lewis's pockets, I did. I patted him down quickly, but he wasn't carrying so much as a wallet, let alone his phone.

"Nope." I stood and, like Bob, I wiped my hands on my pants. "He must have left it in the other room."

"Heart attack, you think?" Troy asked. "He seemed pretty uptight."

"Could be," I said. "I didn't see a wound on him." I glanced at Bob, who shook his head. He hadn't either.

"Okay. All right." I ran my fingers through my hair. "Does anyone know if someone else is monitoring us?" A quick look around the room didn't reveal a camera, but if the guy worked security, like Yuri said, then he'd likely know how to hide them effectively.

"Lewis always worked alone," Rita said. "His wife died young, and they never had kids, so there's no family."

"So, no one can let us out?" I asked, which was probably the wrong thing to say at that point in time, but it was too late to take it back.

"Oh!" Carol made a strangled sound. "I . . . I can't . . ." She spun on her heel, nearly tripped over the Rudolph, and then rushed back into her room. She slammed the door closed, and I heard it click as the lock engaged.

"We can't get out?" June asked, voice rising in pitch. "Are you serious?"

"There's a lock on the door," Yuri said. "Has anyone done this escape room before? Please tell me someone knows the combination."

"Let me try." Troy strode across the room and quickly punched in a code. Instead of three digits, there was a full eight. As he hit the last number, he tried the door.

It didn't open.

Jerry groaned and sank to the floor. Next to him, Bob put both his hands on his own head and scowled.

Troy stepped back, frowned at the door, and then tried the code again. The door remained stubbornly closed.

"What are we going to do?" June asked.

"Stay calm," I said. "We can't panic." I turned my attention to where Lewis lay. "Let's figure out what happened to him and go from there."

"We should cover him," Yuri said. "I can't stand looking at him like this."

"Did anyone have a blanket in their room?" I asked.

"I did," Rita said. "It has a reindeer on it."

"I'll get it." Troy hurried away from the door, and went into Rita's room.

"Maybe the door code is on him?" Jerry said, nodding toward where Lewis lay.

"Let's find out." Bob started forward, but I stopped him.

"He had nothing in his pockets. And well . . ." A thought was working its way through my head, one I didn't like one bit. I walked slowly around the central table, taking in the details. "There's a gift for each of us," I said, speaking out loud for everyone else's benefit. "And each person has a cup of hot cocoa waiting on them."

"Which I could use right about now." Yuri stepped forward and reached for one of the mugs.

"Don't touch it!" I shouted, causing him to leap back like it might explode. "Look." I pointed to the mug lying next to Lewis.

The room fell silent. No one commented on what I was seeing, so I explained, just in case they weren't seeing it.

"Eight gifts. All named for us, so we knew which was ours. But look, Bob's gift is crooked, like someone moved it. And his mug." I pointed at the mug on the floor. "It's not the same as the others."

"What are you trying to say?" Troy asked, stepping forward. He carried Rita's reindeer blanket in his arms.

"I don't think this is the right mug."

"I know Lewis," Rita said. "He's a perfectionist. He wouldn't have left one mug different than the rest. If one of them broke, he'd buy an entirely new set."

Yuri nodded in agreement.

"Unless it was a clue," Bob said. "Like, maybe that mug has something hidden in it."

"I don't think so." I crouched down, keeping well back from the spilled hot cocoa. "I doubt Lewis drank from the mug, so we don't have to worry about its contents." Or, at least, I hoped we didn't.

"Then what's the big deal?" Yuri asked. "If he wasn't poisoned, he might have died of a heart attack like he said." He jerked a thumb at Troy. "Or maybe it was an aneurysm. High-strung people like Lewis die like that all the time."

"Maybe." But it didn't sit right with me. Why was Lewis in the room, to begin with? Why had he picked up the mug? Nothing lay next to him, like a half-full carafe, so he wasn't filling them at the time.

"We need to find a way out of here," June said. "I can't stay in here with him."

"It's all right." Troy handed the blanket to Rita so he could hug June. "We'll be okay. There's nothing to be frightened of."

Isn't there? I wondered, eyeing Lewis. The hot cocoa spread around him like a brown bloodstain.

"The mug is different," I said again, running it through my mind. "There has to be a reason for it." I leaned in closer, and then I saw it.

The mug was ceramic, and appeared as if it was made

by a local craftsman, rather than mass-produced. It had that handmade look to it, with tiny imperfections that gave it character. It would be the sort of mug you'd buy at a craft bazaar, or at a local potter's shop.

But there was one more difference to this mug than what you'd find on any other mug, no matter how it was made.

"Does he have a prick on his finger?" I asked.

"Excuse me?" Bob asked.

"A pinprick or a dot of blood?"

When no one made a move to check, I huffed and moved to where Lewis lay. I checked his right hand, but there was nothing there.

His left hand was a different story, however. There was the tiniest hole on the pad of his index finger. It was small enough that I'd missed it in my first brief examination of him.

I closed my eyes and mentally forced myself to keep from trembling. Or from screaming—because that was what I really wanted to do.

"What is it?" Bob asked. His voice was loud in the closed space. "What did you find?"

"The mug," I said, standing. I moved so I could see the faces of everyone in the room in the hopes I could read something on them. "It's been booby-trapped."

"*Booby-trapped?*" Jerry asked. "How?"

"There's a small pin built into the mug, on the inside of the handle."

Both Bob and Yuri leaned forward, squinting at the mug, but neither got close enough to make anything out.

"I don't see it," Yuri said.

"It's there. There's also a small hole on Lewis's finger. This wasn't his mug. He must have seen it and picked it up to investigate." And then he collapsed, which meant . . .

"He was poisoned?" Rita asked, eyes going wide. She hugged the blanket close to her chest as she turned her attention fully to Lewis.

"I can't say for sure." Though the evidence was pretty compelling. "But it tracks. The mug might be a coincidence, so he still might have died from a heart attack or a stroke. We don't need to panic."

"A little late for that, don't you think?" Jerry asked. He stared long and hard at Lewis before he rushed to the door and punched in a series of numbers. He yanked on the door, which remained closed, but that didn't stop him. He kept tugging, yanking so hard his head whipped back with every pull. Muffled, panicked sounds came from him as he did.

"J., stop." When he didn't, Bob raised his voice. "Get a hold of yourself, man!" He grabbed Jerry roughly by the arm and jerked him away from the door.

"Leave me alone!" Jerry shouted, but when he backed away from Bob, he didn't go back to the door. He pressed himself against the wall, hand going to his mouth, where he bit down on the meaty bit just under his pinky.

"It'll be all right," Rita said. "Krissy Hancock is here. She'll take care of everything."

"And what's she going to do?" Yuri asked. "A man's dead. We're trapped."

"Go ahead, Rita," I said, indicating the blanket. Like Yuri, I couldn't stand to look at Lewis's pale face any longer.

"Shouldn't we leave everything untouched?" June asked. "You know, for the police?"

"Probably," I said. "But covering him up shouldn't cause too much trouble, as long as we don't disturb the scene too much." Or so I hoped.

Rita started spreading the blanket, careful not to touch

Lewis. Yuri stepped forward and helped her. Instantly, one corner soaked up some of the hot cocoa, but at least now, we could think without a dead man watching our every move.

Once he was covered, Yuri retreated back to his spot near the wall. Rita moved to stand next to me.

"Now what?" Bob said. "He's right, we're trapped."

"We are, aren't we?" June asked. She scanned our faces, her expression grave. "We're stuck in here with a dead man." Tears formed in the corner of her eyes, and in them, I saw genuine fear. "We're trapped in here, with no way out, and one of us is a murderer."

Chapter Four

Rita and I stood in a corner of the room, watching the others, who had broken off into their own small groups. Jerry and Bob were together, talking in hushed voices, as were June and Troy. Yuri remained alone in the corner, and Carol had yet to leave her room. They were the only ones who didn't have someone to confer with.

"No one trusts anyone else," I said, noting how Yuri kept shooting June and Troy suspicious glances, while they, in turn, did the same to Jerry and Bob.

"It's no wonder—now, is it, dear?" Rita asked. "A man's dead and no one has any idea who did it. And you say he was poisoned?" She tsked. "All the books I've read say poison is a woman's weapon, though I find that to be hogwash. It's the weapon of someone who doesn't want to get caught."

I had to agree. Guns could be traced. Knives could leave fingerprints if the killer wasn't wearing gloves. And both of them require the killer to be present during the murder.

But poison? You could pour it into a drink—or, in this case, put it on a concealed needle—and be long gone before the victim ever stepped into the room. If that was indeed what happened, this wasn't going to be an easy case to solve. The killer could already be a hundred miles away by now.

"We aren't sure it was poison," I said, trying to keep my options open. "The needle on the mug could have been an accident, a defect that looks far more sinister than it really is."

Rita gave me a flat look. "What? Do you think our potter was sewing before making the mug and accidentally dropped a needle into the clay?"

"Well, no." A part of me wished that was the case, but it was too far-fetched, even for me. "But maybe it was a joke. Like, they made it like that to trick friends, give them a little prick on the finger in April or something."

"And Lewis just happened to end up with the mug, picked it up, and startled so badly from the poke, he up and died?"

"Yeah." I heaved a weary sigh. "It doesn't really hold up, does it?"

"Not one bit," Rita agreed.

Which meant, we were almost definitely dealing with a murder.

Why couldn't anything be easy around here?

"What do you know about the others?" I asked, eyeing the people in the room with us. Rita was Pine Hills's foremost gossip. If anyone had dirt on our little gathering, it would be her.

"Not a lot, if you can believe it," she said. "I knew Lewis, of course. He was a bit of an odd duck, was a smidge OCD, and was a big control freak. You know, he used to tell people how to bag his purchases at the grocery. I saw him do it once. Stood right there and told the bagger how to puzzle-piece it together so nothing got broken or smashed, like it wasn't the young man's job in the first place."

"It would explain why he would check the odd mug, I guess," I said.

"It would. He wouldn't have stood for it, not Lewis. The moment he saw the oddity, he wouldn't be able to help himself. He'd have to have done something about it."

It made me wonder if that was part of the plan. Did the killer know about Lewis's compulsive behavior and used it against him? He'd almost have to, since you didn't kill someone with a booby-trapped mug in a fit of rage.

No, if this was indeed murder, it was most definitely of the premeditated sort.

"What about the others?" I asked.

"Other than you and Lewis?" Rita asked. "The only other person I know here is Carol Kline. Everyone else is a stranger, if you can believe it!"

Actually, no, I couldn't. Rita seemed to know everyone, and not just in Pine Hills, but in all the surrounding towns.

I glanced toward the door Carol had vanished into. No one had tried to talk her out of it since she'd gone in. In fact, I hadn't heard so much as a peep out of her since she locked herself away. "She's taking this pretty hard," I said.

"That, she is." Rita shook her head sadly. "Carol isn't a bad woman. From what I hear, she was a pretty good teacher, tough but fair. Although, I have heard she can be impulsive at times."

Impulsive, like the kind of person who might kill someone over a slight? "Did she know Lewis?"

"I don't rightly know," Rita said. "She was a teacher, so I suppose they might have crossed paths at some point. We could ask her if she taught him or one of his relatives."

With no other plan in place, I thought it sounded like a splendid idea.

Before Rita or I could make a move for Carol's closed door, a shout erupted from the other side of the room.

"I didn't do anything!"

Jerry was standing with his back to the wall, both hands raised. Bob stood in front of him, his own hands balled into fists. His face was red, jaw bunched and working.

"It was *my* mug!" Bob shouted, pointing toward where the mug lay next to Lewis's covered body. "How do you explain that?"

"I can't!"

"Uh-oh," Rita said. "That doesn't look good."

"No, it doesn't." I turned away from Carol's door and hurried across the room. We so didn't need a fight breaking out, not with tensions already running high. It wouldn't take much for it to escalate.

"What's going on?" I asked, stepping between the two men.

"He's lost it," Jerry said.

Bob's already-red face turned a deeper, darker scarlet. "J., so help me, I'll knock you right out if you keep it up."

"Me?" Jerry said. "You're the one accusing me of trying to kill you!"

"What?" I asked. Across the room, Yuri was poised, as if he might leap into the fray. Next to him, June clutched at Troy, who looked just about ready to lock both him and his girlfriend in one of the rooms until this whole thing was over.

"It's the mug," Bob said. "It was mine."

"You made it?" I asked.

"No, of course not. But it was the one that sat next to my gift, the one with my name on it."

"That doesn't mean anything," Jerry said.

"It means someone was trying to kill me!" Bob shouted. "Why else put it there? If our host wouldn't have come in and investigated, *I* would have been the one lying dead on the floor. Both you and I know it!"

"You think the poison was meant for you?" I asked, turning it over in my mind. It did make sense. Why else place the mug where Bob would be the most likely person to pick it up? If the killer didn't know about Lewis's OCD, then they wouldn't know he'd feel compelled to come in to check the mugs. He might not have been the target at all.

"Of course it was," Bob said. "And the only person here who would have done it is him!" He pointed at Jerry with such force, the other man leapt back, smacking his head against the wall in the process.

"Let's not jump to conclusions," I said, taking Bob by the arm so conclusions wouldn't be the only thing he leapt at. "Why would Jerry want to kill you?"

Bob's entire body tensed briefly, before he sucked in a breath and took a step back. I let my hand fall away, but remained positioned so that he couldn't get to Jerry without going through me.

"We work together," Bob said. He glanced around the room, noted everyone was watching him, and then lowered his voice. "Have for the last five, six years."

"So you've known each other for a while."

Bob nodded. "We work at the same accounting firm in Levington."

Levington was the closest city to Pine Hills. It wasn't large by any stretch of the imagination, but compared to our small town, it was nearly a metropolis.

"Last month, I got promoted," Bob went on. "I've worked at the place for twice as long as J., and I deserved it."

Jerry, who'd been listening in, spoke up. "I worked twice as hard as you. No." He shook his head angrily. "Five times. You used to just sit there and watch the rest of us work, and somehow, you get rewarded?"

"I put my time in!" Bob roared. I tensed, waiting for him to throw himself at the smaller man, but he managed to compose himself before losing his temper completely. "I'm better at seeing the big picture than the small stuff. The head honcho saw that, and he rewarded me for it."

I looked to Jerry. "You wanted the promotion?"

He bit his lower lip, looked ready to make a run for it, before he finally nodded. "I didn't just want it. I *needed* it. I'm drowning in debt. You know how it is. Went to college, needed loans." He pressed both hands to his temples, face bunching like he might cry. "Degree amounted to nothing, and come to learn I was a victim of some predatory practices by the loan company. I need the extra money so I can stay above water."

Bob snorted and crossed his arms. He refused to meet Jerry's eye, even as the man gave him a pleading look. It was like Jerry thought that if he begged hard enough, Bob might give up the job right here and now.

"Okay," I said. "I understand why Jerry might be upset. And I can see why you might think he would want to get you out of the way." The last was targeted at Bob. "But do you really think he'd go to all this trouble, just to kill you for a job?"

"People do strange things all the time," Bob said. "And since it doesn't look like there'll be another opening for years without someone dying, killing me would be the only way he could ever hope for a promotion now."

I focused on Jerry, forced him to meet my eye. "Did you try to poison Bob?"

"No! I swear. I didn't get out of my room until after the man was dead. There's no way I could have done it."

"You could have snuck in before we started," Bob said.

"When? I was with you the whole time!"

That caused Bob's brow to furrow. "I suppose you were," he said grudgingly. "But I still don't trust you."

"I didn't do it." Jerry looked around the room. "You have to believe me. I'd never hurt anyone, no matter the reason. I don't have it in me."

I found I believed him. Nothing in Jerry's demeanor screamed "killer" to me. He might be upset that Bob got the promotion over him, but to come all the way to Pine Hills just to murder him? It didn't make much sense. He might have had the motive, but the opportunity? I wasn't so sure.

Still, just because I didn't think Jerry was our killer, it didn't mean Bob wasn't the intended target.

"Do you know anyone else here?" I asked him, keeping my voice low. "Anyone who might want to hurt you?"

He glanced around the room, then shrugged. "If I met anyone before now, I don't remember it. I'm not from here. And if they are a client with the firm, I often do business over the phone, not face-to-face. I wouldn't recognize anyone by sight, and the names aren't familiar, so I doubt it."

I glanced at Jerry.

"I don't know anyone either," he said.

"You say you were with Bob the entire time you were here," I asked him.

"I was. Other than when we were sent to our own rooms, that is."

"When did you escape your room?"

"Well . . ." A flush ran up his neck.

"J.?" Bob asked. The heat returned to his voice.

"I got my door open first," Jerry said. He seemed to shrink in on himself, as if trying to make himself smaller to avoid Bob's wrath. "But I didn't leave my room right away."

"Why not?" I asked. Carol said she'd found the body,

but did that actually mean she was the first to do so? It wouldn't be the first time someone found a dead body and didn't report it right away out of fear of being blamed for the crime.

"I've never liked to be the first at anything," Jerry said. "Even back in school, I'd wait until someone else turned their test in before taking mine to the desk. I don't like all those eyes on me. People get jealous, angry even, when they think you believe you're better than them."

"So, you waited until Carol came out before you exited?"

He nodded, looked to the floor as if ashamed.

"Where was your room?" I asked.

Jerry pointed to the door next to him.

"Okay, let me think." I moved to stand just inside Jerry's room and then turned to study the main room.

The big gift in the center of the table was visible, of course, as were a few of the smaller gifts surrounding it. I could read only a few of the names in front of them, including Jerry's. I couldn't see the spilled hot cocoa, but I *could* see Lewis's covered foot.

But what if he didn't look down? If Jerry had opened the door, saw no one else had escaped, and then chose to remain inside, he might not have thought to look at the floor. The big gift would have drawn his eye. He might not have even glanced Lewis's way.

"Carol was the next one out of her room?" I asked, to be sure. Her door was across the way, and one to the left of where I stood. That would put her door right in line with the body.

"She was," Jerry said.

I played it over in my mind again. I heard the scream and was last out of my room. That meant everyone had escaped at near the same time, all within a few seconds of one another. There wouldn't have been time for anyone to swap out the mugs, if that was indeed what had happened.

A thought hit. "Bob, when I tried to contact you using the mic in my room, it took you a while to respond."

"So?"

"So, what were you doing?"

He glared at me. "What do you think? I was trying to find a way out and it took me a minute to find the mic."

"You didn't sneak out early?"

"How could I? I didn't have the code."

As far as I knew, none of us did. It was possible someone had found a way out of their room, but the more I thought about it, the more unlikely it seemed. It took three people to produce a code to escape our initial rooms. And while it was possible to guess the code, it wouldn't be easy.

Another memory surfaced then: Carol coming from the escape room *before* the event had started.

Could she not only have discovered Lewis's body, but have also been responsible for causing his death as well?

There was only one way to find out.

Chapter Five

"Carol?" I knocked on her door with the back of my hand. "You in there?"

The room behind me was silent. Everyone was watching. Rita stood next to me, hands on her hips, foot tapping. I was afraid that if Carol tried to hide in the room much longer, Rita might break the door down and drag her out of there, like an angry mother might a disobedient child.

A shuffle from inside told me that Carol hadn't found another way to escape the room. That was a positive, I supposed.

"Carol," I said as gently as I could. "We need to talk."

"Leave me alone," she said. It sounded like she was leaning against the door, not cowering across the room. "I didn't do anything wrong."

"No one said you did." I shot a warning look at Rita, who'd opened her mouth to speak. "We're trying to piece things together, and since you were in here before we started, you might have seen something that can help us do that."

Another shuffle. "I'm not coming out."

While I could ask my questions through the door, I didn't want to. Lies could sometimes be seen on a person's face.

Their eyes might dart away, their cheeks, ears, and neck might redden. I needed to know I could trust Carol Kline, and I couldn't do that with a slab of wood between us.

"Please," I said. "No one is going to hurt you."

Her laugh was sharp and was void of humor. "Tell that to Mr. Coates."

I glanced at the gathering behind me. Only June and Troy stood close to one another. Everyone else was spread around the room, shooting distrustful looks at everyone else. If we didn't get to the bottom of Lewis's death soon, I was afraid we'd start having more outbreaks like the one between Jerry and Bob.

"We're all out here now," I said, turning my focus back to Carol and the door she hid behind. "Whoever killed Lewis isn't going to try anything with all of us here. I promise you'll be safe."

"Unless she's the one who killed him," Yuri muttered. I scowled at him, which caused him to raise both hands in front of him in mock surrender.

"Carol," I said when the door didn't open. "Please. You can't hide in there forever. We're going to need to work together to get out of here. We need you for that."

"Someone will come for us."

"Who?" I asked. "It could be hours before anyone realizes something is amiss." All my friends would assume Rita and I had stopped for something to eat after the escape room if I didn't show soon. I was pretty sure it would be much the same for everyone else. "Come on out. We can talk and plan our next move together. I promise we'll keep you safe."

There was a long stretch of silence where I started to wonder if perhaps she'd moved away from the door and was quietly searching for another way out of the room, one that would prevent her from having to face the rest of us. Then there was a faint sound, a muted click. A moment later, the door opened and Carol Kline stepped out of her room.

Lewis's death had affected her greatly. Already, her eyes were red and sunken in as if she'd spent hours crying. Her once-vibrant face looked hollow and drawn. She didn't look like a woman mourning a stranger, but, rather, a close friend.

"I didn't do anything," she said, meeting my eye. "This is too much for me." Her gaze flickered to Lewis before she squeezed her eyes shut.

I took her gently by the arm and led her away from the door, to an empty corner of the room where Lewis's body wasn't visible. The red and green Christmas lights did her no favors as she stood beneath them, next to a child's rocking horse made up to look like a Clydesdale.

"I'm trying to figure out exactly what happened," I told her. "So I'm going to ask you a few questions. I'm not accusing you of anything. I'm simply trying to get the facts and organize a timeline. Would that be okay?"

She nodded, but her expression didn't change. "You might not be accusing me of anything, but they are."

I glanced back toward where both Yuri and Bob had drawn near. I gave them each a warning look to keep back, before turning my focus back to Carol.

"Everyone's scared," I said. "Don't worry about them and just tell the truth. If you do that, there's nothing to be frightened of."

Carol took a moment to simply breathe before she spoke again. "I don't know what I can tell you. I didn't see anything other than Mr. Coates. He was already dead by then."

"You didn't see anyone else in the room at the time?"

She shook her head. "As far as I am aware, I was the

first to escape." Her eyes drifted back toward her door. I could tell she longed to lock herself back inside.

"You didn't see Jerry?" I asked, pointing him out in case she'd forgotten who he was.

"I didn't," she said. "When I opened my door, all I saw was Mr. Coates. It took me a few seconds to process what I was seeing, and I may have screamed." Her face flushed at that. "I didn't mean to. It was just so shocking."

"I totally understand," I said. "I might have done the same if it had been me."

"I wasn't sure what to do with myself." Carol wrapped her arms around her midsection. "Then everyone started piling out of their rooms, causing a ruckus. I hoped that it was all part of the game, that Lewis would pop up and tell us everything was okay, but he didn't." Tears welled in her eyes as she repeated, "He didn't."

"Did you know Lewis well?" I asked.

Carol shook her head. "I'd never met him before today. I knew his name, of course, but this was the first time we had a chance to meet."

I wondered if she was telling the truth, since she seemed pretty upset by his death. Then again, finding a dead body did things to a person, whether you knew the victim or not. Carol Kline seemed as if she might be empathic, so it's entirely possible she'd have the same reaction to someone she'd never laid eyes upon before in her life.

"You came into the room before we got started, right?" I asked her, moving on to what I'd originally wanted to know.

"I did," she said, lowering her eyes to look at her folded arms. "I didn't realize how angry Mr. Coates would be if he caught me. I just wanted a peek. There was nothing malicious in it."

"Did you come all the way into the room?" I asked her. "Or did you stop in the hall outside our individual rooms?"

"All the doors were open at the time," she said. "So I came in. I knew I wasn't supposed to, but figured there would be little harm in it. I suppose I was trying to cheat a little too, get a head start, if you know what I mean? I wanted us to escape and thought that if I saw the layout before we got started, I could work through it faster."

"I doubt anyone would hold that against you," I said, offering her a reassuring smile before going on. "Did you see anything when you came in?"

"See anything?" she asked. "Like what?"

"Was someone else in the room? A stranger perhaps?"

"*A stranger?* Do you mean like someone who snuck in?"

Honestly, I wasn't sure what I'd meant, but I nodded anyway.

"No," Carol said. "I was the only one inside. I suppose someone else might have been here, since I didn't go through all the little side rooms, but if they were, I sure didn't see them."

"What about the main room itself?" I asked. "Was it the same as when you saw it the first time, after you escaped?"

She frowned, eyes going briefly distant. "I'm not sure. I mean, I think it was, but it wasn't like I stuck around for long. I came in, took a quick walk around the big gift in the middle of the room, and then I headed out to join the rest of you. After I escaped my room, I didn't see much else other than Mr. Coates." She paled slightly, but seemed to be handling his death a little better now that she was talking it out.

"Take a quick look." I took a step to the side so she could see the room better. "Is anything different? Anything at all?"

Carol scanned the room. Her gaze lingered on the others, as if weighing their thoughts before she truly started focusing on the objects set up around the room.

While she did that, Rita leaned in close and whispered, "Do you think she did it?"

"I don't know," I said, watching Carol carefully. If she killed Lewis, I was hoping she'd give something away while looking around the room. What? I had no idea. I wasn't even sure I'd know it when I saw it.

Carol walked around the outside edge of the space, taking everything in bit by bit. I followed in her wake, giving her room to work without feeling stifled, but not straying too far away, just in case she made a run for it.

Then her breath caught and she took a hesitant step forward, brow furrowing. She glanced at me, then back toward where Lewis lay.

"What is it?" I asked her. I met Yuri's eye. He was frowning hard at where Carol was looking.

"The mug," she said. "It's different."

"We already figured that out," Bob said.

"No, I mean, it was like all the others earlier," she said. "It didn't register until now."

"Are you sure?" I asked. If what she was saying was true, that meant the killer was likely in the room with us now. A part of me had hoped the poisoned mug had been placed *before* the escape room had begun.

"I'm sure," she said. "When I walked around the table, I read every name." She glanced up and shrugged when she saw how some of the others were looking at her. "I was curious to see if I recognized any of you, had you in class."

"Did you?" I asked.

Another shrug. "First names don't really help," she said. "As a former teacher, I've seen them all at least a dozen times over." She took another step toward the table, but kept well away from Lewis's body. "I had to lean in close to read the names, though. I see well enough normally, but I do need reading glasses."

I looked to the table, at one of the undisturbed mugs. The tag hanging from the gift there hung down low, right next to the mug of the now-cool hot cocoa. If Carol had leaned in to read them, it would have put her face right next to the mugs themselves.

"There was nothing in the mugs at the time," she went on. "I remember thinking it odd, but figured he'd eventually fill them with something." The pained look she gave me was heartbreaking. "I guess he did that when he left us alone to get to know one another, didn't he?"

I wanted to comfort her, to tell her everything would be fine, but I pressed her instead. "Are you sure all the mugs were the same earlier?"

"I'm positive they were."

This time, I met Rita's eye. She was thinking the same thing I was.

If the mugs were the same when we were led into our rooms, that meant that they were changed sometime after, while we were all supposedly trying to escape.

If no one else had snuck in while we were searching our individual rooms, then that meant that the killer was one of us.

And the original mug might still be with them.

I sorted through what I knew and tried to pinpoint when the mugs could have been swapped. If Carol was telling the truth, it would need to have happened after we were locked up in our rooms. Lewis came into the central room at some point before we escaped, picked up the odd mug, and then died from what I assumed was a pretty strong poison.

That gave the killer less than fifteen minutes to work with. It wasn't a lot of time, but if the murder had been planned—and it would have had to have been, since poison was likely involved—then it was more than enough time to make a quick swap and then sneak away.

My gaze rose to meet Jerry's. He was the first person to get his door open. While he claimed he didn't leave his room until after Carol had escaped her own room, that didn't necessarily make it true. Guilty people lied all the time.

"Thank you, Carol," I said, patting her on the arm before crossing the room to where Jerry stood. He looked wildly around, as if seeking an escape as I approached. "Anything to say?" I asked him.

"Me? No."

"J.?" Bob asked. "If you were trying to kill me . . ."

"I didn't do anything!"

"Then you wouldn't mind us checking your room," I said. If the killer had indeed swapped mugs while we were working our way out of our rooms, they would likely have hidden it afterward. What better place than a room full of knickknacks?

"My room?" Jerry asked. His eyes kept getting bigger and bigger and they darted every which way, not settling on any one person or thing. "Why?"

"To look for the original mug."

Bob sucked in a breath, and then before anyone, let alone Jerry, could object, he marched past us, into the room. The rest of us followed after and stood in a loose huddle around the entrance, while Bob tore the room apart.

After only a few minutes, he threw his hands up into the air. "Nothing."

Jerry sagged against the door frame, as if he hadn't been sure what his coworker might find.

"We should check everyone's room," Troy said. He stood to the back of the group, standing apart from June for the first time since they'd arrived. "If someone here changed out the mugs, they might have left it in their room."

"I agree," I said. "We should split up, choose a room of someone you don't know. I'll take Carol's room."

With only a little bit of grumbling, everyone chose a room, and within moments, we were all searching for a mug I wasn't entirely convinced existed. If Carol was wrong, and the mug hadn't been swapped, we were wasting our time.

But if she was right, we could be seconds away from discovering a murderer. That would create an entirely new set of problems for us to deal with, considering we were still locked in together. I, for one, wasn't looking forward to dealing with a killer with no way to escape them if they decided to go on a rampage.

Walking into a Christmas-themed room, knowing evidence to a murder might be lying around, made my heart ache. This was supposed to be a happy time of the year, and now a man was dead. A part of me wished I'd stayed home and prepared for my dad's visit, rather than letting Rita drag me all the way out here.

Yet, at the same time, I was glad I'd come. If I could put another killer behind bars, then all the heartache, all the hassle, would all be worth it.

"Here!" The shout came from a room a few doors down.

Everyone spilled out of the rooms they were checking, to follow the sound of the call. Yuri stood just outside the room he'd searched, pointing inside.

"The mug is in here," he said.

"Whose room is it?" Bob asked. He held a pillow decorated with a large, grinning snowflake. He looked as if he was prepared to use it as a weapon if the need arose.

It took me a moment to reorient myself. All the doorways looked the same. And with no other visible entrance—though there must be one, since Lewis got inside—it was hard to figure out which room was which without going in and checking for familiar signs.

Someone spoke, just as I figured it out.

"Mine." Rita's voice was a shadow of itself as she stepped forward. "The room was mine."

Chapter Six

"Wait!" I said. "Let's think this through." Everyone was staring at Rita, and both Yuri and Bob had started toward her as if to restrain her.

"There's nothing to think about," Yuri said. "The mug was in her room. She did it. She killed Lewis."

"I did no such thing!" Rita was backing up, but before long, she'd have nowhere to go.

"She couldn't have done it," I said, mind racing to come up with a way to get Rita out of this. "She didn't have a chance to swap the mugs."

"Really?" This came from Bob. "And the rest of us did?"

Rita bumped up against the wall between two doors. Carol stood next to her. The older woman appeared undecided, as if she wasn't sure if she should grab Rita to keep her from running, or if she should protect her from the angry men converging on them.

"Perhaps we should hear her out," I said. "Let her explain herself. It's not like she can go anywhere."

"I agree," Carol said. "We can't condemn her yet, not until we know all the facts."

Both men stopped advancing, though neither looked happy about it.

I breathed a sigh of relief and moved to stand next to

Rita. I took her hand and squeezed it to let her know I was still on her side.

"All right, then." Yuri crossed his arms and tapped his foot. "If you didn't do it, explain to us how the mug got into your room."

"Well, I don't rightly know," Rita said. "It wasn't there when I'd searched the room earlier, I'd swear to it. Someone must have planted it there after we escaped!"

Bob snorted. "Who would do something like that?" he asked. "This isn't some movie."

"The killer might have," Carol said. "History is rife with people planting evidence in order to frame someone else for their crimes."

"Rita didn't have the opportunity to swap the mugs," I insisted. "She didn't escape her room until after Lewis was discovered."

"As far as you know, she didn't," Troy said. "She could have gotten out early, killed Mr. Coates, and then snuck back in."

"I never would have done such a thing!" Rita said. "Krissy is right. I never left my room, not until after he was found."

"I think we should tie her up," Yuri said. "Keep her from hurting anyone else."

"And if she didn't do it?" Carol asked. "Then you're detaining an innocent woman."

"Better than leaving a killer run free," Bob said.

"That's enough!" I shouted. "This is getting us nowhere." All eyes turned to me and I lowered my voice. "Rita was talking the entire time she was in her room. If she would have left to kill Lewis, I would have noticed."

"And why should we believe you?" Yuri asked. "You're her friend. You could be covering for her."

"Maybe she's in on it too," Troy said.

"If Rita killed Lewis, I wouldn't protect her," I said. "I'd turn her in to the police myself if I had to."

"What?" Rita turned hurt eyes on me. "I can't believe you'd abandon me like that. After everything I've done for you . . ." She sniffed as if genuinely hurt.

"I'm not abandoning you," I told her before turning back to the group at large. "She's innocent. Yes, I know her, which means, I also know she's incapable of hurting anyone. Something else is going on here."

Glares were shared around the room. Yuri, Troy, and Bob were watching Rita like they thought she might sprout horns and a tail at any moment. Jerry stood quietly alone against the wall, not meeting anyone's eye.

Only June and Carol seemed sympathetic toward Rita, though June would likely side with whatever Troy decided. The mere fact that the men *wanted* her to be guilty was going to make this harder than it should be.

But at least they weren't tying her up with Christmas lights just yet. I had time to make things right.

"Did you touch the mug?" I asked Yuri.

His scowl moved from Rita to me. "No. I'm smarter than that."

"Good. Did anyone have mittens in their room?"

"I did," June said, raising her hand. When everyone looked at her, she reddened.

"Could you get them for me?"

"Why?" Troy asked, holding June tight so she couldn't do as I asked. She looked uncomfortable in his grip, but didn't complain.

"We should investigate the mug," I said. "We can't check it for fingerprints here, but maybe there'll be some clue on it that will help us figure out who actually killed Lewis Coates. The mittens will allow me to pick it up without leaving prints of my own." And would hopefully protect any that were there for when we could finally call the police.

Troy didn't look convinced, but he let June go. She gave him a worried look before she hurried into her room to find the mittens.

"We all need to remain calm," I said. "If we keep throwing accusations around before we have any sort of proof of who is actually guilty, we're only going to make things worse."

Jerry chuckled and shook his head. As a target of similar accusations, including ones from me, it was no wonder he found my words amusing.

June returned with the mittens then. They were thick, nearly full-on snow gloves, and were a size too big for my hands, but I pulled them on anyway.

"Show me," I told Yuri.

He shot Rita one more sharp glare before he turned away. "In here."

Rita's room was a mess. The knickknacks, which had sat upon the shelves at the start of the escape room, had been knocked to the floor. Whether by Rita during her search, or when Yuri had entered her room to look for the mug, I didn't know. I had to step over a broken ceramic reindeer on my way in.

"Where?" I asked, appalled by the mess. If Lewis hadn't been murdered, seeing the destruction might have killed him.

Yuri pointed to the corner where a red sleigh leaned against the wall. "Behind that."

I crossed the room and knelt beside the sleigh. It was one of those smaller ones that are more often referred to as a sled, but it amounted to the same thing. It could fit two sitting adults, maybe three if they were small and were smooshed together.

Thanks to the Christmas lights on the wall above, and

the slats of the sleigh itself, there was light sifting in behind it. The mug sat on the floor, half covered by a baby's blanket, the kind with an animal head on one end. This one was a polar bear. Its wide black eyes stared back at me, almost accusingly, as I brushed it aside so I could pull the mug out from behind the sleigh.

As I rose, I noted the mug was indeed a match for the others in the central room. Using just my fingertips on the handle, I carried it out into the main room, where everyone else was waiting. I moved to stand where the light was best and turned the mug over in my hand.

"Well?" Bob asked.

The inside of the mug glimmered faintly as I looked inside it. The number 7 was written in black ink inside, on the bottom, but it was the shimmer that I was most interested in.

I ran a finger along the inside of the mug. "It's damp inside." The mittens were black, with a wreath design on the back, so I couldn't see much in the way of color. I brought my finger up to my nose and sniffed. "Chocolate."

"As in hot cocoa?" Carol asked, even as she took a step away from Rita.

I nodded and spun the mug around in my hand a few more times. "There's nothing else on it that will tell us who might have hidden it in Rita's room." I'd been hoping for a clue of some sort, but, apparently, our killer was smarter than that. "It does tell us something important, though."

"What's that?" Yuri asked.

"The mug was swapped *after* Lewis filled it with hot cocoa. That means Carol didn't make the change when she came in here before the event started."

Carol's hand fluttered to her chest and a relieved look came over her face. "I told you I had nothing to do with it."

"Just because she didn't do it then, doesn't mean she didn't do it later," Bob said. "She *was* the first out of the room."

"As far as we know," I said, glancing at Jerry. "What we do know is that the mug was on the table with the others when Lewis came in to fill them. Afterward, he led us to our rooms, where we entered, alone. During that time, someone snuck out and swapped the mugs before anyone else escaped. It's the only thing that makes sense."

"It has to be her," Troy said, pointing at Rita. "The mug was in her room. She snuck out, swapped them out, and then took it back to her room to hide it."

"We can't be sure of that yet," I said. "What we do know is that Lewis must have seen the mug. I don't see a camera anywhere, but I imagine he had a way to keep tabs on us."

June's eyes widened as she looked around the room.

"If he was watching, then wouldn't he have seen who swapped the mugs?" Jerry asked.

"It's possible," I said. "He could have been watching the whole thing, including the swap."

"And what?" Carol asked. "He came in to investigate?"

"He'd almost have to, wouldn't he?" I said. "Someone messed with his game. He might not have thought it was anything sinister, just a prank, but he would have come in to see why the mug was changed out."

"If he wasn't watching, he wouldn't have known to come in," June said.

"Which brings us back to the idea that perhaps Lewis wasn't the intended victim," Yuri said.

All eyes swiveled to Jerry.

"I didn't do it!" It came out as a whine. "How many times do I have to say it?"

"I need a box," I said. Just holding the mug was giving

me the heebie-jeebies. It might not have been the murder weapon, but it *had* played a role in Lewis's death. "Something we can use to store evidence for the police."

"One sec." Carol vanished into her room and returned a moment later with a holiday-themed popcorn tin. "Will this work?"

I took the tin from her and checked inside to make sure it was empty. "It's perfect." I carefully placed the mug inside, standing it up so the hot cocoa remnants wouldn't leak out. I then went to Lewis's body. Using the rim, rather than the booby-trapped handle, I picked up the murder weapon and set it inside with the other. After a moment's thought, I added both mittens, just in case I'd gotten something on them when touching the mugs.

"You're probably contaminating evidence putting them together like that," Bob grumbled, but he didn't make a move to stop me.

Carol handed me the lid to the tin and I sealed it closed. I placed it in a corner where we could all keep an eye on it. If the killer decided to try to dispose of it, someone would inevitably see them.

Once that was done, I turned to face Yuri. "When did you escape your room?" I asked him.

"Me?" he asked. "Why?"

"I know for a fact Rita didn't kill Lewis." Both Bob and Troy made disgruntled sounds at that, but I ignored them. "Which means, someone else did."

"And you think it was me?" Yuri asked with a laugh. "Why would I kill him?"

"I don't know," I said. "And I never said you did. But instead of us standing around, accusing each other of murder, don't you think it would be best if we all explained how we *couldn't* have done it?"

Yuri narrowed his eyes at me, as if suspecting I had ulterior motives, which, admittedly, I did. I wanted to take the heat off of Rita, and, hopefully, get to the bottom of this mess before someone did something stupid.

"I didn't pay attention to who escaped before me," he said. "All I know for sure was it was after Carol screamed, but before a lot of you got out."

"Was anyone with you when you went into Rita's room?"

He opened his mouth, and then closed it again without speaking. Instead, he crossed his arms and glared. He knew exactly why I was asking.

"If we assume Rita had nothing to do with the murder, then that means the mug was planted, right?"

No answer, not that I expected one.

"Since you knew the rooms were going to be searched, it isn't hard to imagine you grabbing the mug and taking it into Rita's room to hide it. Then, while the rest of us are searching elsewhere, you conveniently find it, putting her in the crosshairs."

"I did no such thing," Yuri said.

"You *were* alone in there," Bob said.

"That doesn't mean I hid the mug," he said. "I found it, that's all. Besides, when would I have retrieved the mug anyway? I didn't go into my room, and I surely wasn't carrying it around with me this entire time."

It was my turn to open my mouth and then close it without a word. His shirt fit snugly around his torso, and his pants were likewise tight. There was no way he could have hidden a bulky mug on him; none of us could have.

"You could have hidden it in the room here," June said. Her voice was small, frightened, as if she was afraid that accusing Yuri of anything might turn her into the next target. "And then grabbed it when no one was looking."

"Impossible," Yuri said. "I might have gone into the

room by myself, but he saw me do it." He pointed at Bob. "He knows I didn't have time to dig the thing out from wherever you think I might have hidden it before starting my search, not without getting caught."

"That's true," Bob said.

"Maybe we should focus on who had an opportunity to swap the mugs in the first place," Carol said. "That's the most important element here, don't you think?"

As much as I'd hoped to find a clue on who hid the mug in Rita's room, Carol was right. If we figured out who wasn't where they were supposed to be while the rest of us were trying to escape our individual rooms, then we'd likely have our killer.

My gaze swept across the room, hoping to glean something from the faces of the people there. Rita looked both worried and annoyed to have been thrust into the focus of the investigation, but was thankfully not in any more risk, as of yet. Yuri looked angry. June and Troy were clutching at one another like they feared they'd be torn apart.

Then, as my eyes passed over Bob, I was once again reminded of his delay in answering me when we were trapped in our initial rooms. He'd said it was because he couldn't find the mic, but they weren't exactly hidden. As soon as he heard my voice, he'd know where to look.

Bob's head turned my way, as if he could feel my stare. His eyes were bloodshot, narrowed. We maintained eye contact for a good five seconds before he spoke.

"I need a moment to clear my head," he said, before he turned and walked into the room he'd been locked in earlier. He pushed the door closed, but not all the way, so it didn't lock.

"What are we going to do?" Carol asked.

I stared after Bob, and then made up my mind. "Bob's

right. We all need to clear our heads. Let's take five minutes to think things through."

No one seemed happy about it, but that was none of my concern. I had other reasons for wanting a few minutes without everyone breathing down my neck.

Making sure no one was watching me too carefully, I crossed the room, and then slipped into the room Bob Mackey had vanished into a moment before.

Chapter Seven

Bob stood at the far end of the room, shoulders hunched. His back was to me, so I couldn't tell what he was doing, though I assumed it wasn't anything good. A small, ceramic Christmas tree sat on a table next to him. Its plug hung over the edge of the table to dangle just above the floor.

"Couldn't take it," Bob said, glancing back at me. The look in his eye told me he wasn't surprised I'd followed him. He patted his suit jacket pocket before he wiped his nose with the back of his hand and turned. "The blinking. The lights. They made my head hurt."

"Do you need to take something?" I asked. I had ibuprofen in my purse, which I couldn't get to anyway, but I hadn't intended the question to be taken seriously.

Bob's smile didn't reach his eyes. It was pained, almost self-deprecating in nature. "Oh, I already have everything I need. I'm just not sure it's actually helping anything. It rarely does, to be honest."

We stood facing one another from across the room in tense silence. I wasn't sure how to broach the subject of his whereabouts during our initial escape without sounding accusatory. Out in the main room, I could hear the others talking amongst themselves. No one was yelling, which I took as a good sign.

Bob ran a hand over his mouth, and then looked at it like he expected to find something there. "What is it you want from me?" he asked. "You didn't follow me in here because you wanted to admire the view. Might have thought it possible a few years back, when I was younger and fitter, but not now." His laugh was bitter.

"I wanted to ask you a few questions about earlier, when we were escaping these rooms." I indicated the overly jolly room. "For clarification purposes."

Bob blinked at me. He, otherwise, didn't respond.

Okay, then. There was something going on with him, something I couldn't pinpoint. This wasn't the same loud man who'd shouted down his coworker. A darkness hung over him, and I had to wonder if it had something to do with Lewis's murder.

"Do you remember when we were trapped in our individual rooms, how I talked to you through the mic?"

"I do. You needed Christmas trees." He nudged the ceramic one next to him with his elbow.

"I did. But when I first tried to talk to you, you didn't respond right away."

Another long blink before, "And? I already told you what happened."

"You did," I said. "But I don't quite buy it. It should have only taken you a couple of seconds to find the mic and respond, but it took nearly a minute."

Bob grunted a laugh and ran his fingers through his hair before looking to the ceiling. "I knew I shouldn't have come here. Dark is better. Dark is safer, yet I was so sick of movies and alleyways. I thought . . . Honestly, I don't know what I thought. I needed somewhere to go, and this sounded like something that might help, I don't know, ease my mind."

"*Ease your mind?* What do you mean by that?"

Bob's gaze dropped to mine. That self-deprecating smile was back. He reached into his inner suit pocket, causing me to tense, but it wasn't a weapon he pulled free.

It was a flask.

"Wife hates it." He unscrewed the cap and took a long pull from the flask before capping it. "I hate it. But you know how it is. Once you start, it's not like you can just up and quit. Mouth goes dry, and mind gets stuck on repeat. Can't help yourself."

He stared at the flask before tucking it back into his pocket.

"I've never hit my wife, or gotten too drunk to stand. But the smell, it sticks with you. No matter how many mints I eat, how much mouthwash I use, it's there. And then my health . . ." He shook his head, then spread his hands. "Look at me. I'm sure it's slowly killing me—these things always do."

"You're an alcoholic." It was a statement, not a question, but he answered anyway.

"I suppose you could say that. I've never thought of myself as such, but look at me now. Who else, other than an alcoholic, would come to an escape room, just to find a safe place to drink?"

"You came here *to drink*?"

He laughed at the disbelief in my voice. "It wasn't my intent at first, but as soon as J. asked me to come along with him, I figured, why not? I did my research, learned we'd start in little rooms by ourselves, and thought I could take a couple minutes to myself and have a few quiet sips without anyone nagging me. Barely had time to take the first pull before you were asking me to scour the room for trees."

"That's why you sounded breathless," I said. If he was tipping the flask back, knowing he only had a few minutes before he'd be forced to join the main group, he'd have rushed, would have drunk faster than he rightfully should.

"I barely had time to enjoy it," Bob said. He wiped his nose again, before he reached into his jacket. His hand paused, halfway to grabbing the flask again, before he removed it, empty. "Maybe it's a sign. Maybe if I'd been more concerned about escaping my room, rather than seeing how much I could drink before time ran out, I could have saved that guy."

"You can't blame yourself," I said. "I'm not sure any of us could have stopped what happened." And that's not to mention the fact that if he'd gotten out of his room earlier, *he* might have been the one with the pricked finger.

Bob shrugged one shoulder. "Guess we'll never know."

"You said Jerry asked you to come to this?" I asked, not wanting to dwell on the "could have" possibilities.

"He did."

"Was that normal?"

Bob glanced up at me. "I didn't think much about it at the time." His eyes hardened. "But now, I'm starting to wonder if he asked me to come here with him so he could kill me." Both his fists clenched, and with the flush on his cheeks, I was afraid he'd had a little too much to drink, despite his claims that he'd barely gotten started. Drunk people did stupid things all the time.

Even if Jerry *was* guilty of Lewis's murder, I couldn't let Bob enact drunken justice on him. It would only make matters worse, and likely get him into trouble with the police afterward.

"How did you find out that you'd have time to yourself here?" I asked him. I'd looked the escape room up, but hadn't found much online about it. Lewis had a website, but there were no pictures of any of the rooms he'd run, let alone descriptions of what to expect.

"One of J.'s friends did this last week. It's how J. knew about it. The guy works with us, so I took the guy aside and asked him about it. He was all too eager to tell me exactly how this thing was supposed to go. I think he was hoping it would score him a few extra points with me, like it would somehow speed his advancement at the firm." He glanced around the room and frowned. "Though there are some pretty significant changes from what he'd told me, so his info didn't help me all that much."

"What do you mean?" I asked.

"I don't know." He touched the ceramic Christmas tree, fingers barely brushing it as if he was afraid it might break. "The items are different. The number of them. I guess he changes things up between sessions."

Which was understandable. If you kept everything static, it wouldn't be long before everyone would know exactly what to do. I imagined it wasn't only the numbers that changed, but the method of obtaining them as well.

"Do you think the guy who killed that Lewis guy knew what to do?" Bob asked. "Like, he'd learned the codes ahead of time?"

"I don't know," I said. "It's possible."

Bob nodded, then scrubbed his hands over his face. "We should probably get back before the others start to wonder what we're up to. I don't need those kinds of rumors floating about, especially since J. wouldn't hesitate to spread them around the office. Wife wouldn't think twice about kicking me out of the house if she learned about this." He patted his pocket. "She'd be happier if I *was* cheating."

"I won't tell," I promised him.

Bob and I left the room and found the others standing almost exactly where we'd left them. Troy was by the door, attempting to crack the code once again. He typed in a few numbers, tried the door, and then punched it when his latest attempt failed.

"We should talk." Jerry approached Bob with a somber look on his face. "Alone."

Bob heaved a sigh, but nodded. They both looked at me expectantly.

I was able to take a hint. With a slight nod to Bob, I left them to it, choosing to join Rita where she stood with Carol.

"Discover anything that will help us get out of this mess?" Rita asked.

"Not really," I said. "I don't think Bob was involved, however. How about you? Did you learn anything new?"

"There's nothing *to* learn," Carol said. "Everyone's keeping to themselves, won't talk to anyone they don't know."

"Almost everyone," Rita amended. "That Yuri fellow tried to mess with Lewis's body while you were gone. We stopped him."

"Didn't think it was right to be messing about like that," Carol said. "Let the dead lie in peace, I say."

Yuri was leaning against the wall in the far corner. He was watching everyone with a suspicious gleam in his eye. When his gaze passed over me, those eyes further narrowed, before moving on to watch Troy try yet another code.

"Why do you think he was wanting to look at the body?" I asked.

"Well, how would I know that?" Rita said. "He didn't exactly tell us what he was doing. Just scowled and walked away when we stopped him."

"I think Yuri knew Mr. Coates pretty well," Carol said. "Didn't the two of them talk before we got started?"

I thought back and realized that, yes, Lewis and Yuri *had* acted like they'd known one another. Yuri had called Lewis his "friend," but by the scowl on Lewis's face at the time, I don't think it was an entirely accurate statement.

"I'll be right back," I said, before walking over to join Yuri.

"What do you want?" he asked, crossing his arms. His glare intensified, as if he thought he could scare me away just by looking mean.

"You knew Lewis Coates," I said. "Before all of this."

"And?"

No denial. Just the one word. I hesitated, not quite sure how to continue. It wasn't like Yuri had hidden his relationship with Lewis. He'd admitted to knowing the guy from the start. Would someone do that if they planned on killing a guy later?

"Did you get along with him?" I asked.

Yuri's shoulders eased and he dropped his arms. "Look, I knew him. We weren't friends, if that's what you were thinking. The guy didn't much care for me, and I felt the same about him. But that doesn't mean I killed him."

"When you first saw him today, you called him 'my friend,' " I reminded him.

"I liked to tweak his nose," Yuri said. "Give him a hard time. It wasn't like we were mortal enemies or anything."

"Have you done any of his escape rooms before? Or know someone who had?" I asked, thinking back to what Bob had said. If someone knew the codes ahead of time, it would make it easy for them to slip out, swap the mugs, and get back before anyone was the wiser.

"One or two. Never this one." He nodded toward the big gift in the center of the room. "I'm not usually into Christmas stuff like this. It's too . . . cheerful." He made a disgusted face.

"So, you've done a few? Is that how you met Lewis?"

Yuri crossed his arms again. "I said I've done escape rooms. Didn't say I did one of his. The first was in Vegas a few years back. Another at a wedding, if you can believe it."

"So, then, how do you and Lewis know one another?" If it wasn't through the escape rooms, but something else that connected them more intimately, it would go a long way in proving a motive.

"Our paths crossed a time or two," Yuri said. "He works security, uses computers. I use them too, just in a different capacity. But we were never competitors, never had cause to fight. He was uptight, rude, and always acted as if he was better than everyone else. I felt the need to knock him down a few pegs over the years. Gives me a laugh."

"He didn't seem very happy to see you," I said. "Were you two arguing?"

"That's none of your business," Yuri said.

"Come on, Yuri. The man's dead. Secrets aren't exactly your friend right now."

He sneered, but answered. "We didn't get along. What do you think he said? He told me I should leave him alone. I made a joke about him slipping in his job or some such. He hardly heard me, though. He was distracted, kept missing what I said. Felt like he was angry at something else."

"Like?" I prodded.

"How should I know? The guy wouldn't meet my eye. Kept looking past me and scowling. Then that woman over there came out of the room, which set him off further." Yuri leaned forward, lowered his voice. "Honestly, if Lewis *was* the intended victim, I think he knew who the killer was from the start."

"You think he knew someone was trying to kill him?"

"That, or intended him some ill will. He was more fidgety than normal, quicker to anger. Can't say who it was, though. I don't know the lot of you, and don't plan to." He leaned against the wall, turned his head away from me.

Apparently, our conversation was over.

Bob and Jerry shook hands and parted at the same time I turned away from Yuri. Neither looked thrilled about whatever they'd discussed, but at least they weren't at one another's throats.

"This is getting us nowhere," Troy said, stepping away from the lock. "We need to get out of here."

"And how do you propose we do that?" Yuri asked. "Break the door down?"

"Why don't we do what we all came here to do in the first place?" Bob asked.

All eyes drifted to the table and the waiting gifts.

"What if they're booby-trapped like the mug?" June asked, hugging herself. "Can we take that risk?"

"Do we have any choice?" Carol said. "I don't want to die any more than you do, but if we don't do something, we aren't getting out of here any time soon."

"I would rather not starve to death," Yuri said, shooting a glance at Lewis's body.

I doubted we'd be trapped here for *that* long, but I understood the point.

"Bob's right," I said, taking a step toward the table. "We need to get out of here." I eyed the gifts, the mugs of now-cold hot cocoa. "And from the look of things, there's only one way we're going to do that."

"Okay, then," June said. "Who's going to go first?"

Everyone looked to everyone else. No one volunteered, which wasn't exactly surprising. One man was dead already. None of us wanted to join him.

But someone had to take that first step, or else we'd be waiting until police officer Paul Dalton or someone else decided to come looking for us. That could still be hours from now.

I couldn't handle hours more of waiting, especially with a killer in the room.

I took a deep breath and walked around the table until I found my name. "I'll do it," I said. And then, with everyone else watching with bated breath, I reached for the Christmas gift with my name on it.

Chapter Eight

The package was one of those prewrapped gifts, the kind where the lid was wrapped separately and could be lifted from the rest without unwrapping anything. I did just that.

Nothing exploded. No needles shot into my finger. And, thankfully, nothing leapt out at me like a demented jack-in-the-box.

I let out the pent-up breath, which I didn't realize I'd been holding, and peered over the edge.

"What's inside it?" Rita asked.

I checked every corner to make sure nothing was hidden in the packaging and then I removed a small Rudolph with a tag hanging from it. I twice turned the reindeer over in my hand, before checking the tag. I read aloud: " 'My nose is bright. I light the way. But the glow does not make me what I am today.' "

"What does that mean?" Yuri asked.

"I'm not sure," I said. I fiddled with Rudolph's nose, turned him over twice more, but I saw nothing that told me how the clue worked with the figure.

"Maybe we need to look at the other gifts before we can make sense of it," Carol said.

No one made a move for the table.

"We need to do this if we want to get out of here," I reminded them. "If you're careful when you open your presents, you should be fine."

"Unless it's rigged to blow," Yuri said.

"I don't think that's going to happen," I said. "The mug was poisoned. That's a very specific, very direct way to kill someone. I don't think the killer wanted to hurt anyone else."

I looked from face to face, hoping that Lewis's killer would show some sign that they agreed with me, but no one reacted in any way I found suspicious.

"Oh, I'll do it," Rita said. She marched up to the package with her name on it and gave everyone a stern look. "You're all acting like a bunch of cowards, you know that?"

As she reached for her lid, June stepped forward, toward her own gift. Both Troy and Jerry quickly followed suit. They were then joined by a more tentative Carol and Yuri.

Bob, however, remained standing where he was.

"Not happening," he said. "If my mug was booby-trapped, there's a chance my gift will be as well. I'm not going to risk dying over some stupid game."

"It looks the same as the others," Carol said. "I don't think it was swapped out like the mug."

"I don't care." He crossed his arms. "Someone else can open it if they want. I'm not touching the thing."

Lids popped off and trinkets were removed. Rita had a Christmas tree, Yuri a snow globe featuring a gingerbread house. Every item was Christmas themed, and each and every one had a short poem written on their tags.

" 'Beneath a star, a globe burns bright'?" Rita said. "What is that supposed to mean?"

"Mine isn't much clearer," Carol said. She held out her tag to Rita, who read it and shook her head.

I met Bob's eye, daring him to open his gift. He stared right back without blinking. So, with a frustrated sigh, I walked over to stand next to Lewis's body, making sure not to step in the spilled hot cocoa. My hand hovered just over the box, but a stab of fear shot through me, keeping me from touching it.

What if it is *booby-trapped?* The killer could have set traps on both items, just in case one of them missed the mark. It wouldn't be hard to slip a needle into the lid, or on whatever item was inside. One wrong move and I wouldn't care one way or another if we ever got out of here; I wouldn't be caring about much of anything anymore.

But everyone was watching me. I knew if I didn't open the gift, we wouldn't know what to do to obtain the code to the door. Of course we could probably guess the final digit once we had the rest figured out. But what if this step merely allowed us to retrieve Santa's gift, and we would need to do something else in order to open the final door? We couldn't do that without Bob's clue.

My hand hit the top of the box. I grabbed the lid, wincing only slightly. When nothing poked my finger, I jerked upward, fully expecting something to fly out at me.

Nothing did.

The tension released from my shoulders, and then I leaned over the table to look inside the box.

"It's a snowman," I said. I picked it up to show everyone. "Is it safe?" June asked.

I turned it over in my hand, carefully inspecting it. "No needles," I said. Then, before reading what the tag said, I tossed it to Bob.

His eyes widened, and his body tensed as if he might leap out of the way like I'd thrown a grenade at him. Instead, he caught the snowman, wincing like he expected it to hurt; then, with a relieved grin, he checked the tag.

"Something about button eyes and coats," he said, his grin melting into a frown. "I can't make heads or tails of it."

I glanced around the room. "There's a tree," I said, indicating the Christmas tree across the room. "And there's a reindeer with a red nose."

"Do you think that's what we need to do?" Jerry asked. "Check the decorations around the room?"

"I doubt we need to return to our starting rooms, so yeah," I said. "Find the object that matches your figure and examine it."

"I can't wait to get out of here," Troy muttered as he made for the string of Christmas lights hanging around the room. He had a small string of them in his hands, and I noted the color pattern wasn't alternating, but had two red bulbs next to one another, followed by a green, then a single red. I was sure he'd noticed the same, so I let him get to work.

While the others checked their own items, I headed for the Rudolph in the corner, but my mind wasn't on the riddle. I kept thinking that once the door was open, the killer would walk right out of our lives. Once that happened, the chances of them getting caught would plummet.

I had no doubt the mug that killed Lewis would be clean of prints. Why go to the trouble of murdering someone that way, and then leave evidence that could easily be traced? Gloves would solve that. And while the suspect list was rather short, we weren't even sure Lewis was the intended victim.

I ran my hand over Rudolph's back. Brown felt covered the reindeer in place of fur. His nose was a simple red lightbulb, much like the ones decorating the rest of the room. I unscrewed it, but there was nothing inside the hole left in his face, nor was there anything on the light itself.

I returned the bulb, and then read the riddle again.

" 'But the glow does not make me what I am today,' " I said aloud. So it was not the nose, then.

I stepped back and looked Rudolph over. I doubted it was the felt covering him. There were no seams, no way to remove it to get to his insides. His tail didn't move, and his hooves were a part of the whole, and didn't come off.

My gaze traveled from his hooves and tail, all the way up to his head.

And the antlers there.

The story came back to me. Rudolph was young, his antlers mere stubs that would eventually grow out.

The reindeer in front of me had a full rack sitting atop his head.

I ran my hand along Rudolph's antlers, looking for anything that stood out. Near the tip of the longest antler on the left side, I found a seam. Careful, as not to break anything, I wiggled it back and forth, until it clicked. The antler opened, revealing a hidden compartment within.

"Got ya," I said as I stuck a finger inside. I immediately regretted it, remembering the needle in the mug, but my finger didn't get pricked. Instead, I felt the edge of a piece of paper tucked just inside the cavity. I worked it free, and then, with a triumphant grin, opened it.

3.

"Oh!" Rita exclaimed as I shoved the number into my

pocket. "I think I have it." She removed a glitter-covered ornament from the tree. When the light struck it, it seemed to glow like a star. She popped off the top and removed a number of her own. "Seven!"

Others around the room began finding their numbers, calling them out excitedly as they did. For a brief few minutes, it appeared as if everyone had forgotten about the murder and were enjoying the escape room like they'd originally intended. There were smiles, brief chuckles.

But then the humor dried up as we all turned back to face one another.

"How do we know what to do with them?" June asked.

"We input them into the code box," Bob said. "Did everyone find theirs?"

A round of affirmative answers followed.

"Yeah, but what order do we put them in?" she asked. "There's what? Eight of us? Think of how many combinations there are with eight numbers. It could take all day."

"But we'd get out of here," Bob said.

"The hot cocoa mugs," Troy said. "We should empty them."

"Why?" Jerry asked, eyeing his mug with a healthy dose of distrust. I couldn't say I blamed him after what had happened to Lewis.

The number I'd seen in the bottom of Bob's mug came back to me. There had to be a reason for the hot cocoa to be there. I mean, nearly everything else was part of the game, so why not the cocoa and mug? Once the mugs were emptied, the numbers would be revealed. Could that be our order? Or were the numbers tucked inside our clues our order?

"What about the big gift in the center?" Carol asked as

I tried to work it through. "Shouldn't we be doing something about it too?"

"It's probably part of the story," Bob said. "But I doubt we need it for getting out of here." He pointed to where the gift was connected to the table by a chain. "There's a lock that requires a key. So, unless our numbers open some other box around here, I don't think we need to worry about it."

"I think we should check the mugs," Troy insisted. "They're there for a reason." He strode forward and picked up his mug. At least half of us sucked in a sharp breath, as if afraid he'd suddenly collapse and fall dead like Lewis.

Instead, he upended the cold cocoa on the floor. With hardly a glance, he flipped the mug around to show us all the number within.

"See," he said. "Our order."

"How in the world did you figure that out?" Bob muttered.

"Who cares? I want out of here." Jerry scurried forward and emptied his mug onto the floor like Troy.

"What if that's there for the gift?" June asked. "I think we should check it, just to be sure."

"Forget the gift," Bob said. "We need to get out of here." He looked at the empty spot where his mug had been, then at the popcorn tin in which it now sat. He paled. "Guess we can figure mine out once we have the rest."

I already knew the number, having seen it when I'd put the mug in the tin, but I wasn't going to tell him that.

Another thought had hit me, one that pushed all thoughts of escaping right out of my head.

"I know," I said, unable to believe I hadn't figured it out before then. All the clues were there; I'd been too distracted with the escape room to notice them until now.

"Know what, dear?" Rita asked. She had her mug in hand, but had yet to dump it.

I took a deep breath, and then let it out between my teeth before looking at each and every face in the room. When I spoke, I did so slowly, clearly, so that everyone could understand me.

"I know who killed Lewis Coates."

Chapter Nine

Tension filled the room as everyone stopped to stare at me. My nerves were jumping as I ran it over in my head again and again. Each time I did, I came to the same conclusion; I knew who killed poor Lewis, though I didn't know why as of yet.

But I hoped to figure that out soon enough.

There wasn't much the killer could do to me with everyone watching, but that didn't mean I was entirely safe. There were objects all over the room, things with sharp points, heavy blunt ends. If I wasn't careful, I could join Lewis on the floor before anyone could step in and stop it.

"What do you mean, you know who killed him?" Bob asked. "How long have you known?"

"Not long," I said. "In fact, the pieces just now fell into place."

Suspicious glances went around the room.

I kept hold of my Rudolph, clutching it like it was the only thing keeping me safe. I glanced at Lewis's covered body, wishing I would have somehow been able to save him, but it wasn't to be. Even if I'd seen the out-of-place mug before he'd touched it, I wouldn't have known what it meant until it was too late.

"Who was it, dear?" Rita asked. "Don't leave us all in suspense!"

I could have pointed a finger and then hoped for the best, but I needed to talk through it first. Not only did I need to hear it out loud myself, but I hoped in doing so, I'd stumble my way to a motive. That would go a long way toward me not sounding like a lunatic.

"It wasn't easy to figure out," I said, meeting everyone's eyes one at a time. No one, not even Lewis's killer, reacted. "There was so much going on, it distracted me from the truth."

I moved to stand so I could see everyone. It put me farther away from the door, but it wasn't like I'd be able to escape that way. It also had the benefit of putting me farther away from the killer, so I'd take it.

"There needed to be an opportunity," I said. "Carol coming into the room early must have felt like a blessing. She didn't know it, but her curiosity caused her to play right into the killer's hands. How easy would it be to pin the murder on someone who was somewhere they shouldn't be, someone who was snooping where the murder would soon take place?"

"I was just looking," Carol muttered, looking down at the folded piece of paper in her hands.

"Then she was the first to escape her room, which meant it would be even easier to accuse her of being the killer." I paused, then looked to Jerry. "But she wasn't the first to get her door open, was she?"

"I didn't do it," Jerry said, eyes widening. He looked wildly from me, to Bob, and then back again. "I didn't kill anyone."

"No, you didn't," I said. "But you were the first of us to escape legitimately. You didn't leave your room, but it did allow you to see that no one else was messing with the mugs. You might not have seen Lewis's body, but because you saw Carol escape, it made it harder to blame her for murder."

Jerry sagged against the wall. Bob, however, wasn't convinced.

"The mug was mine," he said. "If Carol didn't sneak in here earlier to swap it, wouldn't it be more likely that J. did it to get back at me for getting that promotion over him?"

"That was another convenience that played right into the killer's hands," I said. "You two knew one another, so it made sense to replace one of your mugs so we would suspect one of you of going after the other. I don't know if he knew about your promotion over Jerry, or if that was just a happy coincidence, but he knew that if it came down to accusations, Jerry would be the first person you'd look at."

"You said *he*," June said.

"That's right." All eyes turned toward the last two remaining men in the room. "Rita didn't do it. She babbled so much while searching her room, I would have noticed if she'd snuck out."

"I don't babble!" Rita said. She sounded genuinely offended by the comment.

"And June?" Yuri asked. "Why does she get a free pass?"

"She doesn't," I said. "And while I can't prove that she *didn't* do it, I know she's innocent. Like I said, I know who killed Lewis, and June isn't our murderer."

It wasn't a ringing endorsement, but it was the best I could do. She relaxed visibly, so it appeared it was good enough for her.

"Yuri, then," Bob said, turning to the man in question. "We all saw you go up to Lewis before this thing started. You knew the guy. I think that makes you the most likely killer."

"I agree," Troy said.

"We knew each other." Yuri scowled. His hands balled into fists, his posture ready for a confrontation. "I explained all of this to her." The look he shot me could melt steel.

"True," I said. "You did explain it. And while it would be easy to dismiss your words, claim that you were lying to protect yourself, I find I believe you. You knew Lewis before this, had interactions with him outside of the escape room. Yet, why kill him? What would be your motive?"

"Does anyone here have a motive?" Jerry asked. "I mean, we're all strangers, right?"

"Not quite," I said, eyes moving to the last man in the room.

Troy stood across from me, arms crossed over his chest. Everything in his posture screamed intimidation. "What are you trying to say?" he asked. "That I did it?"

"I am." I kept my back straight, my gaze steady, though I was a jumble of nerves inside. What if I was wrong? What if he had a weapon hidden on him somewhere? This could go wrong in so many ways, yet I couldn't keep it to myself, not with Lewis lying dead at my feet.

"*Troy?*" June said with a shake of her head. "He couldn't have done it. Why would he?"

"Exactly," he said. "Why would I? I didn't know the guy. I don't know any of you."

"Don't you?" I asked. "I have a feeling that isn't entirely true."

Troy snorted and moved to put his arm around June. She took a quick step away from him, eyes wide, uncertain. He scowled at her a moment, before turning his attention back to me.

"Fine," he said. "Lay it on me." There was a confidence

to his posture that had me briefly questioning my conclusions. If I was wrong, I was accusing an innocent man of murder. It could ruin his life. The killer had planned so much, worked things so that we'd think others guilty. What made me think he didn't plan this too?

I refused to let my doubts sway me, however. Lewis was dead. I might not be able to bring him back, but I could help provide him with some sort of justice.

"Let's start from the moment you arrived," I said. "You played it off like you were here for a little fun with your girlfriend. And then when Lewis joined us, he immediately saw someone he didn't like."

"Yeah, Yuri," Bob said. "We all saw the way he reacted to him."

"That's what I thought at first, but that wasn't the case, was it?"

Troy didn't respond. The muscles in his arms bunched, and the corners of his mouth twitched. He was barely suppressing his anger, which made me want to goad him all the more. If he broke and screamed something like, "He deserved it!" then I wouldn't need to prove anything. Instead, he'd do it for me.

"Lewis did scowl," I said. "And he did have a confrontation with Yuri. But I bet if Yuri had stayed where he was, Lewis would have looked right past him. That scowl wasn't meant for Yuri—it was meant for you."

"Says you," Troy said. "I didn't know the guy."

"Are you sure?" I asked him. "Because people don't usually react so negatively toward people they don't know."

"I'm sure."

"Okay, then, let's move on to the mug," I said. "It was swapped out, that we can all agree upon."

Everyone but Troy nodded.

"The real mug, the one that was supposed to be sitting on the table with the others, was found in Rita's room."

"Yuri found it," June said. Her voice trembled, and worry filled her eyes. She wanted to believe Troy innocent, yet a part of her seemed to realize that he wasn't telling the truth. My heart broke for her, but I didn't stop.

"He did," I agreed. "Once again, the killer planted evidence that pointed to someone else. This time, both Rita and Yuri would look guilty. Rita, since the mug was found in her room, and Yuri, because he was the one who'd found it there. Since he searched the room alone, he could have easily planted it."

"Are you saying he didn't?" Troy asked. "I never went into her room."

"That's not true," Jerry said, pushing away from the wall.

I was glad I wasn't the only one who'd remembered. Jerry's added support gave me the courage to keep pressing. "When we wanted to cover Lewis, Rita said there was a blanket in her room. You must have realized we'd search for the mug, so you took the opportunity to hide it in her room while you were in there, grabbing the blanket for us."

"That's preposterous," Troy said. "I was doing a good thing. I was helping."

"You were," I said. "Helping yourself."

A vein started to pulse in the middle of Troy's forehead.

"While a lot of what happened was convenience, you had much of it planned out. Everything you did, every step you made, in turn, made someone else look guilty."

"Everyone but us," June whispered.

"June, I . . ."

"You didn't want me to come," she said, taking a step

away from him. "You didn't even want to tell me where you were going. If I wouldn't have found out, wouldn't have insisted, you would have left me at home."

Troy floundered for something to say to June, before turning to me. "Why would I kill him?" he asked. "I had no reason to do it."

"That, I'm not sure about," I said. "We're all pretty much strangers here. Maybe that's why you chose this place to kill him. You thought that perhaps we'd turn on one another." Which, admittedly, we almost had. "You hoped that one of your many plants would keep the police from looking too deep into your connections with Lewis Coates."

"I have no connections!" Troy shouted, spreading his arms wide. His composure was cracking. I could see the fear behind his eyes, the guilt.

"Their jobs," Yuri said with a snap of his fingers.

The lightbulb went on in my head.

"Lewis worked in security," I said, piecing it together. "You work at a bank, don't you?"

Troy showed no reaction, but June nodded. "Investments." Her voice was barely audible.

"If the police were to check, would they learn that Lewis handled computer security at your bank?" I asked. "Did he catch you doing something you shouldn't? Did he try to blackmail you? Or did you merely suspect he knew something and decided to put an end to him before he could tell anyone?"

Troy went completely still, other than his eyes. They moved around the room, seeking an escape, an excuse. He knew he was caught, knew that while I didn't have the exact why, or even the how, the police would eventually figure it out.

"Did you come here before?" I asked. "Run the room?" I nodded, noting the way he sucked in a breath. "You did, didn't you? You learned Lewis was running this thing, showed up, and had a look around. Maybe you only talked to him then, begged him not to turn you in."

"You don't know anything," Troy said, without conviction.

"Whatever happened, it made you unhappy. After that first visit, you decided to kill him and registered again, but this time, under an old nickname you no longer use. Then you hid the mug in the room, quickly figured out your escape, and snuck out to make the swap."

I wasn't sure how he'd escaped so fast, but assumed he'd learned the code ahead of time. Lewis probably kept the codes tucked away somewhere, just in case he needed to help people along, so perhaps Troy found it and used it. It was likely I'd never know for sure how he'd managed it, but, honestly, that was none of my concern.

"You were so quiet at the start," June said. "I thought you were busy searching your room."

"I . . ." Troy glanced at her, looked back to me.

"Then, once Lewis's body was discovered, you went straight for the door. Without hesitation, you input a code. Maybe you would have played it off like a lucky guess, and with a man dead, we might have believed you."

"But he changed it," Bob said, taking a step toward Troy, his own fists bunching.

Troy eased away from the other man. His eyes were wild now as they scoured the room for a way out of this.

"Why'd you do it?" I asked him, keeping my voice calm. "Why kill Lewis Coates?"

Troy shook his head. It looked like an involuntary motion. His eyes fell on June, softened. "I'm sorry," he said.

And then he made his move.

Quick as lightning, he flung himself at Rita. She yelped and tried to jump out of the way, but he was far younger, and far quicker. He got behind her and whipped the string of Christmas lights he'd been holding this entire time around her neck.

"Stay back," he said, giving a sharp tug on the strand, causing Rita's eyes to widen. "I don't want to hurt anyone else."

Everyone in the room froze.

"You can't get out," Bob said. "The door's locked."

"But we have the codes, don't we?" Troy said. "Everyone simply needs to input their numbers in the correct order, and then we'll all walk out of here nice and easy."

"And then what?" I asked, meeting Rita's eye. She looked scared, but also really, really annoyed. "The cops won't let you walk away from this."

"They aren't here," he said. "I know you'll call them the moment you are able, but you can give me a head start."

"Why would we do that?" Bob asked.

Troy's only answer was to pull the string of lights tighter.

"They'll find you," Yuri said. "The rest of us will make sure of that."

"Put the cord down," I said. "Let Rita go." I held out a hand, took a tentative step toward him.

He lifted his elbows, tightening the cord. Rita was forced to stand on her tiptoes, lest her breath be cut off entirely.

"Troy, no!" June shouted, lifting her own hand toward him. "She didn't do anything to you."

He met her eye, his entire posture softening. "I'm so sorry, June," he said. "I was scared. I didn't want to get caught. I didn't mean for you to get caught up in it like this."

"I know," she said. "But I did." She glanced around the

room. "We all did. You can't change that." A tear slid down her cheek. "Please. Let her go. This isn't you."

He closed his eyes, his arms slackening ever so slightly.

Rita made him pay for the lapse.

Her fist bunched the moment she felt the cord loosen on her throat, and she pistoned her arm backward, directly into Troy's stomach.

His breath left him in an expelled "Oof!" and he staggered back a step, his grip on the cord loosening completely. He opened his mouth to say something, but before he could, Rita spun around and kicked him hard on the shin.

"Don't you ever touch me like that again!" she shouted, kicking him again.

Troy scuttled away from her, right into Bob's and Yuri's waiting arms. Instead of fighting them off, he sagged into their grip.

"Come on," I said, putting an arm around Rita to keep her from going after the detained man. Both her fists were bunched, and she was panting like an angry bull. "Let's get out of here."

Rita huffed, checked to make sure her hair was in place, and then, together, we gathered everyone's codes.

Everyone handed them over quietly. Even Troy motioned to his pocket, where he'd shoved his, without resisting. Bob pulled the slip of paper free and handed it over.

Since Bob and Yuri's hands were full, I did the honors and punched in the numbers. The door opened, and everyone piled out, making straight for the lockers and their cell phones.

I paused just outside the door and looked back into the

room. The big gift still sat unopened in the middle of the table.

"I wonder what's inside," Rita said, rubbing at her throat. "Do you think we should open it? You know, finish the room?"

I glanced at the others. Bob and Yuri had a firm grip on Troy. June stood nearby, watching her boyfriend, and, very likely, keeping him from doing anything stupid. Both Carol and Jerry were on their phones. I hoped one of them was calling the police.

"I think we're done," I said, putting a comforting arm around Rita's shoulders. "Let's leave some mystery for Santa."

Rita grinned. "Lewis would have liked that," she said.

Sirens rose in the distance. I squeezed Rita close, glad she was okay. "Yeah, I think you're right."

Then, together, we waited for the police to arrive.

Chapter Ten

Troy Carpenter didn't protest as the police took him into custody. Paul Dalton was one of the cops who showed, as was John Buchannan, who wasn't one of my biggest fans.

"Of course *you're* here," Buchannan said as soon as he saw me. "It never fails." He shook his head and wandered into the main room to secure the scene.

The next hour was spent answering questions and waiting for the chance to go home. I'd hoped Paul would take my statement, but he was busy with Troy, so instead, a young, unfamiliar cop who looked overwhelmed by this whole thing took me aside. After only a few moments, I realized he was new to the force and this was his first murder. Lucky for him, I'd already solved the case, so he wouldn't get to experience the joys of searching for suspects.

Once Rita and I had given our statements, we were given permission to go. We left just as the ambulance drove off with Lewis Coates inside. I sent a quick prayer after him, hoping that wherever he was now, he was happier.

After dropping Rita off at home, I headed for my own place, anxious for things to get back to normal.

"Hey, Misfit," I said as I stepped inside the house. My fluffy orange cat was sprawled on the couch, dozing. He didn't look up as I entered. Christmas tree ornaments were scattered around the floor, but at least the tree was still standing, for which I was thankful. I swear Misfit must be part-tree cat for as much as he liked to climb it.

As I cleaned up and readied the bedrooms for Dad and Laura's visit, I kept thinking about Lewis Coates, Troy Carpenter, and the rest of the escape room participants. During such a happy time of the year, how could someone let their fears drive them to murder? It was enough to make *me* depressed.

The house came together, the sun went down, and the snow began to fall in earnest.

It would have been perfect, but the quiet was getting to me. I tried turning on the TV, tried talking to Misfit, but it just wasn't working this time. While my house would be full to bursting over the next week or so, I couldn't stand being alone now.

That was how I found myself sitting at a table at Death by Coffee twenty minutes after closing time, a hot mug of coffee in my grip, relating my harrowing experience with an escape room to my best friend and her husband.

"That sounds horrible," Vicki said. Her black-and-white cat, Trouble, was snoozing in her lap. She'd somehow gotten him into a cat-sized Christmas sweater, and had come away with all her fingers intact.

"It was," I said. "And to be trapped with a killer like that." I shuddered. Things could have been a lot worse if June hadn't been there to talk Troy down.

"It's a good thing you were there." Mason sat next to Vicki, an empty mug in his hand.

"I guess. I just wish I could get through a holiday without someone dying."

"No one died on Thanksgiving," Vicki said.

"Or Easter," Mason added.

"Halloween was pretty quiet this year too," Vicki said with a grin.

"Okay, I get it," I grumbled, swirling my coffee around. Small chunks of the cookie I use instead of sugar and creamer floated up from the bottom of the mug. Yum.

The lights were off in the bookstore section of the shop, as were the ones to the back. The CLOSED sign hung in the window, and the only light on was the one above where we sat. Which was why it was a surprise when there was a knock at the glass door.

It was too dark outside to make out who it was. Mason popped up and answered as I finished off my coffee and began spooning gooey chunks of cookie into my mouth.

"It's all over now." Vicki reached across the table and briefly took my hand. "You can relax."

"I'm trying," I said, showing her a soggy bit of cookie before eating it.

She made a disgusted face as Mason returned with another man in tow.

"I hope it's okay I stopped by," Paul Dalton said. "I saw the light on and thought that maybe Krissy would be here." His eyes fell on me and he smiled, though it was a tired smile. It had been a long day for all of us.

Warmth flowed through me hearing my name come from his lips. "I'm here," I said, hurriedly wiping my mouth in case I'd smeared chocolate on it.

"Krissy was telling us about what happened," Vicki said.

"Can I get you something? Coffee? Hot cocoa?" Mason asked.

I cringed at the mention of hot cocoa, but, thankfully, Paul asked for a coffee.

As Mason went to get it for him, I asked, "Did Troy confess?"

Paul sank into a chair and took off his hat. His hair was a mess, and his eyes were a little sunken in, but I still found myself staring, wishing I could run my fingers through that hair of his. He was barely able to suppress a yawn when he spoke.

"He did. There wasn't much else he could do. Mr. Coates recorded everything, apparently. It didn't take long to find a clip of Mr. Carpenter swapping the mugs. He stared right at the camera when he did it, too, as if daring Lewis to do something about it."

So there *was* a camera in the room somewhere. "If you go back a few days, you'll probably find another recording of Troy. I don't think today was his first trip to the escape room."

"We might not need it," Paul said. "With the video we have now, plus everyone's statements, *and* Mr. Carpenter's confession, there's not much he can do to talk his way out of this one."

"If there was a camera, how did he think he would get away with it?" Vicki asked.

"He probably planned on deleting everything once he escaped the room," I said.

Paul nodded. "Or he could have simply stolen the laptop. Everything was saved to a hard drive, and not on the cloud. It was how he knew how to escape his room. He snuck in earlier and found the codes needed on the laptop."

"But Lewis changed the last code, didn't he?"

"Must have," Paul said. "I don't know why he did, and doubt we'll ever know for sure."

It was a good thing he did. If we'd escaped right away, there was a good chance Troy would have been long gone before anyone pieced together what had happened.

"Why'd he do it anyway?" Mason asked, handing Paul his coffee.

"I don't have all the details yet," Paul said. "But it looks like Mr. Carpenter was skimming money from clients. When the bank hired Mr. Coates to upgrade their computers' security systems, he came across some incriminating evidence. Or, that's what Mr. Carpenter thought. There's no evidence Lewis Coates ever confronted him about anything, or turned him in."

"Are you saying it might have all been a misunderstanding?" Vicki asked.

"Could be." Paul shook his head sadly. "He got paranoid, confronted Mr. Coates about it, and when Lewis didn't admit to finding anything, he decided to silence him, just in case. I won't know for sure until we talk to Carpenter some more."

We all stared into our coffee mugs for a few minutes. I kept thinking about June, about that look on her face when she realized her boyfriend was a murderer. I wondered if she had anyone else she could go to for the holidays. It was going to be a rough couple of months for her.

Snow was still falling outside. It wasn't coming down hard, but since the ground was already covered, it was beginning to pile up. A salt truck drifted down the road, closely followed by a car filled with a family singing loud enough to be heard inside Death by Coffee.

"I should probably go," I said when they were gone.

"We should too." Vicki looked down at Trouble, but didn't make a move to rise.

Paul glanced over his shoulder, out the window. "It was kind of slick out there when I got here. We should probably wait and let the salt do its work."

When he turned back to the table, his eyes met mine.

Quite suddenly, the room felt a little too hot, and time seemed to slow to a crawl.

"You're probably right," Mason said, popping up from his chair. "Let me get everyone a refill."

No one complained, so he did just that.

Seconds passed where no one spoke. Mason filled each and every mug and then sat back down. Unlike at home, the silence now felt right. Comforting. I could have sat there, sipping my coffee, and would have been content.

Mason was the one to raise his mug. "To family," he said.

Mugs were raised around the table.

"To family," Vicki said.

My eyes met Paul's. When we spoke, we did so together. "To family."

I brought my mug to my lips, and knew that those weren't mere idle words, but a promise.

And it was one I expected to keep.